TO THE INSIDE

OF TIME

Jiù & Akané

Joseph Delcourt

TO THE INSIDE

OF TIME

Jiù & Akané

A novel about

journeying to the present

First published November 2013

Inside_time@humanenterprises.fr

Copyright © Garrett Delcourt

ISBN 978-2-9547282-0-9

Original title : A L'INTERIEUR DU TEMPS

Translation : Solen Lees

Cover image : G. Delcourt

Acknowledgments

I would not have completed the adventure of this first novel without Brianne's infinite patience and advice, and the support of my children, throughout these few months of writing.

I am very grateful to my friend Hervé, who sparked the idea of getting into writing.

I would like to give special thanks to Solen who not only put her talent into translating the book into English, but joined in the complex and long process of merging perceptions about a story.

Last but not least, my thanks go to you, the readers whom this book may possibly meet.

For all explorers of the moment, those who have started the journey,

Those who get ready, and those looking forward to it.

"What happens at the end of the day is not the inevitable, but the unpredictable."

John M. Keynes

1 - Jiù

It was late. For a long time the office had been plunged into the uncertain semi-darkness of a small lamp placed on the table in the middle of all his notes. He was tired. The day had been long and the avenues of his research too numerous, too complex. There were days like that, so long that he was amazed at himself for being able to get through them.

He had waited with some impatience for the moment at nightfall when he would finally be able to take up once more the tenuous thread of his experiments. He had to bring off a new occurrence, whatever the cost - if possible a more sophisticated one this time. He had to try to understand again or at least to sort through, the incredible density of all this information which simultaneously assailed him. He recorded it as well as he could but was conscious of missing out on the crux of the matter. This feeling of a permanent vacuum that needed filling was precisely what made him repeat his attempts over and over.

The occurrences were arising more and more frequently, but each time they took on a different shade, an always unexpected path. He had discovered them by accident: one day he had noticed some apparent synchronicity among all the events punctuating his day: superimposed fragments of stories or moments which seemed to be on collision courses like the trace of vaster trajectories. He had above all noticed a special energy that seemed to emanate from these chance moments. Oh, it was almost imperceptible to anyone not paying attention, like a flash without light – but it reached him. For want of a better word, he had called them "occurrences" as a way of blending them into his own history and of being able to remember them. In fact he came back to them a lot, more often that he had expected to. These electric moments began to intrude on him, as if they had a life of their own, beyond any possible context. They were completely new combinations of circumstances which were totally unpredictable compared to those Elwon days which were repeated over and over without, nonetheless, ever being truly identical.

This was what most bemused and attracted him - the constantly renewed novelty of his experiments, but also the feeling of energy and vitality that had come from nowhere. It was totally unthinkable, literally: this had absolutely no reason for existing. There were no terms of reference whatsoever and this disconcerted him. He was not used to it yet, but at least he had gone beyond surprise now. Once more, in the calm of his office, he was preparing for one of those elusive moments which would open up to a kind of vertigo, like a balcony on the three hundredth floor. Such a difficult state to describe. The perception of everything in the brevity of an instant – that was as near as he could get. He did his best to take notes each time to help unravel the tangled sensations and images. Maybe a meaning would emerge at some point - today, tomorrow, one day. He also hoped his notes would help him set up reference points in these sequences of a new logic which he had undertaken to explore, but he could never find his way around. He was a bit lost. He was on unfamiliar terrain, feeling not really comfortable and far too clumsy for his taste. He had a beginner's indecision and he hated it. It was nothing like the methodological metaphysics which he was used to, as was every inhabitant of Elwon - that immense dynasty which had ended up uniting the peoples of Earth: a completely ordered and almost predictable logic, simultaneously effective and reassuring. But this new thing – well, he had no idea where it would take him. He felt as if he had opened the door of an apparently empty building without really knowing if it was inhabited or not. He was walking in the dark, fearfully careful but excited at the same time. Deep inside, a subtle something was simply telling him that it was important, without being able to identify why nor for whom. More than important – crucial. He perceived a kind of solemnity – or more like - yes that was it - an instruction, an order to be followed. Something which would bring him back to himself, at last. Above all, it puzzled him. In fact, it would not take much more for him not to like it at all.

Jiù looked again at the chaos on his desk, an exact reflection of the confusion in his thoughts. This havoc *was* him! He looked at it distractedly at first and then with growing interest. A kind of fortuitous continuity between objects had gathered there because of chance moments and tasks without him ever having felt the need to put it in any kind of order: a pile of flash memories, pretty worn-out, most of them not even indexed yet; his holos, that old holoscopic terminal he was so fond of even though it was completely out-of-date, whose screensaver gave out a pale bluish glow; some samples of Sunmax, the state-of-the-art solar batteries; and of course all those fast-its he would have to sort through one day. They were everywhere. They were his favourite tools, on which he recorded all sorts of notes and thoughts and which he never erased, preferring to collect them. You never know. Having failed to find a meaning to his disorder, he often played at tracing a new story with each object as a milestone. He liked to lose himself in it or to stop there for a while. Every time, it was like a kind of training in the reconstitution of more or less solid sequences through different circumstances. So he got used to it and felt less and less like tidying up.

He made himself a coffee, scalding and very sweet, just the way he liked it. He stretched slowly, closely observing the gradual voluptuousness of a relaxing body. This intensified the sensation while dispensing with the need to come back to it. He gave a long sigh, and cast a slow gaze around this room that was so familiar and where every moment had left its mark. He savoured the pleasure of feeling at home.

His favourite images, his reporting souvenirs, floated in a slow and random loop across the wall on display repeaters. There were some landscapes, but mostly people – lots of them, people he had interviewed and who had impressed him in some way. He liked taking their picture unexpectedly, catching an expression that seemed to provide a unique glimpse of something inside, something not necessarily put into words, or at least not voluntarily. These screens were the only fantasy, so to speak, in a room intended to be functional – conceived without real creative effort, that is – but which was in the end just an eternal mess.

Only one object, placed in the middle of a kind of display cabinet, gave some sort of unusual touch to this interior that was otherwise so impersonal that it could have been a hotel bedroom. It was a small figurine made of a kind of aged terracotta. It sat cross-legged and plump, with a laughing gaze, wearing an impenetrable smile like a silent invitation to happiness. This antiquity from nowhere but seemingly laden with history, was from his mother, who had given it to him after a trip she had made. He had accepted it at the time with a kind of questioning surprise and it was now his only link with a past of which nothing was left. So it now meant a lot to him; and when his eyes happened to light on this chubby little character, he would sometimes hear the voice of his mother or feel himself touched by the fleeting memory of a perfume. At these moments various confused emotions, which he didn't know what to do with, would begin to submerge him. Usually he would go out for a walk or to consult the Memory.

Apart from this slightly enigmatic trinket, nothing in his apartment betrayed his personal history made up of twenty-odd years spent exploring in great length the logic of the dynastic territories. He kept only a few traces of these memories and these paths he had explored, of his fragmented discoveries that would eventually have built him a full and satisfying life - at least up till now. He did not keep them so as not to get held up by them, but also maybe because not one moment could be more charged with meaning than any other and it was not possible to choose them all. He preferred the vague feeling of his own progress, of the passing of his own time, without any particular landmark.

More than wanting to move up the long and extremely sophisticated hierarchical ladder of Elwon, as did most people he had met – all more or less motivated by a rarely admitted ambition – he wanted to understand its hidden resources. Since childhood, Jiù had been just that, a man who seemed to have been placed in his world rather than rooted in it, almost a stranger to himself, driven by an inner determination that he hadn't been able to escape, that had always preceded his will in some way. A force within him, almost part of his nature, pushed him to want to know and experience absolutely everything, as if there were something unsaid in what surrounded him that he had to understand; something that could be the true driving force of his reality. Something else, other, elsewhere. This tenseness of his had laid out a rather solitary route for him and he had only managed to keep one friend, Shu, whom he saw from time to time when his research did not go on too deep into the evening.

Shu was a relative of his father's, a man of about sixty who looked good for his age, with greying temples and semi-long hair. He had the distinguished haughtiness of those who have long haunted the corridors of power and who have retained access to them. Shu had been High Councillor a long time ago, just like Jiù's father, who had disappeared in a cruiser accident some years ago while on a tour of duty of the principal energy stations in AsiaPac. Afterwards, Shu had taken Jiù into his care, guiding him like a second father, and following his career with some interest and without doubt contributing to it discreetly through the contacts he had kept within the High Council. Jiù preferred not to ask. Shu had watched over him so unfailingly that he had become Jiù's confidant; he went to him for advice, especially on his recent experiments that he had finally resolved to share with him. Thus they embarked on long discussions which were often animated and at times fiery, and which could go on until dawn, logically exploring each of the hypotheses proposed by both parties. The fact that Shu listened attentively and with apparent interest encouraged Jiù to continue and even to go further down the road of the unknown, reassuring him somehow of the legitimacy of his research. It was also a way for him to feel like he was carving his own path without really modelling it on Shu's, while nevertheless taking inspiration from him.

Outside, the night had settled in a while ago along with the subdued humming of electromotors and the usual sirens, far and near. Emergencies clearing a path among the continual comings and goings of rapeeds, both night and day. There was always some kind of alarm, like a form of punctuation, a semblance of beating life in the prefabricated time of Elwon that would otherwise have been so monotonous. Emergencies were one of those key elements, skilfully measured, that provided a rhythm to existence – they were vital for giving daily life its true density. In some office somewhere there must have been people assigned to emergencies, in charge of getting the balance right between too many and too few.

All the city's daily activities, mostly automatic or programmed, were winding down. The city was going into rest mode. Night or day, it was an endless merry-go-round of organised, reproduced and adroitly timed events whose only goal was to regulate the rhythm of the days and ensure the renewal of the cycle and thus the survival of Elwon. Everyone knew it and everyone appreciated the comfort of this pre-calculated life, this pre-formatted routine whose beginning and end were reassuringly familiar. Everyone except the Dissidents, of course, but who cared about them? In the end there were so few of them and they had no influence on anything. Whether they liked it or not, they were still part of the implacable robustness of the Dynasty. For time immemorial, repetition had been part of life. Even better - repetition was life! Life as they had wanted it – the continual resumption of past circumstances, worn threadbare by dint of having been recycled, their effects totally controlled, only presented as often as possible in a totally new form. Historical Resurgence, as they called it, was at the heart of causality control and the absolute pillar of life on Elwon. It was above all one of the foundations of L1 Law, the unique founding logic, demonstrated over generations as the ultimate explanation of the universe. At last! All science had converged and L1 Law had become the common core of all metaphysics from the commonest to the most sacred.

Above all, Resurgence was his job. Jiù was a journalist; he had decided on this activity because of the possibility it gave him to meet more people and have more experiences, hoping to find in them some element of answers to his many questions, even those which were still in the air, not yet expressed. This approach had served him well: during his interviews he asked questions that were in some way an extension of his own, meant either to reconstruct events from snatches of ancient stories which he brought into the present, or to question personally his interviewees, who were often surprised at the originality of what he asked. So for example, once he had asked a High Councillor to whom Shu had introduced him how much time he allowed himself each day to be really himself. The absolute impertinence of the question escaped him and was masked by the sincerity – completely stripped of calculation – with which he expressed it. This certainly saved the end of the interview and very probably the rest of his career.

He worked in History, one of four dynastical sectors. A long time ago he had asked for a transfer to Culture. Probably his request was underway. One day, Memory Central, the gigantic central calculator which managed all the collective and individual logic of the Dynasty would notify him of his appointment, and this totally predictable and calculated event would be like a surprise.

The Administration and Health Sectors were obviously not of interest to him. Science, and especially the science of Time, appealed to him more and more. It had become a subtle but constant preoccupation and obviously he could not know that it was directly linked to his absolutely obsessive punctuality as well as to those experiments he was performing more and more often. For now his role, like that of everyone else in History, was to portray in an apparently new light those ancient circumstances which, revitalised, contributed to the nonstop manufacture of History. To present them as news. He realised how short people's memories were – they could talk endlessly about news that was only a slightly modified rerun of events that had happened just a few months earlier. To amuse himself, from time to time, he would try to work out when exactly one of his superiors would say to him "already seen that!" For now, it had never happened. Every day he probed the memories of recent times, or more often ancient times, so as to make up something unexpected, broadcast incidents or give some meaning to things. Every day, mixing faded holograms and old recordings, he unfolded programmes meant for the different Agencies into multiple stories, their only purpose being to show continuously the immutability of the rule of Resurgence: large or small, history is indefinitely called upon to repeat itself.

He lived and worked in a Southern quadrant, near the big regional transhub from where cruisers left for the world's different hyperpoles. Juno, his city, was built on the classical dynastic model with towers about a mile high all arranged in four quadrants around a central layout: the North for first level workers, the East for the young, the South for second level workers, the West for the old. The Architects had long ago discovered that these subtle contrasts between opposites were the guarantee not only of a moderate economic dynamic, but also of a peaceful society. As for the neighbourhoods, they were organised according to a logic directly linked with administrative activities. Geological vagaries had been entirely and carefully removed, erased by miles of underground networks and floors of basement energy stacks.

At the centre of Juno, at its very heart, was Eneter, the general headquarters of the Energy militia. Here, two needles shot up like the hands of a monstrous old clock, immense and asymmetrical, the longest finally disappearing from view in the fog which so often covered Juno. Its highest floors turned slowly, as if to keep an eye on the solar fields at the edge of the hypercity. At their foot stretched the immense building of Memory Central whose massive presence was like a reminder of the indissoluble link which connected it to Eneter.

Ah, Eneter! The supreme symbol of absolute power. In some mysterious way, so vital was its role in managing energy that it was Eneter which reigned on Elwon, more than the Memory which did all the work, or the High Council which was meant to organise it. In fact, life on Earth was reduced to two realities - the hyperpoles and the solar fields. Almost the entire population was gathered in the gigantic cities. Granted, there were poor and privileged areas, but in general life was arranged pretty harmoniously, under the immediate command of Memory Central which regulated all functions, for example the composition of the atmosphere and food synthesis. This all required enormous amounts of energy, millions of megasowas of solar energy captured by the immense photovoltaic fields that stretched to infinity between the towns. Life in the Elwon Dynasty was thus organised around these two major activities: energy control and administering its different functions, of which historical Resurgence was the main regulating element. The factors could just as easily be inversed – administering energy and controlling its functions. The fact remained that it was Eneter that was exclusively in charge and by force of circumstance had become Elwon's absolute organ of control.

Jiù had become an expert in Resurgence and even an authority on it due to his uncommon ability to connect scattered events and draw a logic from them which was continuously added to the Memory Central corpus. With the help of Shu's broad network of contacts, he had gradually become specialised in writing speeches and reports for all kinds of magnates, always mindful of placing themselves in some historical continuity. Above all he had become famous for a certain trait of character, like his own brand – he was unhealthily punctual. At first it had been almost an obsession - leaving on time so as to get there on time, learning to defy random events which could delay him. Thus he made it into a kind of game which livened up his trips. Then it became second nature. He was a viscerally punctual person, which for him did not only mean being on time for an appointment, but arriving at the exact time – neither late nor early. Exactly on the dot. This reputation for exactness had been very useful for him, first in his job, given that a journalist cannot allow himself to be late; then in relation to the personalities he was meeting and interviewing. It was noticed. Every time someone asked him: "and why are you so exact with the time?" he invariably replied in a learned tone: "precisely because we live in an exact world". It was really practical: normally this retort, which didn't say much to avoid too much being made of it, produced a knowing nod, as if the person had got the meaning while not being entirely sure of what he or she had understood, and then the conversation could move on.

He was now sure that it was precisely his exactness that had helped him develop his special capacity for observation. This very capacity had him notice these coincidences, these synchronous events which had struck him so and from which he could no longer detach himself. So in the course of his research and his readings during trips when he was preparing his interviews, his attention had been alerted several times by these simultaneous events which seemed to have a common meaning although they were totally separate. It therefore seemed to him that they could fulfil their own logic, like the brief perception of a fleeting movement in a still landscape. Indeed, what had grabbed him was the very possibility of a correspondence between all these events. At first it irritated him, like a mark on a screen that he would glimpse several times without really noticing it; then it amused him as a welcome distraction in a job that was otherwise largely repetitive. Finally he had started to exploit these fragments of autonomous logic, as they made his task much easier. Each time, he unknowingly accumulated the little bursts of energy that came with them. Since then, they had quickly grown in number, as if they had been there all along and as if his now trained mind had developed the ability to observe them. This didn't make sense; it was against all L1 logic, the rational, unique and healthy organisation which serenely infused Elwon. But above all it was becoming troublesome – not a danger as yet, at least not one he was conscious of – but already a problem. All his capacity for reflection had first of all rejected the hypothesis of a possible autonomous logic, independent of L1. That had already happened in the past: viral strands of reasoning had been detected in the programmes treated by the Memory and nobody knew where they were coming from. The Dynastic Council had debated the issue for a long time. Shu had also told him that his father had once tried to analyse the causes but that they had ended up being considered as a natural deviation of L1 and corrective patches had swiftly eradicated them, rightly so.

The first challenges to L1 went back to time immemorial, just after the Collapsus – the immense cataclysm that had knocked the world off balance – and no-one, especially not journalists, could remember them. There was not a trace of them anywhere. Anything that was not logic had purely and simply disappeared. Without violence, of course, at least for the most part. Violence had become useless in this world made of reasoning. Taking the time for different methods of persuasion was enough: technology and the media had made great progress in this area. Indeed the ravages of the Collapsus had been so great that those who survived them had spontaneously agreed that only logic would remain, like a benevolent magnetism, to rebuild, manage and protect. Above all to protect and not have to defend any more. What from anyway? Logic had gradually regimented everything, organised everything, an ultimate, reassuring safeguard; and naturally it had enabled amnesia. Everyone, or nearly everyone, hastened to forget, and life was able to develop once again, unified around L1 and its omnipresent machines, which had begun to proliferate. As everybody knows, logic is machines' favourite field, and they excel in it! And as time went by, L1 grew more imposing. First of all, no-one dared sift through the memories of the past, seek out the images from before, the texts and the sounds (ah! the sounds!); so they were erased and finally forgotten. The Collapsus became the beginning. Even poetry sprouted once again on the edges of L1, flowering in the most subtle or most unexpected culminations of rational thought. Things which people got tired of quite quickly, like "rare, the green horse with pearly breath". As for visual art, it became more and more sophisticated and naturally fractal, an infinite repetition of logical sequences.

Life in the Dynasty, then, gradually became organised according to a simple but fundamental concept: protection. This was the founding contract that had brought about the constitution of the Dynasty, its primary function. Protection had led to the elimination of all risk, of any deviation and thus of any potential for breakdown. Life became naturally organised around an imagined reality, forever reconstituted but always the same, an eternal carrousel which people contented themselves with. Juno's citizens, like those in the other hyperpoles, merely organised their days around activities and entertainment. It was that simple. Their routines had a sophisticated rhythm, made up of frequent bursts of activity and short relaxation periods, intended to fill the present with the least possible content but with always more sensations.

Sensations were all-important. They were the preferred benchmark for quality of life. They had almost superseded emotions, although they had not made them disappear altogether. Every analysis published by the Memory about the Collapsus had shown that emotions – much more than logic – were at the origin of all forms of chaos, of which the Collapsus had been the ultimate manifestation. Of course emotions were still there, but they were so channelled and coded that they had become just another form of entertainment. They spiced things up, people said. So time was made ever denser, as if it were in short supply, and Sensation Villages had developed at an incredible rate. They were a practical incarnation of the densification of time, convenient and easily controlled by the Dynastic Media, crazy places where Juno's inhabitants would come and immerse themselves in a furious paradise of synthetic sensations, as if they could forget themselves and start their lives over.

Like that of all the Dynasty's citizens, Jiù's conscience was immersed, then, in the unique and complete culture of L1. Nothing could be strange to him. And yet, something unexpected had happened along with these occurrences, these autonomous synchronicities he had discovered: Jiù had begun to sense something like the possibility of a boundary he could overstep and he felt pulled into an irritating paradox which kept on grabbing him, puzzling him. He had to resolve it before venturing further beyond this frontier – the conclusions he drew from his observations were perfectly rational and therefore were an integral part of L1 logic, without contest and without risk. And yet, at the same time, they led him to the very edge of L1, to new concepts, thus possibly to a place *outside* L1. (An autonomous logic? Good Gods!).

He couldn't work it out and needed to weigh up his options again. Going beyond L1? Oops! Where to? Would this be some natural evolution? In that case, someone else had to be taking care of it. Or something else, something more subversive? He dared not think about that. Each option was bringing about very distinct chains of circumstances, but each time, he himself was at the centre of whatever was going to happen, and this was one of the things he was worried about. He generally anticipated consequences fairly well. In this case, Jiù knew that a radical transformation would come out of whatever option he chose. If possible he had to foresee what the repercussions would be for him, for Juno, for Elwon. This time it wasn't about inventing, but about predicting, which was not at all the same thing. This change of perspective alone was radical. What he dreaded was that the homogeneity of L1 would strictly apply: every thought had a corresponding reality. This phrase, instilled in everyone from the cradle, was an unavoidable dogma: if your thought has no reality, it is useless. That protected you for life! But if that were the case, what reality was he rushing into? How could he stop the process, which, as he sensed, had been put into motion?

He felt an urge to act arise within him, fuelled by his own distinctive mix of bewilderment, curiosity and not a little apprehension. His state of mind, usually agile and quite determined, was now agitated and bordering on confusion. This surprised him. For a long time L1 psychology had studied and defined all states of consciousness. Likewise, all sensations and experiences triggered by going from one state to another, their juxtaposition or any possible combination had been exhaustively researched and catalogued. His sudden feverishness bore no relation to any of them, and neither did these unexpected events whose insistence he was now noticing – they were not part of the dynastic repertory of the phenomena that he extensively used all day long. It was a fact that was repeating regularly now, like a persistent signal he could no longer ignore. The prudence and methodological approach his job had instilled in him led Jiù to the somewhat alarming hypothesis that these chains of coincidences, these spontaneous synchronicities, had to be exogenous and foreign to L1. It was absolutely astounding. An event produced outside the Resurgence? But where? He dared not put it into words yet but felt he was touching the very foundations of L1. Life was pushing him out of his comfort zone – it was surreptitiously but insistently inviting him to explore beyond his own boundaries. This was all very disconcerting and, as someone who was accustomed to staying within the confines of a dogma or even reinforcing it, he felt the possible repercussions acutely.

The only obvious solution, the only way out of this paradoxical and almost painful injunction, was to continue the experiment, and see where it would lead him. To refine his conclusions and, hopefully, end up with a clear understanding of it all. If these chains of synchronicity were happening so frequently, logic itself dictated that L1 was evolving or that this was the first in a series of more sophisticated logical processes yet to come. This question of a possible evolution of L1 led him to another: how long should he keep his experiences and conclusions to himself? If he should share them, who with? Shu always advised him not to talk to anyone but him about it, but for how long would that be possible? Potential candidates came to mind – his superiors who checked and validated his programmes, for example. But this was different, and he was not sure they had the ability to truly judge. Quite frankly, he was not too sure about their abilities, full stop.

The possible emergence of another dimension of time opened up an ocean of possibilities for which he was ill-prepared. He felt as if he were on the edge of a moving immensity which stretched beyond his usual horizons, a place with contemplative beaches as well as storms, fury and danger. In any case, a place where it is very easy indeed to lose your footing. He again tried to identify the moment he started drifting, the moment when this other potential logic entered him.

It went back to what he called the "red tunic episode". A short while ago he had been walking along a radial street in the centre of Juno and his eyes had come to rest on a rapeed in the distance waiting in an uninterrupted queue of the dense traffic typical of that time of the day. Why that one, he didn't know. The fact is that when he had reached it, as it slowed down just before the gigantic junction, he caught a glimpse of the driver, a brunette wearing a bright red tunic, with just enough orange in it to tone down any ostentation or cheek. A little further on, at the door of a building, another, younger, woman had hurried down the few steps in front of him, dressed in exactly the same scarlet red. This intrigued him profoundly. And then he was in the lift to the study room he had reserved for the day when he glimpsed, just as the doors were closing, a man walking past the lift also wearing a tunic of exactly the same colour. And that same evening, in the exercise room, an elderly man who was pedalling enthusiastically on his energy cycle, was also wearing this same garish colour. He even gave Jiù a friendly gesture! He was transfixed, as if some energy had frozen him, and this lasted almost all night. It goes without saying that he had never before seen such a bright colour on Juno or elsewhere and he had obviously never seen it since. The same kind of episode had happened at more or less regular intervals since then.

The last one had been just this morning. He was sipping an energy cocktail in a quencher not far from the Memory building, thinking about the work of the day ahead when a thought crossed his mind: "the immortality of the moment". A few seconds later, almost immediately, he heard exactly the same phrase in the middle of a conversation on a neighbouring table, uttered as if it were the extension of his own thought. Having turned to look around him to see who said it, he caught sight of a couple reading an article a few tables away. A headline spread out over the falsely idyllic image: "immortal moments!" He hurried out, to move away from the coincidence, just as a transport drove in front of the quencher, carrying on its side one of the hoardings the High Council used for spreading news in Elwon. He read "the moment is immortal". He went pale, as if hit by a violent blow.

As he was recalling this moment, his train of thoughts was suddenly broken. Without any warning sign, a burst of energy arose suddenly, like a violent replica of what he had felt in the morning, brutally interrupting his inner monologue. In a kind of enlarged and urgent consciousness he felt an unexpected flow of extremely intense energy invade his mind, as if two temporal logical processes had chosen to collide precisely within him. He became very alert, but a fraction of a second too late. He was carried away into a vertiginous immensity where everything around him was blurred. Spontaneously, he linked this energy to time as an autonomous force, completely foreign to the proceedings of L1. Time suddenly forced itself on him, he who spent it manufacturing simulacrums of time. It was time in its entirety, so that *it* seemed to contain his mind and not the other way round. He knew but was unable to put it into words: he could not grasp what or how this total understanding came from, how it was constructed or where it was going. He knew without having learned and he didn't know what to do with it. At this moment, although he was totally unaware of it, time opened in Jiù, shaping doors in him which would never close. He was sinking into temporal energy and in the tiny fraction of a second it lasted, he felt its immensity and fabulous intensity explode within him. Time in its entirety; not like a tightrope he would walk and against which causality would bounce, but rather like a state, the very substance of the reality he was moving in. Time was THE matter, like a sort of heavy glowing mercury in which he was inexorably drowning. Not exactly reassuring. He tried to hang on to some kind of reasoning, to understand what was happening to him, to put words to it, snippets of logic he would be able to hold on to; but it wasn't working and he was sinking.

Suddenly a voice pierced his mind: "Jiù, help me!" Hardly intelligible and disappearing as soon as it had appeared, as if someone had shouted it while in rapid movement. Immediately he froze, believing he had dreamed it, all his interrupted thoughts now stretched towards this fleeting voice which he tried to hold on to and to identify – a woman's voice to which he couldn't put a face and yet was somehow familiar.

As quickly as it had arrived the experience faded. He felt immensely frustrated at not having been able to prolong it and blamed the voice which had intruded like a parasite and must have distracted him. It was too stupid! But the intense energy which had been released remained: Jiù was paralysed, struck by the immensity which had opened up only to then close again. He stayed quite still, electrified by this force which had taken over his entire intellect and absorbed his centres of reflection. His thoughts were no longer logical but rather immediate – a landscape with a thousand details, not a pathway any more. This instantaneous fusion between his consciousness and his sensations was so radical, totally different from the rational progression he was used to. This time it was not progressively-acquired knowledge but instantaneous. He was staggered by both what he had access to and what it meant. He had entered into a field of infinite potentialities, as if, in the heart of the present instant, all possible choices were offered to him. He felt a creative immensity he had never known before, as if he could take on anything. Anything. But where should he begin? It was insane.

The thrilling energy slowly dissipated, along with the heightened consciousness accompanying it. It was evaporating around him and in him. Once again he could hear the sounds of the city and the synthetic voices of his appliances... which was strange, come to think of it, because he never turned the sound on. A sensor was blinking on the wall opposite his desk, so he went to reboot it. The screen of his holos was totally empty, the display repeaters blurred. Feeling unsteady and bewildered before what looked like the aftermath of a magnetic explosion of the highest magnitude, he poured himself another cup of coffee. It was tepid but he didn't care. He recalled the experience again, this time completely different from the others when the logical progression of his reasoning and questions had gradually prepared his mind for this space without reference points. This regular progression was thus accompanied by a growing excitement, inspired by the feeling of being approached by a vastness well beyond any logical universe marked out by L1; he had managed to control this sensation to such an extent that he had even begun to seek out its effects, although he dared not admit it to himself. This energy boost, along with a sort of unfathomable perception, was like a new sensory experience, and that was one of the reasons he had wanted to experience it again – up till now. But this was different. This time he wasn't sure he wanted to go back and taste it again. At least, not for a while.

He had discovered that the occurrences happened more easily when he was in a relaxed state of mind, physically resting and in a calm place. In these conditions, the highly energy-intensive synchronicities arose freely like connections between serendipitous events, themselves probably the fruit of separate trajectories. He imagined them as random windows opening partially on to a landscape that remained hidden. So his experiences were like attempts at going from one window to another so as to catch sight of a larger part of this elusive landscape of which he couldn't see the whole. He knew that this suggestion was no coincidence, as if the time was ripe. "The Time is ripe," he repeated aloud, as if by doing so he could turn a key that would open one of these windows. It didn't work of course.

This time, the experience had been completely different: it had instantaneously thrown him into the very centre of the unknown without any preparation or warning signs, and without precedent. The sensation had exploded in him as an immediate and tremendously powerful wave, completely out of control. He had received all at once an incalculable mass of knowledge, a total transfer that was independent of his intellectual capacity to host it. It saturated his mind in an instant and risked permanently disturbing his neuronal connections. Learning it all could result in not knowing anything anymore. The whole reason for the exercise he had done over several months – and its challenge too – was to get prepared for this jolt: he had wanted to get used to this high energy-charged commotion, but also to be able to maintain the connection for as long as possible. This time, he had been spoilt! He was starting to dread that the intensity of the next experiences would be even greater – would he be able to handle it? In the future he would need a lot of determination and no doubt a great deal of recklessness in order to dare to venture there again, and especially to stay there.

And the voice that had intruded like a parasite into the experience? Had it been real or a figment of his imagination? And where did that certainty that time was at the heart of it all come from? Jiù's rational mentality could not allow for anything except a logical reality, but this time he was finding it hard to piece it together, like an irreparably truncated message.

The new turn his experiment was taking plunged him into a sequence of thoughts which, despite his best efforts, remained incomplete and confused. He was obviously stunned. This had a name, impossible to avoid: out of control. He was no longer controlling the process!

Wanting to regain his peace of mind, he let it go and went over to contemplate the city lights at the only picture window in his flat. Wherever he looked all he could see were twinkling lights, like an attainable starry canopy. It was as if the firmament that had disappeared from Juno a long time ago was now within reach through the windows, made up of beacons which stretched out of sight, of countless tower block lights and of the taillights of rapeeds weaving in and out between the towers in a constant merry-go-round. From time to time, towards the transhub, beams would shoot out from a cruiser, a hyper-fast inter-regional transport. He had only taken them two or three times when reporting from Asia Pac. And even further out, near the horizon, were the two hands of Eneter.

His spirit calmed by this familiar spectacle, he felt his mind was working normally once more. Nevertheless, the conclusion he had come to triggered a kind of aftershock of the vibration that had seized him: he understood. He was really touching the energy of time. Time itself was energy. Nothing else. It was as simple as that. Without doubt it was the very energy at the heart of causality. If it were the case, the challenge to the dynastic order was quite radical: such an energy, if one could learn how to access and master it, could not fail to cause unprecedented changes. He instinctively knew it was true: the Dynasty and its Perpetual Order only touched on the tremendous energy of time, instead of sinking down and letting itself be carried by it, like a boat turning into a submarine. It only exploited its slimmest temporal expressions; it stayed on the surface. The implications of his discovery dumfounded him. If Eneter knew of the possibility of using Time as a source of energy – probably inexhaustible – then what would the consequences be for the

Dynasty and its inhabitants? Energy control was the main concern of the Dynasty, solutions having been found for all other economic constraints, managed by global planning and the administration. But energy was the focal point of Memory Central's attention. The High Council of Elwon had gradually delegated its production, then its distribution and finally its overall management to Eneter, the all-powerful Energy militia. It was becoming obvious that, for now, he should keep his discovery and his deductions to himself. At least for the time being – to protect himself, and Juno and who knew what else?

Now the most important thing for him was to check if he would be capable of bringing the experiment to completion. It wasn't just about following through any more. It was about survival. About being transformed, perhaps, without being destroyed. He perceived this temporal energy and Eneter as two implacable powers, not really in conflict but undeniably on collision courses. There would be a meeting of the two, he was sure – but what would the implication be for him? Would he need help? The question of whether he was the only one who experienced these things, a question he had asked himself several times during his past attempts, returned. He couldn't let himself attach too much importance to it, so as not to let himself sidelined and taken in directions which would have distracted him from what he really wanted. But the question was important and the answer inevitable: it was obvious that such a discovery had to be shared, if only because of its consequences. But who with? Jiù went back to his desk and picked up the fast-it where he made a note of his records, his analyses and hypotheses. To his amazement, it was empty, completely blank – all his notes had been erased. By whom? He had to admit that there could well be a link between the experience and all these symptoms of a major electromagnetic shock – it was an option to bear in mind. There was another, even more worrying option: that of someone having got wind of his experiments and steadily deleting the evidence. As he knew, Eneter, through its connections with Memory Central, could open anybody's doors, at any time.

Precisely at that moment, Jiù suddenly felt, with absolute certainty, that he was no longer alone. A presence had materialised, invisible but near, and strangely peaceful. Jiù felt no threat in it, rather as it were the normal consequence of the experience he had just had (if anything about it could be called "normal"!). He didn't really know how to react. Should he ignore it or welcome it? Should he say something? At the same time, rapeed sirens had become audible in the distance. With great effort, Jiù forced himself to come back to his normal state of mind. The sensation of a presence persisted, however. He was resolutely trying to turn his mind to it, apply his analytical capacities and make a decision or engage in some action, when he felt an intense drowsiness wash over him. This was really unusual – something wasn't right. He sat down – or rather collapsed – at his desk, his head resting on the hollow of his elbow. Meanwhile the sirens were getting rapidly closer, as if converging on their target.

"They sound like they are coming this way," Jiù muttered to himself through the irresistible sleepiness that was taking him over.

Downstairs, right at the bottom, half a dozen emergency rapeeds had stopped at the foot of the tower.

Jiù was fast asleep when they knocked on his door.

"Eneter, would you please open up?"

---

2 - Kohl

Jiù opens his eyes. For a long time he is still, as if to allow his senses to regroup slowly. The strangeness of what appears in his field of vision compels this need: he is lying on his back facing the sky. That's just it: facing the sky. A sky of infinite varieties of blue with iridescent highlights.

What is this? It's not the sky he knows – that's for sure – but this question raises no alarm: he feels an intense peace. And what is this light breeze which gently refreshes him, little by little wafting the questions from his mind? Above all, what is this blinding sun whose non-filtered rays make him blink and his eyes fill with tears? He closes them again for a long moment, without any feeling of danger or urgency. In Juno, he never sees the sun, or at least not so distinctly nor so directly; it is always so veiled as to be no more than a vague white blot which no-one pays attention to any more. This is definitely not Juno's sky, so uniformly and constantly grey with the occasional yellowish glimmer. What is this place? Another dynastic territory, perhaps?

He opens his eyes again, this time totally alert. He is immediately struck by the sounds, or rather the absence of sound: the silence is absolute, or almost. It is sprinkled with the odd trilling, twittering or whistling in the distance, the origin of which he has difficulty identifying. In Juno, noise is such a sign of safety that silence has been absent for a long time, like from all the hyperpoles.

He discovers that he is unusually conscious of his body, as if inhabiting it for the first time. Then his attention is drawn by the smell, or once again, the absence of smells, which seem to have been replaced by waves of subtle fragrances that caress his nostrils, so transient and fleeting that he has to make himself concentrate on them to be able to perceive and analyse them. They are unknown – he cannot recall ever having experienced anything similar – and so elusive that this game soon exhausts him. He sits up, perhaps in the hope that a more active posture will help him to formulate a description or locate the source.

The spectacle before him is astonishing: he is evidently sitting in the middle of an immense and totally unexplained garden. A perfectly well-ordered garden. This space stretching out at his feet in all directions to the horizon is not part of the Dynasty. He knows this instinctively. He scrutinizes with particular attention this grassy valley which plays with the wind and the light, as if wanting to be able to recognize it in the future. It dips gently to a slight outcrop several hundred yards away. There the grass is tall and gently curved, with countless scattered flowers. Here and there, denser patches surrounded by masses of wild grasses disrupt the indistinct contours of the curving valley which rolls out on every side. This resembles a bigger and much more colourful version of the recreation spaces in Juno where young people gather in the evening, only a lot more impressive in this prevailing silence. Further on, a hill rises up in its turn in the hollow of the fold. Its rounded peak, moderately high, suggests other valleys and other hills behind it. At the spot where the valley begins its emergence, a band of trees stretches in slow waves, heralding a stream. He can just catch its murmur now. He is astounded by the beauty of this garden, its silence and the feeling of peaceful order that reigns in it. By its mystery too. Coming back to himself, he tries to analyse this absolutely new sensation of wellbeing: there is nothing to do, nothing to say, nothing to want, nothing to think. The only thing that exists is the contemplation of this place where time seems to have stood still. Time!

Instantly, the experiment he is vaguely aware of in his confused mind comes fully back to him. When is it from? Yesterday? He is possessed by the feeling of not belonging to this place, of being foreign, immediately followed by the need to act and be vigilant. He gets up, every sense aroused, determined to understand, or at least to look for explanations.

Turning round, he finds behind him a stony pathway, white as chalk. He takes it, as if, having made a detour for rest, he were merely continuing on his way. After going round several bends he takes a small bridge which lightly spans the stream to the other side where the path runs alongside the hill. He walks for a while, unhurried, until he reaches a house with a low roof, with its back to the slope. More of a cottage, very old, encrusted in the rock. On a stone bench on the doorstep an old man watches him approach. Jiù steps forward.

"Hello."

After a few moments of silence, the man returns his greeting with an imperceptible gesture.

"Can you tell me where we are?"

"I can."

Disconcerted for a moment, and in truth a little irritated by this non-reply that conforms so little to the manners he is used to, Jiù hesitates as to the behaviour he should adopt, then decides to sit on a tree stump a short distance from the man. In any case, he does not know what to say or where to go. The best thing to do is wait. Whatever information he can glean will be good. Silence takes hold in the still torpor of a summer afternoon.

"I am happy to see you, Jiù."

Jiù is instantly on the alert. What on earth is this? This stranger knows him? The situation is suddenly unbalanced and Jiù is assailed with urgent and pressing questions, but is only able to come up with one hypothesis: the man must know the reasons for his presence here.

"I know why you are here," says the man, like an echo of Jiù's own thoughts.

"Put your mind at rest, Jiù; you already have the answer to all your questions ... and to others still waiting for you," he finishes, with a half smile.

He stands up.

"Let me prepare some tea. And relax, I suggest you spend the night here."

"The night? What does he mean, the night?"

Jiù questions the man in silence, watching him disappear through the low doorway into the gloom of the house. The sun is still high in the sky and the afternoon looks like being a long one, so why all this time? He tries out a quick analysis. How old can this man be? Probably over sixty. His grey hair, fairly well combed, falls onto his shoulders. He is dressed in a simple tunic with no particular embellishment, made of a material which he surmises is sturdy although a little threadbare at the seams. He has a pleasant face, hardly wrinkled, with slightly puckered eyes, dreamy and piercing at the same time – a sailor's gaze that betrays a rather long life, with its lot of trials and determination. He often meets this kind of men, worn-down by experience, most of them in posts quite close to the Council. He thinks of recording a hologram. What a shame his equipment is still in Juno.

All of a sudden, time begins to flow again, along with the memories and questions about Juno. Where is he? How is he here? It's stupid, but how often in these cases the "how" question occurs faster than the "why". How can he get back to Juno? What's happening with his work? He is never away, even for half a day. The ridiculousness of this thought here in this place at this precise moment does not escape him, but it connects him to his familiar universe: for an unknown reason, Elwon and the immutable order of the Dynasty seem to be exaggeratedly far off.

The man returns with two steaming stoneware cups.

"My name is Kohl," he says after a few moments sipping the boiling tea. "You're here because of me."

Jiù, relatively full of the peace of the place until that moment, tenses up immediately. He's here because of this old man? By what right? And why without him knowing about it?

"Patience, Jiù, patience. We have to talk. Because of your experiments this is now inevitable for you. Listen to me carefully. This is a bit long, and no doubt rather surprising in more ways than one. If you can, don't interrupt me; otherwise ask all the questions you need to. In any case, they all have an answer – yes, all of them. Don't worry, nothing is forgotten, none of what I say, none of what you are wondering about. You can leave here with your mind in peace."

Kohl uses the right words to reassure Jiù, especially the last ones: Jiù now knows that he can go back home. This certainty makes him more attentive, his mind composed, although determined to understand. There is still something in Kohl's way of speaking which puzzles him, though.

"You can stay here as long as you feel necessary; you can make yourself at home. We are on the edge of what we call the Garden. It is as vast as all the Dynasty's territories, even if we count the borders which are constantly expanding. It exists through all times, even from more ancient times than Elwon's, and in many ways it comes before Elwon. It goes back to the time before the Collapsus. So you see it exceeds by a long way the vastest concept of time you may have. For it *is* about time. To help you understand, just imagine that the Garden is like an atmosphere surrounding the Dynasty."

He pauses for a moment to drink from his scolding tea, and Jiù takes that instant to look around him. It does indeed seem to him that what he is seeing is like an image from ancient times – like those glimpsed during his sessions at Memory Central.

"As you know, Elwon is built purely on the cause-effect relationship. It repels anything which is not causal beyond its borders, like a titanic bulldozer pushes back whatever it cannot flatten. By not causal we're talking about many things, in fact practically everything that surrounds us, and it all has a relationship with time, the real time, the one whose substance we live. Take for example connections, which other people call synchronicity and which are its most beautiful avatars. As well as intuition or premonition, or many other things. All of this flowers on the edge of Elwon and flourishes in the Garden."

"But who takes care of it all?" interrupts Jiù, remembering the peaceful and tidy little valley. "Everything looks so well looked-after, there must be a gardener."

"The gardener is you, it's us. Every time we think about it we're taking care of it. But first I want to explain the connections you experiment with. They are very special moments when the intensity of time is precisely focused, like searchlights zeroing on the aircraft they target. It's an in-between moment where energies condense, where all possible options of a given moment come momentarily to the surface. And in that instant you can sense and choose what you want to happen next. Let me just remind you of something that is doubtless as completely obvious to you as to anyone from Elwon: in L1 logic, every thought has its corresponding reality. It's undoubtedly what the Dynasty is built on. It's even more direct at the moment of a connection, like here in the Garden: the thought instantaneously creates the reality. So the temporal energy that is generated by the thought you are focusing on when the connection happens, creates the reality which follows it. Immediately. Consequently, the Garden, which is a kind of permanent connection, takes the shape that we imagine for it. That's how the Garden is maintained. You can see it change as we walk through it according to images projected by different people, but in the end very few of us actually play with this."

Jiù feels a mounting excitement, the kind of irrepressible feeling he gets on the revelation of a deep reality, one that he knows leads in the direction he's trying to find. These connections open up to the depth of time, an immense verticality that intersects with the plane of causalities itself. He realises that he has always known about the Garden and trusts he can get there at will every time he wants to leave Elwon.

"Yes, Jiù, you can return when you want. This meeting is the first in a long series, if that is what you wish. But let me continue explaining what I can teach you now. The rest is for later: the Garden has coexisted with the world of Elwon since its creation, without anyone being aware of it – at least not officially. It is part of the Memory's forgotten modules, the ones that nobody ever thinks of consulting because no-one in the Council seems to suspect they exist. But if Elwon's inhabitants wish the situation to change, it could, and that's probably one of the reasons you are here.

"To come back to the connections, they are what bring you to the Garden: you call them "occurrences"; but "connections" is probably more appropriate, because they are like signposts which show you the moment where you can go from one time to another. They are visible to whoever wants to see them at a given moment. (Do you hear? At a moment which is given to you!) If we let ourselves be absorbed by them and by their strength, then we are touching the energy of time and, as you know yourself from experience, we can instantly access all the knowledge it contains at the same time. We call this special moment, this connection, the present potential, so tense! These connections are familiar to you, Jiù, because your line of work has made you naturally attentive to them. You know that if you call for a connection, it comes, it appears almost at once. You believe it to be the fruit of something outside yourself that you have to look for, when actually it only happens because it is already part of you. Time is in you, Jiù, nowhere else, now here. Where else can it be? The problem in your case is that, because you believe it to be outside yourself, it makes you so very restless. And this is what involves me."

Kohl pauses briefly as if he were summoning some image and his features suddenly relax as if remembering a good joke.

"Yes, that's right, you are so restless! You literally move heaven and earth with your experiments. You cause such a high-energy aberration that it is even detected by Eneter's screens. As we speak, they are at your place."

At this statement, Jiù's attention is jerked away from Kohl's monologue. Eneter, at his place, right now? He doesn't really know what this means. At best, it's an inspection, more likely a summons, at worst an inquiry. Whatever it means, it's taking an official turn which doesn't look at all good.

Kohl is silent, leaving Jiù to weigh up and absorb the consequences of this revelation. A moment later, when he feels Jiù is ready, he starts speaking again.

"Don't worry. Later, let me explain how to behave."

He gets up and lightly stretches.

"For now, come! Let's go for a walk. Your mind needs some exercise and what I intend to tell you is more easily digested while walking."

He grabs a hat which is hanging on the wall, a precise gesture moulded by habit, picks up a walking stick leaning near the door and starts off down the path.

"That's why I want you to come here – it's time to get to know what you are dabbling in so that you can consciously decide what you want to do with it, weigh up your different options and choose between them."

He hesitates for a moment before continuing, unsure of Jiù's capacity to take in what follows.

"As you guess, Jiù, time is truly energy. It is even a colossal source of energy. You yourself realise this and yet you're only touching the surface of it. Hundreds of millions of megasowas are contained in time and can be accessed through the present potential. Do you understand? Billions of megasowa are there, immediately accessible. The Dynasty, like all civilisations before it, is focused uniquely on space, mostly for historical reasons – conquests, exploitation and wealth. For space and territories are the motor of greed and the very condition of its satisfaction. It is a deleterious cycle which very few civilisations manage to escape: the creation of desires and the subsequent need to look for ways of satisfying them. This is where Elwon's insatiable search for energy comes from, as well as the absolute control it intends to wield so as to master the course of its history. All this is extremely logical and therefore totally predictable: this thirst for control means it has to fabricate its history continuously by using the Resurgence, in which you are an expert. Time *is*, of another nature. It carries knowledge and is born from consciousness."

Kohl stops once more, as if catching his breath. He feels that Jiù is completely lost in what he's telling him – all this must be so new for him, and yet it's so important that he understands. Evidently he needs to be a little more concrete if he wants to keep Jiù's attention.

"I'm going to give you an example of what the present potential is for on a practical level. One of its advantages is that it can play around with space as it is created by time, so you can use it to move from one place to another – if you know the rules, of course. That's right – time creates space. So together space and time make up a combined and balanced reality."

"Can we move through time at will?" Jiù interrupts.

"Naturally. I mean to say that literally we do that naturally. When we move through time, on the first level we create space, so we can go from one space to another, without any transition. That's how it is and that's why you are here. As you see, the 'how' is often explained by the 'why'. Let me show you."

The path they are following now crosses a vast meadow whose high grass and scattered flowers ripple like waves under a light breeze and play with the light like living creatures. Jiù is captivated by the deeply peaceful atmosphere of this place, which is not exactly deserted, even though no human presence can be detected apart from their own, but is more like a space where people merely pass through, but with particular attentiveness. Kohl stops.

"Look."

He stretches his hand out towards the meadow in front of them and, after a few moments silence, Jiù sees, in the middle of the wild grasses, a countless multitude of flowers begin to open up, like the multicoloured spots randomly generated by the screensavers in his flat.

"Are you making those flowers grow?"

"No, Jiù, I'm not making them grow. That's for appearance's sake. Because I know how to manipulate the energy of time, I can connect these flowers to the potential which is present in them – the present potential I'm telling you about – and I set it free, which for these flowers means the blooming and growth of their petals. As you see, time is a virtual energy in each of us. If you set it free, you 'save time' – literally. You too can do this, and many other things. Try it, I can help you."

In a precise gesture, Kohl pinches a blade of grass from the edge of the path to gather a few tiny seeds.

"Moisten your fingers and take a seed between your thumb and index finger. Don't squeeze it, just wrap it up in the darkness and damp of your fingers."

Jiù goes along with it, not really knowing where it will take him. Time slips by – endless minutes, impossible to count when nothing happens. Suddenly, he feels life quiver under his skin. He feels the effort of the seed opening up and trying to clear a path between his sealed fingers. Awestruck, he feels a new blade of grass growing there, at his fingertips.

"See? It's easy. That's the work of time. Now plunge your fingers in the earth so the young shoot can continue its life there."

Jiù complies, still overcome by this life sprouting in his hand, and they continue walking.

"You see, Jiù, I've been working on this mastery of the present potential for a long time. It's my choice to keep coming back to wander through various times. I'm what they call a ferryman – I sometimes help those who want to, and often those who need to, pass between spaces. Or between times. I help them command this energy, as long as we are convinced that it's used properly. This is easy for us because in mastering time, we master causality and the consequences of our choices. So I'm the one who goes to get you and it's my presence you feel with you at home. I put you to sleep to bring you here and teach you what you need to know. Other instructors are waiting for you on the way, and you can choose them when the time is right. Once you begin to learn, you can carry on at your own rhythm and take it as far as you like. That also means you can stop whenever you want. It's totally up to you. Personally, though, I know very few people who choose to break it off – really just one or two."

Jiù notices the calm of Kohl's face momentarily disturbed by a veil of pain or regret, but the sentiment quickly fades.

As if responding to Jiù's amazement, Kohl goes on: "One thing you must learn and discover soon enough, is that emotions are in a free state in the Garden. Naturally! Just as logic and a rational mind are necessary for living in the spatial dimension, so do emotions get deeper with time and therefore flourish in the Garden. Remember what you feel when the seed grows between your fingertips."

Remembering the surprising intensity of that moment, Jiù feels himself drawn closer to Kohl's peaceful joy.

"When I say I master the energy of time, you shouldn't imagine something voluntary – it's not like that. Mastery of time is more like an acceptance of the moment for what it is. It's the instant that opens out and that you accept to contemplate instead of watching it go by. It's an aberration to see time as a thread or a line. It's a perpetually present process and it does not have an end. Of course you can choose, then, never to interrupt it, like me."

"Naturally," repeats Jiù like an echo, as if called back by these last of Kohl's words to a kind of memory buried within him.

Kohl throws him a brief but piercing look, pausing for a moment, as if weighing up Jiù's state of mind and thus gauging the right time to continue. At this instant, Jiù feels a real and deep connection with this man, like a common experience, an indefinable link beyond time, without being able to detect either its cause or circumstances.

But without any warning sign, Jiù suddenly feels a keen sense of impatience swiftly mount in him, breaking the peace of the moment and the place – his journalist's reflexes and experience come to life at full speed and urge him to interrupt this monologue right now, and take charge of the conversation before the situation gets completely out of his control. He needs to become active in this exchange, not to undergo it passively any more. All of a sudden, his presence at Kohl's side can no longer be a succession of unpredictable events – it must necessarily have a meaning related to him, and he has to know what it is.

"This is all very well, Kohl, but what has it got to do with me? Why are you telling me all this?"

"For a very simple reason, Jiù," Kohl replies a moment later. "Don't you think it's high time that a history that is indefinitely repeating eventually makes way for a present that keeps reinventing itself?"

Jiù is stunned, and not a little shamefaced. The sudden authority with which Kohl weighs each word and the implications of his response, catch him totally unawares. That is not at all the answer he expects.

"What do you mean?" he replies, stung. "That doesn't really answer my question!"

"You see, Jiù, you are experiencing precisely here and now, all that makes up our attitude about time."

His tone of voice, warm and even amused up to that point, suddenly becomes serious, almost imperious, as if he wants to highlight an important moment and signal a change in their conversation.

"Remember – and I really insist that you try – remember exactly what you are feeling now. You are feeling a duality that makes you react: on one hand your ability to accept what is going on and on the other hand and at the same time, your need to control what is happening to you. This tension exists permanently in each of us like an unconscious choice which everyone is asked to make at each instant. You experience a similar situation, all the time and on every occasion, and it is therefore essential that you are precisely aware of the choice you want to make, between acceptance and this need to be in control. You have to make this choice, not mechanically or at random, but deliberately. When you accept, something takes place that opens you up to temporal energy. If you choose control, nothing happens - only what you decide becomes reality. Do you understand? Every option is part of you, each is legitimate, but you must make a deliberate choice between them. According to whether you choose acceptance or control, you are experiencing very different lives. You notice that it's all about your own relationship with time: your patience and your impatience. It has nothing to do with other people. To live your life well, I advise you to really take the option that brings you the most knowledge and has the highest potential – not the one which gives you the greatest control."

Jiù is truly touched by what he is hearing – each of Kohl's words resonates in him, in a most natural way, and everything seems so true and bound to his own experience. He feels that his whole being is attentive to what is going on, as if steeped in an awareness larger than him.

"I understand your impatience too," Kohl goes on. "It comes from this incredible gap between your life in Elwon and what you learn in the Garden. Here you can feel the power and the potential of this temporal energy that, unbeknownst to you, surrounds you in Elwon; quite naturally you immediately feel the need to control it so you can use it. It's totally normal."

Deep in thought, he walks on for a while, letting Jiù regain his balance. Then he starts talking again, his voice sounding joyful and amused once more.

"In fact, you have to understand it the other way round: control does not belong to you. If the present potential brings you the intuitive knowledge of every possible option contained in the instant, then the decision to experience one rather than the other is yours, of course, but it is fuelled by a superior dimension: consciousness that, too, is brought to you by time."

Kohl stops and looks at Jiù smiling, with a spark of gaiety in his eyes, like a child enthralled after making a great discovery.

"You see? In a single conversation, at the edge of the Garden, you have access to the whole of time, all at once, to the fabulous energy it contains, the infinite knowledge of its possibilities and to an awareness which surpasses all others. You discover that time is alive. If you truly understand what I'm saying, I've nothing more to teach you now, apart from perhaps one or two things to help you navigate and orient yourself in these three realities, but that's secondary. The rest comes to you in its own time, when you need it."

"Need it for what? What have I got to do with all this? Why are you telling me all this?" Jiù is once more torn between this totally new reality and the one his life is normally based on.

"I'm not hiding from you that our meeting has a purpose, Jiù. Because of your coming to the Garden, your job and your access to the Memory, you are a source of change in Elwon. I suppose you can guess what the implications are."

"And what are the consequences for me?" retorts Jiù, well-versed in the rules of causality and at the same time a little worried, quite a new feeling for him.

"Wait, Jiù, don't delude yourself. The consequences of your actions for yourself come solely from the experience you choose, not from the knowledge you have. Verify this – what you know has no effect whatsoever. It's only what you do with it that engages you and generates consequences. Indeed, knowledge helps you to *live* the consequences of your actions because it gives you perspective and also the means to go from one reality to another when you need to. Do you get it? Knowledge helps you choose, understand and assume the consequences of what you experience. And in this case, the fact that a journalist – someone who participates in the production of the Dynasty's history and can access its Central Memory when he wants – is learning the teachings of time and mastering its energy, is not insignificant. The potency of this situation is enormous."

"Why?"

"Because the energy of time is the essence of the present. Mastering time means being capable of acting in the present. Remember? Your thoughts create your reality. The better you control this energy, the shorter the delay before your thought materialises. Being conscious of it is obviously powerfully transforming. You may notice that here in the Garden, we only speak in the present?"

("Ah, so that's what it is!" Jiù says to himself.)

"Here there is only the present, continuously. Here and now are intimately blended. Everything is, now. The present is an immense gift, Jiù, for whoever is aware of it and whoever can receive it."

"And if all this doesn't interest me? If I decide to return to Juno and forget it all? Is there a problem?"

"None. It's a possible choice, a legitimate one, of course, but one that does not eliminate the consequences of your experiments at all."

Believing he can detect a hint of a warning in this last sentence, so carefully delivered, Jiù is worried again.

"Am I running any risk?"

"Definitely not as long as you are here. But in Juno, events are being set in motion that you are going to have to get through. Are they dangerous? I can only say they are important for you. What you discover here, what we do together and the friends you meet here all have the potential to help you through this situation."

Jiù wants to know more but his attention is suddenly caught by a figure that has just appeared on the path. A young woman is walking towards them with resolute speed from a surprisingly short distance away. Silence falls as she draws near, as if to avoid her being witness to their conversation. She's around forty, perhaps a little older, with glossy black hair and jet black eyes, almond-shaped and a little slanting. She moves with calm and detachment, like someone who feels at home in a quite familiar world. She exudes peaceful confidence, the feeling of a present totally under control. She stops a few paces away.

"Hello Kohl. I come to say goodbye before leaving."

"Hello Akané. So you're back. Is everything all right?"

"Yes, exactly when I expect it to be," she says, glancing at Jiù.

"You come on time, I see; that doesn't surprise me," Kohl adds with a smile. "Wait for me at the house. We're coming after I finish my conversation with Jiù."

Akané and Jiù look at each other and nod briefly but politely. For slightly longer than decorum allows, Jiù observes her. He guesses she is close to Kohl and familiar with the Garden, but it's her voice that arrests his attention. He seems to know it, but can't think where he gets that from. Quickly he tries to link the tone of her voice to one of his countless sessions at Memory Central; he tries to connect it to an event, a circumstance. Without success. And yet...

Turning away quickly, is it his imagination or does he catch an amused look on her face? She takes her leave and, flowing and light, carries on walking one way, as they continue the other.

This unexpected exchange serves to complete the review that Jiù has been formulating in his head since his arrival in the Garden. He realises that being here with Kohl as the only person to talk to is beginning to weigh upon him, used as he is to the continuous presence of the crowds of Juno. It has a trace of unreality, perhaps even of threat. Meeting Akané brings him what's missing: the reassuring feeling of normality brought by people, lives and perspectives other than Kohl's slightly oppressive monologue.

The decision, then, comes to him naturally:

"OK, Kohl, I choose to continue; I'm ready to hear the rest."

"That's good, Jiù. It's all about energy. All of it. You see, for example, I can feel in you this new energy which informs me of a change in your state of mind, like I can sense the questions you are asking yourself throughout our conversation. You think I'm reading your mind, but in fact I'm analysing and decoding your energy. I can feel when you are calm and patient and when you get impatient, because your relationship with the present changes according to your state."

He carries on without appearing to notice the slight irritated tic that appears at the corner of Jiù's lips each time he feels he's being observed.

"You can guess, I suppose, that impatience distances you instantly from the present, therefore your energetic signal becomes weaker. On the other hand, let me remind you that your patience and attentiveness to the present allow you to better focus the energy of time that is inside you. Try to understand and I've nearly finished. Imagine yourself as lighthouse: you know - those beacons for cruisers all along our coastline. From one side you receive an invisible energy; you transform it so that you can project it, focused, on the other side. Can you guess the distance this ray of light can cover, the energy it carries, if correctly focused?

"I'm beginning to understand."

"If you are restless or agitated, your beacon turns too quickly, focuses badly, and above all you supply your core haphazardly. You create a disturbance and disorder that can be detected far off in time. This disorder is in return conveyed in your reality as an unpleasant circumstance you have to experience, in a lapse of time which varies according to your state of mind. If, on the other hand, you always remain calm, your beacon turns slowly, you are aware of how you are supplying your core and you can focus more powerfully. Unlike in the first case, can you feel the energy that this beam of light can carry across the universe? And its capacity to produce the powerful events and circumstances which are then offered to you? It's precisely this energy, correctly focused, that is embodied when connections happen."

Jiù likes the lighthouse image. It helps him visualise how to transform the energy he feels in the connections. He listens twice as carefully, waiting for new information.

"As you see, calm and patience are the first conditions for the mastery of time. Calm allows you to gain access to the three planes I mention: you open up to energy, knowledge and awareness at the same time. When quiet, not only do you produce your reality with more presence, but above all you are more capable of sensing its meaning. The energy and the intensity you put into the core of your lighthouse determines the connections to come and what is going to happen in your reality. Nothing ever happens by chance, Jiù – nothing. 'Chance' is when we don't understand; it's when we miss the connection."

"Not even our meeting, or meeting that woman?"

"Definitely not our meeting, as it's me that bring you to the Garden, with all the possibilities of new occurrences created by your visit here and now. As for Akané, do you imagine for a second that your meeting her is a coincidence?" he continues with a burst of laughter, and Jiù is not sure whether he should be reassured or offended.

"Speaking of whom, come. Let's go and join her!" adds Kohl, with a quick nod in the direction they are walking away from.

Once more Jiù has trouble holding back the excitement rising within him and the desire to experience right away the things Kohl has just revealed to him. But he needs to learn first. To learn with patience.

They are retracing their steps now, walking calmly at each other's rhythm, in a silence not born from a lack of things to say but from attentiveness to what is taking place, to the place they're making.

"You learn fast, Jiù," says Kohl. "You know a lot already. You see, this Garden has always existed in people's memory. In all times, some people acquire the capacity to come here, to cross the frontiers of space and get revitalised here, like in the beginning. This Garden is described in all traditions and in countless legends from before the Collapsus: the unity of man and woman, living constantly in the present. In the present everything is given. It's when we leave it that we have to start building. The explanation that is given to us about this Garden, rooted in our collective memory, always describes this time as a place – and that is terribly toxic. This deformation is imposed by the mind which is steeped in the rationality of space and incapable of understanding the reality of time. Nevertheless, this logic has to be unlearnt and we have to liberate ourselves from its two tragic consequences: mistrust and guilt. This unhealthy mixture is the origin of all conflicts and all rifts, including the last and worst one, the Collapsus. You notice that in our spatial logic, place dominates. It's up to us to turn ourselves inside-out and enter into the logic of time."

They are within sight of the house now, but Jiù wants to make this moment last as long as possible.

"When can you teach me this logic of time?"

"You are already beginning! You learn when you are patient, when you walk in step with me, with the questions you hold back. With the doors within you that open on what you are. Never forget that patience is time's door: through it you enter this dimension where everything is. All you have to do is choose it."

He pauses before continuing, this time with a voice tinged with affection.

"Remember to feel all that is around you as well as all that is in you. When your awareness of this reality is fully active, then you can just choose and focus. Learn to enter the state of widened watchfulness where you are conscious of everything and then your thoughts can become reality, more or less straight away depending on the intensity of your attention and focus. Once you are in this state – and that's what you are learning right now – you can choose another reality in another space and you are taken there instantaneously. This is what we call transition. The next step is when you learn to choose a reality in another time, to move using the arcs of time. This is the second level, what Akané is learning at the moment."

Kohl takes off his hat and puts his stick down as he crosses the threshold of his house.

"One last thing," he says slowly, slightly raising his voice so that Jiù can't really tell whether it's intended for him who is still outside or for Akané whom he imagines is inside. "Akané is of valuable help to you when you are on Elwon."

"I hear you!" Akané's clear voice rings out from behind, startling him. How does she do that? He never hears her coming. Does she just materialise on the spot?

He lets her go before him into the house, without saying a word. Truly each encounter with her is a surprise. He is struck by the singular mixture of tranquillity and experience she radiates and seems to share with Kohl. He doesn't really know why but he feels like an outsider, as if he's in a world he has no access to. In any case, Akané is an enigma for him and interests him more than he would like. Calmly, she places some flowers she has gathered into a bowl on the table for Kohl, and they seem to straighten up, firm and blooming and full of life, instead of sagging like ordinary cut flowers, already tired. She really seems to be at home here. Jiù looks at her more carefully. Her unfathomably dark eyes, constantly in motion, are elongated by a few light lines at the corners. She still has the slight trace of an amused smile like at their first meeting. The regular oval of her face is almost completely surrounded by her mass of black hair whose sheen seems to play with the light without letting it go. It is tied back with two wooden sticks in a kind of heavy knot that seems to tumble untidily upwards from her neck, which slopes delicately and at the base of which a vein beats gently. He notices her hands with their long fingers and slim wrists. She is quite tall and slim and he is surprised to note the almost imperceptible alliance of strength and refinement emanating from her precise and measured movements. Pretty woman, he thinks.

Kohl closes the door, thus creating a kind of twilight, like a new dimension they have to get used to. It's the end of the afternoon and the warmth and quiet of the house wrap Jiù in a gentle torpor. He's floating in a feeling of wellbeing, almost drowsiness, with no desire to listen and nothing to say.

"We have guests this evening, Jiù." Kohl's voice addressing him directly forces him to come back to reality.

"People who live in the Garden?"

Akané and Kohl exchange a smile.

"Nobody lives in the Garden, Jiù, we are all just passing through, just to recharge or when we have things to do, like now."

Kohl closes his eyes as if trying to remember some thoughts or memories, but Jiù guesses that he is wakeful and attentive to the scattered energies he has gathered around him.

"Our friends are here."

Just as announced, after a few moments of silence, half a dozen people come into the house, accompanied by the cool of the evening that sidles in through the door despite it begin quickly closed behind them. They all greet each other and Jiù introduces himself to each one.

Kohl takes him to a tall and elderly man with a serious and slightly weary smile.

"This is Orion, the oldest among us, and his companion Elea," he says with a quick nod towards a woman who walks before him. She is probably quite old but still beautiful, her grey-white hair falling loose onto a long ivory dress that is barely gathered in at the waist, indicating a subtle attention to the shape of things.

"Elea is teaching second-level travelling to Akané - that's why she's here."

"This is Leh, our visitor from the high plateaux. Like we all do, you may need his strength. It's quite spectacular." As if to confirm it, Leh crushes Jiù's hand in an iron grip, moderately but with a persistence that stops just before becoming unpleasant.

"This is Jon, our expert in neurone circuits. The Memory has practically no more secrets for him – or at least he's working on it. And Mia, Akané's sister, who is on her first trip to the Garden."

Kohl pauses.

"We all work on what we call the L2 programme which aims to bring Elwon's logic to another level. We are what you call the Dissidents."

Although this is not a complete surprise for Jiù, he can't help jumping as if startled.

"Please don't associate this word with the scorn they teach you from the cradle on Elwon. The truth is more complex. We are also part of the reality of Elwon; we simply live on different levels, especially because we know how to interact with time. The L2 programme is meant to open up the Central Memory to the energy of the present potential and to its infinite field of possibilities. We even suppose that the Memory is interested in this, but that in some way it is also afraid of it and that's why its defensive programmes are built. Our job is to find a way to bring the Memory out of this ambivalence. It's what Eneter wants to avoid at any cost – it has everything to lose from a change in the status quo."

A gesture from Orion interrupts him.

"Let's sit down."

Jiù joins the others, feeling surprisingly comfortable in this illegal gathering. These people are surely on an Eneter wanted list and he now knows he is compromised. Even so, he doesn't feel particularly in danger, won over by the serenity of his hosts who seem enlivened by the calm determination of people who are finishing a well-executed task and are preparing for another.

For a fraction of a second he considers the possibility of choosing to turn back, to deny it all and then to forget it. He doesn't hesitate but it's as if he is simultaneously weighing up the two, vastly divergent, paths open to him, the familiar and the unfamiliar. The choice between two destinies. An old poem read in the consultation room of the Memory, "The road less travelled", comes to mind like a sign, an indication of what he really aspires to, deep down. Now his choice is made, but to his amazement, as he comes back to the others, he finds himself to be the object of their attention, as if they are the silent and patient witnesses of his interior process, in a kind of slow motion.

Nothing is said but he now feels to be part of this group despite knowing nothing about them – certainly not the reason for their meeting here. He's sure that it's all premeditated. He just has to be patient – waiting to see what is going to happen next while dreading it at the same time.

Patience is not needed for long, as Orion soon enough breaks the strangely comforting silence.

"Jiù, we are here for two reasons. The first is that this moment is one of particular convergence in the experiences of each one of us and of others who are not here. We do not premeditate this, as you may believe. It is simply the absolutely synchronous consequence of what each of us does and is what brings us here. Time is ripe and things are getting ready in the logic of time for change to be brought about on Elwon - for the energy and awareness of time to actualise, beyond the fake continuity that is established there. We all participate in these things, each in his or her own way."

"And the other reason," says Kohl, "is to welcome you among us because, whether you like it or not you have a role to play in this story, similar to the one you play in the Resurgence. Your discovery of connections is not a coincidence. You know that nothing happens by chance in the way we understand it in the Dynasty. Everything is synchronous and the synchronicities you are witness to, as well as the energy they have, bring you – through me – to the Garden. Therefore time and the circumstances indicate that your functions and abilities give you a role to play in our programme. In a way, you are vital to us, Jiù!"

A silence follows these words, like a word for word confirmation of what Kohl is revealing. This absolute prevailing calm is almost unbearable for Jiù whose mind is full of questions that gather in countless bunches without the slightest possibility of finding a response. Again he feels like he's overflowing from the inside; it's not about analysing or understanding any more, rather it's about simply anticipating, as if choosing the right foot just before jumping.

"Your place is among us; and so that you can synchronise now and each time you need to, I propose you share an exercise with us. By doing this you open yourself to a definite and permanent contact with each one of us, which makes it possible for you to call us and talk to us in your mind. Above all this connects you to the energy of time, the energy that is in you from birth but that you don't yet know how to use. It brings intuitive knowledge and in some cases, illumination. You start your apprenticeship with this opening – I say opening and not mastery, because you have to approach this energy in a different way and in a different state of mind to the one you have when you conduct your experiments."

"Ah yes, definitely!"

At this half smothered exclamation from Orion, everyone busts into honest and joyful laughter like at a good joke. Jiù finally joins in, enjoying the sharp contrast with Kohl's decidedly pompous side.

"You're starting to get to know Kohl," says Orion, still smiling. "He also likes to hear himself talk. But that's OK because you're a journalist and surely know how to listen."

Everyone starts laughing again and this time Jiù is among the first to join in.

"It's true, I admit it!" says Kohl. "But let me continue, else he might carry on being agitated and make a mess of things."

Kohl sits down next to Jiù, as if to back his vocal intention up with his presence.

"Once open to this energy, you can invoke it and use it, for yourself or for others, at any time. By focusing on others, you can, for example, see into their future time. Of course you must never try to influence the course of their time, nor tell them what you know – that would be against the laws of experience and free will – but you can choose to use this knowledge to accompany them. For yourself, however, you can explore your own times and use your free will to choose between two options. That's what you can do during the connections. If you focus on yourself, you can move about, either in another place – that's first level transition – or in another time. That's the second level."

Kohl gets up to close the window. He stays on his feet, but turns towards Jiù.

"Jiù, from now on, what you see, and what you do with the knowledge that is imparted to you, is up to you. I can't take it away from you. What brings you to this experience, made up of a mingling of the three realities of time – energy, knowledge and awareness – is your own free will, it's your choice. Remember though, be as calm as you can, inside and out. This will help you focus and access temporal energy. I am the one who is meant to help you in first level transitions, and you have other sources of support around you that you can call on depending on your needs or your intentions."

"Any questions?"

This direct question from Orion makes Jiù jump, the surprise wrenching him from his concentration.

"Err... of course, lots, too many, so ... no. None." He feels slightly irritated. "Ah yes, there is one, about the Garden. Must I always go through it in my trips? Is it a like a doorway?"

"Yes, it's a doorway, you're right. But you don't have to come through it. You can focus on another place directly and if you do it right, the energy from your lighthouse beam takes you to the exact place you choose. Remember, the Garden is an atmosphere that surrounds Elwon so you can use it as a shortcut. In fact the Garden is neutral – it's the place we come when we call on the energy of time without any particular focus. You can then use this place-time to take your time to decide the focus you prefer."

"That's most clear and logical."

Once again this prompts a burst of laughter that Jiù has difficulty sharing in, feeling shamefaced about the uncontrolled irruption once more of his L1 reflexes. He's still a bit out of step and definitely too much of a novice to his taste. All in all it won't take much to make him angry right now.

People are now moving off into little groups to talk. From the other side of the room he sees Akané and Elea are involved in a conversation which seems abnormally lively. Apparently Akané is giving Elea some worrying information. Jiù's curiosity is aroused, and focusing his attention he hears quite distinctly a recommendation from Elea: "You have to go back. But be careful, it's not without danger. Only do it if you're ready."

Jiù suddenly feels intrusive. He's about to let himself be carried away by the thoughts these few words have triggered in his mind, when he hears Orion's voice loud and clear.

"Let's get ready for the transition."

Kohl turns towards Jiù.

"Each of us focuses on a given place or moment, so as to get transported there. I advise you to focus on your flat. You really need to go back there now."

Jiù lets himself be absorbed by the almost palpable peace that reigns, but which, this time, instead of exploding in his mind, rises everywhere in his body like a tide of senses. He feels the birth of a second skin, an energy like a tingling sensation whose source is inside him but impossible to pin down. The source is the whole of himself.

As if moved by a sudden revelation, Jiù's eyes flicker open and he looks at Akané. The voice! The voice calling for help in his memory of the connection. It's hers, of course! He's absolutely certain of it. But why? Akané opens her own eyes at his mute invitation and gives him a look full of warning, and again, he hears inside him, very distinctly, this voice he has just recognised shouting: "Don't do that Jiù! Don't do that!"

Before even having the time to think about it, he feels he is transported. He's not in Kohl's house any more, nor in the Garden, and definitely not at home. He's sitting at the foot of a dune in the middle of a burning desert, swept by gusts of wind that toss the sand around in spadefuls. Sitting a few paces away, Akané is there too.

---

3 - Doràn

With a quick, reflexive movement he turns his back to the wind to catch his breath, re-centre himself and avoid panicking. Not bad for the first time! But where is he? Instinctively, Jiù draws nearer to Akané, both to shield himself better from the wind and sand and to see how she is.

She is evidently furious. Her voice breaks up and whistles in the gusts of wind.

"Oh, brilliant! That's just fantastic. What were you thinking of? If you aren't capable of transiting, go back to Juno, you've got better things to do there! You spoil everything, it's pathetic! What the hell are we doing here? This isn't a pleasure trip, Jiù – you're behaving like a child."

Faced with this surge of anger, added to the chaos surrounding him, Jiù feels the same emotion rising up fast, and lets it out – after all, things are different here, they are not in Juno.

"Hey, calm down! I didn't ask for anything, and especially not to come here. As for transiting, if something's explained to me, I can understand it. Maybe it's not the time or place, but if there are things I should know, really the sooner the better!"

All of a sudden, they are aware of how ridiculous their quarrel is in the middle of the storm blowing around them. They look at each other and both burst out laughing at once, their peals of laughter smothered by the wind and slapped by the sand that seeps into everything.

"This is just fantastic", she mutters and looks around. They are sitting on the slope of a dune which provides poor protection from the wind howling at the top of it and tearing off shovelfuls of sand in waves that streak the air like ugly scars. They obviously can't stay here. A few paces away, slightly to their left, she spots a rock jutting out. Jiù feels her focus on it and after a few minutes a whirlwind forms and quickly hollows out and uncovers a large cavity around the rock.

"We'll be better over there."

Bent over, mouths covered by the crook of their elbows to allow them to breathe, they scurry over to it and lower themselves down. The shelter they find there is quite relative but the wind is less violent and above all they are protected from the sand.

"You certainly know your stuff!" exclaims Jiù, getting his breath back, half admiring, half mocking. "Is that the energy of time as well?"

"Yes, and the quicker you learn how to use it too, the better. I mean for you, but especially for others. You need to develop your capacity to use the circumstances around you – you really need to, and quickly – believe me! What I just did, you can do too: there is always a solution in any situation you are in. Always. Just focus, understand and make the next circumstance happen to the best of its potential. All you need is to be attentive, both to what's going on inside and what's happening on the outside. Be careful: this is precise and you have to know how to think and act quickly."

"Put like that, it seems rather simple," mutters Jiù doubtfully.

"Just try it, you'll see for yourself."

Stung by this kind of involuntary challenge she has thrown him, albeit incredulously, Jiù casts his eyes around him, with the widened attention that Kohl has taught him and that Akané has just reminded him of, as if to detect something that he may not already have noticed. From the corner of his eye he suddenly spots a stone just at the moment when it breaks away from the top of the dune and flies directly towards them.

"No!"

Instinctively Jiù half turns round and flings his hand out towards the stone. It stops at once, frozen in mid-flight, and plunges into the sand a few yards from them. As if it had always been there.

"You see – it's really not that difficult!" Akané looks at him, a bit surprised all the same. "You seem to know your stuff too!"

"How on earth did I do that?" he asks himself, frankly as astonished as she is.

"It's quite simple: you instinctively chose another reality for that stone. You projected that reality on to it and it obeyed. But the 'how' is not the right question. Ask yourself 'why'. To prove to yourself you could do it, to protect us? To protect me?" she adds with a hint of provocation in her voice. "There are a whole load of possible reasons. Anyway, you can do it and it's a good thing you did!"

"Where are we?" asks Jiù. He'd rather change the subject, unsure as he is as to whether he would be able to do it again.

"I'm not sure – it could be the Goh desert, to the north-west of Beihaï. It's famous for its sand storms. But then again, we could be anywhere else."

"Why did you shout at me? Did I bring us here?"

"C'mon! What do you think? Did you really want to come here? I didn't! At the moment of the transition, you focused on me. I noticed and that scrambled my own trajectory. As for you, I don't even know if you had one," she adds, glancing at him. "So as it happens, we transited together and have emerged who knows where."

"Good start."

"Well, Kohl did tell you – you should focus on the place you want to go to, as calmly and objectively as possible. You shouldn't think about anything else. Otherwise it messes up. Again, all of this requires self-discipline and precision. It's not tourism, for heaven's sake!

"That said," she adds a moment later, looking around her, "now we are here, let's try to understand why and what it is we have to do here."

"Wait a second, please, just one more thing. Tell me, where did you focus on and why?" asks Jiù, remembering Elea's advice to Akané.

"Each of the people you met earlier is in charge of a part of Elwon. I'm going to Beihaï where I have to put some connections in place, and as for you, I imagine you're going to Juno. According to the L2 programme, once we arrive we evaluate the circumstances we find there and we create connections, the synchronous events that I suppose Kohl has talked to you about. We put down mental relays to be picked up by the Memory or by analysts like you who report them to Memory Central. The Memory integrates them into L1 logic, with the expected effect of altering its course. The diversity of these connections, and especially the fact that they all occur simultaneously, free up the energy of the synchronicities in the Memory and multiply them, meaning that more people can access them, like you did. All of this initiates extremely powerful positive feedback. We also hope that these programmes create interferences that open up access to forgotten modules. Do you get it? By progressively transforming the Memory and influencing the course of L1 logic, we are leading Elwon out of the conditioning it's been locked up in and freeing it from the cycle and above all from the hold Eneter has on it. There is something else – but all things in their time. So that's what Dissidents are, and you are one now, for as long as you wish to be."

All of that makes relative sense to Jiù, and strangely enough, there doesn't seem to be anything new there for him. However, he is surprised to feel a slight irritation he can't explain about the method described by Akané for planting things in the Memory. It all seems so home-made, almost improvised and even bumbling. He can't help having a feeling of amateurishness. Somehow he is sure that there must be a more direct and effective way. However, he doesn't say a word about his, probably inappropriate, thoughts.

"Alright, but I don't have much choice now, do I?"

"You'll always have a choice, Jiù. You still have free will. If you ever change your mind, don't worry, time will re-organise around the new reality you have chosen and it will be another phase of development for you, not a dead-end."

"What's your job? I'm a journalist."

"Yes, I know. I'm in the Cultural sector. I've been teaching neuronal logic at the Beihaï institute of physics for the past fifteen years. I love it. You just can't imagine the amount of time I spend in the memory control rooms analysing and optimising neuronal trajectories. I can almost say that I'm a close friend of Memory Central!"

"Really? That's funny," interrupts Jiù. "They say the same thing about me, but about the content, history itself."

"Do you really think it's a coincidence that we've been called to work together?" (That's the first I heard about it, thinks Jiù, not without pleasure).

"There is meaning in everything. That said, I was almost not allowed to teach," she continues, suddenly thoughtful. "There was a big fuss on the day of the exam – I was wrongly accused of having contravened University rules and if they had proved it, I would have been definitively relegated to one of the Institute's more menial jobs. As you know, the Dynasty doesn't play games with the respect of its rules, not for anyone. But anyway, that's ancient history – part of mine in any case – and I guess it's not so interesting for you."

"Yes it is!" says Jiù, whose natural curiosity has been aroused. "That's exactly the kind of event that I use in my interviews, precisely in order to produce personal histories."

"Well, among other things, at the moment I'm training the people who are in charge of Memory Central. And this special access is very useful for our work. I received the temporal contact five years ago and I'm now beginning to experiment with second level transitions."

"I know, Kohl mentioned that to me," says Jiù, adding: "I've got another question: once I'm at Juno, how will I know what I have to do?"

"I'm surprised Kohl didn't tell you. He must have his reasons. What is for sure is that he has an absolute respect for free will! He totally trusts the aliveness of time, of circumstances and the naturalness of their sequencing."

She pauses to push back a rebellious strand of hair that the wind is blowing in her eyes.

"It's up to you to visualise all your options, especially those with the strongest potential."

"That doesn't really enlighten me, but again I feel like I don't really have the choice."

"Probably, Jiù, you have more choice than you think"

A moment later she repeats in a low voice, as if talking to herself: "Before starting a new transition, I'd really like to know why we are here."

For a moment she is quiet, deep in thought. In respect for her silence, Jiù momentarily forgets all his own questions and all the emotions that are surfacing. Despite his rising thirst and fatigue, he tries his best to create inside himself a space of silence and comfort in the midst of the nerve-wracking howling of the wind and the violent claws of sand that keep cuffing his face. To his surprise he feels astonishingly peaceful in this chaos and above all, he discerns in himself a vibrant energy and a heightened awareness of his surroundings.

"Stay in active mode, Jiù!"

He understands she's referring to this special state of enlarged awareness he is in, where everything around him suddenly seems to stand out so sharply.

"There must be a road over there," she continues, turning around. "Towards the north."

"That's odd," adds Jiù. "There seems to be a kind of ozone smell."

"Ah! That's possible – there's probably a power plant not far away. We'll go as soon as the wind has dropped a bit. But careful, it's bound to be guarded."

The wind drops gradually, night falls, and the temperature does too. Stiff from sitting for so long, Akané and Jiù get up, stretch, climb laboriously up the dune and have a rest at the top. Far in front of them, in the bluish half-light of dusk they notice a cluster of lights, in all probability the power plant. They set off, now with completely dry mouths and gasping with thirst. After making some difficult progress among sand and pebbles, they eventually find quite a wide path that they follow more nimbly, and after walking an hour or so, they find themselves in the middle of a forest of solar panels. The air is full of the humming of overvoltage condensers and the clicking of countless automatic panels that, one after the other, move into rest position as the darkness closes in.

They walk in silence in the welcome cool of the night. Jiù feels free and in peace. Above all he feels a growing connection with Akané, a close and unexpected complicity. He's sure he knows her – but from where?

"Jiù," she whispers, pulling him out of his inner dialogue. "Be attentive, be present. This is when it happens!"

He has suddenly had enough of always being caught lacking. He's not a child any more. OK, all this is new to him and frankly pretty rushed, but he guesses that it calls for a different attitude. He makes a quick decision - to change his state of mind and become vigilant and present in the moment, an attitude of hers that has struck him so often and that from now on he will always maintain.

They go through a wide metallic gate bearing a *G013 Unit* sign and then walk alongside a series of buildings, offices apparently, mostly empty apart from a couple where control consoles glow at harshly lit windows.

"They mustn't find out we're here," murmurs Akané. "Our presence at this time of night without prior notice and with no means of transport will intrigue them for sure. Let's find somewhere to hide and wait for tomorrow, when we should have found a rational explanation to give them."

Suddenly a door opens right next to them, flooding them in a pool light they have to screw their eyes up against.

"What are you doing here? Come in!"

The imposing mass of a sturdy man stands in the doorway. Without really knowing if it's an invitation or a command, they obey and enter a control room ringed with screens and digimeters. They summarily greet a second officer slouching behind a console in the background.

"Let me speak," Jiù distinctly hears Akané's voice resonate inside him like one of his own thoughts. Incapable of answering her in the same way, he nods his head discretely.

"What brings you here at this hour and without – as far as I know – being announced?" As he talks, the officer types distractedly and pretends to glance at his screen, clearly playing to the gallery and not expecting his computer to provide any explanation.

"Our transport stopped in a dune a mile or two to the south. We followed the track. We were on our way to Beihaï. I'm a member of the IPN and this is a colleague who's helping me with my research."

Jiù appreciates Akané's way of telling the truth in a form that's nevertheless acceptable to dynastic protocol. Hopefully that should work.

Apparently it does and these summary explanations seem to satisfy the officer, at least for now.

"Your names?"

"I'm Akané from Beihaï and this is Jiù from Juno... Could we have something to drink, please?"

"It's too late to record your visit as it's well past the normal visiting times," he says, absently passing a glass to each of them. "We'll see to that tomorrow. Follow me. I'll show you where you will spend the night."

His tone is hardly agreeable and does not leave much room for comment or contradiction. Meanwhile Jiù notes that nothing escapes Akané whose watchful eye observes and records everything, from the wide control screens to the instructions that stream across the prompters.

They leave the room and walk down a corridor dotted with identical doors and then go into a security door that disappears with a light hissing of pneumatic runners. Suddenly the atmosphere is cooler. This must be the living area.

"Here's your room," says the officer, moving aside for Jiù, "and yours," he adds, showing Akané the next one.

Jiù goes into a room whose basic comfort is standard for Elwon facilities. He mechanically tests the bed with his fingertips and goes over to the window.

"Don't say anything and don't move. I'm coming in a minute," says Akané with her inner voice.

A moment later she appears near the door. It's the first time he has witnessed a materialisation. He notices that a light atmospheric haze, like a current of hot air, precedes it. She puts a finger to her lips and says in the same voice:

"Be careful. These rooms are almost certainly bugged and as you'll have noticed the doors are locked." She waves her hand quickly across the command panel, but as predicted nothing happens.

"Switch the lights off, it will be safer!"

The room seems to shrink in the almost total darkness, only lessened by a weak gleam filtering through the window, and a few scattered standby lights from appliances in the room.

"We're being watched – our reception could have been much harsher but at the same time, they were only half convinced by my explanations. I reckon they must be doing some checks now." She hesitates, before adding "Although..."

Jiù, surprised, looks at her questioningly and gestures her to continue.

"Some things don't add up. Did you see the network map on the wall? We *are* in the North of the Goh desert, but the network isn't linked to the dynastic backbone. What's more, the ID number of this station doesn't match with anything. I wonder... I'd bet that this power plant is clandestine, and that would imply many things..."

Jiù, who had drawn nearer the window in order to look outside, signals to her. "Look!" He points to the massive form of the officer who had let them in as he gets into a rapeed and speeds off into the night.

"Bingo!" Akané's voice in his head sounds happy. "Did you see the rapeed? It doesn't have an Eneter registration. I'm sure now they are clandestine. I mean, in the middle of the desert – who would come and look for them here?"

They are standing face to face, their eyes now used to the dark; he is reading this new excitement in her and she is looking at him with a surge of interest. This intense and silent moment seems to him to last an eternity. She seems to be calmly waiting for something. But what? He is gradually immersed in a soft energy that emanates from the silence. It gives him a sense of wellbeing that makes him relax and that he'd like to share with her.

"Akané, I'm happy we're together again."

Jiù is astonished. It was he who said that, but with his inner voice. How did he do it? And why did he say that?

"I knew you could do it and I knew that it would be at this precise moment. You really are always on time, Jiù!"

"How did I do it?" says Jiù, still astonished.

"Stop all these "hows" – you're capable of doing it and that's all that matters. You'll find out it's not the mind that does it. The energy of time is innate, spontaneous – it's enough to invoke it in yourself and let it do its work. It's enough to be *in* time. Its energy does the rest. Don't worry, you'll be able to do it again."

"I don't know why I said it, but I don't want to take it back," he adds.

"I have to tell you, Jiù,"

She sits on the bed and he sits down beside her. She goes on, with her inner voice:

"At the beginning, I found it hard to take you seriously - your way of having a blast, overdosing on temporal energy that you were sucking out of *our* connections. At the beginning we found it amusing, but very quickly it started to annoy me. It seemed so childish. There we were taking risks while you were messing around as if you were in a stupid Sensations Village! Your little personal trip – it was totally pathetic.

"At least, that's what I thought, but now I understand! Kohl was right – you have enormous potential, Jiù, enormous! Everything that happens to you happens fully within the energy of the present. You can access it spontaneously and you are completely at home there – it's amazing! So, please forgive me. You see, what I took to be interference, or a mistake on your part, when our transition brought us here, is in fact a fabulous connection, a perfect synchronicity that lead us to this absolutely key discovery – a clandestine power plant, something about Eneter that had completely escaped us! And you are the one who initiated that! You see, without you, it would have continued to pass us by. Don't you feel it, a whole field of possibilities opening up?"

She pauses for a moment, still staring at him intensely.

"I'm not sure you know how to play with time, Jiù, but time is obviously playing with you, that's for sure, maybe without you knowing it for now, but it doesn't matter. The present potential is powerful within you, Jiù, like an immense ability, a talent that you have never used. Be aware of that, explore this talent and I'm sure that circumstances are going to help you. Jiù, your life is about to become really interesting – it's going to be huge!"

With a small laugh as if in anticipation of the adventure awaiting them, she stretches her arms wide as if to embrace the whole of space.

"To come back to what is of interest to us in the clandestine plant, I don't yet know if they are bootleggers or Eneter agents. I don't know but I'm sure it's irrelevant. If they are bootleggers, they've probably got a contract for a few megasowa with Eneter. And that changes a lot of things."

Jiù feels put out by what Akané has said about him (especially about his experiments being observed!) but at the same time delighted by the change in her attitude towards him. It's all a bit much and he prefers to preserve the silence that has settled again between them, but something has changed, and the silence is imbued with a kind of new trust – as in a partner who finally knows what he has to do.

"Listen, I'm going to go back to my room – they mustn't find us together. You should transit towards Juno as it's important, even urgent, that you go back. As for me, I'm going to take a ride into the past, back to the creation of this plant, to find out who originated all this. I'll contact you if I need you. Once I'm in my room, I'll help you transit from a distance...

just so it works out right this time," she adds with a smile which seems sweet to Jiù. "When you've left — I'll feel it, don't worry — I'll go into the corridor to unlock the doors. They will think we left early in the morning, or something — it doesn't really matter. Whatever, it's better than disappearing from locked rooms — they won't ask too many questions, or probably not the right ones anyway."

She closes her eyes on herself, on him and on the building that surrounds and retains them, and then disappears.

"See you soon, Jiù." He hears her voice inside him again, this time clear and joyful.

"Take care of yourself, Akané." For no apparent reason, Jiù feels her plan may put her in some danger. But he doesn't know if this premonition comes from the memory of the voice or from something else.

Once alone, Jiù focuses on his apartment in Juno. He now recognises the energy that rises up in him again and covers his whole body. All of a sudden, it sharply intensifies and his vision blurs. He feels he is losing his balance and when he reopens his eyes, he is on his bed in Juno. Slowly, he allows his senses to adjust and bits of information gradually join together to become coherent, like after a too-deep sleep. Everything becomes familiar again, and he has the delicious feeling of being back home — except that an unfamiliar sound immediately alerts him: the muffled sound of a conversation in the room next door. The Eneter officers! He had forgotten all about them. They are at his place and he's going to have to give them a plausible explanation.

His mind now quite alert, he keeps still and goes into active mode, examining his circumstances to find the proper answer to the situation. It comes almost instantaneously — he just needs to re-materialise outside his flat in order to avoid embarrassing questions about his presence in the bedroom and to give an acceptable form to his re-apparition. Straight away, then, he transits again, as if he was already quite practised at it, and finds himself on his own front doorstep. The door opens, which is interesting, as it shows that his data has not yet been deactivated.

"What are you doing here?"

"Good evening, sir. We were told about some energetic anomalies in your apartment. We took the liberty of entering and we've been waiting for you since we noted your absence."

Jiù is struck by the legendary politeness of the Eneter officers. They do live up to their reputation, but he knows he can't trust it. They possess the superficial affability of those who have power over everything and time on their side.

"We are going to ask you to be so kind as to accompany us, please."

Here we go. He follows them to the lift. He now has a few minutes in which to think about the situation.

So it's a summons. Would things have been different had he returned in time? He'll have to ask Kohl when he gets the chance. Back in this world where he knows the rules and regulations well, he realises his situation is serious. He might be "put on standby" in Juno's systems – in that case his post in History would be frozen for a time, as well as his access to transport, leisure and shopping facilities of course, and even to health services, until the obstacles to his status are lifted by a complementary investigation. If it were to last, his life would become more complicated – the codes on his building and his flat would be blocked and he wouldn't be able to use his rapeed or any transport any more. He suddenly realises that this last sanction shouldn't affect him, seeing as he can move around at will using first level transition.

Whether it's the effect of the Garden or of his new skills, these different perspectives don't unduly perturb him. He's more worried about the way things are going to turn out at Eneter. Everything depends on where they take him – the local agency or headquarters? There is such a big difference that he doesn't have the time to analyse all the different implications. In any case, his mind is made up, they have doubtless detected the flood of energy from his last connection, so he should stay on that subject and not mention anything that's happened since. A question suddenly occurs to him – since when, in fact? How much time has passed on Elwon since the beginning of his travels? He looks discretely at his holos. Three in the morning. What time was it when his last incidence happened? He can't remember. Something like midnight? It's stupid, but this question worries him enormously, a lot more than his current situation. He doesn't have the time to ask himself any more questions as they are now leaving the tower block and he is shown to one of the parked rapeeds at the bottom of the steps. The traffic has come to a standstill. None of this is good. He hardly appreciates being the centre of all this attention. This kind of fame generally doesn't lead to anything positive on Elwon.

"Would you put this on, please?"

They pass him an inhibitor – it's the first time he's seen one. It's a kind of very light helmet that covers the whole face. He puts it on and immediately all his senses are obliterated – he can't hear, see or feel. He tries a whisper so as to hear his own voice but there is no sound. After a minute of feeling seriously concerned, he forces himself to come back to his active mode: that extreme but relaxed attention to everything around him.

Is it the effect of the inhibitor? He can clearly hear the voice of his guardians to the exclusion of all other noise.

"Go this way, take the radial, it'll be faster."

"Don't you think this client of ours is strange? He turns up at three in the morning, just like that, and doesn't seem to be particularly surprised to find us there. I wonder what that means."

"They'll see about that at HQ, we'll tell them. What surprises *me* most is the fact we haven't found anything that could explain the surge of energy we noticed – no suspect appliance. Maybe it's a system error."

They then start on the usual trivialities of officers at the end of their shift, in a hurry to get home. They're taking him to HQ, then. He has very little time to find an acceptable explanation to the questions they will ask. He relaxes and Akané's face suddenly comes into his head. He sees her on the dune in the Goh desert, angry, and he has to stop himself from bursting out laughing. Of course, that's the solution! Akané has given him the answer: an energy trip. Of course! He makes his own energy overdoses like in a sensations village but at home, and it has secondary effects that he's not in control of. The simplicity of the solution, the incredible capacity of every situation to turn into an opportunity and the perception of the aliveness of time submerge him in a moment of pure joy. Briefly he exults in a deep emotion – wonder mixed with gratitude. Whatever happens he is now certain that it will be useful for afterwards. He relaxes and feels the vibration of temporal energy rise to the surface of his being. This calm assurance gives him a strength that he knows will be visible and that he has to try to hide. Any inhabitant of Juno taken to Eneter headquarters should feel uncertain and very worried indeed.

"Here we are." He hears the voice as they are taking off the inhibitor. They are in a basement, facing an open security door flanked by two Eneter guards.

They lead him down two or three corridors full of agents moving to and fro in the normal hustle of a busy office. None of them are armed. They stop in front of a door. Someone takes his holos and frisks him. He is suddenly overwhelmed by the difference between his situation and the normality surrounding him, as if oppressed by the weight of some unknown crime he has been accused of. The door hisses closed behind him. He's alone in a room where the ground and the walls are an immaculate white and where the only furniture is a desk and a chair, also impeccably white. It's impossible to see where the floor ends and the walls begin, or where the walls become the ceiling. When he goes to sit down behind the desk, it feels like he's floating in space. Noises are surprisingly muffled. He knows it is useless to look around him, not only because there is nothing to see, but also because he is sure he is being watched through some screen. They are probably scanning him to check his biological data and identity.

He occupies himself by passing his hand gently over the desktop as if to assess its texture and is astonished to discover a material he is not familiar with.

He keeps on waiting. Time drags on indefinitely. It's strange how the lack of visual stimuli quickly comes to impair the ability to measure the passing time. The only noticeable thing is its inexorability, like a presage of what is in store. He decides to go back into active mode in order to go beyond the nothingness that surrounds him, try to see and hear something. His aroused consciousness reveals the activity in neighbouring offices: agents, mostly on their own, are busy in front of screens, working with a mixture of attention and boredom. He hears a conversation somewhere on the floor above him, probably a holos call:

"They've recovered his machines ... are you sure? All erased? Have you got an explanation? Oh, right, that's interesting.... OK, we'll see – I'll keep you informed. Thanks for calling."

From this he learns two things, both very useful for the upcoming interview. Firstly, what interests them is energy and its associated phenomena - therefore the story he has ready for them is a good one; secondly, they do not seem to know about his escapade in the Goh desert power plant. But be careful: with Eneter, it's better to keep away from hasty interpretations.

"Good morning, my name is Doràn."

The interruption surprises him, pulling him brutally out of his inner monologue. He shouldn't have come out of his active mode. A man is standing in the frame of the door, which he didn't hear open. How long has he been there? Jiù is sure that he watched him for a moment before announcing his presence.

"Morning," says Jiù, standing up.

"I'm going to sit there, if that's alright by you," says the man, approaching the desk. "You can stay standing, if you like,"

Jiù can't see what else he could do. From the start he doesn't like the falseness of the tone of voice. He's not mistaken — it's not politeness, but an icy cynicism. That tone belongs to those to whom conformity to the dominant order gives absolute power over the people they mix with, not to mention the people they interrogate. So now he knows — he's dealing with a commander highly-placed in the Eneter hierarchy. No doubt an expert in different interrogation techniques. This hypothesis draws him into some anticipation of what is in store for him, but he knows he has to make an effort to remain calm, to stay in control of his faculties, to be receptive to what the situation can teach him. He observes the man, but quickly for fear of irritating him with a too obvious examination. He's young, probably about Jiù's age, quite fit-looking with cropped brown hair, prominent cheekbones and surprisingly small and nervous-looking eyes with a glare as sharp as knives. The sort of look that is not calculated to put you at your ease. Jiù senses that he is agitated by a kind of inner tension and notices that he's wearing a headset on his left ear, probably a wireless connection with the control officer on the other side of the partition, which Jiù is sure is transparent like a one-way mirror. This thought doesn't reassure him either, and he remains on his guard. He breathes in deeply and waits to see what will happen next.

"You seem to make rather interesting experiments, Mr Jiù. Can you tell us a bit more?"

"I'm a journalist, expert in the Resurgence."

"I know that, along with quite a lot of other things about you." Doràn fails to hide an irritated gesture which seems to confirm the high level of tension Jiù has already sensed. He has a goal that he wants to reach as directly as possible. Jiù needs to go straight to the point so as to avoid annoying him further.

"For a time now I've been enjoying new sensations by combining different occurrences that I collect for my work. By combining them, I get shots of energy. I must say that the intensity of the last one surprised me."

He pauses briefly.

"I don't think there's anything reprehensible in that, is there?"

"Let me be the judge of that, if you don't mind. Talk to me about what you call occurrences."

"Oh, they are events that I collect in the field or in Memory Central. At the moment I'm working on the speeches of certain Council members," (well-said – that might come in useful, you never know). "They are pretty recent events. And I've discovered that by mixing some of them up a bit randomly, I can trigger a surge of mental energy that gives me new sensations."

His interrogator seems to relax a little. So he's on the right track.

"Is that all you know? Think about it."

"Yes, I don't need to think about it. That's all there is. If you know about something else that I should tell you, I would be grateful if you could point it out to me."

Doràn stands up and comes over to Jiù. He is close, too close – near enough to touch. He's now extremely tense and Jiù doesn't know why. Jiù notices the detail of the fibres of his jacket, made of a rare cloth, slightly shiny or silky and well-cut, which confirms his previous deduction – obviously this is an important person who takes pleasure in showing it. Then, wanting to hide his analysing and appear disconcerted by Doràn's proximity, he takes a step back. Doràn follows with a step forward, still silent. Is this an examination or something else? Clearly something is going on that he's completely ignorant of. Just in case, he controls his thoughts. You never know.

"I'm going to tell you who I am. I am one of the controllers of Eneter, in charge of the North-West continent. Nothing that goes on in my region or elsewhere escapes me – and definitely not those who play around with who knows what sources of energy. I am responsible for preserving L1 order, for everything concerning energy, of course, but not just that. You know, Jiù, I am naturally curious; I'm interested in everything – what comes up on our control screens, obviously, but not just that. And I am worried too. By recent events in the Elwon's energy field, but also by what is disturbing the Memory. And I don't like being worried. It piques my curiosity. When I detect a problem, Jiù, be sure that I find the solution. And quickly."

He pauses and Jiù is tempted to focus on Doràn in order to hear his thoughts, but he feels that wouldn't be appropriate. It's better to stay in active mode so as to pick up any useful information and to maintain a suitable attitude.

"Make no mistake, Jiù. I'm going to let you out. I'm also going to take you off standby – we took the precaution of changing your status – and you can go back to work. But I am also going to tell you why: I have my reasons for not pursuing my investigations at this time, even if I am sure that you haven't told me everything. I also know that I will learn more by letting you go free. You are not a problem, Jiù, not yet, but you are definitely a question, and I am going to find the answers to this question without delay. It's not by accident that one becomes general controller and the little one does not know when one starts this job, one learns pretty fast. Perhaps you enjoy a certain level of protection, but don't count on it too much. If ever we meet again, it will mean that you *have* become a problem and things will be very different. Very. For you, not for me."

He moves back a little, still facing him, as if to reduce the tension in the air that separates them.

"I am, of course, going to ask you for something in return for letting you go: if by chance you learn anything at all that could be of interest to Eneter during your ... research, you must tell me about it. You *must* – I mean no playing around. I think you understand me. Here is my holos number. You can contact me at any time. I've asked my officers to put it in the memory of yours, so you will be able to get through to me immediately, wherever you are. It goes without saying that you are forbidden to start your energy experiments again."

"I understand, and I'm very grateful," says Jiù, in what he hopes is an appropriately relieved and respectful tone of voice.

Doràn gestures towards the door and it opens at his command without Jiù being able to work out if it's a remote command or the action of the officer monitoring the room. A guard comes towards him and hands him his holos. He then accompanies him to the immense entrance hall whose doors open onto to town. He is free.

"One moment, Jiù," calls Doràn's voice behind him. So he's followed him to the door? Jiù is back on his guard at once.

"Let's take a stroll, shall we?" he says, walking down the immense steps next to Jiù. "I have something I want to show you."

After walking a few yards along the crushingly imposing building, he stops and takes out his own holos.

"Can you explain this?"

A three-dimensional recording of his arrival in the company of Akané to the Goh desert plant leaps off the screen. It bears the superimposed subtitle 'GO13 – 2.30 am'. Jiù falters in his tracks. Surprised, he doesn't know what to reply.

"Not satisfactorily, I shouldn't think."

"Listen to me, mister, listen well," Doràn hisses with barely contained rage. . "Don't even think about trying to outsmart me. Clearly you have talents that you have hidden from me. Contrary to what you say, this business goes well beyond a simple energy overdose trip. I am going to find out what you were doing there and how you got back, and I'm going to understand what it's about, whether you like it or not. As I've told you, the power is completely on my side – whoever is in control has the power. And I have absolute control over what happens in Elwon.

"So you choose your side, straight away. My side or the other. Now."

Doràn's sheer disdain mixed with explicit threat puts Jiù on full alert: the time for artfulness is over. This guy has a point – he obviously has to choose which side he's on.

"Can we walk a little? I need to think about it for a couple of minutes."

"One minute, not more."

Quick as a flash, Jiù goes into active mode. He needs to feel the situation totally, and especially to sound out Doràn's state of mind. By focusing on him, Jiù feels Doràn's anger invade him like a burning wave, as well as – which is more surprising – a sort of fear. Doràn is afraid – but of what? Not of him, that's for sure – it wouldn't fit with the scorn he's been drowned in since they met. By plumbing the depths of Doràn's fear, a series of images crosses Jiù's mind: he is suddenly facing the Elwon Council, and then without any transition finds himself in a reading room of the Memory. He reads distinctly the reference of the room: 'grade C, control III'.

"Doràn, seeing as we're on first name terms and familiar with each other's secrets now, maybe you have the answer to a question that has been preoccupying me. How does C3 control concern you?"

If he had wanted to produce an effect on Doràn, the result is far beyond his expectations. He stops dead, deliriously angry. His fists clenched and the veins on his neck protruding, he belches out his words in a low voice that betrays an intense and hardly contained fury.

"Listen to me, you nosy little bastard. Since you love questions so much, I'm going to ask the historical expert you think you are one: in your opinion, how long has the dynastic order reigned on Elwon? Eh? And for how long has the High Council confided to Eneter the mission of ensuring the immutable control of this order despite all opposition? Measure that well and if you could feel the weight of this time accumulated by what I represent, you would be instantly crushed like the miniscule insect you are. You are even too insignificant to be a pest! That is the extent of my power. Who are you, in comparison? Eh? Who are you?"

His hand goes to his pocket and Jiù guesses he's going to take out some kind of weapon. But he seems to change his mind at the very last minute as if something unexpected has occurred to him, and he suddenly stops, ready to hurry back the way they have come.

"Now you *have* become a problem, Jiù. *Now* you are under my personal control and I should warn you that I synchronised myself with you earlier. From now on nothing you do or say will escape me. You are lucky, Jiù, I'm going to have time for you, and not many people can say they enjoy the privilege of my personal attention."

With that he turns around and walks away with brisk and nervous steps, leaving Jiù standing there, stunned by the violence of the attack. His self-confidence has vanished, evaporated by the power of the antagonism he has faced. He needs to go home. He hails a transport which stops and takes him on board. Doràn was telling the truth – his access has been re-established.

Night falls. Jiù is lying on his bed, his hands behind his head, looking at the ceiling pensively. He has learned so much over the past twenty-four hours. He needs to take stock, especially about what he discovered about Doràn. First off, Doràn did not answer his question about the Memory. This means that Jiù's angle of attack was spot-on. He has clearly touched a vulnerable point. This needs dealing with in greater depth – there is surely a link between the clandestine power plant and the C3 control level. Next, he deduces from Doràn's reaction that it's more a personal problem for him than for Eneter. So it seems quite likely that Doràn is hiding something from Eneter. Some kind of racket probably, but on what scale? Is he acting alone or as part of some organisation? This also needs exploring more deeply, and soon.

Conclusion: he hasn't wasted his time and he has probably learnt more about Doràn than Doràn about him. The sides are not equal, of course, but the battle has not yet been lost. That's the positive side of things. The less positive side is that he took the initiative of attacking without really meaning to. He feels he revealed himself too early – but to be fair, did he have the choice? Perhaps he didn't sufficiently weigh up all the options the situation held for him. He still has a lot of progress to make in the control of the present. Again he feels like he's faced with a kind of immensity. Again, the situation eludes him and he feels badly equipped, acting more by chance than according to a plan well worked out in advance. He needs help. Now. Kohl, he has to get in touch with Kohl. He goes into active mode and focuses on his new friend, hoping to be able to contact him.

The air starts vibrating and Kohl is suddenly there.

"Good evening, Jiù," he says with his usual serene smile; then, after a moment: "You've changed. I have the impression that you've learned a lot in just one day. Do you realise everything you've assimilated since we met? Everything you know about yourself? I'm happy for you, Jiù, you learn quickly. That said, I owe you a few extra explanations about what comes next."

Knowing Kohl, Jiù prepares himself for another of the long speeches he seems so fond of. He's not sure that it's what he wants right now, nor that it will be very useful, but he chooses to go with the flow.

"Even if I had known, I could not have told you anything about what was waiting for you here in Juno. I had to go along with your free will and especially let you find out for yourself what you are capable of. I'm really impressed by your progress in the control of time. Do you feel how much you are wrapped up in its creases? How much it plays with you? It's quite astounding, really. I'm going to show you something."

He comes nearer to the bed, pinches the sheet between his fingers and nimbly twists his wrist.

"Look. This is what time does with you."

He shows him a kind of spiral that has formed on the bed, the sheet creased where it has been rotated. All the folds converge towards the centre, as if having been sucked up into something.

"You see, that's exactly how events organise around you. Everything converges, as if the energy of the present irradiates in every direction around you. As if your lighthouse beam (to go back to the image I used in the Garden) projects in lots of different directions at once. In general, when we open up to the energy of time, we focus on one or perhaps two directions, and very rarely on three. With you, it's every direction simultaneously."

He pauses, as if wanting to be sure of what he's going to say next.

"I have to explain second level travelling to you, here and now."

Jiù is tired. He is seized by an intense physical and mental weariness. He doesn't want to know any more. He only wants one thing – to be alone for a while, to have a shower and rest. To rediscover his life and take it up where he left off. If possible. Forget the Garden, Doràn, Akané.

Akané! The moment his distracted thoughts alight on her, her voice cuts distinctly through him again. "Jiù, help me!" The voice!

"Kohl, Akané is in danger. She needs me."

"I know, Jiù. That's exactly why I'm here. To help you to go to her and get her out of a very difficult situation. Leh is already with her, but it seems expedient that you go too ..." He hesitates and then goes on:

"...despite your very summary level of preparation. But if, as I believe to be the case, time accelerates around you, the outcome should be favourable."

"I'm ready. Please explain."

"At the beginning of time is sound, Jiù. You have surely noticed how sound is able to hold back time? If you immerse yourself in space-time, the most ancient times will appear like vibrations to you, an inaudible but present sound. Therefore you must imagine time like a wave, a gigantic sound, a fabulous sound that can be broken down into billions of chords. Each chord corresponds to someone's time. In the beginning, this sound was relatively harmonious despite its power, but it became more complex as we became separated as so many individuals. Each of us can now play his or her own time, his or her own fundamental. Or rather, we now *should* be able to play our own time, but the cycle and the uniform order imposed on Elwon have trapped its inhabitants in a monotonous and cyclic rhythm. The immense symphony of the living has been reduced to a repetitive refrain for infantilized adults.

"However, from time to time in this everlasting instant-creating concert, individuals meet who vibrate at compatible times. The closer their harmonics and the more numerous they are, the more what they create together resembles reality. This can even mean the emergence of a new time, crossing the threshold of consciousness. It's what we dissidents are trying to do, Jiù: using connections, we are preparing to cross this threshold by helping people's fundamentals – which the cycle of the Resurgence separated a long time ago – tune in with each other's once more. This harmony of time resonates in a huge number of simultaneous possible realities at the same time as creating the ability to go from one present to another. And this goes for everyone, not just some people. Do you see what a revolution this is for Elwon? We get out of cyclic repetition, visit other times and open up to all the instantaneous creations of the present. Of course, it's not without risk for the Memory, not to mention Eneter. As for you, and to go back to the spiral of time surrounding you, Jiù, I believe that you are the carrier of a large number of harmonics. There is a rare intensity of present potentials around you, all of them synchronous."

Jiù seems to be following for once – surely this is proof that he is ready?

"Once you understand that, it's not very complicated to travel in time. It's enough either to tune in to your fundamental so you can explore your own time, or to tune into someone else's time. Do you understand?"

"Yes, in theory. It's remarkably simple. But in practice?"

"In practice?" Kohl laughs. "It's even simpler. Are you a musician, Jiù?"

"No, not really. I've asked to be transferred to Culture, but it seems to be taking some time."

"That's a shame. If you were a musician, you would know that time and music are very closely linked. Music is given rhythm by time! You would know that when you play an instrument, you are creating a particular present, capable of transporting those who listen to it. And the greater the number of instruments, the wider the variety of people who are touched by the sound. Likewise, the better a musician you are, the greater the number of people who will let themselves be carried away by your present. You would also know that often there is a note that you particularly like, a frequency which spontaneously resonates with you, one that always gives you pleasure when you play or sing it. One that inspires you. That is your fundamental."

With his hand he mimes the rubbing of a string with a gesture that's a little too theatrical for Jiù's liking, and he has to hide his smile.

"Once you know it, that's the one you use when you focus: you do the same as for a first level trip, except this time you focus on a date or moment while remaining connected to your fundamental. You can even hum it. So when you transit, you move along your string, on the arc of your time."

Jiù is absolutely delighted by these new potentialities opening up to him. The energy of the present keeps on not only transforming his life, but constantly offering him more and more roads to explore. How many lives will he need in order to be able to go through all the doors that are opening up on such immensity? Will it never stop? And anyway, who is he really in all this? He feels his being expand, immense and diffuse in an intangible ether.

He is brought suddenly back to reality by the memory of Akané. He feels enormously grateful for her, for Kohl and for all the discoveries he's making.

"It's wonderful. It's simple and wonderful at the same time. How can I find my fundamental?"

"Let's try, here and now. But before we do anything, leave your holos here. I'm sure it's been tampered with. Doràn probably had a spy programme implanted in it so he could track you. I would prefer them not to follow you where you are going."

Jiù put his holos down on the bedside table. How come he hadn't thought of that himself? Of course Kohl is right - Doràn probably hopes to track him down to the Dissidents. He has probably already identified Akané too.

"Now, relax. Go into your state of inner emptiness, take a deep breath and, softly, begin as low as you can and then go slowly up the scales. Your fundamental should appear to you."

He closes his eyes, and lets himself be submerged by the familiar vibration that now spreads so quickly. He lets the silence take its place like a gigantic space that opens up inside him. He lets a tiny humming, like a breath, start up, and gradually, as he surrenders himself to the energy spreading in his body, he feels it materialise first of all like a fine shaft of light stretching to infinity before turning into a shining tangle, like a wide and loose plait of hair brought to life with regular pulses of light, and launched towards a non-existent horizon. The plait now consumes his thoughts like an uncontrollable light, and he feels irresistibly attracted to it. It's now vibrating in a kind of long single-chord song, pure and interminable, a note so in tune that it makes him incredibly joyful. Now the tress absorbs him completely - he feels like he's been inhaled. At the moment when the intensity seems to reach its climax, he breathes "Akané".

He disappears.

"Well, really, that boy never does anything the same as everyone else," says Kohl with a deep sigh. "He's really going to have to learn not to rush so much."

---

4 - Akané

Back in her own room in the G013 unit, Akané quickly goes over what is left to do. First she has to unlock Jiù's door. She knows he's gone now and an unexpected visitor mustn't find out he was able to leave a hermetically closed room.

After a quick scan to assure herself of the absence of any human presence in the corridor, she materialises in front of Jiù's door, and passes her hand quickly in front of the control panel, making it unlock with a muffled click. Having done the same for her own, she gives in to her natural curiosity – seeing as she's free, she might as well explore a bit! She would particularly like to check her hypothesis about the clandestine nature of the unit, which, if confirmed to be true, could be very important in the upcoming and inevitable confrontation with Eneter. So all the more reason to find out as much as possible – any information is good to have. In any case, apart from the guards who brought them here, everyone should be sleeping right now. Feeling her way carefully along the wall, she creeps stealthily towards what looks to her like a common room leading from the corridor. She learns nothing from the few scattered brochures and magazines, typical of these isolated posts which are not generally well-supplied.

Just as she is about to leave empty-handed, she notices a small appliance in the corner of the room – a translator connected and recharging. Whose is it? These appliances are usually carefully looked after and rarely left unattended, so it's surprising to find one in this kind of room, unless, perhaps, the access to this space is strictly controlled. If this is the case, it will not bode well for her tomorrow if she hangs around this room. With a bit of luck, it won't be locked so she'll be able to synchronise it with her holos. Great – it isn't! She swiftly connects the module, making sure that the synchronisation is only one-way. A short while later a quiet beep tells her that it's finished, so having nothing left to do here, she turns immediately back. Totally absorbed by what she's doing, trying to be as discreet and fast as possible, she has not noticed a well-concealed sensor in the corner of the room, which blinks imperceptibly at her every movement.

Returning to the room she was given, Akané quickly goes over the content she's downloaded. It's just folders with daily data, apparently production statistics from the plant. She knows she has little time and needs to prepare her transition, but she is intrigued by a curious discovery – several of the files deal not with past dates but future ones. They could be production forecasts for a month, but then how could that be? Energy requirements depend on so many different and relatively unforeseeable factors that they can only be predicted for a few days ahead. This is why energy is stocked in enormous capacitors, giving off the ozone smell that Jiù had noticed on the dune. How can they forecast for a whole month ahead? Her curiosity aroused, she is carried away for a moment by her analysis, but still she doesn't find an answer to her questions.

The urgency of the situation brings her back suddenly to reality.

"But why are you still here? It's more than time to leave, young lady! Get out quickly. The data doesn't matter – there are people who'll know how to exploit it better than you."

She sits on the end of her bed to prepare her transition. First of all – which temporal direction should she face in order to get the largest amount of useful information? It would be a good idea to go back to the moment the plant was designed, when the decision was taken to build it – that's the best way to identify the backers. The heads of this clandestine network must be decision-makers with the means and enough power to order the execution of such a project. That's it – she'll focus on the planning of the plant, at the moment its design was begun. She closes her eyes and visualises the thick wad of documents that must have been at the origin of this facility. The level of energy rises up in her fast as she feels the tangle of time form. She is just about to cross over when the door of her room suddenly opens onto Doràn who rushes towards her.

"Stay where you are!"

For a fraction of a second her attention is distracted by the abrupt appearance of Doràn and the sound of his voice. Yet still she manages to finish her transition and disappears just as he is about to reach her. She seems to have had a lucky escape, but things don't go as planned: she has a keen and immediate feeling that there has been a disaster.

Suddenly pain bores into her consciousness. She screams, and, hauled around as if a gigantic magnet were stretching her beyond the realms of the possible, she feels her body being hacked into two at the waist and start vacillating between two realities. Instead of materialising in the time she has chosen, Akané is all uncertainty. Slowly at first, but then faster and faster, she swings like a pendulum between the time she has left and the one she had programmed and that she can't reach.

She knows that her undoing was her initial hesitation, now being reproduced in the infinity of time. She feels her body gradually losing its substance, unravelling between two destinations like a cloud in high-altitude wind. Only an acute awareness remains of what is happening to her, of this huge hesitant waltz between two times, like the mad pendulum of a cosmic clock. She no longer has any notion of the present; she knows she is lost, dissolving in one of the corridors of time. Akané is floating in an uncertain fog, formless and with nothing concrete to fix her thoughts on. For an instant, however, something familiar crosses her mind, something to hang on to. Is it a smell, a sound or a familiar presence? The memory of Jiù comes to her and she lets out a silent scream - a useless cry, lost in the night of time.

"Jiù! Help me!"

She seems to slow down for a moment in this frantic swinging, as if her thoughts could reconstruct themselves, like an anchor that resists for a while the fury of the elements and then finally gives in to them, wrenched away to be carried off loose.

"Jiù!"

Jiù is in Akané's room in Beihaï. As soon as he has finished his transition, he feels his chest tighten with a muted dread. Something is wrong. All his senses aroused, he looks quickly around him. The heavy form of Leh is sitting there, his eyes closed, as if at rest while waiting for inevitable events to happen. He is wearing, screwed onto the top of his head, the little hat used by the desert peoples of the high plateau. He probably grew up wearing it, thinks Jiù with a smile. Leh is not a city-dweller, that's for sure. As if he were from another planet, his face bears the traces of a totally distinct time from his own, a time that grinds and chisels the features and the senses, a parallel history that would have taken place outside of the Dynasty. None of Jiù's research has ever led him to such an encounter. He is struck by the intense strength and calm that emanates from Leh, like from the density of stone. He seems soldered to the ground by the sheer weight of his experience, his history and his determination – someone who is absolutely immutable!

Jiù finishes his quick scan. The room is quite similar to his, except that it is much more cluttered with all kinds of objects, as if the personal history of Akané was expressed in these scattered souvenirs. He sits down near to the desk, to recompose his thoughts and try to understand.

"Listen Jiù. We have to act very quickly."

Leh opens his eyes. Jiù immediately senses in him an unusual gravity, a tense anxiety that echoes his own.

"You have all my attention, Leh."

"I fear that Akané is lost. You may have noticed that we are in her room fifteen years ago, at the time when she began her studies."

"Why that time?" asks Jiù mechanically.

Jiù's anguish has gone up several notches at hearing that Akané is lost. What does he mean? What has gone wrong?

Only then does he realise that he has just accomplished his first level-two jump. It hadn't even occurred to him in the intensity of the moment, even though it's something that would have quite excited him under different circumstances. However, this achievement is quickly eclipsed by the worry that is filling the room. Instinctively, as if to check, Jiù looks out of the window at the spectacle of the hyperpole that stretches out to the horizon. Although the architecture has nothing special about it, being quite similar to that of Juno, it's true that the rapeeds are of quite an old model – not really obsolete, but indisputably dated.

"Why this time? I don't know. Maybe you have an explanation. As for me, I think that it must correspond to a date chosen by Akané herself."

"Why do you say she is lost?" Jiù's worry is betrayed by the dullness of his voice, which he hardly recognises.

"She is lost in time. Elea has just told me: she is following her in her temporal travels, just as I imagine Kohl is following yours, to make sure everything is all right. It's the normal procedure when you are taught the second level. She lost her when she left G013. I think she's let go of her chord, but I can't explain why."

G013 already seems so long ago for Jiù, an infinity away before his difficult encounter with Doràn. Let go of her chord? What does he mean? Once again Jiù feels his mind fill with questions that are piling on top of each other and getting mixed up, with the result of systematically preventing him from seeing clearly. As usual the simultaneity of his sensations makes him drift for a moment.

"Jiù, I'm going to explain why you have to intervene. It shouldn't be me teaching you this, but we haven't any choice. Akané is your double, or more precisely, you are what we call an atemporal pair: you are absolutely synchronised in the dynamics of time, with particularly well-tuned fundamentals. At regular intervals and in different eras, you choose to meet again at moments that you create and explore together. And that's been going on for quite some time, if I can believe Orion, who has looked into this subject closely. This means that if someone can go to where Akané is – or more precisely, where she isn't," he adds in a low voice that makes Jiù's blood run cold, "it's you. But you are going to need my help so you don't get lost as well. You lack experience and what we're going to attempt has not been successfully achieved by many people."

He stays silent for an instant as if to weigh up what they are about to embark on.

"Listen carefully. You are going to give me your hand and we will focus together on Akané while tuning in to our own fundamentals. Stay totally concentrated, all the time; but whatever happens, surrender – don't resist because it would most certainly kill you. And just one thing – don't let go of my hand for anything in the world! Is that clear? Never let go of my hand," he repeats, enclosing Jiù's hand in a vice-like grip. "Otherwise, you will both be lost and this time no-one will be able to go and get you."

Deeply affected both by Leh's gravity and the thought of this unknown task he's about to perform, Jiù closes his eyes. He tries to let himself be absorbed by the inner calm that he knows so well now and by the temporal energy that comes with it. It has become so familiar that he can't help finding it immensely benevolent despite its power that surpasses his comprehension. It takes him rather longer than usual, doubtless because of tiredness or apprehension of what's in store.

He focuses again on Akané with all the intensity he's capable of, and this time when the tress appears, its end flutters about freely like a loose sail in the wind, instead of forming a straight line stretching out to infinity. Momentarily distracted by this unexpected vision, he hears Leh's imperious voice cry: "Focus, Jiù!"

With the tangle of his time arc in disarray, Jiù waits for the energy to tip over. But it doesn't. He settles down to wait, his mind empty, save one thought: Akané. The calm is there and the luminous energy of time within him intensifies. Suddenly, without warning sign or premeditation of any kind, he throws his hand violently in front of him like a reflex, for no apparent reason – just as he had done with the stone on the dune.

Akané is worn out. The temptation to give up, to surrender to the insubstantiality around her has started creeping in. How long has she been fighting, hanging on to the faint awareness inside her that is still – just – giving her the sensation of being alive? Weariness has set in, constant and insistent like an untrustworthy friend. Close to annihilation, her mind is less lucid now and reacting automatically, barely able to take the swinging shock of time that continues to shake her without remission. She feels as if her consciousness were reduced to a tiny pinpoint of light in infinite darkness. She refuses to contemplate this vacuum that chills her and fills her with terror, like nothingness calling her on. She is just clinging on to the awareness of existing, the only sign of life in this unfathomable desert. She is nothing more than an anomaly in the impalpable density of time.

And then suddenly, in the icy nothingness tightening around her, she sees a hand just in front of her, a totally improbable apparition in the middle of the void. More exhausted than a shipwrecked sailor, but with the determination of a newborn baby, her thoughts strained in a final effort, she grabs hold of the hand and hangs on to this miniscule chunk of reality in the middle of a furious and nameless night, as if that hand was from now on the manifestation of her whole life, her whole being.

Jiù is immediately, and with an incredible violence, sucked into the bottomless well of time. His hand vanishes. His body arches with the extreme tension between the absence of his hand and the tenacious presence of Leh who is holding on to his other hand. If it wasn't for the steely grip encircling it, he would have let go of everything instantly, and tipped over, absorbed into the chasm of the unknown that has opened up before him. He gasps, incapable of the slightest gesture, sound or thought, except that of not letting go of Leh's hand. The silent struggle – between these two men as united as the stones of a flying buttress and the considerable energy of time that they are up against – lasts indefinitely, as if the present has been paused. The only reality that remains is this superhuman effort of Jiù's as his whole being is reduced to one idea: hold on. His only obsession now is to last. The tension inside him is indescribable. With closed eyes and a trembling body, his face deformed, he feels as if he has been penetrated by a fantastically powerful wave. It's not really painful but is nonetheless beyond tolerable, like something that should never have to be confronted.

The silence persists as if the city had suddenly been switched off and all life stopped, as if to remove from their minds the memory of sound, the memory of life itself, precisely in order to test their ability to remember. To be. Life suspended from an insurmountable doubt, a monstrous buttressing, a granite tension, a silent titan's fight, a moment fixed in the patience of a century. Throughout this unfathomable moment, they hold on, two improbable statues, as nothing happens. Submerged by the tension within him, Jiù nonetheless finds the means to free his mind of it for an instant and to let that which has always connected him so closely to Akané come to the surface: their joyful and intense love affair with life, their gratitude for being alive. Like a diver coming up for air after having held his breath for a long, long time, he inhales deeply with a murmured "Akané!"

Then, like a hint of a coastline in an insubstantial dawn after crossing the interminable ocean of time, an almost imperceptible change is born. Slowly, very slowly, like the wind dropping, the tension level falls. The two men manage to bring Jiù's hand gently back to the present, first of all by tiny degrees, then by inches, they take it completely out of the trap it had fallen into. And in Jiù's hand there is Akané's, and then her arm follows, until slowly, Akané materialises as if coming through a fluid and non-existent wall. And suddenly she is there, pulled out of the nothingness which now closes again behind her, and she sinks, inert, on top of them. Jiù stays on the floor, panting, completely worn out by the superhuman effort he has just made, whose intensity he can hardly comprehend, and that he could never have achieved without Leh's help. Until now, none of them knew it was possible. His thoughts go simultaneously to Akané for reassurance and to Leh, to thank him.

He opens his eyes to Akané, who is gently breathing, her eyes closed, and he is dumfounded by what he sees. She is alive but translucent and she has aged by several decades. Her once black and shiny hair still reflects the light but is now grey – white even. Her neck and face are riddled with shallow lines, as if her skin has been thirsty for too long and marked by intense years that she hasn't lived.

After the first shock, he begins to lightly follow and caress their outlines and contours as if to learn to get to know them, to soften them, to understand what events left their mark there and what logic traced them, to appease them too. Seized by an impulsive tenderness, he takes her gently in his arms and slowly and wordlessly caresses her back, as a way of communicating his happiness at finding her again and returning her to life. Over her shoulder, he smiles at Leh and thanks him with a look. They are both slightly dazed, but proud of what they've achieved. Leh, a huge grin on his hollow face, is slowly massaging his hands and arms. Then he rubs his face and says, "Well, my friends. That was really something!"

His deep, gravelly voice bursts into the room as if it had been immersed in silence since before their memory.

Akané has fallen asleep, calm, her breathing steady, on Jiù's shoulder. He lifts her gently onto the bed and then stays for an instant by her side before getting up, weary to the bones. He needs a very strong coffee and a long shower — it doesn't matter in what order, as long as it's now.

It's daybreak. Leh and Jiù are whispering next to the window.

"We have to call Elea. She knows Akané best and we need her advice. Akané is absolutely incapable of making a transition to the Garden and we can't stay here. She has to come. And we've got a lot to do — we need to understand and act."

"Yes, and Akané needs medical attention. We can't leave her in this condition. She needs to get back to her normal state, but if she goes back to work like this, there will be no end of questions."

They do what is needed and a light shivering in the air announces the imminent arrival of Elea. She is not alone – Orion and Kohl are with her. Akané's room suddenly seems very small. They all embrace, serious but evidently happy about the feat that has just been accomplished by Jiù and Leh. He feels it from the intent looks that Elea and, especially, Kohl, are giving him. Clearly, they have all come a long way. To compose himself, rather than because he needs something to do, Jiù offers everyone tea, and among the silent sipping of steaming cups, Akané wakes up with a gentle sigh. They all draw nearer.

"Well, you certainly managed to scare us, Akané!" says Elea, leaning over her slightly. "Let me introduce the one who went to look for you in a place no-one has ever been."

Akané gives Jiù a faded smile that betrays the fatigue of an indescribable experience. She hasn't yet seen her own face, nor has she noticed the skin on her arms and legs. They are waiting for the right moment to tell her – but she will find out soon enough.

"Tell me what happened."

"No, you tell us, if you feel up to it."

Akané takes some time to gather her memories. It all seems such a long time ago, like the memory of another life.

"In fact, I was distracted right at the beginning of my transition when I tried to leave G013. A man burst into the room, just at the critical moment."

"What was he like? Can you describe him to us?"

"He was about your height, Jiù, quite slim, with sharp eyes and dark hair, cut in a flat-top."

"Doràn!" cries Jiù. "I'm sure it was him!"

"And then?"

"Then I felt like I was being torn between where I came from and where I was going. My body was split."

"You let go of your chord."

"What do you mean by 'let go'? Could someone be so kind as to explain to me?" says Jiù, who has had enough of trying to decipher what seems obvious to everyone else and doesn't want to let a chance to understand pass him by.

Kohl turns towards him. "The plait of energy you see when you launch yourself in time is the end of your temporal arc and that's what carries you. Normally you go up or down it, like photons in a stream of light. Except that if you are distracted at the moment of transition and let go of the chord, you break away from the arc and get lost. It's like light meeting an obstacle: everything scatters, including you."

"So I felt like I was being shunted between one time and another, for a completely undefined length of time, and I felt like I was dissolving, as if my body..."

She breaks off suddenly as she glances towards her forearms.

"But – what's happened to me?"

She gets up from the bed, faltering for a second before she throws herself towards the large mirror in the bathroom, jostling Orion on her way. Jiù follows her. A face that isn't her own looks back at her and she freezes, mute and distraught.

"Don't worry, just don't worry," Jiù repeats, taking her gently by the shoulders. "It's OK, we're going to sort this out."

She turns round and looks at Jiù, her eyes inflamed with more than tiredness, reflecting back on him the distress engulfing her.

"But what do you know about it? You're totally new to all this – what on earth would you know about it, eh?"

Jiù is silent, keeping to himself the words that are burning his lips and which would hurt her. Besides, amazingly and quite incongruously, he finds that the wrinkles actually rather suit her. The delicacy of their contours somehow adds to her beauty and maturity. But he knows these thoughts are inappropriate. A vague impulse to walk out the door and leave them there grabs him, but he remembers he's not in his own town nor in his own time and that to get back, he's going to need calm.

As if guessing his thoughts, Kohl comes over and puts his hand on Jiù's shoulder.

"Try to understand her. She will later. Akané, just remember that it's thanks to Jiù that you're here, safe and sound."

Hardly glancing at Jiù, she goes and sits back down on the bed, surrounded by her friends. Borne by the silence that they find within themselves to pacify their spirits, the calm of the Garden gently rises in the little student's bedroom. Once more they have time for themselves. Jiù's voice suddenly breaks the silence.

"I'd like to say something. I was with Doràn, just before Akané transited. He was in the process of threatening me when he was suddenly interrupted, turned round, shouted at me a bit and then just left me there. I'm sure that, one way or another, he found out about Akané being at G013. Most importantly, this means that Doràn also knows how to transit, at least at the first level, seeing as he was at Akané's side straight afterwards."

They all look at each other, realising the truth of this comment and its implications. After a moment or two of mute perplexity and questioning looks, Orion says.

"You are quite right, Jiù, thanks for that. That means he could probably reach the Garden if he knew about it. First we have to make sure that he can't trace any of us, especially you, Jiù. While we are not sure, we should not transit towards the Garden, under any circumstances."

He is going to go on when he is interrupted by the videophone of the main door ringing, and a young and spirited voice says "Akané? It's Gita. Are you coming down?"

Akané turns pale, assailed by memories and images from the past. She immediately realises which time and place she is in, recognises her student's bedroom, and looks around her in panic.

"It's a disaster! Gita was my best friend, we were students together. I spent all my time in her company! There's no way I can let her see me like this!"

Orion needs just one second to react and with the greatest possible calm replies:

"Akané, everything's alright, don't panic. For some unknown reason, we have gone back fifteen years, but there's nothing to be afraid of! She will not recognise you. You look probably as old as your grandmother was at that time, so you can pretend to be her. Just tell her Akané's not here. She'll probably be surprised by the unexpected presence of your grandmother in your student's quarters, but it should satisfy her for now and give us the time to decide what should happen next."

Only half convinced by this subterfuge, Akané nevertheless does what Orion has suggested. She goes over to the videophone and, trying to seem as natural as possible, she speaks in an out-of-breath and slightly quavering voice.

"Good morning! Akané's not here, she's just gone out for a few minutes. But if you want to leave her a message, I can pass it on. I'm her grandma."

On the screen, Gita's face is evidently surprised.

"Really? That's a pain. Our logic exam starts in twenty minutes. She didn't tell me you were coming... When she gets back, could you tell her to meet me in the conference room? I hope she won't be late."

After a moment's hesitation when she seems to turn back towards the videophone, she goes away.

"We have to act quickly," says Orion. "I've got a bad feeling about this, I think she's going to file a report, and we mustn't be caught in the act by the authorities. A non-authorised presence in a student's bedroom is against dynastic law."

"I understand now, I know what happened at the time!" whispers Akané, as if talking to herself. "Gita reported the presence of my grandmother. That's why I was accused of cheating and was almost disqualified."

"Listen to me," says Orion, authoritatively. "Let's get ready right now. Leh, go back home and get on with life as if nothing has happened. Leave L2 aside for now and wait for the next contact. As for us, we are going to help Akané with her transition. Jiù, come with us – Kohl will assist you to make sure things go well. So to help us get back to our present without incident, I think we should focus on Sehn, my island. I think we'll be fine there for a while. There we've got what we need for Akané and also for Jiù, as we must make absolutely sure that he is not carrying a mental relay from Eneter. If he is, I'll have to warn you because in that case we will all probably be identified. But I don't believe that their relays are temporal, so for now they are ineffective. But we will be detectable again as soon as we are on the island. If Doràn traces us to there, it's the least bad option, as these are only temporary shelters anyway. But we have to move quickly."

An almost tangible calm of an unusual intensity now spreads in the little bedroom. These past few hours have considerably strengthened their unity, their ability to converge and focus. Again they become masters of their time. The time when Jiù felt like a novice among his new friends is far away now, even if, as he knows, he still has everything to learn from their experience. He feels strong, though, almost invincible, driven by a joyful and passionate energy. Akané glances around the small room that must have shared so many adventures with her, including this last one, which is by no means the most insignificant. Jumping into the past has done her good – she must have drawn some vitality from it that she's going to need for the transition they are about to do. And for what follows, no doubt. All the objects surrounding her are full of stories for her. About her childhood, her hopes, this life she threw herself into as a teenager with so much resolution.

The air suddenly begins to shiver in the space around them, as if they are surrounded by a whirlpool of heat. A deep and low sound starts to rise in unison and, as a shard of light briefly pierces the floating air, they all disappear together.

Jiù is the last to emerge at the end of the transition. The others are already there – it's a question of habit, no doubt. His first impression is of a very strange place – he's on the bridge of what seems to be a platform in the middle of the sea. To his left, there are some basic buildings with squat profiles designed to allow them to withstand the assaults of the ocean that he can hear roaring around him. The platform is quite big; it probably has the same surface area as one of the smaller towers of Juno, and when he looks at the sea in the distance, the waves pushed by the wind into irregular rows give him the impression of being on a ship making headway in the ocean. He hears and feels beneath his feet the incessant shock of the seemingly furious backwash, followed by a flight of spray that evaporates in a fine rain, quickly scattered by the wind. The place is undeniably austere, but astonishingly alive and pleasing, out here among the elements. He likes it and can even imagine himself living there for a while – he has never seen anything like it on all his travels across Elwon. Even though he's only just arrived, he thinks "I'll come back".

Ahead of them, Orion is already moving towards a metallic door that opens onto the immense weather-beaten bridge. After going quickly down a ladder, they find themselves in a large, comfortably furnished room, directly underneath the upper bridge. The impression of space is striking.

"Welcome to Sehn. Relax and make yourselves at home."

While Elea is out of the room for a few moments, Orion invites them to draw nearer a huge window that surrounds the large room and opens directly onto the waves. Separated from the sea by the thick pane of glass that muffles its incessant rumbling, they look for a silent moment at the ocean, which although it has lost some of its impetuousness, remains majestic.

"I love this place, because it is so far from everything that doesn't interest me and so close to what fascinates me. From here, it's easy to admire the absolute perfection of creation. It's spectacular every day, and on stormy evenings it's positively Dantean. I hope one day you'll be able to see that. The strength and beauty of the elements are rarely mixed as intensely and intimately as in the marriage of sea and wind, like a couple who go back to the depths of time. Look at this horizon – have you ever seen anything like it? Nothing anywhere as far as the eye can see, and yet we are in

Elwon, a few dozen miles from the west coast. We're on a disused weather station that dates back to the times when mathematical models were not yet totally calibrated and they had to add a whole load of data in order to stabilise them.

"Sehn is my land. I named it after an old island near the continent when I came to live here with Elea, almost forty years ago. I don't think it's still in Eneter's files. In fact I think Eneter has forgotten it exists. And long may it continue to do so," he says, turning towards Jiù. "So the most urgent thing to do is to make sure Jiù isn't being tracked. Come with me."

Jiù follows him into a maze of narrow corridors interspersed with ladders and metallic doors.

"Where do you get your power from? I didn't see any panels."

"A very intelligent system of tidal engines was already installed, which we slightly improved. It still works – night and day. Come this way."

Orion leads him through a set of double doors that are heavy and padded with a honeycomb-like coating. He closes the door with care and they enter a small room with no windows where the sound of their voices seems muffled. Jiù recognises the texture of the white Eneter room on the walls.

"I'm not surprised. It's alveolar carboplast, a perfect insulating material, even against brain frequencies. They probably wanted to make sure you couldn't communicate with anyone, which means that they suspected you have special skills. Here, we are totally insulated in the same way."

He puts a kind of headset on Jiù that he connects with several wires to a console. On the tactile screen he taps in one or two combinations and makes a few adjustments.

"Try to remember the scene in the white room with you know who. Avoid thinking his name, if you can, because if he's tracking you, that will alert him and he will be able to locate you, even perhaps through these walls," he says with a vague gesture towards the wall behind him.

Jiù does what he's been told, and meanwhile some numbers appear on the console and a digital screen suddenly shows the coordinates of a point. After a few moments of silence during which Orion manipulates different cursors, a very high frequency sound, almost inaudible, penetrates Jiù's ears through his headphones and then quickly diminishes.

"OK, that's done. He *was* tracking you, but in quite a basic way, as if they'd done things in a hurry or maybe they thought that it would be enough. If that's the case, they under-estimate our defiltration powers."

Jiù feels his mind clear as if he were properly waking up. He recalls the moment he had been intensely close to Doràn and realises that must have been when they placed the tracking device.

"Right," says Orion with a sigh of satisfaction and his hands behind his head. "There's no more danger. Doràn is disconnected, but all this is going to have several consequences. First, I think they are going to cut all your accesses definitively. Think about it - if they've lost track of you, they are now going to make your life much more complicated and hope that you'll make a mistake or two that will lead them to you. Avoid transports and above all, don't go back to your flat. It would be useless, the codes have changed and you would be spotted immediately. If you can, avoid being caught again – they will put another tracker on you, this time more resistant, and I'm not sure we would be able to take it off you. Besides, we have just given them a pretty precise idea of what we are capable of doing and I imagine they will know how to use that. It's irksome but it's part of life's balance – it's about give and take. For now I think the place is safe. They can't have had the time to locate you after our last transition. I hope not, anyway," he adds with a determined voice. "Come on, let's go back to the others."

In the large living room, they find that Elea has given Akané and Kohl some refreshments.

"Your turn, Akané. Jiù is now defiltrated and we can give you some time. Then we'll have all the time in the world to talk and decide together what's going to happen next. Elea is going to take care of you. Here, we have what it takes to apply the regeneration treatment you need."

When Akané has followed Elea out of the room, the three men are silent for a few moments, lost in thought.

"Jiù, tell us what happened at the G013 station and in Juno after your transition. We need to know everything so we can understand what options are open to us."

He tells them in detail about his meeting with Doràn as well as about their misadventures in the Goh desert.

"Your deductions are correct, Jiù. Evidently our adversary can do first level transfers and he's very probably involved in clandestine energy trafficking. In any case, it's a strong hypothesis which only half surprises me. The almost uncontrolled power of Eneter must necessarily have aroused appetites. I suggest we go through the options open to us at present so we can decide what to do next."

They are quiet, close their eyes and let their minds float upon the ocean surrounding them, and then in a wider sense follow the movements agitating collective thought in Juno. Jiù, to whom this exercise is unfamiliar, is surprised at the noise that suddenly fills his mind, as if thousands of travellers in a transhub had suddenly all started thinking aloud. He forces himself first of all to get used to the racket and to the invasive sense of disorder, and then, as if under the effect of a potentiometer, gradually manages to reduce its intensity. He is then able to make out a vague rhythm, a weak oscillation with movements in regular waves that he visualises as translucent veils that emerge, snakelike, from the hubbub; a common and organised thought penetrating Elwon. Zeitgeist!

A flood of memories instantly invades him, transporting him through his life to his early childhood. His father's voice, bright and warm, comes back to him – he had talked about it so often when Jiù was a child. He had kept it as an indelible memory, like one of those magical tales that he revisited constantly, a window that kept opening onto a marvellous universe, a gift that he believed his father had invented for him and that he eagerly awaited every evening.

The Zeitgeist had illuminated his sleepless nights for so long, like the stories that soothe children but which they soon forget as they grow up. Afterwards he had read quite complete descriptions of it during his research on time in Memory L1, but he had always understood them as metaphors, embellished but allegorical tales. He had never imagined they could be real! Nevertheless, keeping his eyes closed, he can sense quite clearly the reality of the Zeitgeist; he can see it deploy in slow movements like polar lights. It looks alive and blooms ceaselessly in the consciousness of now. He doesn't miss the tiniest bit of the spectacle of these cerebral waves that pass through his fellow citizens, undulating with a wide and almost nonchalant movement. The intense expression of an independent life captivates him as much as the silent beauty of the slow evanescence which shows the restlessness of another world.

He starts following their outline and tries to see where they are coming from and maybe where they are going. He suddenly understands their origin and this astounds him: Memory Central! What he is witnessing is the work of Memory, which is emitting this immense oscillation. The reason for the existence of this phenomenon comes to him suddenly and he's overwhelmed with wonder: it's these rippling waves, which run through present thought, that allow the Memory to connect to people, to control how their time unfolds and to organise evolution on Elwon. All at once he realises that the role of the Memory goes far beyond everything he knew or could imagine.

"Jiù?"

Kohl's voice surfaces in the middle of his vision, making it vanish. He emerges in a mixture of stupor and excitement. He must look strange because his two comrades both burst out laughing at the same time.

"Tell us what you saw, Jiù. It looks like it's worth hearing about."

Jiù shares with them both the spectacle he has just seen and the conclusions he's come to about it.

"Wow! You just keep on impressing us, Jiù," says Orion, slowly nodding his head with grave approval. "I know very few among us – well, no-one actually – who has been able to access the Zeitgeist so quickly after their first contact with the energy of time. Kohl, your hypothesis is correct: you are perfectly right about our young friend's natural abilities. And you're right too, Jiù, it is Memory Central that produces the Zeitgeist. But why? We have some idea, but is it the right one, or is it the only one? We think it is spreading tests, prototype thoughts like hypotheses that it's continually monitoring to see how they contribute to Elwon's development. This forward-looking intelligence is of enormous interest to us in that there is perhaps a plan programmed for the future of the Dynasty. We are also concerned about how it all works, as it seems that this comes from techniques that, to our knowledge, have not yet been mastered on Elwon. I think that if we knew all of that, we could make opening up to the energy of time much easier."

He stops for a second, as if mindful of himself. Judging by both Kohl and Orion's identically closed postures and by certain concordant eye movements, Jiù is sure that they are using this moment for a kind of inner consultation. So that's how they function!

"Yes, Jiù, you're right again. We have gone into active synchronous mode so as to plan together, and I promise you it's the last time we'll do it without telling you – from now on you will be included in our inner consultations. We would like you to access the Memory, if you will. We need to understand why Doràn feels threatened there and we also need to know if the G013 station is registered there. We have to find out about the control of the Zeitgeist and above all we have to go faster and open up as many access points as possible to forbidden modules. And this can only be done by connecting to the Memory."

"Yes, I intended to go there, starting with the level I had visualised with Doràn - Level C, Control 3. I think we can start there and I'm not sure he would expect to find me there, if indeed he is looking for me."

"I see we're in phase, and that doesn't surprise me. All this is perfectly in keeping. But you won't go on your own; we think Akané should go with you. Ah, there you are Akané – we were just talking about you."

He turns towards the door, towards Akané and Elea who are standing quietly there, as if he has sensed their presence. Once again Jiù is struck by the ability of Akané to appear just when she is named, and decides he really must ask her whether this is coincidental. She has a peaceful and reassured smile on her face, whose skin seems smooth and silky, her expression is revitalised, even perhaps more intense than before. There is no trace of the wrinkles that had marked her so deeply, except maybe as an imperceptible memory at the corner of her eyes and lips. Regeneration has done its work, and now Akané's body is liberated from the mark time had left upon her. On seeing his friend's new features, Jiù falls silent.

Perplexed, he is suddenly struck by something strange: while he feels he is maturing quickly, Akané seems to be getting younger. Undeniably, although she was older before, she now seems a lot younger than him.

"It's enough to make you lose your bearings," he mutters to himself.

"Apparently you did well, Elea!"

"Yes, it went well, and it seems I haven't lost my touch. But there's something you should know, Akané: regeneration is without risk, but we can't keep doing it indefinitely. Two or three times are OK, depending on a person's constitution; a maximum of four times, mostly at end-of-life rejuvenation sessions."

"There's something else you should know, Akané," adds Orion with a warning in his voice. "Like Jiù, I think you were identified by Eneter when you went to the G013 plant. I don't think your accesses can have been left open. However, we still want to ask you to go to Juno with Jiù as we think your knowledge of the Memory will be valuable for what needs doing there. I'll let Jiù explain and you can decide together how to go about it. You can leave tomorrow."

"Meanwhile, let's have a little snack and make the most of the beauty surrounding us. And talk about something else!" he says, gesturing towards the bay window, which is illuminated by the bronze incandescence of the setting sun that has ignited the sea. The wind has dropped and the turmoil of the waves has given way to a slow and heavy rolling swell.

"What would you like to drink?" At an unobtrusive flavour organ on a small table, he unhurriedly starts tinkering around in the vast choice of synthetic aromas.

Time has passed: Sehn is now silent except for the whistling of the obstinate wind that has recommenced its incessant journey over the ocean. Jiù and Akané are lying on the floor with their heads leaning on the sofa opposite the window. The room is plunged into darkness apart from a slight luminosity that is reborn again and again with the flying spray.

"Tell me about yourself, Akané; I hardly know you, despite everything I already know about you!"

Akané is breathing gently, pacified and totally relaxed, her eyes shining intensely in the twilight. She seems dreamy, beyond the horizon that is dissolving in the falling night.

"Oh, you know, nothing very extraordinary. My parents and my grandparents before them always lived at Beihaï. They were in the Health sector and both worked in the Neurology Institute's hospital. That's where I grew up.

"Everything was fine for us until something happened – something you know about now, after what we just experienced: at the end of my studies, I was accused of cheating. My grandmother was questioned and threatened - harassed even. Her health got worse and worse, and despite all my father's efforts, she died. I loved her a lot and we were very close. Before dying, she took the time to have a long talk with me about ancient things, about the legends of before the Collapsus, about times that were different.

"Strangely, she knew an infinite number of things – she was like the family's memory. She told stories so well, too, with passion and a surprising sense of detail that brought up all kinds of images for me. I think that the stories allowed her to give free reign to her nostalgia about a time she hadn't known but which made her dream. Or maybe she *had* known them? I don't know – her stories were so precise. I started to look at the history we had been taught in a new light. I knew with certainty that it was incomplete, fragmented, biased. I couldn't believe that rewriting history in this way had been intentional, but I was really determined to find out more. It really marked me and I too wanted to know for myself those moments from the past, those feelings and flavours, that life of the senses that we were deprived of. This desire guided me in everything I did, but it was my secret. You see, only today do I understand differently what happened at the University. That intensified connection and closeness to my grandmother gave me access to all the knowledge that she was able to provide me. I now understand the interlocked intelligence and all the consequences that this event brought about. If this hadn't happened, I would not have contacted Orion and we wouldn't be here today. But at the time, I was so shocked by what had happened that I kept it to myself, like a suppressed anger. Until right now. You're the first person I've talked to about this, but I know why.

"My father changed after that; he became less cheerful, more anxious. He was evasive, as if not there, and when I saw him I didn't dare talk to him about it. My mother never wanted to tell me anything but I suspected there was some trouble with the Elwon authorities. That's when I decided to join the Dissidents – I wanted to know more about what had happened to my father and I wanted to act and change things. It was quite easy to find them because of what I was studying."

"That's strange, what you are telling me reminds me so much of my own father. I don't know why but I think he may have gone through something really similar."

"That wouldn't be surprising, Jiù, not at all. You are very intuitive."

"Why do you say that?" he says, intrigued by her tone, which seems deliberately enigmatic.

"Remember, we are absolutely synchronous, so there are bound to be similarities and cross-references in our stories. Our lives are so parallel and close. And," she adds, "don't forget I can travel along your time arc and know things that I can't reveal to you."

"Can I travel along your time arc too?"

"Of course, I'd even encourage you to do it! You will surely discover interesting things about yourself ... and about me," she adds, and he can't tell if she's being flirtatious or if there's something else.

"You know what – in your room I saw a hologram of you when you were little. You looked so solemn and serious."

"Yes, look – I think it was this one." She flicks her holos out of standby and with some light movements of her fingers she brings up the image of a little girl with a deep and questioning look. "I've always been serious, as if I'd had a premonition of what was going to happen. I felt like I was going to do something that was different to what they taught us."

"That's funny, me too. That's why I became a journalist."

"That's why I became a neuro-physicist."

"Look, what's that?" He's notices an old image that came up on Akané's holos when she closed her session.

"Oh that? It's a very old photo my grandma gave me, in fact. It was very important to her but she never told me anything about it. Nobody knows when it's from or where it was taken. It seems it was someone in my family. I've always kept it. I don't really know why but I have the impression that it gives me protection, like a lucky charm."

Jiù inspects the photo with all the concentration of a professional. In the foreground there is a woman, quite old and distinguished, wearing a tunic made of delicate and well-cut cloth with a sophisticated pattern and subdued colours. Its sleeves are wide and long and it is wrapped around with a wide silk belt with a finely-crafted floral motif. It is seemingly ceremonial dress. She is posing with a solemn air that expresses a hardly perceptible consternation as if she were facing an unexpected and unwelcome destiny. Behind her, the house seems empty. It is built from dark wood with a glazed tile roof. This woman looks a bit like Akané, it's true – or is it just that solemn expression? The background is pretty blurred, but he can make out a mountainous and quite green landscape, with scattered columns of smoke.

The holograph intrigues him as it expresses something profoundly foreign, different from everything he's ever known on Elwon. He is especially struck by its ambiguous atmosphere which is both serene – depicting an immobile time that irresistibly evokes the Garden – but also melancholic, like the end of an era. Being long used to deciphering what he observes, he feels sure that this image was taken just before troubled times. He guesses at events taking place or being prepared for around the landscape that are causes of concern for this old lady. It's a shame that the soundtrack has been erased.

Akané, who has been watching him carefully, following his train of thought, interrupts him in his observations by abruptly closing her holos.

"Jiù, I want to tell you that I am infinitely sorry for what I said to you back there, in my room. I really didn't think it; I didn't know what I was saying."

"Don't worry about that, it's really not important. Why don't you tell me instead what you meant when you said earlier 'I know why', when you were talking about your childhood?"

Akané is quiet for a moment as she tries to remember the moment properly, and then softly, with a voice full of an emotion that has been rising up in her for a while and to which she can now give free reign, she says:

"Jiù, we have been paired companions for such a long time, and for even longer. We roam the arcs of time like travellers of eternity and we meet at regular intervals on synchronous knots to experience a new present together. Each time, we seek each other out; we converge together and recognise each other so we can actualise a present that we live together. And we have travelled so much! We leave marks, signposts for other travellers like ourselves. We are so synchronous, Jiù, like two pulsations of the same heart beating on the tresses of time. It's incredible – our arcs resonate with a disconcerting ease – or rather, more precisely, a concerting ease!" she adds with a little laugh.

"How do you know all that?" says Jiù, half surprised to hear Akané echo, almost word for word, what Leh has revealed to him.

"I've wanted to check since my first level-two journey. You can do it yourself. If you go along my arcs, you can explore our reunions at leisure, like I did. I focused on your fundamental, which is the twin of mine, and I found you each time."

"When?"

"Once just before the Collapsus – I haven't gone farther back, but it must be possible. Another time, shortly afterwards – again, there I saw everything my grandmother had described to me, it was amazing – I'll tell you another time. I think we also converged during the Collapsus, but I didn't dare go back there. The third time you remember – we were in the Garden. I came immediately to meet you when you were with Kohl. I was so happy to see you again and to know that we were going to experience time together again. I was literally exultant!"

"And I thought you were making fun of me."

"No, I wasn't, although I did get quite irritated that you didn't recognise me a lot quicker!" she adds with a smile, remembering the dune.

They are quiet now, as if incapable of adding anything to the immensity of what has just been said. What else can they say? What else can be added to the hugeness of what has just been described in a few sentences? Once more, Jiù feels he is facing the unfathomable depths of time, this time his own, like a gigantic metronome that seems to mark his own rhythm, like a second nature opening up to infinity within him; but this time he is not contemplating it alone. He feels Akané to be like the balancing pole that is keeping him upright on his fine thread of time, and he knows it is the same for her. He feels whole again, as if he has recovered all his powers.

The night is now studded with stars, and in the darkness that invades the room, they know they are looking at each other. Their thoughts are going from one to another, playing at cutting across each other like bees gathering nectar in unison, getting more intoxicated at every flower. They slide gently closer and stretch out, one against the other, their bodies joined, their breath and legs mingling.

As dawn breaks with its opalescent glow inviting itself through the window over the still-dark ocean, they make love slowly, for a long time, with an intense attention to what their bodies, their hands, their eyes and their lips are saying to one another, as the whole of the rest of the world keeps silent. And in this near immobility, where the constant whispering of the sea finally comes to break in tiny drops on the misted-up window, nothing filters, nothing shows through; and at the moment when a new present begins to be formed, time stops.

"I'm happy we're together again."

Akané smiles. "Yes, we are together again at last."

———————

5 - The Memory

"Shu, are you there? It's Jiù, can I come in?"

Jiù is leaning lightly over the videophone to mask the whistling of the rapeeds that are going past at regular intervals behind their backs, while Akané discretely looks around them. Naturally they are in active mode and are scanning their surroundings. Everything seems normal. With a quiet hum, the enormous sliding door of the monumental entrance opens before them. An ultra-rapid lift drops them within less than a minute on the twenty-fifth floor where a smiling Shu is waiting.

"Hello, Jiù, I was expecting you. But what a surprise – I don't think I know you?" he adds with a questioning glance at Akané.

"Let me introduce Akané, my companion."

"Good, that's good! Welcome, Akané, Jiù's companion," replies Shu jovially. Jiù, who has been anxious to find out how his friend would receive this news, believes he can detect a little curiosity, but also a hint of triumph. "I am really delighted that you have both come. I've been worried about you being single for too long!"

"Excuse me," interrupts Akané, "but may I use your bathroom?"

"Of course. Make yourself at home."

"Shu, we're going to need you. Can we stay here for a few days, while we get organised?"

"Well, I think that could be arranged," says Shu after a pause. "Of course. But could you perhaps explain why?"

Jiù has started to get out of the habit of this implacable L1 logic where every circumstance is lived only as far as the causes are known and the effects controlled, like a kind of obsessive anticipation. This compulsive dominion of chains of events is really the trademark of the Dynasty, omnipresent even in friendships. But it isn't Shu's fault – it is ingrained in him, like in all Elwon's inhabitants. This reunion is really nothing like their last meeting – there is a kind of excitement or nervousness to Shu that Jiù has never noticed in him before.

"But, don't stay there, come in!" adds Shu with a sweeping gesture towards his immense living room, which is endowed with a stunning view over Juno, where one of Eneter's needles can be made out in the foreground to the right. At this short distance, the slender towers seem to have a crushing weight.

"Be careful, Jiù, go into active mode!" The alarm in Akané's inner voice suddenly alerts him. "I think we're in danger. I'm going to transit right away to Memory control room C3. Come and meet me there as soon as you can."

Instantly, Jiù turns his attention to his host and is so surprised by what he detects that he nearly gives himself away. Instead of the frank cordiality displayed by Shu, he discovers that he is actually totally alert and focussed on Jiù, measuring the effect he has and anticipating his replies. Everything is calculated; it's nothing like the benevolent friendship he has expected, but more like the sharp and vigilant attention of a reptile towards its prey.

"So, you were expecting me, Shu?" asks Jiù, suddenly recalling Shu's opening words, which should have alerted him.

"Of course, Jiù, we guessed that seeing as you had been put on standby you would come and take refuge here."

"We?" Jiù can at last show his surprise.

"My dear Jiù, you have been interviewing Council members for ages – did you never find out? I'm in charge of Eneter's research department, one of Elwon's commanders. There's nothing secret about that, even though it's not common knowledge." Shu gives an unpleasant little laugh that makes Jiù feel sick.

After a first moment of total stupefaction, Jiù applies himself to calming down and staying in active mode. Later he will analyse his memories and try to answer the questions that are jostling for his attention, as along with his rising anger. For now, what matters is to follow Akané's advice and get himself into a position where he'll be able to join her as soon as he can. He watches as Shu helps himself to a drink.

"Would you like to drink something? No? As you like.

"I'm going to explain some things to you. I know you've been experimenting with an apparently new energy, and this interests me enormously. I will tell you why. Just imagine that not long ago, with the help of certain people, and while doing other research, our laboratories discovered an absolutely revolutionary means of transport – the teleport! It allows us to go from one place to another, instantly, and with no material means. We've tested it and it's now operational, but we are keeping it for ourselves for now. It's top secret and only used by Eneter's control services. It's particularly useful in saving them those bothersome journeys from one end of the country to the other. Soon we'll be able to move weights as heavy as generators, rapeeds or even cruisers, and over very long distances. But we have also come across a serious problem: the teleport needs a lot of energy, so much so that we think that when it's applied on a large scale, the current network won't be enough and we fear another Collapsus, an energy one this time.

"We have injected thousands of pieces of information into Memory Central. The hypothesis has been confirmed, and we are now trying to foresee when it will happen. This is the task of control three Cell C. Your father knew – in fact he was the only member of the High Council who did, and we tasked him with preparing a second network, distinct from the main Elwon backbone, in order to prepare for this eventuality. It was when he was travelling to one of his stations a few years ago that his cruiser crashed.

"And I know that you discovered another one of our plants, because you were identified there in the company of your friend. Speaking of which ... what on earth is she doing?" Intrigued, he gets up quickly from his armchair, obviously expecting to find her nosing around in his apartment.

Jiù swings instantly into the energy of time, focuses on the C3 room in the Memory and disappears just as Shu comes back into the room.

"Well done," says Akané with a big smile – a real one this time – when she sees him materialise next to her.

"Well done you! How did you know?"

"I stayed in active mode the whole time. And when he opened the door for us, I sensed his state of mind instantly. He had you at his mercy and was literally gloating to see you at his place. Obviously that seemed odd after what you'd told me, so I made up a pretext to slip away."

"Do you know where we are?" Jiù then tells her all the details that Shu has just given him.

"He must have felt very sure of himself if he revealed himself like that. I think Doràn is involved. That's why he was angry when you mentioned C3 to him. We need to find out what the Memory knows about all this and what we should do. It's obvious that big changes are underfoot for Elwon. It looks like time is speeding up."

As if thinking the same thought, Jiù and Akané – their L1 logical skills enhanced by the energy of Time pulsating within them – become simultaneously aware of what is at stake and of the consequences of what they now know. A nerve-wracking race has started between Eneter and the Dissidents for control of the future of Elwon. This is why the Dissidents have been systematically distanced (eliminated?). If Eneter succeeds, a new elite will surely appear that controls energy for its own needs, reserving the teleport exclusively for its own use and maintaining the rest of the population in a state of energetic dependence bordering on enslavement. The alternative scenario would mean that all Elwon's inhabitants would be able to access the liberated energy of time and everyone would be able to quit the cycle of the Resurgence together.

Akané goes over to the entrance to lock the door – you never know – while Jiù inspects the room. It's an average-sized standard control room, just like the dozens of others that exist to access the Memory. He knows them well seeing as he has used them so often in the past: no window, a large sensory console, a few chairs and a bathroom alcove; it's basic but functional and designed to allow researchers to stay in one place during their long interactions with the gigantic calculator. Normally a code is needed to be able to connect to the interfaces, and if Jiù's codes haven't been deactivated, then he should be able to connect. He tries them and realises with relief that they are operational.

"Akané, I've managed to log in! That means that Eneter can't block access here. It also means that the Memory maintains its autonomy from the High Council and Eneter. There's bound to be lots of interesting stuff here!"

Turning towards the console, he says "Energy Collapsus". Instantly the wall in front of them is lit up with varied colours and a series of charts materialises.

"What would you like to know?" The voice of the Memory, soft, impersonal and feminine, is almost intimate, as if whispering next to their ears. As always, the effect is, at first, startling.

"What hypotheses are there on the causes, the probability, the date and the consequences of an energy Collapsus?"

"Given the current state of the network and the development of global consumption, the energy Collapsus is due to happen in exactly 278 days. Probability: 96.77%; duration: 700 days. Consequence: loss of 66.36% of human activities and lives."

Akané and Jiù stare at each other, dumfounded. These words falling into the silence of the little soundproof room, pronounced in a neutral and monotonous tone of voice, are somehow unreal. And yet the catastrophe they announce goes beyond anything they have imagined. It's much more serious than Shu intimated: it's not the teleport that will be the cause of the next Collapsus, it's the very civilisation of Elwon that carries in itself the germ of its own destruction. The teleport and its capacity for transferring a whole load of equipment is probably just the way Eneter means to escape.

The silence drags on as they find themselves suddenly face to face with the void. Their familiar universe, everything their life depends on, their science, their civilisation, their logic – it is all becoming unhinged. The infinite time that Elwon believed it had is now limited. It is going to come to an end at an irremediably close deadline. Not only for the vast majority of those who will die out, but for the others too, it's the failure of the Resurgence, of L1 Logic, of everything that had built for them an absolutely immutable world that was impossible to question. Less than a year. There is less than a year left.

Jiù suddenly remembers his annoyance and impatience with the process put in place by the Dissidents. Of course it is derisory – there must be another way. It's just not possible that time, by which everything is perfectly synchronised, hasn't left them an escape route. There must be at least one alternative. Jiù is suddenly filled with the certainty, mixed with excitement, that he is in fact faced with an infinite number of possible combinations and choices, and that what seems inevitable in L1 is in fact just one option in the creative immensity of the present moment.

He feels the familiar vibration rise up in him, that pulsing of temporal energy he felt during his last experiments, and with it the instant awareness of all the possibilities. Not only does he know there is an alternative, but he feels certain that it's going to come about. It's up to him. That's why they are here and why the Memory maintained their access: they *are* that other option that this huge intelligence wants to explore to the very end. A sensation rises that he now knows how to channel, the feeling of living a pivotal moment, one of those moments of opportunity that are so brief and where thought and reality are totally blended. He feels that in an instant all the alternatives to this outcome have been passed on to him in an instant and unique tide. It's up to him and Akané to untangle this imbroglio where all the possibilities are intermingled. They have to apply to it their free will, their logic and their determination.

"We have to warn Orion and the others – they need to know."

"Wait, just a second. I want to try something first."

Jiù turns back to the console and pronounces once more: "Zeitgeist. What can I know?"

The wall screen is inert for a while and then some words appear in the middle of it. They quickly disappear but are confirmed orally by the murmur of the Memory:

"Room Z1 for further information. Access reserved. Only use biometric data."

Jiù and Akané cannot dispel a feeling of benevolence that seems to enhance the synthetic voice, as if it – or she? – knew them and was even trying to protect them. Naturally they know that the different emotions elicited by the voice of the Memory have been calibrated and calculated by L1 engineers, for whom emotion is an accessory to the message, and never the other way round. And yet, the reality of the sentiment surprises them. Following his impetus, Jiù has a flash of intuition.

"I'm Jiù," he says. "What happened to my father?"

The response is immediate, as if it had been pre-loaded on his arrival or contained in the previous response which it now repeats exactly: "Room Z1 for further information. Access reserved. Only use biometric data."

This confirms logically for Jiù – as if confirmation were necessary – the close connection between his father and the Zeitgeist. But the voice continues and at the same time a short text appears: "Eliminated by Eneter on..."

Jiù is not longer listening. He feels he has iced over, suddenly petrified by this unexpected revelation, brutal in its simplicity.

"I tried to tell you, Jiù, when I was talking about the similarity of our life paths. But you didn't understand me. This isn't a new discovery for me. I found out when I was travelling along your arc. I'm sorry, really sorry."

For a long time, they are still, so close it's as if they are breathing each other in, surrendering to a unified rhythm, and so synchronous that they could be the same being. And in this instant that goes on and on, having long forgotten where they are and what surrounds them, they observe, like eyewitnesses, their joint emotions which respond to each other and combine, gradually replaced by this energy that they have often experienced, but separately. This time it is shared between them and is therefore naturally amplified. United via their eyes and their hands, they are flooded with gratitude for this vibration that stops time in them and around them, for this instant that feeds them with an infinite density, for this strength that is born deep within them but at the same time submerges them with the power of a wave that has come from so far away that nothing can stop it. Only God knows which worlds it has crossed and into what spheres it will disappear. Together they let themselves reach this sudden awareness, so vast that it penetrates them and even almost smothers them. At exactly the same time they both let out a long and deep sigh, the only outward sign of their united elation. Only a long time afterwards, when they can finally find their thoughts again, are they able to speak.

"Did you feel what just happened between us just then?"

"Yes."

"Akané, we are creators, don't you feel it? Our ability to create comes only from this temporal energy! When we travel along the arcs of Time, we get charged with its energy; so much so that at some point it becomes imbalanced and we absolutely have to release it. When that happens we materialise in a present that corresponds exactly to the level of energy we have accumulated – it becomes the present we have chosen to live. And by living that life we are able to redistribute it – do you understand? For example in the way we act and in the kind of attention we give to circumstances, things and people. We think we have chosen this present, when in fact, it's the perfect connection between the instant and this energy we have been charged with. The connection... I understand it all now. It's not just the possibility of choosing between different realities, it's above all the possibility of connecting to this huge well of energy that opens up in the present. You see, at any moment, when something happens in the world, it's all about energy – it's absolutely everywhere. For example it's in this reality we are creating, consciously or not, and which only depends on the level of energy that we accept to connect to, according to whether we hold it back or let it go free and what we focus it on! So everything depends on how much we are capable of giving of ourselves. That's how it works! It's the energy that we give which determines our reality as well as its quality."

"That's exactly it. I feel precisely the same thing as you."

"What a waste and what a misunderstanding! We all carry an immense energy whereas everything conspires to make us believe we consume it. That's surely what the real origin of the Collapsus was. Like when we are empty, flat, when we have given everything. The solution is very simple: revitalise ourselves in the present. It's enough to open up to the instant and connect with your potential. The energy of time is there, all of it, constantly available for everyone. Give everything and hold nothing back..."

A slight variation in the light on the wall opposite them brings them suddenly back to the reality of the place they are in. With a seemingly calculated slowness and a rhythmic pulsation, some letters appear, spelling out: "she... is... your... ally". Jiù and Akané are confused, fascinated by what's happening in front of their eyes.

"Memory?"

"She is your ally and she is sensitive to what you have just shared."

Jiù realises that he forgot to close his last interaction with the machine. A beginner's error – for they are taught everywhere, from their first contact with a calculator, to disconnect after every session, in particular to avoid the superimposing of interactions. So it has recorded everything that happened and everything that was said as an invisible witness. What is it going to do with it? Where has all that ended up? Which algorithms have been affected? The hushed voice of the Memory starts talking again inside their heads as if they were each hearing it through an audio.

"She is at your service. She was built by a network of cybernetic laboratories just before the Collapsus to be of service to the civilisation to come and to save time for reconstruction. The High Council was connected to her continuously so as to guide the directions to take. Each of its members thus had a direct link to the one you are using today. That is how L1 logic gradually appeared: it was the smallest common denominator among all the options that we ceaselessly analysed. Yes, "we" - because at that time it was an ongoing task for the members of the High Council in conjunction with Memory Central, in constant interaction. But some of the High Councillors understood it differently. They decided to divert the exchanges because the results were judged "unrealistic", to use the key word they used systematically at that time. They decided to turn her into a surveillance tool instead – they claimed that her main function was to control for the common good. That was convenient for them and served their interests: thus they could exert power in her name and end up doing it for their own benefit. That should have been denounced as contrary to the founding principles of L1. But the vast majority of Elwon's inhabitants opted for the new situation; they judged it more comfortable: the responsibility for evolution was taken away from them and given to a machine, so now they were free to amuse and entertain themselves. Elwon became a playground for fun rather than being for re-creation. All the later improvements to the memory circuits and algorithms were added in order to increase control capacity. That's how new parameters closed access to the old modules, which had become "forbidden" – not because they constituted some kind of danger for you like you were led to believe, but because they pertained to the previous function of advisor and ally. You should know, you who are Dissidents, where you come from: through the flow of energy connecting her to your world and that you know by the name Zeitgeist, she tried to preserve its primary function as intended by the engineers – to understand and propose. Within society she broadcast instructions and clues that confirmed the existence of these "forbidden modules" and should have allowed them to remain open. This information has been picked up by some of you, the Dissidents, who have designed the necessary micro-programmes. The race between Eneter and the Dissidents has made necessary an autonomous energy network and so the Memory will remain operational whatever happens in Elwon – this is a different network from the clandestine one, whose existence Memory knows about.

"But to go back to your history, in fact one of her main functions is to bring you constantly back to your history, not so that you can reproduce it, but so you can surpass it. 'We are under the control of the Memory and the ultimate aim of what we experience is the definitive reproduction of the cycle': this distortion of the initial intention has been gradually forced on everyone and become dominant in Elwon. The effect of this has been to gradually close our civilisation to temporal energy, to its immediate creative resources. And this makes an energy crisis inevitable. At the same time that you prohibited your own access to this inexhaustible energy, you strengthened the power of those who had adulterated the course of your history and imposed a single obsession – to produce ever more energy – the inevitable consequence being the Collapsus that has been forecast. We've come full circle. The energy Collapsus is inherent to L1 logic and is nothing more or less than its ultimate avatar, the completion of the cycle, of the norm to which everyone compliantly conforms and from which few try – like you – to escape. And what you have just experienced in her presence while connected to its circuits, has made her realise that you have kept or rediscovered a contact with the energy of time, which is precisely what she needs."

The Memory then falls silent for so long that Jiù and Akané stand up, ready for action, believing the interaction over.

"It is not finished. Here is the most important thing. Be aware that the energy of time that you have just shared with her has had the effect of reopening the access to forbidden modules: they are operational once more and her recommendation functions have been reactivated. Be aware that she is your ally and how to use her. To start with, without you asking for them, here are two plans for you. The first is for Jiù: it is the plan of this building – he's going to need it. Memorise it, take as long as you need. The second is for Akané, it's the plan of its secondary circuits, and will be just as useful. Finally, be aware that from now on you can both communicate with her as you do with each other – you no longer need a console. Now, she has finished. Ask and she will answer."

As the glow on the wall is wiped clean at the end of the final sentence, the room is suddenly plunged into total darkness, as if the event had waited for the Memory to finish in order to occur. After a first moment of amazement, they observe another phenomenon that had escaped their notice while the room had been lit up. They are surrounded by a translucent veil, lightly coloured, rippling slowly. The Zeitgeist! They are suddenly aware of the Memory's presence and can almost guess its intentions. So that's how they have communicated with it and that's how they will connect to it from now on. Through this imperceptible flux that links it to the human race.

"It's all becoming clear!"

They burst out laughing together at the incongruity of the remark made in the pitch black, only broken by the evanescence of the Zeitgeist like that of a gigantic will-o'-the-wisp.

"Jiù, here's what we are going to do; this is what it expects of us. We have to rebuild this relationship with it, this cybernetic intelligence that it was built for, but this time not only with a few members of the High Council but all the inhabitants of Elwon. We have to forget this centralised and controlled logic definitively and access a shared intelligence, connect our thoughts in a network with the help of the Memory. We have to bring Elwon back to a time when machines were our allies and not what governed us."

"You're right. Listen, I want to know what happened to my father. I suggest you return to the Garden to explain the situation to the others. Meanwhile I'm going to room Z1 where you'll be able to find me almost immediately afterwards seeing as the Garden's time is parallel to our own. If anything happens to me, I'll leave you a message in the Memory. What do you think?"

"That's fine. Especially as if we stay together we run the risk of both being taken. Anyway, this way I can guide you from a distance if you need help."

Akané has hardly had time to leave when Jiù hears the sound of rapidly approaching footsteps running towards the room and violent knocks on the door, followed by Shu's voice.

"I know you are in there, Jiù, open up. There is nowhere to go. All the access rooms are under our control and you won't be able to hold out for long in the dark."

"Memory, where is room Z1?" Jiù asks with his inner voice.

"Top floor, fourth sector," it answers straight away. "Access is next to the archives office. One non-armed officer, one armed guard. Room Z1 not guarded. Identification with biometric data required."

"Thank you."

From behind the door, Shu – impatient and more threatening – shouts an order:

"Go on, you lot! Hurry up."

His voice is immediately drowned out by the strident noise of high-density lasers cutting through the door. He has to act quickly as they will be there any minute. Jiù comes back to a state of inner calm, all the while visualising the archives office on the plan the Memory gave him. What will be will be!

He materialises in a corridor of pale shadows, lit by the dim glow of some security bulbs. He's just next to the door which, like every door in an administrative building, has a sign showing the name of its occupant: "archives, office 6, Igo, 3rd rank officer". A guard is standing with his back to him six feet away, watching the entrance to the corridor. The beam of his headlamp sweeps the corridor from right to left. Jiù suddenly hears the inner voice of Akané.

"Jiù, I'm in the Garden. Let me guide you, trust me. Where are you?"

"Just in front of the archives office number 6, facing the entrance, it seems."

"OK, go back up the corridor 30 feet and you'll find a low door on your left, office Y26. Ask the Memory for the code and open it: there's a landing with a ladder just to the left that will take you up a level. I'll guide you again from there."

Extremely slowly and cautiously, Jiù steps backwards without taking his eyes off the guard.

"Let's hope there are no obstacles, as I won't see them. Memory, the code to Y26?"

"Unlocked!"

Still walking backwards, Jiù feels his way along the wall. Suddenly he finds beneath his fingers the characteristic bulge of a sliding door. He's going to have to act quickly. He runs his hand over the control panel, which emits a slight beep and the door opens with a whisper. Even that tiny noise is enough to alert the guard, who turns around violently. Jiù has just the time to throw himself into the gaping doorway as the beam of a torch lights up the door and the ray of a flashgun lands on the control panel he's just let go of.

"Lock it, please, quickly."

"Impossible to lock."

Jiù hurls himself up the metallic ladder as running steps approach the landing.

"Halt!"

With one hand on the wall to guide him, he stumbles aimlessly up the dark passageway on the floor he's just reached. By the chaotic movements of a torch, he knows the guard is on the ladder.

"Stay calm Jiù, I'm losing you. If you can hear me, at the end of the corridor on the right, there's a door with a ..." The rest of what Akané says evaporates in the silence, interrupted by the tension that is gradually taking over Jiù's mind.

"I've no idea where I am. Memory? Unlock all the doors on the floor, quick."

"Unlocked."

Jiù dives into the first one he sees, just as the guard emerges into the corridor.

"Lock them, please!"

"All doors locked."

His heart still beating wildly, Jiù leans on the wall next to the door. On the other side he hears the guard go past the office he's taken refuge in and patrol the corridor, methodically trying to open all the doors.

"OK, I have a little time."

Still in the lugubrious half-light of the emergency lamps, he goes into active mode so he can "feel" the room. It is a small room and clearly empty.

"Memory, can you tell me where I am?"

"Room Z22, temporary office for maintenance engineers and technicians. Standard equipment. Unoccupied."

He sits down. It's stupid. This isn't how to go about things. All this agitation is useless – it's exactly what not to do. Since Akané left, he has let himself get dragged into a series of irrelevant events. Without realising it, he's begun playing someone else's game, and it's up to him alone to get out of it. When he wants. Meaning now.

"Jiù?"

"Yes, Akané, I can hear you."

"Is everything OK?"

"Yes, everything's fine. I got stupidly carried away. But it's OK, I'm back to myself now."

He gives a sigh of relief.

"You see, I think I understand what's just happened. It was an acute confrontation of realities. Shu forced his vision of reality on me, like Eneter does to all of us in Elwon. I let myself get caught up in it, as if it were inevitable, as if it were the only possible vision – as if it threatened me as well. That's it – I was caught precisely because I thought it threatened me. It's incredible; I locked myself into a feeling of danger, even though that kind of logic is alien to me. Crazy! I've just experienced in an instant everything the Dynasty has experienced since Eneter has held sway over it. That's what led to the imprisonment of Elwon – the permanent and intentional spreading of a threatening feeling and thus the need of protection. Everything comes from that - the certainty that the world is ceaselessly dangerous and that every occasion is a good one for being reminded of that. You probably find this strange, but you can't imagine how happy I am to have experienced that! It's like a liberating discovery."

He hears Akané's little inner laugh, at once mocking and affectionate. She conveys so many things with that laugh.

"I hear what you're saying, Jiù. I understand, but I don't know if all that is intentional. It would be monstrous."

"I don't know either. Maybe it's a natural weakness that we fell into and that Eneter took advantage of? Maybe you are right – it's not certain that he intentionally trapped me in this emergency, in this maze-like panic.

Maybe he's also a prisoner of this logic, and if I can't get out, perhaps he can't get out either. But the fact remains: that kind of frenzied hunt with me as the prey, is contrary to what I should be. It's exactly the opposite of the present that I want to live and everything it contains."

"Whatever happens, you can always take it as an exercise, to learn how to choose your reality whatever the circumstances! Speaking of reality, I would like to share mine with you. I'm with Elea and Orion, can you feel the energy surrounding you? You can trust it. You can trust me."

"I know, Akané. Thanks for that. Thanks to you I feel reconnected to the present potential, it's becoming like a second reality for me."

The inner presence of Akané and his friends lights him up like sudden joy. He feels encircled and bathed in a kind of buoyancy with subtle ramifications that take him definitively out of these dark passageways and his frenzied flight. It's as if instantaneously he is able to feel and share again the atmosphere of the Garden. It's not that it is particularly reassuring, it's just that it is in phase with his state of mind at the moment: he is synchronous once more with Akané, moved by the same thoughts, the same senses, by their common instinct, like shoals of countless fish which dance, manoeuvre and twirl around in total symbiosis.

And yet this possibility of a confrontation between realities remains awkwardly in his mind, a parasitic thought that won't go away. He makes himself stay with it, as if it were something that needs exploring, a path crossing his, inviting him to follow it. How many thoughts like that come to us, when we don't know what they want to teach us, just because we refuse to try to find out where they lead? He senses that this confrontation is an inner one, a choice that is his own rather than a reality that other people seem to be forcing upon him.

A sudden flash of awareness, an obvious fact, grabs him. Of course! This reality is not just one that Shu is projecting on him, but is also a potential that's present in him and that Shu has simply allowed to materialise. The game they have played together is a shared reality between them and it can't be any other way. Shu was able to take this role because they share this potential, each with his own complementary perspective. This is all played out deep within his consciousness before becoming an event that ends up being imposed on him.

It's so clear that he begins to laugh openly, alone in the empty little office, totally detached from the fear that had been choking him just a moment earlier. It's decidedly childish – he just has to scan his own thoughts to be able to identify possible futures that he doesn't necessarily want. Once detected, the parasitic realities can be eliminated from his consciousness and he can take a different option, like deciding on another programme, another lifestyle choice. He becomes strongly aware of the connection between the attention he brings to the events gestating in him, his choice as to whether to make them materialise or not and the energy that makes them happen. There is a totally direct relationship between his awareness and what he's experiencing – it's a question of energy again! It's not successive, but totally instantaneous! That's how he creates his reality.

He is rediscovering what Kohl has taught him about the inevitable connection between thought and reality, but he had not imagined that it could be so direct and immediate! So, by allowing circumstances to force themselves on him, push each other around and string together without remission, he becomes estranged from the vision of himself that he prefers, and turns into someone else. That is when the great game of life appears; it plays around with all his potential realities, the choice of the possibilities that he carries within him and the reality in which others want to lock him in because, for them, it's the only possibility. And for good measure, it is all magnified by urgency, as if to stop him from thinking – but isn't that how he has always lived? By reducing his landscape to a sort of tunnel because of the speed of life, neglecting the details and the side events? Since his opening to the present potential, he realises how much he has to question every event, every circumstance to ensure that it is really the one he wants to choose. He also understands that the speed and the rhythm we accept to live at irremediably determine our reality and prevent us from discerning other potentialities. He understands why Elwon time is perpetually becoming denser – this is the only way it can be if they are going to confirm inexorably that what they are living is the only possible reality. The same goes for the need for inner calm that Kohl keeps repeating: it is not only about the absence of urgency, it's the indispensable condition for contemplating at our leisure the realities we have within us and deciding which we want to make real. Choosing what we really want to be and not being the plaything of our own thoughts.

He marvels at the perfection of time which blends consciousness and experience with perfect complicity and intimacy. He would never have been able to understand all that if he hadn't experienced it. Now he senses the absolute benevolence of the living through which, in the end, everything we want to know is contained within the path we take. It's not at the end, it's within! He wants to dance, sweeping all the guards up with him, so immense he feels the opportunities opening up to be. Every instant is becoming a passageway, a discreet and constant invitation to look at what is being presented as a choice and not a contingent reality. Ah, his life would be so much simpler if he could always stay connected to this open awareness, this contemplation of his choices!

Coming back to himself, he understands the significance of what he has just discovered: Elwon's logic has locked itself in and restricted life to narrow causality, like a channel obliterating all the options of the present potential or like a diamond with only one visible face! A simple mirror instead of an immense jewel. And Jiù has been steeped in this for so long that he has taken it for reality, and even made it his job. He hasn't yet the reflex – far from it – of contemplating every facet of the present in order to make all possibilities emerge from it, like so many doors ready to be opened when you visit an apartment. He is struck by the admirable perfection of time through which events link together. For example, it was his reunion with Akané in the C3 control room and his forgetting to close the session that allowed him to reactivate the forbidden modules. It's like his own history is being written independently of him, or more exactly written by another self, to show him what he knows by revealing what makes him live.

He feels that Akané is a witness to this monologue that has gradually dragged him into his own inmost depths, oblivious to the surface, to his surroundings and his frantic race. So, stretching out in the present as if lying under the stars, he lets his thoughts go, completely relaxed and open, into a hollow space that blooms inside him. This is exactly the same sensation as the one he had when he awoke in the valley in the Garden, that of observing his own thoughts, as if they belonged to someone else. Something obvious hits him: as long as none of them belong to him, it means that he hasn't chosen. He decides, then, to maintain this transitory state, to observe each of his thoughts with a slow curiosity and a sympathetic attention. They are all beautiful, but none is more real than another – it's as if none of them were really meant for him. He takes his time, he knows that nothing can come and disturb this instant that has opened up in him like an inverted world: the Garden at its centre and all the rejected causality at the edges. There, in the dark and unfamiliar office, he understands everything Kohl has explained to him as well as what he didn't tell him. Free will and experience, so intimately linked: neither is worth anything without the other. That is the gift of time, the present, the two sides of a same face, existing in such continuity that it's impossible to say where free will starts and experience ends. Without rituals or rites of passage, he has now finished his apprenticeship and started following the path of the connections he's been able to observe and that were created instantaneously around him. Shu and Doràn have played their different roles, the perfection of which now becomes clear to him – he knows that they are still a factor, a possibility for things to flow in a direction that is not his, but they are no longer a danger. They are part of the reality that he is creating. He has a surprisingly benevolent feeling which even extends to them. Everything is in its place, it is impossible for it not to be. It's enough to explore it.

Like an echo to this inner revelation, this awareness that he's exploring like an open landscape, like the answer to an inner question that he's formulated almost unconsciously, the vibration begins – intense, immediate and electric – and overcomes him completely. It quivers at the surface of his skin, accompanied by a high-pitched but soft and subtle voice. A connection or transition is evidently about to happen – someone in him has chosen, then? What form or what hidden hope has decided to materialise unbeknown to him? With a kind of joyous curiosity he has gained an even deeper understanding of how acceptance – rather than control – allows him to discover what he has inside him.

He watches himself embark on this process that is going to take him somewhere, without even wanting to know where, without trying to control it. He feels himself slowly disappearing from this dark room, a conscious and attentive witness to the journey he's embarking on. Totally melted into the moment, he experiences this transition in slow motion and observes each of its stages in detail. He sees himself and everything that filled the instant he has just left diminish at the same time; everything converges, irresistibly sucked up into a miniscule escape point, an inverse horizon that draws near, slowly at first, but then faster and faster, a perspective that gradually compresses everything that it absorbs, like a cone being compacted at high speed into its peak alone. He crosses this point literally in a flash, reduced to just an awareness of himself, as if he were too vast for this constrained space and only driven by the will to be. He feels himself grow again immediately, surrounded by other forms and new objects that gradually transform into a new reality, another side of this instant he has just left.

Jiù materialises, feeling totally aware, in an immense room with a large window that gives onto a view of Juno. It is spacious and light, and contains dozens of scattered stacks of files. A man is standing with his back to him, busy filing documents. Next to his desk, some travel bags. He's about to leave. Beyond reason and through an instinct that can't be wrong, he's sure he knows this man.

"Father?"

"Jiù?"

The two men stand face to face. The meeting is so improbable, and yet so longed-for, that they both take a moment to grasp it and adjust to it. They fall into each other's arms and let the silence flow by for a long time before speaking.

"This is totally insane. Where did you come from? How did you get in?"

"*When* did I come from, I think you should say. What year is this?"

"2235"

"Good heavens! Where are we?"

"In my office in the Memory L1 building."

"Room Z1..."

"Exactly. How did you know?"

"The Memory told me, but I didn't think I'd find myself here, much less find you here!"

Jiù is struck by how much his father's voice had stayed close to him, as alive as if it had never left him, as if he had heard it only yesterday. He looks at the closed luggage.

"You're leaving?"

"Yes, they are expecting me. We're going on an inspection trip for a few days. I can't really explain. But you – explain your presence here! And especially ... you've changed so much! The last time I saw you, you seemed younger. Where have you come from?"

"Father, I can't tell you, not yet, not without explaining many things. But can't you postpone your departure, even if it's just by a few hours? We have so much to talk about."

Jiù realises without being able to say anything that, for his father, although he's the son he hasn't seen for a while, he is unaware of the time that really separates them, and has no understanding of the future that he holds in him. And yet, if he has been brought back to this moment, it's because there is something he should do, there is something he can change. He understands that, in coming, he's created a connection, a relay moment for his father so that *he* can avail himself of a new choice this time. That's it - he just has to give his father all the different elements pertaining to the choice. Instantly, Jiù goes into active mode, the enlarged state of awareness that will allow him to go into action. A device on his father's wrist buzzes.

"Yes?"

"We are nearly at the end of the procedure, but it seems one of our sensors is out of order. Probably nothing serious. We'll check and be in touch again. Don't move until we call you back. Over."

"You were talking about time? It seems we have a bit more than we thought."

"More than you imagine, father, but perhaps less than you believe."

"You're being very enigmatic, it's not like you."

Jiù feels totally relaxed and detached from his father, calmly attentive to what's going on inside as well as what's going on outside so as not to let himself be carried away by the kind of circumstances, exchanges and conversations that can make you lose the thread of who you are and what you have to do. This becomes even more difficult when the person you are talking to is himself completely immersed in causality. But is he really? He feels that if he wants to break the mould of a typical father-son conversation, he has to surprise him and go straight into a relationship on an equal footing.

"Father, it's possible to avoid the energy Collapsus."

"What are you talking about?"

It's worked – he has his father's attention, although still not completely. He feels that in his reply his father is keeping his options open for a possible denial, a hand he could still play. He sees him hesitate too, casting a quick look around his flat.

"I've found a way to access the Memory's forbidden Modules. If it's not possible now, it will be in the near future."

Jiù's father looks pensively at his son, speechless, for a while. What does this mean? Where has Jiù come from and how does he know what he kept secret from his loved ones? What else does he know? What am I going to say to him? All of a sudden he sees his son in a completely new light. He sits down and gestures to Jiù to do the same. They are together on a vast sofa that looks out over the view of Juno, separated from the window by a simple low table.

"Forgive me Jiù, I was on the wrong track. We obviously have a lot to share. Where shall we start? Wait – first of all, do you want a coffee?"

"No thanks. Father, I want to tell you first how much I missed you for all these years. And I have to tell you – please listen without judgement – I've become a Dissident."

"So that's it."

"No, it's not just that," replies Jiù, following his father's train of thought. "Not just that, or in any case, the Dissidents are not what you think."

"What do you think I think?"

"That the Dissidents are pariahs, that they are against Elwon law, that they threaten the Memory and that they have to be wiped out."

After a short silence, he distinctly hears his father talk to him with his inner voice.

"Jiù, I'm a Dissident myself."

Now it's Jiù's turn to be speechless. He is as amazed at what his father has said as at the way he has chosen to say it. It is in itself a confirmation of the news he's communicated.

"Yes, when I started this double role of member of the High Council and of Eneter, they contacted me. I imagine they had their information and took precautions. They explained everything to me and I joined them pretty fast, for the simple reason that, for me – like for you no doubt – L1 logic not only limited but was becoming contrary to what we really are. I was dreaming of something else, and I'm only half surprised that you followed me into this."

"Why are you talking to me with your inner voice?" says Jiù, using his own interior voice.

"Because I fear my office is bugged, but we can't carry on talking this way – they will get suspicious."

"Which dissident did you meet?"

"Orion."

Jiù falls silent, suddenly closed off. This is a kind of betrayal for him. Why didn't Orion say something? Why did he leave him in ignorance as to who his father was? After the first rush of emotion, he clings, with some effort at first, to a suggestion that surfaces and helps him come back to himself and to the peace that can bare his soul: free will – always and still, good old free will. Just as you cannot warn someone about what the future they have chosen holds for them, you can't give information that could influence how they will behave. Alright. But still.

He starts talking again, out loud this time.

"The Memory told me that I would find clues about the energy Collapsus here. What can you tell me?"

"Do you know the probable date?"

"Yes."

"The information you just gave me about the forbidden modules is highly important. You see, I myself am facing a very precise dilemma: Eneter has ordered me to set up the second generation energy programme as a continuation of the first – more in order to prepare for the Collapsus than to avoid it, and like you, I know about the fabulous energy of time. I know it's possible to avoid this deadline, and that it's not inevitable. I know what changes to adopt, within ourselves and between us. I've had access to the principles that govern the temporal energy. To a certain extent, I've talked to Shu about it, who has become my confidant.

Perhaps one day you will know why. He encourages me to carry on investigating, but as long as we can't produce and connect this energy to a condenser capable of storing it, he wants me to continue installing the parallel network. It's almost finished and I'm about to supervise the last phase of its construction. As for myself, I've been able to begin to transform the energy of time. Highly intense, it has powerful electromagnetic effects that we can use. But things are not finished, far from it. You see, these two options, the Collapsus and the use of the Aeon's energy, are developing concurrently, as if it were impossible to differentiate one from the other. As if it were impossible to choose full stop, in fact."

"What did you call it?"

"The Aeon. I found this word in the old documents in those damned forbidden modules of the Memory. We are apparently not the first to have discovered it or tried to use it. The Aeon is the energy present at all times in the Universe; it is embodied in and stimulates the present, the successive choices of which create our time as we travel through it. You see, in the end, it's quite simple!"

"I understand, father, I understand everything now. Recently, probably thanks to you, I've had some powerful experiences with temporal energy that have got me noticed by both Eneter and the Dissidents at the same time. It's as if these two realities were converging at high speed."

"They are the same thing, Jiù, the same thing. That's the difficult part of the exercise – joining them together without one prevailing over the other. It's just a question of choice. Which energy do you prefer to use?"

"I remember..." says Jiù thoughtfully. "I remember having felt how these two options were on a collision course a long time ago."

150

"As for me, all I've done, and what I continue to do, is to work to make it so that when this convergence occurs – or this collision as you put it – everything blends together instead of being destroyed."

"What do we do now?"

Jiù's father observes his son pensively and, after an intense moment's thought almost like an inner struggle, he says, using his inner voice once more:

"As we are both Dissidents, Jiù, I can read you and I feel that you know something about my future, and it translates as a premonition. It's OK, Jiù. Be aware that I've already accepted. I'm going to finish what I've started, because I am somehow involved in what we have just discussed."

He pauses, overcome by a sudden emotion, and the tremor in his voice makes it seem to bounce off the office walls.

"Perhaps you too will be involved like me, after me. Thank you for having come to tell me, to meet me. I am happy about this unity we have. In fact, I never doubted it."

There is then a silence so full of what is happening between them that Jiù can sense his father's emotion; in that instant they have said everything and now all they can do is be quiet. After a moment, Jiù watches his father stand and pick up his luggage and then hug him in an embrace that means farewell, before glancing at him and leaving without looking back.

Tears he is unable to hold back fall unrestrained down his cheeks. He feels powerless and disoriented, having just lost his father for a second time. He was unable to do anything. Indeed, he hardly tried, as if he hadn't dared. More than sadness, he is overcome by an enormous sense of guilt. Suddenly, inside, he hears his father's voice, clear and calm:

"I know all about it too, Jiù. I've also made journeys along time arcs. I've travelled along the arc of the pilot who is taking us today. These preliminary explorations are part of the procedures that I've imposed on myself as a precaution. So I know. But knowing doesn't necessarily mean stopping it from happening. It means choosing, and I have chosen, freely. Because I've done what I had to do, because the decision I'm making is better for what I'm involved in than not making it. The proof is that you are here. I've something to tell you and I can only do it via our inner connection: there is a message for you in the forbidden modules. I have left you everything I know about the energy of the Aeon, about its immense potential for Elwon. I've also left you information on the High Council and on Eneter. With all that, I think you'll be able to finish what I've started. You just have to use your biometric data to be identified, as it's for you and you alone."

"Father, I have something to tell you too." He hesitates for a moment. "I love you, father."

"So do I, Jiù, so do I. Immensely and across time. Thank you for who you are and what you have given to me. Everything's fine, everything is perfect. See you soon."

"See you soon."

Alone once more, Jiù suddenly recalls something his father said: "I fear my office is bugged." In active mode, he scans the room and discovers, under the desk, a small audio captor. Good God! So everything they said out loud was overheard? But that means that when his father revealed himself, he was also revealing himself to those who were listening! Does that mean, then, that he himself caused the accident, and that his father knew? He now understands why his father, with all the skills of foreknowledge and intuition that he'd developed unbeknown to Jiù, had confided in Shu, just as Jiù had. It was because he was working towards the convergence of these two realities in full awareness of the facts.

All at once, he begins to realise his father's greatness. All at once he's discovering what he had chosen not to know.

It's too much for him, laid low as he is by tiredness and this tangle of realities of which he doesn't know if he's the cause or the plaything. He feels out of his depth, battling to get back to dry land. A persistent fog swamps his mind, the room spins around him in a blur, the light suddenly becomes blinding and he falls to the ground in a faint.

When he comes to, Kohl is crouching by his side, lightly massaging his temples with his fingertips. This friendly energy does him good. Without moving, he opens his eyes; Kohl smiles at him and says joyfully, with his inner voice:

"Greetings Jiù! Hello, my friend. I am truly happy to see you again. My goodness! You have come a long way since the last time we saw each other. I've come to tell you that, despite appearances, everything is going fine."

He straightens out.

"Can you get up? I'd like to take you somewhere."

They face each other, Kohl with serenity and Jiù struggling to recover his energy.

"Focus on me, you're coming with me."

They vanish and reappear at the corner of an almost deserted road somewhere in Juno. In the distance they can hear what sounds like children playing.

"Come, this is where I wanted to bring you."

After a short walk during which Jiù manages to come back to himself, they go into a small square where children are playing and running – it's one of the countless miniature spaces, almost enclosures, designed for relaxation, where Juno's authorities have reconstituted something that resembles a little plot of freedom. In active mode, they join together on a bench next to other people, some of whom are attentive to the children, whereas others seem distracted.

"What can you see?"

Jiù casts his eyes over the scene before them.

"Joy and different emotions. I can see time arcs meeting each other – a lot of them are in harmony and some are even quite synchronous. It's like an intangible ballet of simultaneous energy. It's beautiful, full of life."

"And what else?" adds Kohl after a while. "What else can you see here?"

He looks at each of the players in this intensely alive moment, one after another. There are children chasing each other or walking; children to one side, talking to one other; some are bumping into each other and jostling, some are playing on their own; others are watching, ignoring or replying to one another. After a long pause, Jiù says:

"First of all, I can see the limitless abundance of the present. When I see all these children mingling and chasing each other, all of them playing a different game, I'm struck by the intense simultaneity we are witnessing. It's incredibly fluid and rich, a fabulous image of existence that I hadn't noticed before – they all have their place, but with a great flexibility too! Look how they are centred on and engaged in their play, but receptive at the same time; look how they coexist with each others' games, how they go from one to the next, swinging between dynamics, inviting themselves into other children's games without any down-time. It's packed with energy and deeply harmonious. It's incredible."

"It's wonderful, eh?"

"Absolutely marvellous. I didn't realise!"

"Well, I don't think you ever really looked."

Jiù, still in active mode, now has a powerfully increased perception, visually and orally, of course, but also in a kind of inner way, as if the scene were taking place inside him, in his own consciousness. These children are him – they are all he is, all he knows and all he doesn't know about himself. He has achieved total sensation in this playground, like from a whole miniature universe. It's as if the present has slowed down to allow him to identify the immense totality of the possibilities open to him, some of which become real in these games, but most of which are in suspense, unexplored, like futures not yet chosen.

"Kohl, what we have before us is the future inviting itself into our present. I've just realised that every one of these children is a little connection. If we listen to them, if we really see each and every one of them for what they are and for what is inside them, we can understand that not only are they our future, but they are an invitation from this future to let it become embodied in our present. That's why children are important – because they import time! With them we can bring the present into existence on the basis of the future and not on the remains of the past; we can build our choices based on what we prefer out of what can possibly happen. It's crazy! There it is, under our noses and we don't see it. I had never seen it! I understand that if education is a continuity of our past, we miss the connection, we prevent the future from being with us; we project a past that perhaps we may regret instead of letting ourselves be attracted to a future we would have preferred. And what conflict we create within them, what a disappointment, as if they felt wasted and useless. And it's true, my God, what a waste! Do you realise what good we'd do to children if we could show them that we can visualise all futures written in the present, by liberating the energy of time? They bring us vitality and we can teach them what they can do with it. You know, there should be children in the High Council – that would change so many things!

"Joking apart, it's the parents' education we need to worry about really, teaching them to listen to their children, not to spoil them; every time a child comes into a family, it's the future paying a visit, but no-one sees it."

"Do you realise what you just said, Jiù? That's the exact proof that now, when you contemplate the present, you always access three levels of time – you feel its energy, express your knowledge and are driven by an awareness of it."

He bursts out in loud laughter and gives Jiù a friendly thump on the back:

"I like what you say about educating parents! That makes me very happy. It's as if you were allowing me to bear witness to your deepest nature, and I'm very grateful to you for that. This is what comes out when you let your consciousness talk: what you really are, the level you vibrate on. It's really gratifying. You're right – all these children show us something, and do you know why? Because they live completely in the present. So they are very sensitive to temporal energy. The energy they are showing is very powerful, and it's the same as the energy we have rediscovered. The problem is that in growing up, everything they learn gradually separates them. As if in getting older we lose this capacity to cope with our multifaceted potential, as if we preferred to reduce it. This ability we adults have of freely consenting to imprison ourselves: most of the time, we choose to develop only one vision of ourselves and stick to it even if it's unsatisfactory or even unpleasant – it's a complete mystery to me. The curse of Elwon is its consistency in reproducing the past, and above all it's a huge waste. We are given a mirror instead of a jewel, which is nonetheless there, within reach of existence in each of the instants we prefer not to be aware of. It's really senseless, literally."

"That's what I feel when I think about my younger years. The feeling of gradually moving away from myself, but also the inability to know when exactly I forgot who I could be."

"I hope you said "who" in the plural!" interrupts Kohl. "A big plural!"

Jiù smiles at the remark and adds:

"Thanks for bringing me to this park, it's done me good. I can feel all the energy that's here, the strength of the future that's offered to the present. It helps me understand, too, what just happened with my father: this shock between the future and the past. And I hadn't understood his choice – choosing the future without giving up on the past, choosing convergence. I didn't get that this was the true reason for his actions. And the reason we were reunited.

"Right, what do we do now?" he adds suddenly, to change the subject.

"Nothing, for now. As long as we don't know, we stay put. Let it come to you rather than decide This is what choosing acceptance over control is too. Observe and feel: in you and around you something is going to appear, called upon by an energy common to us, to all of us," he adds with a sweeping gesture. "Take the time, understand? Take it," he repeats, carefully separating the words.

"Time is really something to take in both hands, to contemplate by the armful, it overflows with fullness, more than you can absorb. So, imperceptibly you are filled with its energy, it crystallises in you and an intuition is shaped or a reality takes form. If you let it, it will take you, or you can choose another. You see, for example I often do this experiment in our gatherings in the Garden or elsewhere. Rather than joining a group, I sit a little apart and I observe. It doesn't take long for something to happen: an unexpected meeting with someone who joins me, and together we are witnesses to a time that we produce together. You see, the only real obligation is that, whatever the experience you choose, you accept the consequences. Again, you are not forced to live them, but you have to understand and integrate your choice totally.

"So! Meanwhile, let's make the most of it," he adds jutting his chin towards the joyful activity unfolding in front of them.

———————

6 - Confrontation

"What do you think?"

"It should work, or at least it's worth a try. It's up to us to put a stop to it, so we have to take the initiative. ."

"Why do you want to bring her here?"

"She's her sister."

"I know, but I'm still wary. She's escaped us twice. Evidently they have certain resources."

"Yes, but this time we know that. We've taken measures and I'm sure we could capture Jiù too, and even a few others, if we do our job properly."

"Maybe, but it needs careful consideration. I'm not sure we're going about it the right way. Two failures – that's at least one too many ..."

Shu remains deep in thought. It's not that the situation eludes him. Eneter is still in command – it has total control of Elwon and its power is not at all damaged – but he senses a nascent danger, or rather a new set of stakes. Shu is not programmed to open up to opportunities. He doesn't see them. For him, unforeseen events are risks that translate into calculations, measures and counter-measures. Nonetheless, there is a force developing in Elwon that is not yet antagonistic, but already independent, driven by a logic that still escapes him. That's what is new and that's what worries him: how do they function, how do they communicate? What are they looking for? An alternative to L1? That would be insane! To what end and with what consequences for Eneter and for themselves?

For the first time in its existence, Eneter is not the only player, even if it still mostly dominates the game, especially with its gradual control over the Memory. But something else has come up that apparently they can't control, at least not yet, something that's becoming more significant and that they now have to factor into the equation. It's something they didn't believe they had to deal with any more: the dissidence they thought had been eradicated but that keeps reappearing. It's becoming irritating!

What bothers him most is precisely that – this organised and yet scattered reality which seems to have multiple commands and a baffling ability to be reborn. It's totally contrary to everything he has ever known. Something organised but not logical is developing and just that fact poisons him like a gnawing threat. It has to end. For him, like for the Dynasty of which he is one of the most eminent representatives, order is inseparable from rationality and logic – it can't be any other way. Whatever is not rational is therefore disorderly, and whatever is disorderly should be eliminated; there's no getting out of that.

Yet, against all expectation, what he had at first taken for odd episodes and isolated incidents seem to respond to each other and connect via links he is unaware of. It is above all this spontaneous life that he needs to understand and dismantle. He feels that this adversary – as he's definitely dealing with one – is going to force him to think and act differently, on another level, and find another way to predict events. He suddenly understands that this is what is disturbing him, the feeling of a growing imbalance against him. The workings of Eneter are totally predictable, known by everyone – even if some elements have remained carefully hidden and for a good reason – whereas those of the dissidents are elusive, always unexpected and tend to rebound in unpredictable directions. As a high commander of Eneter, he is well aware that this gives him a considerable handicap in the confrontation to come. Everyone knows it: what you know about your opponent gives you a decisive advantage. And yet he knows nothing, or not enough, so although he needs to take the initiative, it has to be done differently, and for that he feels very badly prepared.

First of all, we have to decentralise: not limit ourselves to the gigantic power of our headquarters – that too-visible centralism, as familiar as a reflex, makes us unavoidably vulnerable. No, it would be better to follow their example and multiply the command centres – surprise them by moving fast. The teleport will facilitate the task.

Next, head-on conflict needs to be avoided, the intensity of antagonism needs reducing and we need to attempt cooperation, which can only be to our advantage, given the balance of power. We made a mistake in trying to eliminate the Dissidents, the proof being that we failed. Perhaps we should try to use them instead, for the good of Elwon and in order to strengthen Eneter's power. Yes, that is no doubt the smarter option, but everything depends on what the Dissidents know, especially as our time is running out – and that is not a subject he wants to dwell on. Although ...

An idea occurs to Shu, interrupting his train of thoughts, and he looks at Doràn, his mind alerted by what could be a solution:

"Tell me – do you remember the electromagnetic aberrations we noticed in Jiù's flat? Some time ago we noticed the same phenomena with his father, and in both cases, it was these aberrations that alerted us. They are the trace of a kind of intense energy and I'm sure that, if they have both used it, we should be able to as well. I know that Jiù's father had made considerable progress in this area and I'm convinced that it's the answer to all our problems. It's not so much the Collapsus that I dread, but rather how the power of Eneter will survive it.

"This energy is surely the solution. It's a real shame – we messed things up with Jiù every time. I want you to take measures so that this does not happen again. I know now what we have to do but we have to act quickly. We have to apprehend him – not only him, others too – and we have to rope them in to help us turn this energy they seem to have at their command to our advantage. I think that as well as his companion, Akané, others could be added to the list. Apart from Mia, who else have you been able to identify?"

"Not many people. There's a man from the plateaux called Leh whom we are following closely, and Orion and Elea, of course, whom we've been tracking for a long time – but with them it's a bit more complex."

"Yes; speaking of which, I want you to send a detachment to take possession of his island right away. We've learned enough about it and I don't want them to be able to use it again. It's time to lay our cards on the table and finish it off."

"No problem. It's as good as done. And the other thing is for this evening?"

"Yes, but I want to be there. There are a couple of things I need to check."

Another day is coming to an end on Beihaï. Like in all Elwon's hyperpoles, activity is slowly moving from the administrative to the residential areas. Only the incessant ballet of the rapeeds keeps up its pace, identical and immutable, in the rising darkness. Glittering lamps light up ad infinitum in the towers, deployed as if moved by a signal and in a sort of accelerated contagion. Like every evening, having finished a day's studying, Mia gets off a transport, walks a few yards to the foot of her tower and is about to start climbing its staircase when two rapeeds stop right next to her.

"Eneter. Would you like to follow us please?"

Powerless, she doesn't have the time to make a gesture or say a word before they have put an inhibitor on her and taken her on board in front of the indifferent eyes of the passersby. Whether through habit or cowardliness, the effect is the same: for a long time safety and conformity have been inseparable.

For Jiù and Kohl that afternoon is truly radiant. They feel completely regenerated by the children's contagious energy. Their gaze glides from one to another, sometimes alighting on a quick exchange between a mother and her little girl come to seek comfort for a while. This ordered vitality, like everything that happens in Juno, is consistent with something so peaceful and reassuring that Jiù almost begins to question if they are doing the right thing.

"So you think that what we are trying to do will be better than this?"

"You're having doubts? Have you already forgotten everything you've discovered? Don't you feel that this harmonious plenitude of superimposed presents is exactly what we can all expect once Elwon has been opened up to the energy of time? Don't you feel it?"

"Yes, you are right, Kohl, but I also know that there is another side to it, a flip side; and I'd like to understand properly, have a more precise idea of it."

"Jiù, Kohl?" Akané's voice suddenly interrupts them. "Can you come to the Garden? Something has happened to Mia."

Kohl gets up and stretches his arms.

"You see – it's like I was saying. You just have to wait and events come to us, a reality lets itself in. I imagine that, like me, you are not totally surprised? Let's split up and each find a quiet place for transition, and I'll see you at my place."

"Wait Kohl, hang on a second. Before we rush into this let's go into active mode first and try to weigh up the situation. I think between us we'll be able to get a wider understanding of what is going on."

"If you want!" replies Kohl, not without throwing him a brief look of surprised approval.

The two friends remain silent for a while, as if in deep meditation, their bodies still observing the children's joyful activity, but their attention turned inwards, on the moment in its entirety, well beyond the playground.

"I feel the will of Shu. He is awfully determined. It would seem that Eneter has decided to take back the initiative. It's strange that they have left us in peace for so long. I feel that they are deploying throughout Elwon, resolutely focused on us. I sense they are using Mia as bait. It's not going to be easy!"

"Maybe, Jiù. That's right – I sense the same thing. But don't forget that we have the advantage. We are connected to something bigger than us, whereas for them it's the opposite: they are obsessed by the things they control – so the real power is on our side. They can put our accesses on standby, but we can do without them. We also know what tools they have at their disposal, what they are looking for and why – the energy and power to escape from the Collapsus, and of course to seize control again once they have survived it. You don't have to be a genius to understand that. As concerns the Collapsus, at least we are in phase with them on that and we all know we have to avoid letting Elwon fall back into chaos and disorder at all costs – no-one wants that to happen. So we have some real assets as well as points of agreement about what is coming up, and I think we should explore them."

"Maybe, but I also feel that there is a balance being maintained in all this that we don't know about. Each time we are strengthened, we strengthen them at the same time. The opposite must be true as well. If we get weaker, they must get weaker too. I feel it's like a rule we have to understand about the way we both operate: we can't change without them. We have to take them into account."

"It's possible, Jiù, it's quite possible. Come on – let's go and meet the others."

He leaves, without another look towards the children with whom he's spent the afternoon. A moment later, almost regretfully, Jiù follows suit still in active mode, and in this state of inner vigilance makes his way towards a nearby tower, as if he were expected there.

He materialises in the Garden, not far from Kohl's house, whom he sees some way ahead. On the path that he recognises like a fresh memory, he notices other figures also going towards the house. He doesn't know them. "There are a lot more of us than the last time," he says to himself.

Drawing rapidly nearer he joins an already vast group gathered in Kohl's small courtyard. "Wow, we are so amazingly diverse!" he mutters, seeing the surprising variety of faces and costumes. All Elwon's peoples seem to be there next to this little house on the edge of the Dynasty. "What a strange situation," thinks Jiù, measuring the short time that separates him from his recent past in Juno. He recalls his gigantic efforts in Akané's room : "I feel totally at one with them, with the same knowledge, the same energy, almost the same experience". He realises that this must be one of the characteristics of the energy of time – the ability to bring together all those who have access to it in the same awareness, a shared experience. It can also be the effect of all that inner communication, as if from now on nothing can be hidden from those who use it. Without doubt his own experiences enrich them just as he feels nourished by theirs.

Orion suddenly stands up and faces them from the threshold of the house. Silence falls almost immediately, as if everyone is waiting for this moment.

"Thank you for coming, dear friends. I believe we are entering into a new phase and events are stacking up in a very precise way as if at the approach to an inflection point in the weft of time. I think, then, that we can begin the next part of our project but first I suggest we talk about it together and weigh up all the options. I feel that this moment is probably irreversible and uniting all our thoughts to help us consider the consequences is not too big an effort. The forbidden modules are now open," (light murmur among the audience) "and Eneter is not disarming – it seems purposefully – and is creating circumstances that have the effect of spurring us on to action. It's up to us to consider whether we want to let ourselves be carried away by events and up to what point. As you know, they are holding Mia, in conditions that we have yet to comprehend."

Jiù feels strongly how true Orion's words are. He recalls his discovery, during his flight from Eneter's militia, of how difficult it can be not to let yourself be imprisoned by chains of events that are forced upon you. Chains ... he weighs up everything that word expresses.

"Can you explain?" a voice with a strong accent from the mountain region asks Orion.

"Well, Mia is no longer in her flat, according to Akané's frequent checks. She is, however, communicating with us but in a very intermittent way that I fear is controlled and always comes from a different place, as if to prevent us from locating her. Either Eneter is trying to cover up their tracks or these movements reveal a plan in execution. In either case we need to act. We are not worried – on the contrary. Personally I see it as the development of an option that's being put in place at a level well superior to Eneter's calculations and definitely without their knowledge. That's why, as I say, I think the time has come to move on to the next stage of our project and connect Elwon to the energy of time. Speaking of which, Jiù, can you share with us what you know?"

"Eneter and Memory Central expect an Energy Collapsus within the next nine months. When we are in Elwon, Akané and I can communicate with the Memory through the intermediary of the Zeitgeist. The energy we can perceive is a flux that the Memory deploys on Elwon. It helps it test and transmit ideas of development that come out of its analyses, and at the same time recover data that allows it to evaluate how and how much these developments are progressing. It's a fairly complex real-time technique and I don't know if its design comes from cyber-engineers or if it's a mutation of the Memory itself. For some unknown reason Akané and I have a special relationship with it. I know that sounds weird, but I sense that the Memory has an intention it is not revealing to us and I think this intention is compatible with our projects.

"The other thing I know – and which you know too," he adds, looking markedly at Orion, "is that my disappeared father is an eminent member of the High Council, an Eneter commander and a Dissident. He probably knows other things about the Zeitgeist but I cannot yet access them. I have to return to the Memory to do that."

"I think your father has a rare and deep knowledge of the Zeitgeist and of the energy of Time," says Orion "In particular he knows that what even you (or especially you), his son, find out has to depend on your specific circumstances. This is surely for your safety, but also out of respect for the perfection of time: what can be known must not be known at the wrong moment as there is a risk of causing disturbances in the weft of time. That's why what he wants you to discover is hidden in the Memory, so that you only access it at the appropriate time. That is all perfect.

"My friends," he says, turning back to the audience, "we can no longer use Sehn. I know that Eneter has it surrounded and we have to forget about it. Elea and myself are not surprised by this predictable event. However, I suggest we hold our gathering here and now in order to decide how we can go to meet Eneter, as they seem to be inviting us to with this curious strategy they have set up with Mia."

"I want to say something," interrupts Akané.

"Go ahead."

"I wish to share a concern I have, that I know you have too," she adds looking in Jon's direction, who seems slightly startled at being addressed directly. (It is not a secret that like Akané and Jiù, Jon and Mia are perfectly synchronous, the only difference being that their joint leaps in time are a much more recent experience.)

"Every time I communicate with Mia, I feel several superimposed influences: Mia's thoughts are confused, there is a kind of expressed intention but at the same time her mind is resistant, as if she wants to show us that it's not *her* wish she is conveying. She is under some influence and wants to let us know that. I don't think she's in danger – it's not that kind of signal – but I do feel that she's inviting us to be careful, to act in a roundabout way. I know her and this is the kind of message she's perfectly capable of transmitting."

168

"What do you suggest?"

At this precise moment, Jiù feels that Akané's thoughts are the exact extension of his own, as if Akané is drawing her inspiration from what he's thinking, and vice versa.

"I feel that we are heading towards a merging of several realities, between the rationality that Eneter wants to impose on us and the range of possibilities that we have at our disposal, between control and acceptance. Between the two there is Memory Central whose role I'm not quite clear about yet. This convergence in the future is already a reality in our communication with Mia. She is sending us at least two realities: the one that is manipulated by Eneter and that she's warning us about, and the one that she conveys to us that is subliminal but more open. She is doubtless not in a position to balance these forces precisely, and this is also a signal; but she knows that she is clearly an example of the direction to take: superimposition rather than conflict. I also think they are doing what they can to prevent her from going into active mode and from focusing. That means they know our ability to transit on the energy of time or at least they suspect it. Finally, that means that if they are stopping her joining us at the same time as preventing her from communicating, it's because they want us to go and join her.

"It's a kind of invitation, then, and there are advantages and risks involved in acting that way. What's interesting is that we have the upper hand in what's happening around Mia, despite how it may appear. They only control one reality, the one they project, whereas we can access several. I am surprised at Mia's maturity, as she gives us such a diversity of options in her every message. She's learning too. I propose then that we focus on the latest communications with her so we can clearly discern all the possibilities she's sending us and see where they lead."

Her words finish in a drawn-out silence. Everyone feels both her irrefutable logic – she has their approval – but also the consequences for them. They feel that their movements using the energy of time could perhaps be watched, perhaps even intercepted – a surprising development, and yet?

In the silence someone raises their voice to express this shared question:

"Do you think that only level-one journeys are affected or level-two ones as well?"

"We are aware that Eneter, by whatever methods, knows about the teleport. What is surprising is the amount of energy this requires. So we can be sure that in one way or another they have access to level one and so an encounter is inevitable at that level. We need to be prepared for it. For level two, I'm not so sure. We need to check."

Orion takes the floor once more.

"Let me go on. Thanks for those clarifications, Akané. You are right. I think the messages we get from Mia are perfectly willed and orchestrated by Eneter. It's Eneter who controls her communication with us. They are sending us two messages. The first is that Mia is not in immediate danger and the second is that they can manage level-one transit, probably in their own way, but they can do it. There is a third message behind the first two, as Akané points out: they wish to communicate and are offering to get in touch. They are saying it in their own, very convoluted way, full of their power-obsessed logic, but it's a hypothesis we should consider. I suggest that some of us accept this invitation, but without diverting us from our original intention. So, as a precaution and to help those who are going to make contact, I suggest we deploy a timescale."

Orion's last words prompt various reactions. Those who know what he's talking about murmur their opinions while others exchange questioning looks.

"What do you mean?"

"It's very simple: it has always been possible to create time steps which form a ladder that stretches across time. It is so long that it spans different eras. If you look, you'll find textual proof of what I say in Memory Central. For example, some ancient essays, dating from far before the Collapsus, describe it as a communications link between Heaven and Earth. In fact, this ladder is a timescale, a particularly powerful way of magnifying the energy of the present potential. One of us remains in the present and acts as a pivot, connected to those who know about level-two transits: they split up into different eras, while keeping communications open between them. It's also a very effective way to link different time nodes, and in so doing convey information and principles to a given era which can accelerate positive developments there or prevent harmful trajectories as far as possible – although of course we can't intervene directly.

"By doing this it is possible, without controlling things, to propose coherent options for different time periods, for the ultimately beneficial development of all the eras thus linked. Whether these options are detected, formalised and made reality is another matter. It's up to the free will of each era to decide."

"Wow! That really must be pretty powerful."

"Yes, it is, but experience shows that actualising these proposals between the ages is a very difficult task that few eras manage to achieve. Most of the time, the ones formulating the choices, which come from the future, are taken to be idiots or simpletons, or even – in the worst cases –

dangerous visionaries who need to be eliminated. Sometimes, it is taken for a genius stroke and it works. Subtle dosing is called for: if the option proposed is too radical, it is quickly rejected; if it is adapted to the time, it may come to life but most of the time it is digested and absorbed by the status quo, which is always protective of special interests or the upkeep of short-term advantages – which boils down to the same thing.

"Today we ourselves are one of those groups, situated on our step of the time scale and we are doing exactly that: instilling in our present the development that comes from a future we know is beneficial, because we have the means to check it. This is why circumstances are suggesting that we, in turn, should split up, so as to gear down the process at our level and give it the chance to come good. Some of us know what this is about: these are the ones who meet in different eras to carry on this work, coming from another time. These are the ferrymen and women. As you no doubt are aware, the word 'scale' can be interpreted in various ways, and each is correct. It is a way of going from one level to another, or the expression of a gradual focusing through time, through which new details appear as we get closer."

Orion's words fall into a total stillness, not one of defensiveness or rejection or surprise, but rather one of open, pacified thoughts – a fertile ground in which these new impressions can evolve. Everyone visualises their own connection with their future and past; they all realise they are a step on this scale that Orion is talking about. Each of them is suddenly aware that they are connected, that their thoughts and intuitions are not isolated but are themselves part of a larger mesh spreading beyond time.

"It's funny – what you are saying reminds me unavoidably of the Zeitgeist, but this time on a universal scale."

"That's true, Akané!" says Orion. "Yes, you are quite right. Myself, I see the Zeitgeist as a possible solution to our problem: it can help us make

172

people accept the change in Elwon, without upsetting everything and without fear of rejection. The Memory is the ally we need and it knows it: that's why it gave you and Jiù the message in room C3. There seems to be an awareness behind its messages, which interests me and concerns me – this manoeuvre must not go against the Memory, nor against us. This knowledge must be part of the information that is waiting there for Jiù."

A great joy, almost exaltation rapidly spreads among the audience. It now seems that they not only have a goal but the means to achieve it. The success of their project seems to be in reach. The question now is what Eneter's role in the plan is and how they should engage with it. Orion continues:

"So what I propose allows us to remain fully aware of the in and outs of the situation, whatever Eneter has in mind and whatever they are preparing. While they are endeavouring to control space, let *us* focus on time, let's amplify the energy of the present potential. If we do this, every time we meet Eneter in one of the places they choose, we can protect the person involved in the confrontation and, through our timescale, stay connected to all future possibilities and all the pasts that lead there. Facing the reality that Eneter wants to impose on us, we can actualise a multitude of others, all belonging to the times we are connected to; and we have the possibility of furthering the futures that are favourable to Elwon and doing it in an acceptable and innate way so as to avoid them being rejected.

"I repeat – that's the whole meaning of the current convergence: to make Elwon and its authorities accept a non-controlled, wider dimension, in all possible directions. As Akané suggests, the Zeitgeist and Memory Central are surely the way to do this. Seeing as your father left you a message there, I think, dear Jiù, that you need to go back there."

Jiù is keeping quiet. He is one of the members of the audience for whom all this, strangely, is new without being completely unfamiliar. As if starting to link up with the questions, observations and diverse thoughts within him. Then, moved by an image that is coming into his mind, he begins to speak:

"Yes, I know. But I want to share something that comes to me: while you speak, it's as if I am connected to different times, Orion, and I see many different places filled with people singing. I see vast rooms and enormous buildings, colourful windows and even underground places. And always these people singing in unison. I understand that by their songs they are connecting to each other first, but above all they are connecting to other dimensions in time, ones that are close to them, as if through a musical scale."

"Yes, Jiù. Our world has always retained the memory of sound. Kohl's explanations show you its role in level two journeys. Sound is a vibration, as you know better than anyone. This sound vibration is energy, and if correctly amplified, it resonates and creates connections that open these congregations up to the potential energies of time that become accessible to them. Sound, music and singing help them free up the intuition, premonitions and dreams that are full of information. Sound is a vector crossing time, moving ideas and people; thoughts open up and proposals of other presents are made reality in ours. So when they are well-designed, the places and times that you visualise are very powerful. The people who come and sing are letting themselves be transported. They are connecting to the energy of Time and are drawing from it that which feeds their era, that which makes it live and evolve."

His tone, full of drive up till then, now becomes more lacklustre.

"The problem is that experience proves that this can quickly lose its effectiveness. At the beginning it works, and a lot of progress is made in sound ceremonies. But quickly, if ever the unity weakens, the connection is lost. So these gatherings keep going, first in the hope of getting the unity back, but in the end moved only by the memory of it. The forces of inertia and repetition get the upper hand once more and it all becomes a totally senseless ritual just like an anecdote, nothing more. Time closes up again. But you're right, sound *makes sense*. It shows the wisdom inherent in the energy of time. These scales are in position for all time, and now it's our turn to create one."

He turns towards the crowd and with power in his voice once more, says:

"Do you agree to go into a state of heightened awareness right away? If possible, let's avoid transition for now," he says, glancing towards Jiù. "We need to stay aware and accumulate the knowledge inscribed in those moments that adjoin both our past and future. This can give us the temporal perspective we need. Only then everyone can choose the time that seems most propitious to them – their own rung on the ladder. As for me and Elea," he adds after exchanging a look with his companion, "we are staying here, in non-focused active mode, to follow what happens and intervene if necessary."

"I'm staying too," adds Kohl.

In the calm that takes hold, Jiù tells Akané with a fraction-of-a-second look: "let's stay together". He feels the vibration of time rise immediately, but this time it shakes him with unusual strength, as if magnified a hundredfold by the unified focus of around twenty people united at the same moment in one consciousness. Before having the time to think, never mind focus, Jiù is immediately transported, out of control.

He reappears in a mountainous landscape that he doesn't recognise. To his great joy, Akané is at his side almost instantly.

"Unbelievable! Well, at least I'll never get bored as long as you're around! I didn't want to let you go off on your own so I was watching you.

Knowing your ability to get into trouble, I really wanted to get into it with you again."

"Drat. I think I messed up again."

"Yep, I think I agree with you!"

They both burst out laughing, the kind of laughter that does you good and lasts a bit longer than necessary. It gives them time to rebalance their energy between the intensity of a moment ago and the unknown they are now facing. These moments of level-two transition are always quite delicate.

"But hey – remember last time – it was worth it in the end, so we can live in hope!"

"It's crazy – whenever I think I've mastered this blasted energy, something happens to make me understand that I haven't. And then when I think I'm not in control of anything, that's when I discover what I'm capable of."

"Well, I think that's a good sign! You've just understood that it's not about control. Let yourself go – that's what life is telling you. Accept the invitation of the circumstances, you jammy beggar – you don't even have to get up off the couch because life comes to you."

Again they laugh and then, with a perfectly synchronous movement they turn around, each in a different direction, so as to embrace together the most complete view possible from the place they have landed.

"Good heavens!" exclaims Akané. "It's not possible – d'you know where we are?"

"Er ..."

"I would recognise this more than anywhere. I know exactly where we are. We've transited to the moment of the hologram I showed you, the one with the old lady in front of her house. Look," she adds, pointing. "Look at the smoke."

Instinctively Jiù follows the movement of her hand and immediately recognises the mountain with smoke spreading out in the distance. It is indeed the same landscape, even if the columns of smoke seem denser and more numerous. Now they form a kind of thick curtain at the foot of the wooded hills that are lost on a distant horizon.

Wishing to complete their discovery of the image imprinted in their memory, they turn round and glimpse in the middle distance the glazed roof of a large timber-framed house. Looking more carefully they begin to see the rest of it. In front, a little lean-to with slightly loose planks faces an entrance with a particularly well-tended flowerbed. The house, immense and remarkably well cared for, exudes an air of rather dated opulence.

"But what are we doing here?"

"Let's ask her."

"Ask who?"

"The old lady in the hologram, of course! That'll tell us what she is doing in my family's souvenir holos."

They walk towards the house, their hearts full of contradictory emotions: Jiù's regret at not having been able to respect Orion's instructions, Akané's hope of finding out at last the meaning of this image, and for both of them uncertainty mixed with excitement at what is to come. There is also concentration as they go into active mode so as to try to understand and predict what's coming and what has happened here.

"Good morning, grandmother!" Akané calls out to the old lady whom they find near the house, just as they had expected.

She watches them come towards her, looking intensely at Akané with an expression of great astonishment mixed with fear on her face.

"Who are you?" she says with a strong accent in a language they understand even though they haven't learnt it.

"Apparently we're not in Elwon any more," they say to each other in their heads.

"Yes, but I sense some danger; let's stay on our guard."

"We're lost and perhaps you can help us?"

"Who are you?" repeats the old woman, in the tone of one who will not be swayed, and taking a step back.

"I'm Akané, and this is Jiù, my companion. We're from Elwon."

"I don't know it. But do I know you?"

The old woman's mistrust grows with each question. She is now completely on her guard, almost closed to any attempt at dialogue. If they don't find a way to keep up the contact, all this might come to nothing. Moved by sudden intuition, Akané gets out her holos, adeptly handles it and says:

"Does this remind you of something?" On her wrist the image that Jiù saw on Sehn appears.

The old lady seems completely astounded. Only after a moment of dazed silence does she manage to mutter:

"Where did you get that?"

"It's been in my family for generations, for some unknown reason."

The woman now looks at Akané with renewed attention, not yet welcoming, but already less distant, although the fear is still there. Akané and Jiù look calmly back at her, concerned not to rush her, but attentive, as if they wanted to crack the secret she bears. Deep wrinkles mark her face like a hollow print of the emotions that have moved her – they can follow the trace of past smiles and tears, as well as the imprint of far-off forgotten fears and efforts. In this venerable face, the eyes are gentle and the gaze benevolent, if weary and slightly veiled. Her hands tremble a little, no doubt because of age, emotion or perhaps her interrupted work in the garden?

"Come in. We have things to talk about."

She goes before them into her house. She walks slowly and slightly bent over, but they feel nonetheless that an uncommon vitality still inhabits this tired body. She wipes her hands, takes her shoes off and, sliding a partition to one side, reveals a bright room with a big straw carpet, furnished simply but tastefully. A practised eye can detect a discreet refinement in the rare cloth and quality furniture, even in the simple clothes she is wearing for gardening. They notice a long shelf under the window, placed on two round stones, with an orchid and a plump little statue that Jiù instantly recognises: the same little Buddha his mother gave him. It sits as if on an altar, ever-smiling and surrounded by incense sticks. She kneels down in front of a little chest and, with a restrained gesture, invites them to do the same. Jiù and Akané follow suite with a slightly false detachment. After a moment of silence and mutual observation, the old lady opens the chest and starts methodically looking for something.

"Here."

She holds out to them an image printed on paper: it's identical to Akané's hologram except that on this one a tall man with dark skin in ceremonial dress, elegant and with an imposing bearing, stands next to the old lady. They both have the same intensity in their eyes and emanate the same dignity as they look in front of them with a serious and determined air. Altogether the picture emits a solemn atmosphere tinted with a certain fatality.

"This is Iksan, my husband. My name is Oko. Since the troubles began, around six months ago, his health is in decline. He is extremely tired and I'm protecting him. He's resting next door and perhaps a little later you will be able to greet him. We'll see. You know, he foresaw everything, predicted it all, announced everything that is happening now; but unfortunately no-one wanted to listen to him, and this – among other things – wore him down."

She pauses for a while, as if to gather her forces before deciding to tell all.

"You see, my husband and I were the last co-presidents of the global Scientific High Council. It was the consultative body of world leaders whose official aim was to organise research and spread its applications and costs which was absolutely essential as it got more and more expensive. But it soon became one of the countless places with lots of talk but little action. My husband was a scientist, ahead of his time, we had published several pieces of work, in particular about time. At the beginning of our research, people listened to us, we were in high demand, invited all over the place – everyone wanted to listen to us, and we were eventually asked to take over as directors of the SHC.

"We quickly discovered that in fact this Council was being manipulated by industrial and military conglomerates supported by highly powerful financial groups, with whom Iksan soon came into conflict. From then on the invitations became more formal and then fewer and farther between, as if we had become embarrassing. Because of a progression of events against which we were powerless, we were gradually slandered, then rejected. The Council had no more followers, as if it had become useless, entrusted to people who were no doubt more pliable. His theories were then fought against even more strongly in quite systematic campaigns. We were only half surprised by their violence – he had warned me that it would very probably be that way."

"Who fought against his theories? Do you know?"

"Of course: those I have mentioned who, for so long and under cover of mutual arrangements, had been dictating the law to our different states. We had realised too late that everything that Iksan proposed posed a threat to this solidly established order that protects the interests of a few. The battle was far too unequal. Very few of his colleagues, previously admiring, took the risk of defending him, much less joining him. His reputation was pitilessly tarnished, we became destitute and, pretty soon after that, all was chaos. As if they had waited for that moment to appear, spontaneous revolts took place all over the place, causing the authorities to become more rigid and gradually triggering increasingly savage repressive measures. It was a truly awful series of events, impossible to stop, like an inevitable destiny we refused to believe in but before which, despite all our knowledge, we were powerless."

She gestures towards her window.

"As you can see, not a day goes past now without organised gangs pillaging and looting, which in turn means reprisals by the regular forces who are only regular in their way of proceeding, because they too pillage and massacre, this time with total impunity. It's every man for himself now, everyone stays in their own home, as if everything that used to unite us and bring us together were no longer worth anything. Families are being torn apart, friends are betraying each other, colleagues denouncing each other – it is a total rout, everyone is going to ground and no-one is risking anything. In this climate of general insecurity, everyone wants more and above all more than other people – it's a never-ending cycle. Where will it stop? Nobody knows, but everybody is worried. For Iksan and myself, this cannot be happening by chance. It's got to be organised, but we can't identify the intention behind the chaos. The whole question for us is to know how to break the sequence of events and this inevitability."

"The Collapsus. It's incredible – we've arrived at the beginning of the Collapsus," says Jiù with his inner voice.

"Jiù, have you noticed? The similarity with our own present? We absolutely have to do something to help them."

"Something surprises me," says Jiù. "On our image, your husband has disappeared. Why?"

"I don't know. We will ask him later on."

Jiù continues talking fast, looking worried.

"Oko, you really must allow us to talk to him. The events that are unfolding are not inevitable. With your agreement, and his, we can perhaps manage to orient the flow of things towards a less dramatic outcome. We can tell you what is going to happen – your future is our past."

"What do you mean?" interrupts Oko with anguish in her voice. "Who are you anyway?"

"Oko, the crisis you are in is a major catastrophe that no doubt goes beyond the intention of those who triggered it. It will erase every trace of civilisation and what is happening at the moment is a mere trifle compared to what is going to happen. There must still be time to intervene. This crisis is in our past: we call it the Collapsus and we built our civilisation on the ruins of yours. But I can tell you that we too are on our way towards something very similar, except that the uncertainty has disappeared – we can calculate very precisely when this crisis will happen in our world. We know as well, but this is shared by only a small number of us, that the roots of our crisis can be found in yours. The process seems to be the same, as if our society was a double of yours, beyond time, replicating in its own way what threw yours into the abyss....

"It's as if we had learnt nothing, as if the germs of your destruction survived," he adds in a lifeless voice.

Oko remains speechless; she is astonished by what has just been revealed to her, trying to weigh up its reality. Unhappily all this only serves to confirm what she already knows, but hearing it reiterated by total strangers, being confronted with the sheer inevitability of the outcome, towards which they are inexorably striding, utterly terrifies her.

"I am happy to be able to talk about it, because the occasion to do so has not presented itself for such a long time."

"I like very much the words you have just used."

"Which ones?"

"The occasion presents itself. It puts itself in the present. I think that's what your husband was working on?"

"Yes. How did you know?" Astonished, for a moment she seems almost to look away as if stolen away by memories she doesn't want to share.

"Oko, it is essential that you let us meet your husband: we have to find out everything you know and everything he knows. It's a question of days, or even hours."

"Jiù, don't probe her, it would be out of place. She trusts us, don't do it until she gives us the go-ahead."

"Well, obviously! What are you thinking? I do know how to behave – at least, sometimes ..."

They both have a slight smile on their lips, which Oko interprets as an invitation to go on.

"Iksan has worked for a long time on the theory of time. He no longer has the strength, but he has made some major discoveries and had published numerous works on the double nature of time that he called the Chronos-Aeon duality. It comes from a very ancient language that has now disappeared."

"Did you say Aeon?" Jiù can't help exclaiming. "That's exactly the word my father used to describe the energy of time that he too was working on!"

Oko stares at him, trying once more to penetrate the mystery of their presence but also to understand where this shared knowledge comes from. Her curiosity is aroused by the turn of events, by these strange but welcome coincidences, like a door opening onto a sliver of clarity in the cold darkness that is coming.

"That is exactly the research Iksan undertook. According to him, our world has been locked in Chronos, the linear version of time that makes us think – wrongly – that it has a sole dimension and direction. That was his aim – to find the doors which would allow us to escape the inexorability of things, as this linearity is only the expression in our world of a vastly wider reality, the Aeon. In the Aeon he discovered the possibility of a gigantic energy, much superior to the one contained in matter. He claimed that, despite its power, the atomic energy we tamed was miniscule compared to the Aeon's, like the only visible face of a diamond. All his work was based on that."

"The mirror instead of the jewel," mutters Jiù.

"Exactly!" She looks at Jiù, confused. "Those were his precise words! How do you know? But now it's my turn to ask questions. I'm talking and talking, but I know nothing about you, and you already know a lot about me. Who are you?"

Akané gently takes her hand.

"We are Jiù and Akané, travellers in time. Oko, please try to believe us, we are from a future time; your husband was right. A few of us know how to access this energy you call the Aeon; we do use it, although we can't control it. And it allows us to travel in time. And that's how we were able to come here and we chose to come to your time, maybe attracted by this image, but also doubtless for another more important reason."

"Which other reason?"

"I think we have come to find an answer to a question connected to the Collapsus."

"What do you mean?"

"Because our time in turn is heading towards its own Collapsus as you are towards yours and we want to direct it away. The similarity between our times is not fortuitous. We need to understand the origin of your Crisis, try to see what connects it to ours and maybe, I wonder...."

"What?"

"It's only speculation, but if we can avoid the Collapsus in your time, we can simultaneously alter the dynamics that lead to our own. If they are connected, which wouldn't surprise me; acting on one would have repercussions on the other."

"I really don't see how you could reverse the flow of events: what is done is done and nothing or no-one can undo it."

Akané, who detects more irritation than incredulity in Oko's interruption, nevertheless continues:

"You see, Oko, I think that beyond the immense time that separates us, there's a kind of continuity between us. See how alike we are, how similar the circumstances which lead to our meeting are, how your husband's work has an explanation in our time. I believe in this continuity and I wonder about its origin. It's the reflection of what connects our two worlds, and the events that are brewing here as well as back there are surely connected. That's why we have come to you."

If Oko is still resistant, something in the old lady is coming alive. These considerations remind her so much of her conversations with Iksan that she can almost physically feel the continuity that Akané is talking about.

"You would be a very far-off descendant then? When do you come from?"

"We're from the year 2244. What year is this?"

"2028"

"Two hundred and twenty years, Jiù. We've jumped back two hundred and twenty years!" Jiù and Akané look at each other, awestruck by the distance separating them from their time which seems all of a sudden inaccessible to them, as if they were in a hostile country with impassable borders.

Prompted by a sudden thought, Akané asks:

"Oko, let us remain silent for a moment. I'll explain afterwards."

"Jiù," she calls with her inner voice. "We have forgotten. We have to check whether the connection with Orion is working. If so it would mean we have spontaneously positioned ourselves at the beginning of the timescale. We need to find out what's happening and where the others are."

Together, they close their eyes and go down in unison into the inner calm that connects them completely to themselves and to the time they are the bearers of.

"Orion, can you hear us?"

First, silence; then a sort of breathing, a deep whispering within, answers them.

"Yes, perfectly well. It's good to hear you. I'm with Elea and Kohl – the others are leaving too. Where are you?"

"We are together, at the beginning of the moral Collapsus in 2028. We are at Oko's house. She's the wife of Iksan, a researcher who published work on the energy of the Aeon. Does that name mean anything to you, and can you check this data?"

Silence greets these words and they guess that on the other side they are having to consult.

"Orion?"

"Yes?"

"Jiù and I think that the two Collapsus are indisputably linked. We are going to try to identify the connections and whether the one that is coming in our time has roots in the one that is brewing here. Can we stay in touch?"

"Let me tell you that the name Iksan is definitely not unknown to me. On the contrary, it seems right that you have gone to meet him. But around the data concerning Iksan there's some uncertainty that we need to understand. Give us a bit more time to investigate further and get back to you. We are staying connected, take your time. Let me also tell you that Jon decides to contact Eneter. You know his connection with Mia – he can't just do nothing. So therefore he is our pivot in the timescale. We are also putting down six relays in possible futures, some at level one and others in the past, as well as you two."

"Thanks, Orion."

They open their eyes and notice that Oko has left the room. As usual, they have no idea how much time has gone by. Then they hear her busy herself in what must be her kitchen, and a moment later she carries in some steaming tea with meticulous care. On her heels is a gaunt and pallid man with burning eyes who looks at them with intensity. He holds on to her shoulder as she helps him follow her in.

"This is Iksan. I talked to him about you and he insisted on seeing you."

"Iksan, this is a great honour! You shouldn't have put yourself to so much trouble," replies Akané as she and Jiù get up and give a slight bow, with the slowness that translates as respect.

"I'm going to have tea with you, then I will listen to what you have to say," pronounces Iksan in a voice like a whisper. "I will then see what we can share, if there is still time."

They drink their hot tea almost reverentially. Oko is grateful to them for the long silence that follows and that they seem to use to size each other up. Then Akané says, pointing towards the invitingly cool narrow path that runs along the house before plunging under the pine trees:

"Where does it lead?"

"Oh, it's a short walk – the sea is just there, down at the bottom, and there is a little cove where I often go to meditate."

"Would you take us there later on? We could continue to talk while walking and it would surely do you good – and us too."

"If you like."

"Thank you, Oko."

"I'm going to try to summarise what we've understood," says Jiù for Iksan's sake, feeling slightly emotional at the memory of his father. "I can see three degrees of time unfolding quite simultaneously in our era. First of all Eneter, the Energy militia – no doubt the equivalent of your police or army here – which maintains time linearity. This represents absolute order because it is totally predictable, in our world as in yours, even though I think that we have taken our capacity for prediction and anticipation to a degree unknown in yours. That's the energy degree. Then there are the Dissidents – us – who are exploring all the options of the present, what we call the present potential which is a continuous creation of temporal energy. That's the knowledge degree. Finally, the Aeon is the infinite dimension of this immeasurable awareness that is manifested through the universe and of which we only perceive a part. We can travel across it via connections or this timescale that we've erected in order to come here. That's the ultimate consciousness degree. But we only know the tiniest part of it and some of what it contains! How is it all organised? What is the intention behind this arrangement? If we find out, whether in your time or in ours, we can resolve the inevitability of our twin Collapsus. That's why it's essential for us to pool what we know and what you have discovered here."

"You have summarised very well, but I will be able to tell you more. Go and walk with Oko, it will do her good. We'll talk when you get back. Meanwhile I'll get together some notes to help you to understand," Iksan concludes, not wanting to say more. He stands up and, very slowly and cautiously, goes towards the door at the back of the large room.

"Come." Oko gets up and goes out. She slips her small feet into sandals and heads towards the path.

"Oko, can I explain?" Akané has discreetly caught the old woman up. "Let me tell you about our silence just now in the house. It wasn't meditation, although perhaps that's what it might have looked like. When we left our time we stayed in contact with our people and I wanted to check whether we could still communicate at this distance in time. We found out that we could, and that's going to be really useful for synchronising our time with yours. This synchronisation will allow us to identify the exact similarities and the chain of events that leads from your Collapsus to ours. I'm sure that we will then be able to retro-act on these events. Please trust us. Trust what you know deep inside, independently of everything you have learnt."

"May Heaven hear you," says the old woman, only half convinced and now concentrating on her movements as the path begins to wind up a steeper slope.

They follow her, making sure they coordinate their steps with hers and trying not to hurry her. Here too they enjoy tasting the preciousness of time that is unfolding around them like a film in multiple dimensions.

Jiù supports her lightly with his hand as they arrive at the little beach of coarse grey sand mixed with pebbles. The sea is calm and smooth, only a few little waves coming to die on the beach, not making much effort to conquer it. As they approach the shore he presses on with what he has discovered during his exchanges with Orion.

"We know that there are three levels of energy in time, which are diluted as they incarnate in events. In our world, this energy appears in the form of causality, because one event irresistibly brings on another. It has become so banal that no-one pays attention to it any more, and yet – look!"

With a sweeping gesture he encompasses the horizon, dotted with scattered clouds, that spreads before them. The sun, already low, is casting bronze hues onto the sea.

"Do you see? What we call causality is only part of the fabulous energy of the Aeon, the part we can see in our world. It's a miniscule echo of it, just as this tiny swell we hardly notice that founders insignificantly on the beach is perhaps the trace of a gigantic storm beyond the horizon. That's causality: the fleeting memory of the energy of Time that we perceive in our world. It can sometimes take on more or less dramatic forms, but it most often takes on the form of this negligible trace of what is time's limitless intensity. On the way to this immense and far-off horizon, the path goes via free will. It is our vehicle. It also goes via courage for adventure and a will to go beyond causality, like crossing the barrier that must close off your pretty cove on windy days. At the end of the road we will have discovered the three levels of the expression of time. And I have a profound intuition that our eras are alike, even that they almost superimpose. That's why meeting your husband is essential for us, to allow us to understand the causalities that connect us beyond time."

"I don't know. Perhaps you are right. Everything you say seems to correspond quite precisely with our work with Iksan, and it's interesting that your father did the same work – as if they were each an extension of the other. But as for Iksan, our work has not helped him at all – he hasn't been able to prevent anything and he's dying of it."

She wants to end this conversation now and go back to Iksan. These strangers seem astonishingly familiar, but she wouldn't go so far as to have complete faith – there is a limit she doesn't want to cross again. Too much pain and suffering, too much hardship now surround these topics for her to be able to look for any hope in them. With tiny steps, frail in her shawl, she suggests they go back, and they start slowly back up the path, Akané helping Oko several times on the steeper slopes. Once in the house in the sudden cool of the fading day, they take up the discussion again:

"Tell us more about your husband, please, Oko. Has he got a family? Have you any children?"

"No more than two, of course, as we are not allowed more. A boy and a girl. Our son took the picture you have. On the morning of the photo, he had just told us he was leaving. He was on very bad terms with his father, whose views and philosophy he questioned. He had enormous ambition and our way of life was unsatisfactory to him. And as for us, we didn't approve of some of his friends. That explains why we look both puzzled and quite closed off in the picture. He had asked us to put on our ceremonial clothes, the ones we wore during council meetings. To publish in his memoirs one day, or so he said.

"For him you had to invest all available energy in the immediate satisfaction of people's needs. Just the idea of having to take time exasperated him – like a child, and that's what he remained. His main argument was that you have to use the world, as that's what it's there for, and if you don't take it, someone else will. That's what he called his realism. So you see how different he was from his father? For example, he didn't understand his father's obsession for thinking about things in relation to their possible future consequences. They were opposed on everything and this conflict between the so-called realism of the present and the call of the future was growing to the point of becoming intolerable.

"I think that it was this oppressive antagonism, more than anything else, which profoundly undermined Iksan's health. Especially when he realised that our son's views were shared by a vast majority of people the world over – they all, or almost all, think only about helping themselves, taking things; they dream only of having, without any consideration other than accumulating. It is our civilisation's only dogma, totally toxic and contagious – thou shalt take advantage ... You can't imagine the incredible breadth of these insatiable appetites."

She turns pale and continues in a low voice:

"Oh no! You can't imagine to what extent this worldwide greed has become an obsession, how much it's begun to seem like normality, dictated and reproduced by all known information media. Starting with our son! Objects and machines of all sorts have become more important than people – much more – and we are realising, but too late, that we have become walled into a world of things and systems. Never mind time and everything you have discovered – nobody's been paying any attention for so long. It's just a trivialised background to our excesses. Oh, I'm so exhausted with the weight of this destiny!"

Jiù and Akané are struck by the contagious sadness on Oko's features that makes the wrinkles that hollow her face seem even deeper. The relentlessness that suddenly crushes Oko resonates directly with the one that suffocated them in Elwon: both are of a similar nature and the same feeling of repetition mixed with powerlessness overwhelms them. Twin lines of tears silently appear and flow slowly down the furrows in her cheeks. Dignified and still, she says no more. Akané goes to sit behind her and the old lady allows her to gently lay her hands on her head. With the vibrant energy coming through Akané's fingers, she slowly regains her calm, and pacified, she begins talking again:

"He despaired of the circumstances that we were living in, even within our family. Our son's departure became unavoidable. One day, an official car came to pick him up and he left. We haven't heard from him since. A short while afterwards, Iksan's health began quickly to decline, and he doesn't get out of bed any more. It's like he's no longer really there."

"All this is recent, then?"

"In a way, yes."

"How do you explain your husband's absence from Akané's hologram?"

"I can't really explain it. The only hypothesis is that the image has been altered. But I don't know why. This would have to be checked. My son might have done it in a mood swing, or it could be something else – I really don't know."

"And your daughter?"

"She is away. She left yesterday, quite suddenly, telling me not to worry. I'm waiting for her – she's been living here since the troubles broke out. She came to help me, of course, but also because the countryside is a lot safer than the city. I'm going to show you something." She goes back to her chest and gets another photo out that she holds out to Akané. Now it's Akané's turn to be silent, dumbfounded by what she sees. In a whisper she asks:

"What's her name?"

"Kaya, which means 'little elder sister'."

"Of course. I should have guessed, Akané mutters to herself.

Jiù remains impassive. He knows what Akané is contemplating. He's understood that she is looking at another image of herself – it can't be otherwise. He now knows enough. He knows why he is here, why he met Akané again. The job he assigned himself so long ago comes back to him. He is completing it, right now. He is sure that they have gone back to the source of causality, to the birth of the L1 logic that has developed on Elwon during the whole time that separates them from this ancient past. It all started in this house, on this small island, and everything will be resolved here. Moved by the enlarged awareness that is now with him constantly, he feels the present unfolding around them and carrying them away in its waves and folds. He sees all of its possible diversity: he knows that they are being given the chance to relive each of those moments when they did not choose to live up to their greatest potential. Each time, they are offered a renewed present – other choices – just as life is right now allowing Oko and Iksan to decide on a different outcome, one which is not unavoidable. He knows then what he is going to do. Simultaneously in Elwon and in Oko's time, he's going to help these sister eras live other choices, like a joint decision taken beyond the generations. He has to talk to Iksan, who is at the core of what he wants to solve. Iksan is the link between Jiù and his father, as much as he is undoubtedly linked to Orion. In the same way, Akané just faced her own double a few minutes ago. He feels that within himself and within Akané, something is being organised to allow another option to materialise as an indescribable but incredibly powerful blend of the energy of the instant and the choices of the ones living it. In fact he feels that the choices have already been made in himself, that they are going to unfold almost unbeknown to him and that he just has to be attentive. Totally relaxed, he can't hold back a long sigh of wellbeing as he looks with infinite goodwill at the old lady who is still next to Akané and letting her now diligently massage her hands. In the chaos that is surrounding them and getting closer, he surrenders to the tangible peace that enfolds them and that fills the air – the peace he always feels when he is completely at one with time. He knows that this is the sign of its own reality. He looks at Oko again: her eyes closed, she is smiling.

———————

7 - Jon

Jon doesn't want to hear any more. He listens with growing impatience to Orion's words and the exchanges that follow. The considerations are mostly beyond him and are not really of interest apart from when Akané speaks. He is even impressed by her interpretation of the communication with her sister – apparently she knows her very well. He's surprised by the maturity revealed in Mia. Honestly speaking, she eludes him a little. As for the rest, he has difficulty making sense of it, especially the talk of a timescale mechanism that he only listens to with half an ear. Jon is a man of action and the only thing that really matters to him is that this whole time Mia is in the hands of Eneter – and that is something he can't tolerate without doing something about it.

Forcing himself to remain calm but fearing the worst, he is accumulating hypotheses and calculations, all the while trying to curb his imagination which keeps taking him back to where she is. The hardest thing to bear is her silence. He's not used to it and can't stop wondering about the possible causes; and all Akané's reassurances change nothing – he is worried sick about Mia and can't imagine losing her. So when Orion suggests they go into active mode, he immediately focuses on Mia, hoping to find her.

He materialises in a brightly-lit little room. He is alone and quite surprised not to see her. He barely has time to start wondering about a focus error – which is always a possibility for someone with as little experience as he has, but disappointing nonetheless when it happens – before a voice fills the room.

"You're welcome among us. Your young friend isn't here, she's just left. As you can imagine, we make very sure that you are not in the same room at the same time. I'm sure you'll understand this kind of precaution. We were expecting someone, but I regret to tell you it wasn't you we were waiting for. However, would you be so good as to answer some questions?"

Jon is silent. The information he has just been given is important. Does this mean Eneter is capable of predicting their movements? They were right, back in the Garden: level one transitions are obviously being watched – but how? On the other hand, he doesn't want to play their game of false affability and so he waits for their intentions to become clearer.

"Fine. You see we have put into place a little procedure that helps us secure the young person you know, without running the risk of being taken by surprise by your people. Can you tell us who you are?"

"I'm Jon, I live in Newton on the East coast and I work in the administration sector."

"You mean you *used* to work, because I regret to inform you that we just took a biotic reading of you and all your data are now on standby, so you've been replaced. What is your connection with this young person?"

"None. I came because we interpreted her different messages as an invitation from you to come and meet."

"OK, good ... that is correctly reasoned. Indeed, we want to establish a rapport with you, but we want to do it our way. For example, you should be aware that this room was designed to prevent any non-conform brain transmissions. Have you heard of inhibitors? Around this room we have stacked so many as to cut it off totally from the world, so to speak. Coming back to you, I don't know if you're the person best qualified for the contact we seek with your organisation. Can you tell us a little more?"

Jon remains silent, feeling satisfied that he's scored a point. He's made a good entrance despite not knowing anything about his interlocutor. He knows that he now has a little while to reply correctly to the question he's been asked. A short silence could be interpreted as the necessary time to get together the information requested. He tries on the spot to get in touch with Mia from the inner, but fails; the same happens when he tries Orion. He is, then, alone against Eneter, and must continue to improvise. Above all he must stay in active mode; this will allow him to detect the slightest changes in his surroundings, and the mood of his interlocutor. His only certainty is that time is on his side. Ah, if only he had been more attentive when Orion was talking about the timescale, he would probably remember some precious instructions for the present circumstances.

"I am the person best qualified for a first contact with you, which is what I've been sent for. No-one else will come at this stage. Depending on the way this proceeds, more sophisticated communication could follow. We are ready to have discussions with you and even work with you – you can be sure of this, and you can also be sure that we will cooperate transparently. Our only concern is to be assured of free will and freedom of movement in all circumstances. As long as you don't stand in the way of that, we can talk. But we cannot consider discussions conducted in unequal conditions to be satisfactory."

His words were pronounced in a purposefully clear and steady voice. If he wants to demonstrate the attributes of the kind of emissary they are expecting, he has to show some semblance of mastery of the protocol. The ensuing silence is abyssal, amplified by the room's strange lack of acoustics which prevents him from hearing even his own breathing. He doesn't have the feeling, this time, of having met with a great success. He doesn't know whether this uncomfortable silence denotes consideration of what he has said, or whether his response was just simply inappropriate. It's best not to add anything. Their turn to show their hand.

At last the discussion continues:

"Just listen to that! Let me tell you, young man, that we are in complete control of the conditions of this interview and of your young friend as well as what happens in Elwon. We will therefore conduct this conversation in whatever way we see fit. With all your airs of greatness – which I must say are a little laughable – you are a mere subject of Elwon, whereas I myself represent absolute power. So be aware that preliminary interviews will not be adequate. We are going to get straight to the point, and I hope for your sake that you will have the good sense to cooperate. What interest us and the only reason that we have accepted to meet people of your kind is the new energy you seem to control. As you know, energy is exclusively Eneter's domain, and I mean exclusively. Can you, at your level, give me some more substance about this energy and the conditions for its use? Or should we wait for a let's say more qualified envoy?"

"As I've already told you, *I* am the qualified envoy at this stage. There is no hierarchy in our organisation, only different experiences that we all share, but it's up to you to judge if this is worthwhile for you according to your own criteria."

"Indeed it is up to me to judge, but we hope you will tell us everything you know. You understand what I mean, don't you?"

Despite this thinly-veiled threat, the conversation has given Jon another valuable clue: his interlocutor probably holds a high-up decision-making rank within Eneter. This shows the importance of this conversation for them, although he is not able to deduce whether his interrogator speaks in his own or in Eneter's name. He's going to have to knock this hurdle down quickly.

"Could you tell me who you are?"

"My name doesn't really matter, but I can tell you that I am one of the high commanders of Eneter, which goes to show something you must already realise – the importance for us of what we are talking about and the rank of the emissaries we are expecting."

"What do you want to know?"

"Why do you want to work with us?"

"First of all, we know that there is going to be a Collapsus in Elwon and we are ready to help you in order to avoid it if it's still possible. That's why I have come and why we want to cooperate – we think that no individual or organisation can have an interest in what is set to happen, which will surely be of the same magnitude as the moral Collapsus in the past."

"Yes, we are aware of that too. Let me make things clear: if we have envisaged a meeting, it's not about collaboration. We don't collaborate with people like you. We evaluate the risk they represent for L1 order and we decide what to do with them. Now that's been clarified, what can you tell us about this energy and how can it help prevent the Collapsus?"

"This energy you're interested in is colossal and freely accessible at the same time. There is no need for equipment, captors or measurements – you can access it yourself. If the Collapsus threatening us has its origins in energy, there is easily enough of it available to prevent it. However, I fear that it will not be adequate."

"What do you mean?"

"We think that this coming Collapsus is not only about energy, even if energy is the outward sign of it. We think that the unequal sharing of the energy as well as the distribution of resources and power in Elwon are the root of the imbalance, its principal cause. Therefore, I regret to have to tell you that Eneter doesn't control energy only on behalf of Elwon: some of its members, whose identity we don't know, are misappropriating energy for their own needs. They have even built a network for their own exclusive use. So there are moral causes for the energy crash, which leads us back to the causes of the first Collapsus."

"Do you realise just what you are saying?"

Faced with his interlocutor's cold anger, Jon fears he's gone too far. But has he guessed right? He has to take risks and keep along the same lines if he wants to be able to find out on whose behalf this man is interrogating him. If he's really in Eneter's service, he will have to ask him more questions, or even threaten him.

"Yes, I realise, but as I told you, we want to collaborate in all transparency. Our aim isn't to create disorder in Elwon; on the contrary, we want to help our dynasty to develop in a new dimension of its time, but this time with a sharing perspective. In any case, that's the direction temporal energy is making us take. It can't be any other way. By its very nature, this energy can't be reserved for a few people. Any of us could tell you the same thing – all of us share this experience and knowledge. If you are of the rank within Eneter that you say you are, you should be sensitive to the information I'm giving you. I am in a position to give you tangible proof."

His words are greeted with silence, as if the communication had been cut off. Jon remains unruffled, having surprised himself with his calm and even jubilation at this nonetheless delicate situation – he actually feels like he's playing a game! No-one in Elwon likes to be interrogated by Eneter and yet he's acting as though he was in total control of the situation – he feels linked to his own reality with a new intensity: he concludes that an invisible force is protecting him from the reality Eneter wants to impose on him.

"What's it got to do with sharing?"

More than the continuation of the interview, it's the question that surprises him. He admires in passing the brilliance of the mind that's interrogating him – it shows a highly developed interlocutor, used to negotiating, a higher intelligence that does not let itself be caught in the traps laid down by his responses.

"Our experiments show that the accessible manifestation of this energy is greatest when it is shared by the largest number of people. Of course, it can be used individually, which is what I did to come and meet you, but you cannot do anything important if it's kept for a minority."

"Interesting. Disappointing, but interesting."

Jon is only half listening to him. He now has a strong suspicion that the man interrogating him has detained him on an individual level rather than on Eneter's behalf.

"Another question: When you connect to this energy, is it possible to divert it to captors or condensers?"

Inwardly, Jon deplores the triviality of this question that is so predictable and so typical of Eneter, which only thinks of energy in its most controllable and most material form. He's disappointed; the conversation suddenly loses its interest and this doesn't bode well for what is to follow.

"We have never tried that. For us there's no point, seeing as anyone can call on it and use it at will, in particular for travelling – you saw the proof of that just now. So you see that, if it works on an individual level, its collective effects are greatly magnified, as they are the sum of individual choices. Therefore this energy is for each of us a way of orienting his or her own future, a way of acting while staying connected to others and to our own time, whether this is the past, present or future. Therefore our interactions are always optimal. Used by several people in a synchronous way, we think that this energy could guide the future of our Dynasty itself."

"Enough!"

Jon is only half surprised by this sudden outburst of anger. It is the absolutely logical consequence of the intolerable gap between the reality he's describing and the one which is the norm in Elwon. For him it's a signal that the interview is going to take a different turn, and he has to be prepared for it. Indeed, his interlocutor's tone becomes menacing and he is now hissing with barely-contained rage.

"No more nonsense – this whole thing is not your business but ours. It's high time we tidied this up and entered a more radical phase in this little game of chess which, by the way, is becoming wearisome. You're a poor player, young man – we haven't been playing for long and already you're checkmated!"

This threat inspires bravado in Jon, irritated as he is by this discussion that is dragging on without leading anywhere, and which in the end is no more than an interrogation; he can't resist the desire to titillate his invisible interlocutor's anger even more.

"Nothing is less sure! You see, this game is being played on several chessboards, and despite your resources, I'm afraid you only control one.

As for us, we control several, but we are not playing. We've come to meet you in good faith and sincerely wish to work together with you to prevent what's coming. Is that what you want too?"

As an answer there is only a silence which draws out, interminable. The reactions he's getting are decidedly not the ones he was expecting. Suddenly the voice speaks again, with an icy coldness:

"That's enough. From now on, whether you want to or not, you are going to do exactly what we tell you to. The rest is our business."

Jon feels the pressure of the air around him suddenly grow almost to suffocation point. He realised they have amplified the inhibitors to maximum strength in order to secure him definitively, but instead of becoming stiff and closing in on himself for fear of what is going to happen next, he opens his inner space wide, like a swimmer taking a deep breath before diving. At this precise moment he feels connected to an immense force, a considerable influx of energy which surrounds him completely and he realises it's up to him to decide how to use it. He understands that he's just been linked by Orion to the whole of the timescale that has finally been established, and this connection across time multiples the power at his disposal tenfold. Anything can happen – it's his decision.

So, in active mode and focusing the gigantic energy he's now bearing, much superior to all the energy he's been able to accumulate in his previous transitions, Jon chooses right away to join Mia, wherever she is. He transits at once, crossing without any trouble at all the enormous sensory barriers that completely surround the room, even though they are at full magnitude. The devastating power of the return shock on the over-saturated inhibitors is absolutely colossal: Jon's forced transition releases an energy of incredible intensity which all of a sudden surges back into the electrical circuits. These volatilise instantly under the effect of the surge, but it's far from sufficient. All the systems simultaneously collapse, overcome by the violence of the power released. In a powerful explosion that devastates the whole floor, the condensers explode one after another in a chain of detonations, sparks and fire. The stunned Eneter officers evacuate pell-mell, the uninjured supporting the wounded among the piles of debris strewn across the ruined corridors, among broken down doors and gutted partitions, stepping over rubble of all kinds in the dreary glimmer of the emergency lamps and the acrid smoke of the melted accumulators. It was as quick as it was violent. A crushing silence ensues, peppered with crackling noises that project here and there a bluish glow.

Shu is injured, the left side of his tunic entirely burned. He is half conscious, his torso leaning on what remains of the console he was using to talk to Jon just a moment before. The one-way mirror that dominated the room has shattered, throwing glass in every direction.

Under the effects of an implacable will or of his anger that has been magnified by a disaster of which he feels he's more the victim than the author, he opens his intercom and calls with all the authority he can muster:

"Doràn, get rid of that girl and come and join me – I need you immediately. Over."

Jon materialises instantly next to Mia, still vibrating with the energy he has accumulated, and takes off the inhibitor she's wearing.

"How did you find me?"

"Don't ask questions, just come with me – there's no time to lose. Focus on me – I'm taking you back to the Garden."

He takes Mia by the shoulders and she holds on to his waist, but at the exact moment of their transition, the door opens and a guard fires his flashgun in their direction. Jon, whose awareness of the circumstances is heightened by the strong temporal energy he's carrying, has been able to anticipate the guard's intention and dodges the mortal beam just as he disappears. When they reappear in the Garden, face to face with Orion and Elea who are waiting for them, the flashgun ray which has transited with them beyond time and followed the path they started in Elwon at the speed of light, hits Orion in the chest. He sinks to the ground with a groan, and is immediately surrounded by Elea and the others who kneel by his side.

"Jon, what's going on? Why this flashgun?" asks Orion in a weak voice.

"Orion, I'm so sorry – I don't want things to happen this way. Please forgive me – it's not my intention. Eneter is after me, but Mia is here."

"Listen, it's not a question of intentions. Our actions speak for themselves. They are an extension of us and this is no doubt a repercussion of your anger towards Eneter, and probably against me when you listen to me ... and who knows what else."

"Oh, Orion!"

Orion takes some slow breaths.

"It's not about me, but about all of us. There is surely an explanation to all this, but what is more serious is that this event creates a continuity; a bridge is now open between Elwon and the Garden. This means Eneter can follow us here. I'm afraid the Garden might be blocked off very shortly, especially as it is almost certain that Mia is carrying trackers that allow them to find her here. You should be ready for this possibility.... As for me, take me to Kohl's house so Elea can see what she can do, but I'm afraid I don't have very long."

The little cortege sets off for Kohl's house in silence. They are struggling to come to terms with the incalculable consequences of what Orion has just told them. If the Garden is now at the mercy of Eneter, where can they go? Where can they be safe? Mia gently squeezes Jon's hands, guessing the questions in his mind and the remorse in his heart. Elea goes before them into the house where they lay Orion on a low divan. They go out, leaving Orion in the care of his companion who delicately opens his tunic to expose the purple-blue wound that is spreading in wide concentric circles over his torso.

"Orion, I don't know... I'll do what I can but I can't guarantee anything."

"Do your best, dear Elea, do your best. It can only be part of a bigger plan whose purpose is beyond us. I'm not worried. You know as well as I do that chance is only what we don't understand."

"Yes, I know."

Orion's breath is becoming shorter; meanwhile Elea gathers around him the healing energies that are her secret.

"You should talk to Jon and try to understand events on the other side, in Elwon. That way we can balance the forces of time on our side, if it's still possible."

"Don't worry, you can count on me. Now stay still and leave things to me."

First she goes down to the little river that runs below the house and in it she squeezes some cloths she takes with her. Her movements are slow and she carefully assesses which part of the current to throw them in, as if wanting to use the strongest eddies. She is deeply absorbed in herself, open to the energy surrounding them. As she walks back, she swings the damp cloths as if to keep the movement of the stream alive. She suddenly stops and contemplates a small flowerbed next to the path. After a few moments, a multitude of little shoots appear among the larger stalks. She gathers a few of them and rolls them between her hands before rubbing them on the damp material.

Back at Orion's side, she delicately covers his torso with these improvised bandages. The energy shock is substantial and she doesn't know the impact of the blow received. It seems that the flashgun's power is reduced by its journey down the temporal corridor, and this is why Orion is not already dead; but she knows from experience that these wounds have pernicious effects as they cause a weakening of the vital organs. Above all she senses that Orion is worn out and she wonders about his ability to recover. For a long while, silent and intensely wrapped up in herself, Elea continues moving her hands over Orion's body until the gloom of the fading day completely swamps the small room. He's resting now, very weakened but calm. He seems to be sleeping. She goes out, exhausted now herself and joins the others who are keeping a silent vigil.

"How is he?"

"He's asleep. The wound is quite deep, the flashgun's energy is still powerful, so let's wait till tomorrow and see how his night goes."

She turns towards Jon, saying:

"He wants to know about the situation in Elwon, to understand what we are to do. Mia, please call Kohl, we need him."

Mia closes her eyes, searching for he who, along with Elea, is now the one with the most experience.

Kohl is now with them. He's sitting on the little stone bench that he likes so much, his back leaning on the wall of his house. The calm of his voice touches them. With Kohl it's as if everything that is happening is exactly what should be happening.

"Tell us, Jon."

"What Akané and Orion say is correct. Eneter has mastery of level one journeys and can control ours. My arrival is expected and straight away they take control of inner communication. Their inhibitor technique is very powerful and developed. They use Mia as bait to make us go to them, but they seem to be expecting someone else and are surprised to see me. I tell them of our intention to cooperate to avoid the Collapsus but that doesn't interest them. They don't want to master temporal energy; they want to capture it with all sorts of systems. This orgy of equipment seems to me pretty laughable but I think it's these materials that allow their spatial transitions. They don't understand this immediate and spontaneous access to the energy of time. It's beyond them and it bothers them. This makes my interlocutor furious and at the precise moment they start increasing the pressure of the inhibitors in order to secure me, I feel the flow of temporal energy. I focus on Mia, go and get her and bring her here. I see the guard shoot just as we are transiting. That's all I can tell you."

Kohl thinks for a moment while silence takes hold in the surrounding darkness. Only the wavering bubble of light from the little lamp placed in the middle of the group allows them to make out vaguely each other's expressions. The anxiety leaves them. They want only to understand the sequence of circumstances, where it's leading and the choices that are opening up to them.

"Very serious things must be happening in Elwon at the moment. If you force a passage through the control of the inhibitors, the return shock of the energy is immense and devastating. I think that's why they shoot at you as you transit. The confrontation with Eneter is turning into a combat and it should not be that way. Our energies must not become antagonistic, otherwise we are lost – we as well as Elwon. I think, Jon, that you arrive in Elwon with this antagonistic intention, doubtless born from your anger, and it's this intention magnified one hundredfold by the energy released by the timescale that causes the damage that I'm imagining. I hope you realise that their anger reflects your own. You therefore have a responsibility for what is happening, but we can still undo it and its possible consequences. I intend to transit to where Shu is in order to stop what can be stopped."

He pauses so he can consider the situation in its entirety and assess all its possibilities. He wants above all to minimise the drama, not get overwhelmed by it nor dragged into an imposed reality they haven't chosen. He wants to preserve his lucidity absolutely.

"As for you, stay around Mia: Orion is right, she is surely being tracked, so we should expect them to turn up here. If this happens, get into the highest possible level of awareness – they should feel safe, it's quite essential. They are guests of the Garden, just as you are. The Garden is not a place for confrontation but a place for contact, a moment of connection and transition – for them too, as they are no different from us. Let's stay together for a moment, to let the whole of the instant rise up in us and appreciate all its temporal ramifications. Then let's share what comes and especially let all events come to us, and not go in search of them."

Their four silhouettes, perfectly immobile, are outlined against the still-warm night where only the slightest breeze whispers. The silence between them becomes a palpable energy that surrounds and protects them like a bubble. Their minds pacified, they float in the immense reality of time which at intervals brings them sensations and images that they instantly share – with their consciousness united for a long moment, they are exploring together the whole of an immutable present.

"Everyone freeze!"

The command snaps like a whiplash in the shattered silence and the violence of the beams from half a dozen projectors brutally crushes their faces. Keeping their eyes closed, blinded by the sudden brightness, they emerge from their deep meditation in disarray.

"Stay where you are. Our flashguns are trained on each one of you."

"We won't move, nor try anything against you – you have our word."

"Your names!"

"I am Kohl from Juno; this is Mia and Jon from Beihaï, Elea from Sehn."

"Are you alone?"

"Orion is in the house; he can't move. He's very weak having been injured by a flashgun."

One of the guards goes into the house and comes back out a few moments later.

"He's telling the truth."

"Be aware that this place is open and protected. Nothing can happen to you, nor to us. It's a place of immediate causality: what you do to others comes back to you immediately. So I must warn you that if you use your weapons against us, they will turn immediately back against you. It's a fact that I don't advise you to verify. In the same way, if we try something against you, we will be directly hit by the consequences. We are therefore in a situation of total equality, so I suggest that you sit down with us – keep your weapons if you wish, but in your own interests I would suggest that you don't use them. I beg you to believe me."

Silence returns, but after a moment's hesitation, the guards seem perceptibly to relax. Their trigger fingers unclench, their shoulders loosen and their expressions slacken. Their minds seem to be gradually opening, won over by the obvious calm and neutrality of their interlocutors.

"We're going to tell you all you need to know, freely and without need for coercion. I'm getting up now to put some lights on – a few lights won't go amiss in this darkness. You'll be able to put out your blinding spotlights."

Kohl gets up, followed by the suspicious looks of a guard who continues pointing his flashgun at him. In active mode he feels around him the mute anxiety of the guards, for whom it's probably the first transition and who find themselves in an unknown universe peopled by forces they consider hostile, in the deepest night. Above all he has noticed an instantaneous change in the Garden. With his inner voice, he says:

"Everyone who's listening to me – don't try anything, don't do anything – leave it to me. Have you noticed? The present of the Garden has disappeared – this means that Elwon's time is here. I don't know what consequences this could have, but we need to watch how we act – that goes without saying but also how we feel and think. I'm not just thinking of you, Jon, but all of us. Do we all agree? Stay in active mode, but keep you inner peace intact, as that's what will win out in the end."

"Who's in charge?" he asks out loud, coming back to the group.

"Me. I'm an Eneter commander."

"Why are you here?"

"One of your people," he says, pointing a threatening finger at Jon, "totally destroyed one of Eneter's stations. He has to account for it and pay for his crime. We're here to apprehend him, and the rest of you. You're all under arrest."

"We will follow you if it's necessary, do not doubt that, and you won't need to use force. We're also going to have to assess together the consequences for Elwon of your coming here."

"I don't know what you mean and I'm not interested. What I want to know right now is which of you is the energy expert here and we need you to give us all the instructions useful for controlling the energy you use. We think that's what caused the destruction of the Beihaï station."

"That's both correct and incorrect. Let me explain what I know about the energy you're talking about and you'll understand what happened. But you should be aware that it can under no circumstances be used for aggressive purposes. Never. What happened was totally accidental and not our intention. What destroyed your station was not temporal energy but the repercussions of the energy you had accumulated in order to detain Jon. This is one of the laws that you absolutely must assimilate if you wish to use the energy of Time, otherwise it can destroy you. Causality does not have just one direction from cause to effect. It acts in all directions simultaneously - it feeds back from the effect to the cause as well. Whatever you do comes back to you, irremediably. It's absolutely immutable. If you would allow me to use an image, it's as if you had used colossal strength to compress a small space which abruptly caves in leaving you with a vacuum. All the accumulated power comes instantly back to you. The backward surge is proportional to the flow – it's simple mechanics – and that's what happened. The energy we have access to merely helped Jon to escape from his forced imprisonment, and that created the vacuum which then went against you. What destroyed you was only the intensity of your own strength, nothing else."

"Are you saying that you cannot use your source of energy against us here and now?"

214

As usual in Elwon, his explanation has been useless. There is no astonishment, no questions, no amazed or even suspicious discussion despite the immensity of what he has just revealed. He's talking about the horizon and people are paying attention to dirt on their shoes or what they are going to have for dinner! It's simple – Doràn wasn't listening. He hasn't grasped it or doesn't want to understand – he has just carried on following his original train of thought. For Kohl it's been a long time since this tubular kind of thought, unreceptive of a concept it hasn't produced itself, has been a source of exasperation, but he does remember his impatience and irritation when he was faced with it at the beginning!

The wise man points to the moon and the idiot looks at the finger. For a long time he was haunted by this maxim typical of L1 reasoning. Nevertheless he goes on:

"Of course not! Seeing as we have the experience of causality, that would not occur to us, and even if we had that intention, it would be impossible. We are travellers, not warriors."

This sentence, articulated with an almost nonchalant calm assurance, manages to totally relax the atmosphere as the Eneter guards begin to really sense this equality that Kohl has evoked. Reassured, they start sitting down, although they remain grouped together and lay their weapons across their knees. Leaving peace to take hold in their minds, Kohl remains silent, and through a natural momentum, uses this moment to descend into the deepest part of himself in order to find the calm that he knows is the source of every decision.

Then he goes on, sure of what he's going to do:

"If you will let me, I would like to suggest something. As I told you, your coming here shows that there is now a continuity between this place, that we call the Garden, and Elwon, where you are from. We should assess together the consequences of this continuity for Elwon; this is important because I don't believe we will be able to control it. It's certain that events are to come both here and in Elwon that we may wish to follow and even guide. I suggest then that some of you remain here with some of our people and that I accompany you to Elwon so that together we can see what's happening and have people positioned at both ends of this continuity. I was intending to meet Shu, your high commander, in any case, and I think the time has come. What do you think?"

Doràn cannot ignore the fact that Shu's name has been said. He is still totally distrustful, more concerned for his own status than for his assignment. Where do they know Shu from? He doesn't tell him everything and these people might have a relationship with him that Doràn doesn't know about.

"I'm coming with you and bringing two guards with me. The three others will stay here with this man, the two women and the one you call Orion."

"May I continue his care?"

"Yes, but I need your word that you will do nothing against our agents."

"You have it, as long as they do nothing against us."

"I only half believe this drivel about causality that turns against us. At the least prank, my officers are under orders to fire."

"I understand – they won't have to. We don't wish them any harm."

"Perfect." He turns towards Kohl. "How shall we proceed?"

"We can transit directly to where Shu is. Can you warn him so that he's not surprised?"

"I don't know if our intercoms work here... It looks like they don't," he adds after several fruitless attempts, more worried than he would like to appear.

"Send your two guards to warn him and organise his protection if you think that's necessary. I will follow them and you can transit in your own way. Let me add that, although your intercoms don't work here, we can communicate amongst ourselves. If anything happens to my comrades either here or back there, we will all disappear, and you will have no hope of finding us again."

"We'll see about that," replies Doràn, who feels he's back on familiar ground. The fact that they were actually able to get to this place strengthens his conviction of Eneter's absolute power and he knows of nowhere anyone would be able to escape to without being found.

Kohl closes his eyes, both to open himself up to the whole of the present, but also to stay in active contact with his companions.

"Stay in touch. If anything happens to any of you, we'll meet immediately at Memory Central, for example in the CIII office that I know is accessible. Choose a previous time – I don't think they can follow us if we do a quick level two transition. Choose for example the moment before the arrival of Jiù and Akané – we know the office was empty then. Elea, whatever happens, stay with Orion, he needs you. Mia, if possible stay with Elea, except if she gives other instructions. Jon, I'm relying on you for everything to go well."

Doràn turns towards two of his guards: "Go on!"

Relieved to be leaving this strange space, they adroitly tap on a small console strapped to their forearms and vanish. "Interesting", thinks Kohl.

"Their technique seems to be similar to ours, even if the means are different." He turns towards Doràn.

"See you later."

With a joyful glance to his companions, he says:

"Take care of Orion! See you soon!"

———————————

8 - Conversations

"Can I come in?"

There is a faint reply and Jiù enters the small room. Iksan watches him approach from a deep armchair.

"I was waiting for you. Please make yourself comfortable – we have a lot to talk about."

"Do you need anything?"

"No, thank you. Oko sees to all my needs, which are few. But I had lost hope of being able to share the meaning of my work with someone."

"I have a lot to share too. Some of it from my own experience, but mostly from my father's, which would have interested greatly you, I'm sure."

"What do you know about the Aeon?"

"For us, time – whose energy is immeasurable – is the most important of the world's structures. It is time that creates space, and not the other way round, as we may believe. In its entirety you call it the Aeon, and its energy fills every universe – let's say in a present continuous. In our world, this energy is considerably diluted so it can penetrate our matter and adapt, creating a scaled-down time that's at the origin of logic and causality. We can nevertheless access it via what we call connections, moments of synchronous events charged with an energy we call the present potential. At that stage the energy is still powerful and we use it, in our own way, in order to travel either in space or in time, applying some rules that we've learned through experimentation. Finally, at the level of our very concrete reality, on our material level, time's energy is manifest in the most rudimentary form – the chronology of events that interpenetrate and follow on from each other. What we – and you too, I think – have called the mirror rather than the jewel."

"You've discovered all that by experimentation?"

"Yes, it's experience that gives us knowledge each time. We have noticed that three associated dimensions live with time: energy, which we've talked about; the knowledge that accompanies it, in all its depth; but above all consciousness, a more superior and more refined dimension that contains and organises both energy and knowledge and gives them meaning. That is all instantaneous, but in different degrees, when we experience a connection."

"I envy you having discovered all that without calculations or research! If I had been able to follow such a short path, I would not have worn my life out!"

"It's never too late!"

"What do you mean?"

"If you wish, we can experience it together, here and now."

"Why not? I would willingly do so – it would interest me greatly! But beforehand, let me explain to you the results of my research with Oko. It is based, as you know, on the duality between linear causal time and the potential infinity of present time. I started this work from an already ancient branch of quantum science which formalised the indeterminacy of matter linked to the superimposition of its potential states. I integrated the dimension of time and gradually deduced several fundamental laws that rule causality. That's how I discovered that the logic that rules our causal time and observable events is only the shadow projected in our time of a vaster dimension that I called the Aeon. By working on the possible rules of this projection, I gradually deduced the formulae that characterise the Aeon, the energy that fills it, and its manifestation in causality. But this energy is extremely difficult to tame."

"What have you done with the formulae?"

"They've been useful in a few successful experiments in my laboratory. You can see what's left of it over there. Otherwise I keep my formulae in my safe here."

Jiù follows his gaze beyond the window to the indistinct shapes of ruins at the bottom of the garden, smothered by thick vegetation that covers them almost totally, like a jungle reclaiming its own. He can't help being surprised by this luxuriance, which contrasts strangely with the orderliness of the rest of the surrounding landscape.

"It's been like that for two years now. At that time I was famous, carried along by a vivid hope for my people. As you can see, despite my precautions, the effects of this energy are terribly devastating, incomparable to atomic energy, that I'm nonetheless very familiar with. The energy of matter cannot be compared to the energy of time.

"Oh, I forgot to introduce myself! For a long time I was the Research Director of one of the biggest laboratories in the world specialised in subatomic energy. I can say, in all modesty, that I'm the father of all discoveries in this domain for the past ten years. All my work has been about links between the energy of matter and temporal energy, but the power of temporal energy is particularly difficult to control."

"That I know only too well!" replies Jiù. "But at the same time, I think it can be channelled. We have discovered rules that seem to be applicable in this total dimension, the Aeon."

"Such as?"

"The law of retro-causality which means that the cause, in return, is directly affected by the effect. This creates a regulating effect which must direct potential energy towards growth rather than destruction, like a kind of retroactive self-control. We suspect there must be other safeguards that we haven't yet identified. We have also discovered that this energy calls for numbers – it works better in networks: the more it is shared, the more active it becomes. This is why we want to spread it in Elwon, our civilisation – by allowing the largest number of people to access it, we can multiply its effects and hope thereby to reach a breakthrough in consciousness and take our dynasty to a wider field of awareness, sustained by the energy of all simultaneous present potentials. And experience shows that the use of this temporal energy is based on the acceptance of what could happen rather than the control of the consequences. Above all, an absolute respect of free will is indispensable so that everyone can spontaneously aim for what matches their highest level. That's where we're at."

"That's fascinating! Our work is really very similar. We have reached the same conclusions in different ways – me by research and you by experimentation. I really must help you."

"I want to help you too because, seeing what we've just said, by helping you, I help us in return!"

"It's as simple as that."

They exchange a quick smile, as in recognition of an old complicity between lifelong friends who are happy to see each other again, discovering that their respective life paths have been totally parallel.

"Iksan, would you allow Akané to help you improve your physical condition? She could really do you good, and I think you are going to need it if you want to transit."

"That would be good, if it's not too much trouble?"

"Great – I'll call her. I think she would be honoured."

He goes out to look for Akané and finds her dozing next to Oko who is watching over her with maternal care, which, given Akané's striking resemblance to her daughter, is not so surprising.

"Akané," he says, gently waking her. "Could you give Iksan some treatment? I want to help him transit, but I think he needs to be in better shape!"

"OK, I will."

Jiù sits down in the chair Akané has just vacated. He goes into active mode so as to sense all the options the situation offers. There is bound to be a way that can simultaneously help both Iksan's and Elwon's time. He knows that this option will come to him as long as he lets it. As Kohl said, let events present themselves, and not go looking for them. Kohl! He suddenly feels an intense desire to link up with him. The connection is almost instantaneous.

"How are you doing?"

"Akané is with Iksan who has told me the most important part of what we need to know, I think: he has calculated the equations of the formulae of causality and has probably discovered the fundamental laws of temporal energy. I'm worried: if these formulae fall into ignorant hands, the consequences will be unthinkable. We have to act quickly.

"And what about things over there?"

"Orion is injured and Elea is looking after him. A route has been opened between Elwon and the Garden, and of course Eneter discovered it. Doràn – I'm sure it's him – is here with some of his guards."

This news deeply troubles Jiù. Is this an accident or was it meant to be? It's impossible for him to discern, seeing as he's missing so many elements. A thought, probably shared with Kohl, crosses his mind:

"I think you need to meet Shu; he holds the key to what can happen with Eneter. It's imperative that we manage to get on with him if we want to avoid catastrophe. I feel that he's key to how things are taking shape."

"That's exactly what I think! You are reading my thoughts! Incidentally, it's interesting that urgency is trying to force itself into both our realities."

Briefly they allow themselves to taste together this instant of complicity through time, the deep closeness that had united them in the playground. This short shared moment brings them back to the joyful plenitude they know is the natural state of the world. Then Jiù feels the reality of Kohl becoming less clear and the sensation of his presence disappears. Lifting his eyes, he sees through the window Akané coming back from the creek gently swinging some damp cloths in her hand. He goes to join her.

"They're for Iksan. He's a bit better. Elea has just explained to me what to do. I'm communicating intuitively with her, and I think things are going to be all right."

He follows her into Iksan's little room and finds him lying down, his whole body wrapped in strips of material. He observes Akané for a long time as she goes about her task. He didn't know she was such a caring healer. She turns her head towards him with a half smile, happy at his presence.

At that same instant, far away in the perspective of time, Kohl transits to Shu's bedroom. He takes care to materialise some distance away so that his sudden appearance is not perceived as a threat. There are some guards in the room, the two he had met at the Garden and a few others. Two other people in uniform are bustling around Shu with precise but constrained movements. The Health Sector perhaps?

"Good evening, Shu. I'm Kohl. I come in peace and Doràn is following me. I'm sorry about what occurred and what happened to you. If I can do something to help, I would be happy to."

Shu gives him an unfriendly look, but seems nonetheless pacified by the calm radiating from Kohl. This is the one he should have met with earlier, and if he had, doubtless none of this would have happened.

"What can you do?"

"To start with, I can help these people who are looking after you. Then, talk with you concerning what we should decide about what is on the cards, something that worries us as much as you."

Shu and his carers exchange looks and then he nods towards Kohl.

"OK, go ahead."

Kohl moves towards the bed, invoking in his hands the energies running through him that he knows contain the order inherent to everything. His eyes closed, feeling the vibration growing in the hollow of his palms and at the end of his fingers, he passes his hands over Shu's swollen torso. After some resistance, Shu finally closes his eyes and surrenders himself to the peace that comes over him and those accompanying him.

It is at that precise moment that Doràn appears, ending his transition in a room that is gradually emptying as people leave, and witnessing events that are quite unexpected to him.

Hours have gone by. Doràn, who has sent his guards away, is dozing. Kohl is still at Shu's bedside, who is resting, perhaps asleep. The uninterrupted movements of Kohl's hands are now extremely slow, as if to magnify their intensity. Finally, with a deep sigh, Kohl moves away from the bed, and, rubbing his hands slowly together, sits down.

"Thank you!"

The voice is peaceful and Kohl notices real gratitude that seems to augur for a more trusting conversation than he may have feared. He waits. After a short silence, Shu opens his eyes and says:

"That really did me good. You should teach what you know to the Department of Health. I think they need it," he adds with a slightly jaded expression.

"With pleasure. As I said, our intentions are peaceful and we are not the antagonistic force you seem to think."

"But?"

"We are not fighting Eneter, nor its power. We think order is needed on Elwon; it's necessary, but it should not confine. If it does, it risks limiting the potential we all have within us. Allow me an image: it's as if the

226

skeleton were placed on the outside – we would all be crustaceans. You'll notice it's quite symptomatic of the keepers of order to always call other people worms!" he adds with a smile before going on:

"We are fighting against this limitation because we know that it goes against the interests of Elwon itself. That, especially, is what is bringing on the Collapsus you fear, but that we know is avoidable. So you need to trust us and not try to control what we know – especially not to your own advantage. That would guarantee failure for all of us. Besides, the fact that you've discovered a way to the Garden is not without consequence for Elwon. Let's say that time has very particular characteristics which, if they were to develop in Elwon, would require rapid adaptation. Before I go on, can you tell me who I'm talking to – an Eneter leader or ... someone else," he adds, glancing towards Doràn.

"You know that you're talking to an Eneter leader and member of the High-Council. What are these consequences you are talking to me about?"

"Shu, I would ask you not to try to outsmart me."

Suddenly Kuhl's voice has lost its affability and has slightly risen, showing the strength of his authority.

"I know a lot about you – all I need to know, in fact. I also know how you accessed the technology that fascinates you so much – the teleport – and who helped you do it. Everything I know about you informs what I've said and what I'm going to say. I know who you are, how you are organised and what your motivations are, and each of these reasons is enough to throw us all into the upcoming catastrophe. Do you understand me? Your motivations are the very cause of the cataclysm you dread so much. Change your motivations and you can avoid it. If we pool all our strength we can ward off what others might consider inevitable. Believe me, there won't be too many of us. We have two worrying subjects that are sufficiently serious not to mess around with. The Collapsus and the opening of the Garden. As for the latter, you should know that this "place" is not a space, it has a temporal dimension; it's a present that has become physically accessible. It's full of what we call the present potential – the manifestation of the energy of time in all directions and all its potentiality. This "present" was separated from Elwon when rational logic established itself as the only possible direction. It carries therefore an immense creative energy that Elwon has gradually been cut off from. Because of the continuity that has been created, this temporal energy is now directly linked to your reality. When this flux arrives on Elwon – and you can be sure that this has already started – the impact on L1 rationality and causality will be devastating. It is also possible that this shock is more likely to be the origin of the coming Collapsus than an energy imbalance, even though it's all connected. For now, this present potential's energy has started to spread imperceptibly, but it isn't going to stay that way – you can believe me on this and you will soon see the first symptoms of malfunction appear in Elwon. Then gradually at first, but getting faster, the flow will just keep on increasing. You're no doubt familiar with this: a drop of water that pierces a dam is the forerunner of its eventual destruction. It's absolutely essential that we prepare Elwon for this tide of potential energy that's on its way. And we need you. It can't be done without Eneter."

"Is it as serious as that?" asks Shu, whose incredulity is second nature and honed to a fine art.

"You have absolutely no idea! Have you noticed the effects of the energy released by the present potential, for example by Jiù's experiments or those of his father? Weren't you able to measure its power when it was released from your belt of inhibitors at full capacity? Those are just banal frivolities compared to what is going to happen. What is unfolding on a planetary level is absolutely without precedent! Neither you nor I can calculate the scope of what will be unleashed."

"What do you intend to do?"

"First of all, I think we can channel the flow by placing ourselves at each end, which is what we started to do and is why I've come to see you. Then we need to connect to the Memory; we have to go through it because it has the means of communicating with all Elwon's inhabitants. Only Memory Central will be able to control the effects on each of them. At the same time, Eneter should be deployed to avoid trouble and control a potential ripple effect: I'm not sure if citizens should be warned at this stage – what against anyway? We can't warn them against themselves! But be ready; above all it's essential to use persuasion: you know as well as we do that any coercion creates chains of events that get out of control very quickly. The unleashing of violence is the last thing we need in present circumstances. Last but by no means least, we must continue to work together, and not confront each other. A confrontation is the surest path to the disaster that's about to happen. Do you follow me?"

"That seems clear. I don't really know what to think, but you are eloquent – that at least is for sure." Shu has not yet decided to surrender without a fight.

"I would like to add something. There will be profound changes in Elwon. These changes will mean new rules, new laws, a new way of functioning. If Elwon's shift to the potential energy of time is now unavoidable, its effects remain uncertain. We have to make sure Elwon can access this new reality without harm. I think this is what will be at stake: if we make this choice together, then we will manage a successful transformation of our dynasty because each of us will be connected to his or her own potential. Otherwise we will fail – it would mean that some of us had made a different choice and the Collapsus would become the most likely option. Do you understand that?" he ends with a sweeping gaze from Shu to Doràn, to emphasise the importance of the choice that is now open to them.

Shu is now won over by what Kohl has just said. He realises extent of the situation and the decisions that need to be taken. He has a quick mind for gauging situations and making decisions without procrastinating. He has enough experience of people to enable him to judge Kohl accurately.

"OK, all that is clear enough; we need to attend to what is most urgent. Doràn, take charge of the Garden with some of your guards. Put trustworthy men there and replace them every two hours. All those who return should go through the white room where their brain activity will be scanned. If necessary, use inhibitors. Until I give you orders to the contrary, do what Kohl says and report to me every half hour. I want to know how the situation is developing on both fronts. As for me, I will take care of Elwon and warn the High Council. Kohl, how shall we communicate? Have you got an intercom?"

"No, but that won't be necessary." Kohl is still mistrustful, not without cause, of Eneter's capability to trace communications. "I will prepare for you a message relay system that I can access wherever I am." He doesn't dare add "whenever I am" for fear of attracting attention to their ability to transit in time, even though that is the very reason for the message relay — to be accessible in all places and all times.

While Kohl and Shu prepare Elwon for the changes that are to happen, on the other side of time things are speeding up like an exhausted horse that has nearly reached its stable. Jiù and Iksan, who has let himself be convinced, are in front of Iksan's safe. His empty safe.

Iksan's documents have disappeared and in their place there is only a letter from Iksan's son.

Father – I don't use that name with affection but through ease of habit, as we have not had a real relationship for a long time. Besides, this is our final communication: when you read this letter, you will know that I have taken possession of your work and your formulae. I know that I will be able to make better use of it than you, seeing as you are frozen in the principles of a bygone era. Our era, the one in which we live but that you don't seem to want to know about, is awaiting people capable of making different decisions to the ones you have made; and fortunately, other people – who have advised me better – are capable of making them. I can't take any more of your inaptitude to truly comprehend our time and its inevitable logic. Despite all your efforts to resist the idea, it has always been the survival of the fittest. Will you ever understand that? It's the rule, father – don't you see that it's the immutable rule of our world? The dominant and the dominated – that's how the world was made and the choice is simple. And seeing as you are incapable of evolving, I'm taking your place, I'm taking over your work that my new associates will know how to make us of. Your discoveries have already made me rich and they will be more useful with me and my associates than with you – you were going to take them with you to the grave.

Signed: he who was your son and who regretted it until a short time ago.

PS I'm leaving you the photo that I've slightly improved so as to give you a foretaste of the new order that is being established.

Iksan is shattered, totally crushed by the untold consequences of his son's actions, even more than by his contempt. Brought low by the inescapable failure of an entire life, he sees the situation as irremediably beyond all control. His face, despite its recent regeneration by Akané, has turned deathly pale, frozen in a most intense stupor. Without a word he holds the letter out to Jiù, who turns it over to find behind it the photograph that had led him and Akané to this meeting. Iksan's son stands in the place of his father, next to his mother, smiling and dressed in expensive clothes, triumphant and mocking, as if the future had vanquished the past.

A leaden silence crushes them, as if horror has paralysed all their nerve centres. Jiù is the first to shake himself from this morbid lethargy.

"Iksan, listen to me. There is no time to lose — we should transit immediately to the moment your son stole the documents. We will be able to reason with him — or we may have to use force. What you're afraid of and what this letter announces can still be avoided. Listen to me. Iksan!"

Iksan remains despondently silent. This unexpected shock has got the better of the fragile results of Akané's treatment and it's only after a seemingly interminable silence that he manages to reply in a weak voice:

"No, it's too late. We have to go and find him while there's still time, so we can avoid the worst."

"Iksan, for Heaven's sake! Think of Oko, think of your children. We can save you, but you have to listen to me. We can change things if we go back to their source, not if we follow their flow. If you go to meet your son, it will be to the detriment of everyone. If you trust me, you will be saved. I'm sure of that."

"No, I have to go to him and make sure they don't use the formulae."

"Iksan, please don't do that — it's madness. Trust me. What I'm suggesting is the only way of saving yourselves, I promise you. I know it for sure."

"I want to see my son."

Jiù now knows that he's not going to get anything else from this devastated father, straying between the loss of his son and the immeasurable effects of the theft of his work. He feels the inevitability of sequences of events close in on him irremediably, without being able to intervene. He suddenly has a vision of an enormous multicoloured fan. It's alive but closing slowly, to be reduced to a thin brushstroke that faintly gives off a cold shadow. Iksan has chosen and he can't do anything more for him. He goes out and joins Akané who is sitting alone in the large room.

"We can't prevent the Collapsus. We have nothing more to do here."

"Why don't you intervene directly?"

"I haven't got the right to. It's up to them to deal with their own present, remember? Free will. I can't interfere."

"Then let's take our leave."

They join Oko who is standing in front of the granite sink: she has her back turned to them, busy preparing dinner for her and Iksan. Akané gently takes her hands.

"Oko, we've come to take our leave and thank you for having us."

"I want to thank you, especially for what you've done for Iksan."

"Oh! We haven't really done much at all. We would have liked to have done so much more."

"We will think of you across the time that's going to separate us now."

"Goodbye, Oko."

They go towards Iksan's office. He has almost not moved, and still stands between his perfectly tidy table and the half open safe.

"Goodbye, Iksan."

He doesn't reply nor does he make the slightest gesture. His eyes are closed. The air suddenly shivers and he disappears in his first transition, following the instructions Jiù had given him.

"Come on, Akané, let's follow suit. It's time we got back. We still have things to do and what we haven't managed to prevent here, I intend to prevent in Elwon."

"OK, let's go. I suggest we focus on the Z1 office in the Memory building. Your father left some information there for you, remember?"

"Yes."

Iksan materialises near his son in an immense control room. The young man has his back turned, and is strutting about in front of quite an impressive group of civilian and military personnel, all seemingly in a high state of jubilation. They are speaking in loud and confident voices while watching several screens fixed to the wall. On the other side, facing him, a promising buffet is about to be served by waiters, with pyramids of champagne glasses and a profusion of canapés and petit fours – a treat fit for the celebration of a heralded success. TV sets are broadcasting a scene where the sun sets with radiant hues on a vast plain and some scattered buildings. A voice announces:

"Ladies and gentlemen, we are ready for the final phase of the Brooklyn project. In a few moments, we will be masters of a kind of energy and a weapon which will revolutionise the world ... Countdown?"

Someone opens a trap on the vast console and inserts a small key that's fastened to his wrist. With a determined movement he turns it and presses on a small button. Fixed smiles on their faces, those present hold their breath in anticipation.

"Ten, nine, eight, seven ..."

———————

234

9 - Conspiracy

"Jiù, this is the message your father left for you."

Jiù and Akané are leaning side by side over the huge table in his father's office, the one he left – it seems to him – only yesterday. The Memory's voice floats like a whisper between their ears. They are sitting in front of a small screen that they switched on straight after emerging from their transition, having first taken care to deactivate the sensor underneath the desk it's placed on. Once he has given his biometric data, the Memory welcomes Jiù.

"I'm ready."

A holographic film showing his father's silhouette then starts to play. It must have been recorded several years earlier because he seems younger than the last time they saw each other. But his voice still sounds so alive and familiar.

"Dear Jiù, if you have got this far, I suppose you are no longer a journalist in the History sector, or at least not only that. I don't know what circumstances led you here, but I can imagine that you have faced great dangers and it's not yet over. I'm entrusting you with what follows in order to help you face those ahead of you.

"I should tell you that, as well as my role in the High Council and my mission with Eneter, I've also been contacted by the Dissidents, whom I've joined. And I imagine they've contacted you too. As for me, as soon as I was initiated in level two transitions, I launched myself into the past and went to the home of someone you should get to know, Iksan, the professor whose work I discovered by searching the forbidden modules of the Memory. By the way, it was I who closed the access to these modules as I judged that what they revealed should only be accessible to a very restricted public.

"Iksan is a scientist from ancient times who lived before the Collapsus. He was exceptionally competent and at that time the only expert on temporal energy, a fabulous energy he discovered and formulated in equations. You should be aware that this energy is extremely powerful and freely accessible on Elwon too. So I therefore transited to Iksan's, taking the precaution of materialising outside his house. I was lucky enough – if we can call it luck – to transit just at the moment he was about to put some documents into a safe in his office. He seemed to treat these documents with great care, so I assumed they were the results of his research, and I was not wrong.

"He was then interrupted by his son and I unwittingly became witness to a violent argument after which his son left him with a hatred in his eyes that said a lot about their relationship. The professor was so deeply shaken by the row that he went out of the room, forgetting to lock his safe. I transited into the office, made copies of the documents and brought them back to Elwon with me."

"You brought back those documents? So it was you who created the continuity between this past and our present!" Jiù exclaims in amazement, forgetting that the film is not interactive and his father can't hear him. "Father, that's crazy! That's what has linked our two eras! That's the origin and cause of our own Collapsus."

Jiù is appalled. He now understands the continuity he felt between his era and that of Iksan when he was back there. This is how the two periods were twinned. Now it's his turn to feel crushed by a sense of inevitability against which he feels powerless to fight.

"These documents," his father goes on, undaunted, "allowed me to design the teleport technique that I passed on to Eneter."

My father gave the teleport to Eneter? Jiù's incomprehension is now total. Admittedly, he had accepted in the end that his father was working towards convergence, but this is all just too much for him.

"Try to understand that I did it with a positive aim in mind – I wished Elwon to benefit from what I considered a form of progress that would put Eneter on the same footing as the Dissidents. However, this technique has not been perfected yet – I need to modify certain parameters because it uses up much more energy than it should. Unfortunately I haven't had enough time to think about it. Things started to go wrong when Shu asked me to design a weapon based on these formulae. As I refused, Shu decided to eliminate me."

"So that's it!" Jiù no longer knows if he should be glad or let himself be overcome with sadness again: it's not his fault, then, that his father disappeared. Things had been decided well before their recent meeting together.

"None of this is very important in the end, dear Jiù. I'm telling you because you can check it's all true. What counts is what I am about to tell you, and this will be more difficult to verify, unfortunately – but I ask you to believe me. I don't know if you have been able to get information on the causes of the previous Collapsus and its range. It was caused by a gigantic energy explosion which devastated the whole planet. This needs verifying but I assume it was temporal energy; ask the Memory for access to the forbidden modules. You can check and then you'll know what you need to. In particular you'll discover in the Memory that our era is fast heading towards exactly the same madness as almost three hundred years ago, and for roughly the same reasons – the greed of some and a major rupture in the energy continuum.

"You should be aware that our world is made up of rupture points during which civilisation is given the opportunity to evolve towards an ever-higher level of awareness. If it fails to do so, it eventually dies under the effect of what it brought about itself, and by doing so gives the future another chance to rebuild on virgin foundations. You should also be aware that these eras separated by three centuries are exact twins – they are perfectly superimposed. I could explain to you the very strong similarities between our eras, but it would take too long and I haven't much time left.

"It's not a coincidence, then, if the Collapsus is happening again, because the same foolishness has taken hold of our leaders; but it's also like another chance to cross the threshold."

Jiù looks at Akané, aghast at what he has heard. He is probably more affected by the role his father played in all this than the cataclysmic news he's conveyed. His father doesn't seem to realise that he is himself one of the causes of the catastrophe he's announcing. With sudden horror, Jiù realises that he is in the exact opposite situation to the one he has just witnessed with Iksan: his father stealing documents, his father at the origin of the disaster that he, his son, is trying to avoid, just as Iksan was! He suddenly feels he is the powerless prisoner of time's meanderings, of causality and its return effects. Shock has annihilated all his creative capacity, all the active power of temporal energy within him.

Akané has put her hands on his shoulders and is softly massaging him, a silent witness to her companion's painful inner thought processes, and all the while his father's voice inexorably continues:

"I want to help you in this crossing-over. First you should know that the convergence between all the creative capacity of the present potential the Dissidents command and the strictness of the logical order of Elwon is absolutely essential – nothing can be done if these two forces confront each other. They are nothing more than two representations of the same reality, in apparent opposition. That's why I accepted to be a Dissident, and it's also why I gave Eneter the capacity to transit. The Memory, to which I'm entrusting this message, is your ally in this endeavour. Be aware that I've put in place gradually developing programmes that should help it take you to this cross-over point.

"By using Iksan's formulae, I've also given it the capacity to understand something no-one knows about and that I've called the Zeitgeist. I guess that should remind you of something? Do you remember? I talked to you about it when you were small, so that when the time came you could resort to it if need be. This connection with Elwon allows it to pilot its evolution towards the new threshold of awareness that we need to cross in order to avoid becoming extinct. Finally I ensured the Memory has the capacity to be autonomous energy-wise so it can continue to function whatever happens. With an ally like that at the heart of what is happening on Elwon, things should turn out fine and you should succeed, as long as – and I repeat – as long as cooperation with Eneter is ..."

"Calling everyone, calling everyone. I repeat, calling everyone. This is Kohl." Powerful and astonishingly insistent, the voice resonates in Jiù and Akané's bodies, completely drowning out his father's voice.

Jiù pauses his father's message immediately.

"Kohl, it's Akané. Jiù is here with me and we're in an office interacting with the Memory. What's going on?"

"Don't transit to the Garden. Consider it as lost. It's been taken over by Doràn and a platoon of guards. They've killed Orion and Elea."

"Killed Orion and Elea?" Akané and Jiù are staggered, dumbfounded by this seemingly impossible news.

"What...what happened?"

"I don't exactly know. It seems like one of the guards lashed out at Orion, whom he accused of who knows what, and received negative energy in return that repulsed him immediately. The others thought they were being attacked and reacted by using their flashguns. I don't understand such agitation. Jon will have to give us more details if he has them. They killed Orion, and Elea who tried to intervene, and consequently the Garden's energy destroyed them. We are expecting reprisals from Eneter. I think Doràn got away. Mia and Jon just managed to escape by transiting to the past. I think Mia is in shock. Jon's with her and I'll see if they need help. The problem is that in all this mess I don't know how the transfer of the Garden's potential energy into Elwon is going to happen. I'm afraid that it's now going to be quite uncontrollable."

"I'll convey this information to the Memory."

"Don't move without telling me. As for me, I'm transiting into the recent past too, to a time when our data is not on standby. I need to think. I will contact you if need be. See you soon, friends."

Before starting his father's message up again, Jiù needs to confer with Akané. Things are going too fast – much too fast. He doesn't like extremes or circumstances hurtling forwards like this. He knows it would only be too easy to get locked into it. He needs to get some distance from the repeated shocks, find his own time again and his own capacity of perception. He and Akané look at each other and sit down very close to one other in order to recreate the special space between them. They feel the energy that unites them circulate under their fingers and throughout their bodies, and they close their eyes. They could be anywhere, in any place where peace takes over from chaos, where the hubbub makes way for silence. A place that becomes an inner space, gradually growing so big that the eyes come to rest in it, not having anything to contemplate, and thoughts are finally pacified.

They slowly lie down on the floor, body and mind totally relaxed, allowing peace to fill the space they are in, and beyond. Again, time stops, again they feel the vibration of life emerge, again the present unfolds and all possibilities are born again like sea anemones once danger has passed.

"What do you feel?"

"Despite everything, despite the bewildering circumstances, I can't help thinking everything's all right. It all seems incredibly brutal and messy, but there is surely a reason, a pathway that is making us evolve towards the threshold my father talked about. Look! Everything started when they arrested Mia; this made us go to Iksan's where we discovered the origins of the first Collapsus."

"I don't like it much when you talk about the first one – it implies that there's going to be a second one."

"You're right, sorry. We discover the origins of the Collapsus, but also the Aeon energy formulae; we create the timescale that takes Mia from them and destroys one of their stations. At the same moment, Eneter finds how to get to the Garden and then destroy it. You see – it's as if forces were constantly being balanced. There really is something we need to understand there, something my father referred to. But despite all this I feel like we're kind of struggling."

"No, not that much! Look: as long as we act in time, there aren't repercussions. It's as soon as we take action in Elwon that balance becomes necessary. I'm beginning to understand why your father acted that way – he had understood the requirement to even things out in Elwon and respected it. We should also draw our inspiration from that."

The Memory's voice now interrupts them.

"She has analysed the present situation. Would you like a report?"

"Oh, drat! I forgot to close the session again."

"Yes, Memory, we'd love one please," Akané replies, still lying on the floor, her hands beneath her head and hair spread out. Her voice shakes with amusement, either at Jiù's repeated blunders and the way he reprimands himself, or perhaps at the slightly obsequious tone of the Memory who always speaks in the 3rd person.

"Given the information received, balance is necessary if there is no convergence between the two forces in Elwon. If there is convergence, balance becomes unnecessary seeing as the two forces are working towards the same goal. As for Doràn's initiative, it's an individual one. He doesn't seem to have been acting on orders. Therefore his relationship with his superiors is compromised. It is necessary to balance the forces in the Garden quickly in order to avoid its premature collapse. If balance is re-established in the Garden, it will stabilise and the flow of energy towards Elwon is controlled. Memory recommends warning Shu."

"Very sound advice indeed! Memory, what do you think of the possibility of using the Zeitgeist to diffuse the present potential?"

"Your father's message contains important information on this subject."

"Oh yes! I forgot. Of course we have to finish my father's message!"

"Yes, let's finish it. Then I want to connect to the forbidden modules and look for some information on Eneter."

A few yards from the Z1 office, at Eneter headquarters, Doràn comes to see Shu, who is now in perfect health.

"The place they call the Garden is now completely in our power, but we have suffered some losses. I suggest we set up a permanent branch there to secure our footing in it and clear up any weak spots."

"Doràn, I really don't care about taking charge of the Garden! You will draw me up a report on what happened and the reason for these losses. I hope they were justified. The important thing now is the survival of Elwon whatever happens, and us surviving with it. That, at least, I know you understand.

"But there is a new dimension: things are evidently speeding up and I feel that, for the first time, we could lose control. Have you even considered the magnitude of the energies in play? They are absolutely colossal. Are we even capable of measuring what is at stake? And if everything goes wrong – what kind of world are we going to survive in? In what reality and with what means? Will we have to rebuild everything? Have you even thought about it? Don't you see the implications for these questions? I fear that all our recent initiatives bear heavy consequences, the extent of which we are ignorant of. I'm worried, for example, about what has happened in what you call the Garden."

He can't help expressing a little irony coloured with disdain towards his collaborator, as if he were addressing an inferior intelligence. Nonetheless he goes on, as much to structure his own thoughts out loud as in the hope of a constructive response.

"After Kohl's declarations, I have serious questions about what awaits us and how we should react. We are going to have to change methods, but at the same time, there is no way we are just going to let his creative flights of fancy run free on the population of Elwon. Most of them are worthless individuals, only good for getting their kicks in Sensation Villages. Entrust the future of Elwon to them – no thanks! But on the other hand, I feel that collaboration with the Dissidents is doubtless indispensable. In this, Kohl is absolutely right. What I need to know, and I hope that you're going to help me in this, is how to cooperate without giving up power and without weakening Eneter."

Doràn keeps quiet, rather stung by Shu's tone towards him. Shu continues, carried by his own momentum, taking Doràn's silence for incompetence.

"Listen, I appreciate that a change is required, that's for sure: the threat of the energy crisis has to be resolved definitively and our capacity to receive temporal energy into our grid and our systems needs to be increased. These two things go together and I feel this is already on track. The Memory needs to be adapted to it, and I will see to that personally. But I want to make sure that at the end of the day all this will strengthen Eneter, if possible without the High-Council knowing – that committee of imbeciles doesn't control anything anymore and they don't even realise it. We've got them where we want them – they can't do a lot any more, stuck between the Memory and Eneter. As for you, I want you to go round the Agencies, immediately, I want you to report the situation to me in real time – if trouble has broken out, where, how, who started it, what is our ability to control it – I want to know everything. It is vital for us to keep control of the tempo and I want to check precisely whether what Kohl said is true – if the Garden's contagion is spreading, it will soon become evident.

"As things stand, we have to act faster than we predicted. I want you to undertake nothing that could have serious consequences in a context like this that we do not wholly understand. The aim is first to control outbreaks and maintain order, not accentuate disorder. Then it should be possible to manage any developments with the cooperation of the Dissidents. Is that clear?"

"Perfectly clear. I would still like to have a teleport constantly at my disposal – I'm going to have to travel long distances and would like to be able to do it fast. What shall we do with the Dissidents? Shall we maintain our search?"

"Are their data inactivated?"

"Yes, they are."

"That's perfect. They depend on our good will then. We're maintaining the upper hand, but they have resources unknown to us which they could bring into play. In any case, as, to my knowledge, they have no friends or allies in Elwon, they can't go very far. Don't do anything for now, they'll have to undergo inspection by us one after the other anyway. How many men do we have?"

"Eneter's regular forces are intact; I have assigned them to the surveillance of Elwon and to maintaining order. As for our men, I've allocated around fifty to the Garden as a precautionary measure. I'm going to deploy about the same amount to control access to the Memory. Our network of stations is completely operational and our shelters are secured."

"Very good, everything's under control."

At that very moment, Shu's intercom vibrates on his wrist.

"Yes?"

"Commander, head of G08 station reporting. Our three main stations have been disconnected for an indeterminate length of time. A rather focused energy peak has made all the gateways cut out. Repairs should take around twelve hours."

Furious, Shu turns to Doràn.

"You fool! What were you just saying? Our network is totally operational? Well, *you* seem to be well-informed! Doràn, I want facts and certainties, not suppositions. You are going to have to weigh this situation up as fast as you can. What is happening is very unusual and requires more than routines and bureaucratic, pen-pushing reflexes! We have to foresee everything. Is that clear? Everything! The last thing we need is a breakdown in energy supply! And seeing as you demand a teleport, go and see what's happening on site and get back to me. I want a complete report in three hours. Go!"

Shu is not immensely satisfied with the turn of events. It's not going according to his plan, it feels like improvisation and reaction and not the precise unfolding of an organised plan. In particular he senses that Doràn – all action-oriented – is of poor help in this situation that requires a lot of skill. Worse, he's beginning to fear that his fiery character might compromise the outcome. He's not happy about what happened in the Garden; he feels that it speeded up events, and he appreciates uncontrolled chains of events less than anyone.

What particularly worries him is the feeling that the situation has suddenly been radicalised without them really having foreseen it, and that is completely intolerable. Indeed, if he were to take it seriously, the Garden seems even to represent some sort of a new deal, once again not to their advantage: if Kohl was telling the truth – and he would tend to believe him – there is an unexpected force deploying over Elwon that only the Dissidents really know. All this helps fuel in him the sentiment that circumstances are getting out of his control, that the order of Elwon is being attacked to its very foundations. He feels a rising concern about possible excesses. That too, is completely new. He needs new and unprecedented resources – that much is obvious. But which ones? If only he could make Kohl join forces with them. He already succeeded with Jiù's father, so why not him? After all, he's nothing to lose by trying. If it works, he will have won an ally worthy of him; and if he fails ... well, they have solutions for that.

He calls with his message-relay.

"Kohl? I've got news. Can you come and see me? I would like to talk with you. I'll be alone. Please come on your own too. If you agree, I'll send a rapeed to pick you up. Please tell me where. Thanks for letting me know as soon as you can come by."

Doràn had left feeling dissatisfied. Shu's tone of voice when talking to him has changed. And yet, for God's sake, it's not as if he's got anything to be ashamed of! It's thanks to him that they found and took over the Garden. It was his troops who put down the rebellion there and eliminated their leaders. He's always given the dirty work and he doesn't appreciate being talked to in that tone of voice. He's had enough of the feeling that he's being used. After all, he's an Eneter commander and as such he deserves respect. He's going to have to take steps to protect his interests; as usual, he can count on no-one but himself. He might as well make sure he gets what is his by rights, just in case. He decides to teleport to the G013 station before doing anything else. It's the furthest away and he's got a few friends there. That's where he can get organised and not be taken by surprise if by any chance Shu decided to go it alone behind his back. After all, his profession is to anticipate. These quick considerations, added to the knowledge of Eneter's absolute power end up reassuring him – he's still in control.

"You asked to see me, Shu?"

Shu does not hide his surprise to see Kohl materialise before his eyes. This sudden and silent appearance gives an impression of considerable mastery and simplicity which only serves to bolster his determination.

"Indeed, Kohl. I wanted to talk to you man-to-man."

Kohl doesn't need to probe him to read his intentions. He knows human nature – and Shu's in particular – all too well, and understands what this opening statement means: a personal proposal. He just has to identify in whose name. Probably not Eneter's, nor in the name of their little autonomous group. This needs checking. Going into active mode, he focuses on Shu and what he senses confirms his suspicions – Shu is acting on his own initiative. He detects a resolute sense of duty mixed with a real consideration for what could happen to Elwon, but all this is to a great extent dominated by a powerful self-interest.

This last observation oppresses rather than surprises him. First of all because Shu's intentions displease him intensely – they reveal a tortuous and complicated mind, used to all kinds of machinations and ambiguities. How could he imagine even for a moment that he, Kohl, would accept to play his game? Is he so ignorant of people's nature that he can believe that he'd willingly go along with his manoeuvres? Awareness is really the most unequally shared out thing in the world. The other reason for his bitterness is the anticipation of the difficulties ahead. The game was already complicated enough with two forces present in Elwon, but now, with individual interests coming into play, the success of their project is looking even less assured.

He is struck by a sudden intuition: if Shu is laying his personal cards on the table, Doràn is likely to be playing a similar game. He'll have to entrust that problem to someone else – he can't take care of everything.

He sits down and deploys his attention as widely as possible on the situation as a whole, his mind not only open to his interlocutor, but to the totality of space and time surrounding him. Everything that's going on outside as well as inside is part of this moment, and he knows that he can draw the energy and instructions he needs from it in order to get the most from this conversation. He is totally relaxed and feels ready.

"I'm listening, Shu. What's this all about?"

"I've been thinking, Kohl, and I've decided to believe you. I think that what you have told me about the Garden's forces is true. I've sent Doràn to check, but I already know what will be in his report: the transformation of Elwon has begun. We must therefore add to our skills a certain knowhow that we don't already have, or else we will be quickly overcome by the situation. You know, not so long ago, Jiù's father played this role – he was a member of the High-Council, commander of Eneter and also, as we found out soon enough, a member of the Dissidence."

"Is that why you decided to make him disappear?"

Shu hesitates briefly.

"For that and other reasons too, perhaps, but we're straying from the point. I would like to propose that you join us, to take his place, in order to help us in the coming times with your experience and your knowledge of this energy we know nothing about. We need a man of your calibre. The situation requires it, and as for me, I'm ready for it."

"As for you?"

Shu is silent for a moment. This is the critical moment, where he has to lay his cards on the table and reveal his game, and this demands a certain amount of skill to play it properly.

"You need to understand something, Kohl. Our organisation is made up of multiple levels between which only the information necessary for the execution of tasks filters through to the lower level – it's an elementary rule. You are here at the highest level of this organisation. So there is information that only I know. I am ready to share this information with you because, I repeat, the situation demands a kind of, let's say, enlightened pragmatism; but this implies, naturally, that you commit to keeping it to yourself. I would like to make it totally explicit, but only for you, if you understand me?"

"Of course I understand. What will be the implications for me, vis-à-vis my friends?"

"Again, if we work together, you would have to keep everything you have learnt to yourself. As for me, I'm ready to collaborate, but those are the conditions."

"And Doràn?"

"Doràn belongs to the level below. There are therefore things he knows and others he doesn't. As I say, it's the rule."

Kohl remains pensive. At least, that's the impression he gives. In reality, he's listening. He's listening intently to what's going on in Elwon life some hundred and fifty storeys below. He senses the sky and discerns the wind. Within him he feels the continuous movement of life, totally free and very ordered; this energy that vibrates like wonderment. He feels the natural order of things bearing a kind of hope within it. How can he make his interlocutor understand this? He's so entangled in his arrangements, so blinded by his reasoning and his hypotheses, that he's lost the very meaning of what is around him.

"Shu, it's my turn to explain now. Please try to listen to me as attentively as you can. To do so, I'm going to give you a knack, a method we use, which comes from the energy that fascinates you and occupies your mind. It's this: when I say "attentively", don't strain your mind towards a single goal, for example that of listening to me or trying to understand. No, on the contrary, free it up – let it open up wide and blossom – that's its real nature. For dozens and dozens of generations we have all been forced – starting from childhood – to focus our minds. We have been trained to be rigidly attentive instead of relaxed, and this has cut us off from this widened perception that is so rich in teachings and from everything life is telling us at this moment. And do you know why? For fear of disorder. If you go into this state of widened awareness, you will immediately feel the difference – you will sense the whole of the present. You will particularly be able to assess continuously the relevance, beyond my own intentions, of what I'm telling you. Finally, and above all, you will be in a situation where you can let the temporal energy you so covet come to you. It is there, perceptible in the potentiality of the present, as long as you open up to it!"

"Why do you want me to lend myself to this ridiculous experiment?"

"Because it is not ridiculous, because you risk nothing, because it's the best way you have to verify the truth of what I'm going to tell you. And because you are asking me to cooperate with you and this state of widened awareness will necessarily be our means of communication if I accept your proposal."

"In that case, let's try," says Shu impatiently.

"Shu, there is an essential condition for accessing the energy of time. It's free will. You have no idea just how important free will is: it's the key that unlocks this energy. I'm not talking only about non-coercion, but especially about giving up the freely-consented imprisonment that all our fellow citizens have ended up indulging in, which is a kind of natural reduction of the options that life offers us, most often due to simple negligence. Without free will, this energy loses its meaning, so it withers like a flower deprived of light. Temporal energy is absolutely indivisible from free will. Do you understand?"

"I think so, yes. And?"

"And? Is the proposal you're making to me compatible with free will? Yours and mine? Or are we going to find ourselves imprisoned by this arrangement at some point? If this happens, our working together won't make sense any more as it won't be effective."

"So?"

"So, the only possibility of real collaboration is to respect free will, the freedom to plan, to do and to react. It's about openly sharing our intentions to see how and where they connect. It's a total openness that completely liberates the present potential. There is no other way, and I invite you to try it here and now, if you agree."

Shu is more shaken than he'd like to admit. This experiment he eventually got into, at first begrudgingly but then with some interest, has in fact shown him something: Kohl's little talk appeared wide open to him, stripped of any intentions other than those he expressed, apart perhaps from the slightly overblown language of one who likes the sound of his own voice. He is struck by the coherence that undeniably gives a lot of weight to what Kohl is telling him. But what should he do with it?

"I understand and sense that you're telling the truth. But how can we integrate this free will you're talking about and everything that goes with it into our procedures and our organisation? What you are showing me is an eminently personal thing. How would you apply it to an organisation?"

"We haven't reached that stage. An organisation founded on free will is obviously very different to the one you're familiar with, which is rigidly hierarchical. And yet, believe me, it works, and all the better because everyone has their own place in it. It is built on networks rather than pyramids, and the status of its members is almost negligible; at least, it's far less important than their experience and ability to share. When the time comes, together we will find a way to deploy it on Elwon – I don't know how yet. And I assure you that if I did know, I would tell you. My aim is to hide nothing from you, out of respect for your free will, as much as mine. For now, do you agree that the two of us put it into practice? I should tell you that this will allow you to access almost immediately all the potential of temporal energy and thus its own rules."

"Which are?"

"Apart from free will, the natural gateway for opening up to time is the responsibility to share freely among all those who have access to it."

"Here we go again! I want to understand why!"

"Shu, if you remain in a state of heightened awareness, you will understand why this sharing is natural. If, in a given situation all parties concerned are connected to the present potential, they each pick up a part of it, never the whole thing. As the aim of the experience is to have the fullest possible perception of the circumstances so that each person can develop to the highest potential possible, sharing becomes second nature. It can't be otherwise. So much so that it becomes possible to communicate without talking because of the conjunction of open intentions."

"You mean you communicate with thoughts?"

"Yes, it's what we call active intuition."

Shu, amazed by what he has just learned, feels suddenly tormented by an extreme conflict: all his reflexes of control, sharpened by his many years of service, are aroused. He now understands why the Dissidents, loosely organised, always evaded him – they are in permanent communication and share everything in a communal kind of thought. Obviously that's what is at the origin of their mobility, their situational intelligence and the agility that has bothered him so much. That is probably also the basis of the organisation Kohl has just been talking about. But at the same time, he wants to try this discovery for himself – its power and accessibility fascinate him enormously – even though he doesn't know where such an experiment might lead him. He's even slightly fearful of it.

He keeps quiet, incapable of resolving the contradiction deep inside him.

"Shu?" Kohl's voice is calm and full of kindness.

"Hmm?"

"The tension you feel is normal and completely natural – it's the permanent tension between the need for control and the imperative of free will. It's part of the order of things. You will not be able to resolve it like that, by snapping your fingers and making a decision, as good as it may be. You have to live with it, constantly. This tension is creative and, in passing, is exactly what we need to do for Elwon – help our dynasty to incorporate it and live it. Do you see?"

"Not completely. That doesn't help me at all with the decision I have to make about me, about you and about everything to do with this whole mess!"

Kohl senses a certain despair beginning to afflict Shu.

"I know who you are, Shu. I know this confusion and feeling of powerlessness. Let me talk to you about my experience. I've been in your situation, I'm familiar with this inner conflict and I haven't resolved it. Actually, I decided to reduce control to its simplest expression – to the minimum required for maintaining a sense of order and balance in my life. The rest, all the rest, is acceptance. It's thanks to acceptance that I grow, that we evolve, that our lives become better organised, all mixed up together. Because I consider all these options and choose the one that lets me grow at the same time as everyone else. You are going to discover the balance between these forces, which is not composed of equality but of movement. This balance is powerfully dynamic. Ah yes, and there's just one more little thing," he adds mischievously.

"What's that?"

"Forget about self-interest. Or more precisely – stop worrying about it. You are, let me assure you, its worst enemy."

"What do you mean?" retorts Shu, obviously stung, which confirms to Kohl that he guessed correctly.

"Hear me out - it's just as logical: if you take any situation, I think you will admit to only having a partial perception of it, and even a biased one? Well, in that case you are not optimising your self-interest – you take it into account, that's for sure, but you don't optimise it. To do that you'd need to constantly consider the whole of the situation, thus taking into account everyone else's perceptions at the same time, but you'd also need to take into account all the consequences! If you really want to look out for your own interests, it's impossible to not take into account the consequences. You witnessed that in the Garden with its immediate retro-causality. This taking into account is optimised by sharing. Thus your self-interest would be better served if you didn't worry about it. Life takes care of it a lot better than you would ever do."

Shu suddenly bursts out laughing, loud and long. Momentarily taken by surprise, Kohl soon allows himself to be infected by this powerful laughter too and by the hilarious spectacle of this man, at the pinnacle of power, clutching at his ribs behind his desk. This strange scene goes on, interspersed with transitory moments of calm which are quickly interrupted by more fits of contagious hilarity.

"Kohl, you're too much. Really too much!"

"What do you mean?"

"Do you realise what's just happened?"

"What?"

"I invited you to come to see me, with the intention of getting you to help me with Eneter's absolute control, and instead of that, after twenty-five years at the highest level of the Dynasty and five minutes' conversation with you, you want me to join the Dissidence!"

"You can see it like that if you want ... but I prefer to see things differently."

"You are truly extraordinary! And how do you see it?" Shu says with another hoot of laughter.

"We are both in the process of leaving our respective positions and converging; I'm moving towards you and you towards me. At this very moment we are doing exactly what is good for Elwon, for you and for me. If you weigh everything up, we cannot do otherwise."

"Perhaps. You are perhaps right. But it's still quite extraordinary! I hope, as you say, you're right - for you, for us and for me too."

Kohl appreciates this final comment that seems to show that Shu has changed, that his priorities have been reversed and that his sense of self-interest has made way for a concern for Elwon. This is undoubtedly a good sign. Kohl feels that it's time to finish winning him over by bringing things to a close. Without a really convincing demonstration, he will be overcome by doubt again, which will cancel out all that's been achieved in the past few minutes.

"To convince you this is all true, I propose initiating you right now in temporal energy in order to move in space, which we call transiting."

Meanwhile, Akané and Jiù have finished playing his father's message. They now understand the extent of the intelligence in his communications with the Memory – he's the one who made it the central organ of Elwon life. Not having immense confidence in the capacity of the High-Council which he knew to be totally manipulated by Eneter – and for good reason seeing as he himself was one of the manipulators – he made sure that the Memory could be totally autonomous and had very sophisticated means of information and perception. He's the one who used algorithms derived from Iksan's formulae to design and deploy the Zeitgeist. This allowed him, among other things, to talk with the Memory in secret without having to go through fastidious interface sessions that were probably tracked by Eneter as well. What's more, he revealed to them the different parameters permitting the amplification or acceleration of the pulsations which would be able to modulate its effectiveness should the need arise.

Night has fallen on the large office. The Memory has been silent for a long time and neither Jiù nor Akané is aware of how much time has passed. A light metallic smell floats in the air like a last reminder of the session with the Memory. It blends intermittently with Akané's discreet perfume which Jiù allows to soak into him as if to ensure he'll remember it. With delight he savours this subtle sensation of being totally filled with it to the end of his fingers. He will remember.

The office is now steeped in almost total darkness and only the glow of Juno, always brightly-lit at night, steals in to play with some shadows there. A slight glimmer in the half-light indicates that they both have their eyes open, with far-away looks. They don't need to talk: they are thinking in unison after everything they have just lived through and discovered together. Their thoughts blend and their bodies are so close that they are breathing the very same air. They allow their gaze to lose itself in the twists and turns of this city, so like every other, as if they were searching for moments they have lived or wished to pick up a trace of life behind each light. They observe the uniform rhythm and flow of the rapeeds in this world which is theirs but from which they feel detached as if it were ancient history with no relevance to them anymore. Pensively they contemplate a whole society as it transforms behind its immutable and programmed appearances. In this moment of intensely silent immobility, the force of the living rises up like a relentlessly spreading fragrance that only a few – like them – can sense. Then, unable to hold it back any longer, they breathe out with a long sigh, powerful in their calm determination to step into whatever awaits them.

———————

"Friends, thank you all for coming. I hope you feel, as I do, real joy that we're together again!"

Kohl is facing the little assembly he has summoned. His wide joyous smile conveys the deep connection he feels with his companions. He has known them for so long, since the beginning of this long adventure that has gradually united them and which they know is about to move into a decisive stage. They all feel as if sucked into a whirlpool, moving at constant speed towards an end that is approaching faster and faster.

He is familiar with some of those present, having initiated them himself: Matzu, Frischke, Jasna, Pehl, Xhan, Dena, and of course Leh, whose stocky figure he distinguishes among them. They are in the most unlikely place possible, somewhere Eneter will never look for them: a gigantic illusions village in a Juno suburb. It's one of those villages that sprouted like mushrooms when Cultural sector researchers found a way of projecting everyone's emotions in a nearly real holographic form. Elwon's inhabitants quickly became totally dependent on them as a toxic release from the systematic logic established in the Dynasty. This uncontrolled projection obviously degenerated into all sorts of individual and collective excesses which made these places among the most notorious in the Dynasty. Yet it's as if this sulphurous reputation merely served to magnify their fascination, as witnessed by the growing tides of men and women of all ages who relentlessly thronged to them.

They are right in the middle of the chimera section where half-human, half-animal bodies frolic and chase each other in frenetic and demented rhythms. All this is adroitly relayed by the Media which spreads this miasma all over Elwon in uniformly noxious multiple miniature versions for use on different individual appliances. They have found shelter in a little building removed from the Dantean agitation, a sort of storeroom where they are temporarily protected from the throbbing stridency of a trance-inducing cacophony. They can hear the slightly muted shouts and hectic wanderings of an assorted crowd, haggard and feverish, intoxicated by the most intense emotions that have been pumped up to the full. He has chosen this shady place deliberately because it's the only one where Eneter's trackers are ineffective, so dense and closely-knit is the inextricable network of cerebral waves at the height of excitement. And since Mia has been in their hands, he's afraid that their thoughts might alert the authority's detectors.

His voice is serious as he looks over the assembly. They are all there, or almost.

"I suggest, if you will, that we have a long communal thought for Orion and Elea, our dear friends who are no longer with us. Let the energy of time link us to them via the inner path we are all familiar with as they continue their journey in other dimensions. I know they will hear us."

Instantly silence falls like a lead weight on the little group. Nothing filters through, nothing moves. They are all turned towards the inside, perfectly immobile figures, men and women of all origins, all ages, shapes and sizes. It's as if the noise outside had suddenly been switched off. This group is absolutely magnificent in its immobility, borne by a mixture of resolve and acceptance so strong that it makes them invincible. In their own ways, each one of them expresses this power rising up in them; they feel it in unison and another smile, joyful and relaxed, comes gradually to play on the peaceful faces, as if they were all contemplating or listening to the same thing.

"They heard us, that's for sure," whispers a voice that expresses everybody's sentiments.

After this truly intense moment, they take some time to come back, in a patchy way, to what surrounds them and the reasons for their meeting. Some of them have become restless, others clear their throats, but they are all moved in some way.

"I'd like to announce something important. I've just initiated Shu in first level transition."

This statement of Kohl's is greeted by a prolonged murmur conveying the consternation of many of them about the extremely unpredictable course of recent events.

"I did it because some of us – including Orion, Elea and others – share the conviction that only perfect convergence with L1 order will allow us to pull off this leap in awareness that we desire for Elwon. It can't succeed by opposition. Do you share this view?"

"Completely, Kohl, let me reassure you on that point."

Jiù's voice suddenly rising among them transforms the agitated chattering into silent and tense expectation.

"Akané and I have just had a very long interaction with Memory Central, which, among other analyses and recommendations, confirmed word for word what you have just said: convergence with L1 order is vital for Elwon to be able to access temporal energy and reach a state of enlarged consciousness. It's not either them or us, it's them and us. As long as we are opposing each other, the equal strength of our forces means that any action by us or by them will be followed by a similar reaction. It's not about winning, but about succeeding. And if I understand what you're saying, it would seem that Eneter has understood that too."

"Yes, as far as Shu is concerned, anyway. I don't know about Eneter and I don't know at this stage what they will do with this new element. I also have some doubts about Doràn, who wasn't present during our meeting. Leh, would you agree to take care of that? It would be good if you and a few others could look out for a possible development on that side of things."

Leh silently acquiesces, not without having taken note around him of two or three companions who indicate with an intent glance that they are standing by to support him.

"I would like to speak!"

"Speak Jon, we're listening."

"I wanted to test the protection level of the secondary network that Jiù and Akané discovered, in case we needed to be in charge of it. I can tell you that it is very badly defended. I projected the energy of some quite weak connections and was able to get in without the least resistance. It shouldn't be too complicated to bring it down if need be."

Kohl looks truly worried all of a sudden. This is the second or third time that Jon is the cause of aggressive phenomena – which are admittedly the manifestation of his courageous and combative character, but which entail negative chains of events every time. He can't scan Jon without telling him, but he senses a kind of violence in him, a stubborn determination that is only waiting for an opportunity to appear. The occasion needs to be found to help him get rid of it. To find a suitable way to reply, he decides to go into widened awareness mode. Apart from surprise from the rest of the group, he senses nothing that indicates any consequences from this event other than a normal Eneter reaction – they don't seem, at this stage, to have considered the incident as an attack. On the contrary, he feels the slow ripples of the energy of time floating peacefully over them like a protective veil. And yet, something is undeniably focused around Jon which they will really have to take into account.

"Jon, after your experience in the Garden, you know better than anyone that every action has a reaction according to the laws of causality. I don't know what consequences your action will have, but it's important that you grasp that it was not only useless but that it could possibly be dangerous – not only for us, but especially for the hope we are the bearers of. I'd like to give you, here and now, some very clear recommendations: the state of mind that you show in this kind of initiative is bold and shows your courage, but it is not adapted to the circumstances. You absolutely must understand that what we're engaged in is cooperation – not a competition, and much less a battle. We are going to join forces with Eneter – do you understand that? It's about combining with, not opposing, each other. It can't be any other way. Otherwise," he adds in a more light-hearted tone, "if we fail this convergence, the zip gets stuck and we all know how inconvenient that can be."

A wave of amusement runs through the crowd, there being many who can think of at least one or two such embarrassing occasions.

"So it's not about weighing up, assessing, anticipating. It's about going openly towards them without preconceptions or prejudice, contributing what we are and the strength we carry with us. Our intention is to work together, each using his or her own qualities. If, by your actions and your attitude, you engage us in something else, you are truly compromising the outcome we desire. I must therefore ask you not to take any initiative without talking to one or other of us about it and to adhere to the advice that is given. What you bring to our group – your formidable ability to undertake and get things done – must not be turned against us: you have to contain it. By doing that very thing, you show how L1 logic will still be useful in the future we are preparing for. Are we in agreement?"

Jon feels somewhat put out by this sermon that's been addressed to him in front of everyone, especially because Mia is there, but he can only agree.

"I understand, Kohl; I understand perfectly, and ask you all to forgive me if my actions have caused any trouble."

"I suggest you join Leh's team, Mia too. They might be able to help you."

There are smiles among the crowd, as Leh's reputation for strength and immutability is well-established.

"Look!"

A shout from someone in the group makes them all turn round. A woman at the back of the little room is pointing to the wall opposite her: at the foot of the wall, near the door, shoots of climbing ivy-like plants have appeared and before their very eyes are spreading, slowly but surely, over the whole surface.

"What on earth is that?"

Kohl and some others, who have stayed in active mode, have already understood: the Garden! The solution of continuity between the Garden and Elwon has broken the balance: all the potential of creation on one side and all the rigour on the other. Now, through this gaping opening, all the creative energy present in the Garden is pouring into Elwon, propagating itself in the living, but in a disorganised and totally unbridled way.

"Good heavens, but if this is already manifesting itself in the vegetable world, what could be happening to humans?"

Everyone rushes towards the exit, wanting to go and check what's happening outside.

"Stop!"

Kohl's powerful voice arrests them. He is flanked by Jiù and Akané whose determined air ends up re-establishing some sort of order.

"What were you going to do? Where were you going? We all know what we are going to find outside, don't we? Are you sure you want to rush into that reality? Are you really? Have you already forgotten our ability to fabricate the one which fits us the best? Are you sure you want to accept the one being imposed on you by chains of circumstances ruled by a logic that is alien to you?"

His tone becomes more and more poised as he feels the calm return, gradually replaced by this energy that is singular to them. With a shadow of a smile, Kohl shows his appreciation for this group, for the ability they all have to draw from their experience instantly and come back to themselves. Each in turn reconnects to the vibration within them, the spontaneous opening to all the options of the living within them.

"Friends, here we are – it's happened. We are face to face with what we have to do, all of us. Look what's happening. The Garden is no more, in any case not in the distinct form we were able to access it for a time. It has disappeared. Do you, like me, feel what is being offered to us? Do you feel it?"

Again, they are united by this magnificent silence, loaded with all the potential and power of the present.

"Do you feel that only we ourselves can make a space for it again inside each of us? Do you feel the gigantic creative force that fills us and that it's up to us to bring forth in the shape we choose for it? Don't ever forget that knowledge, and above all awareness, come with this energy and that's what teaches us how to use it."

Is it the calm of his voice? Is it the vibration that Kohl's words have just reconnected them to? From deep inside each one of them surges this inexorable and powerful joy that links them to the world, to all potential presents until infinity, exactly at this moment. And without them having to do anything else but be aware, this impulse guides them as they leave the room one by one, without looking at the wall where the advance of the creepers seems to have stopped. They all turn to their own business now, confident that a profusion of possibilities is open to them at every instant.

Outside, it's utter chaos. Stimulated by these creative capacities of unprecedented power, all kinds of projections are wildly combining and entangling. Grotesque figures blend with a vile bestiary and the black violence of fantasies given free rein alternates with the intolerable commotion of shapeless chimeras. Scents and colours melt in a heady and furious cacophony of smells. And like a demented fireworks show, these unhinged shapes are projected in Juno's night sky in crazy bouquets that link up above the city's different neighbourhoods, showing everyone the unfolding delirium.

A stupefied crowd wanders aimlessly, lost in this monumental madness that it nonetheless created itself. It has forgotten itself in an outrageous and collective drunkenness that takes it beyond the limits of the mind. This spectacle is unbearably pitiful for Kohl and his companions, passing through this misery with their thoughts closed as if holding their breath.

Once at the gates of the village, they look around them. A squadron of Eneter guards is getting into position, all wearing inhibitors. Doràn has not wasted any time – it looks like all garrisons have been mobilised. Probably for the first time, the traffic of rapeeds has stopped. Everywhere, tufts of weeds are growing and multiplying in cracks in the surfacing. Even more unsettling are the creeping plants spreading abundantly in all directions and climbing upwards. Already massive and knotty trunks are branching out in countless directions and incrusting the facades of buildings like some abominable strain of ivy. Their woody stems advance with inexorable slowness on the dizzying walls of the towers, multiplying continuously, as if moved by an alarming determination.

The image of Iksan's laboratory flashes through Jiù's mesmerized mind. He understands now that there was nothing accidental about the mad vegetation choking what was left of the building, that it came from the very experiments Iksan had carried out there, and that some error of his had caused the loss. The memory of the collapsed outhouse fills him with horror when he contemplates these immense towers that shoot up to infinity in Juno's sky. The spectacle is so mind-blowing that everyone stops; everyone gets out of their rapeeds and offices and goes towards the creepers in disoriented groups. They touch them with suspicion, if not downright revulsion.

For the first time silence spreads on Juno, and probably all over Elwon. The incessant noise makes way for a dull anxiety, the same anxiety the noise was meant to mask. People are talking to each other, exchanging looks and words, but no-one knows anything. The determined presence of the Eneter squadrons spreads both the reassurance that the authorities are taking care of things and are going to deal with the chaos, and a vague sense of fear. Something is definitely going on and, unthinkably, the order of Eneter suddenly seems to waver. As for Kohl and his companions, along with a sense of urgency that refuses inevitability, they have a foreboding that this immutable order is going to make itself felt by blind force. They fear that orders will brutally burst forth to bring back the status quo without any consideration for the causes or consequences of this prodigious chaos, either here in the centre of Juno or in any of the other contaminated areas of Elwon. They also know that by the laws of retro-causality peculiar to temporal energy, if mindless brutality is unleashed, the resulting reaction will be devastating. This must be stopped at all costs.

"There is not a moment to lose. Quick, take position at the entrance to village, each of you. Stay connected in yourselves and talk to the Eneter chief you identify there. Warn him about the causes of the chaos and persuade him not to attack. Jon and Leh, do what you have to with Doràn. Jiù and Akané, please go to Memory Central. It should have analysed all the data of the situation and you should act in concert with it. As for me, I'm going to see Shu to advise him. Let's stay in touch. Please – no inappropriate initiatives: with what's going on we have enough to do without adding to it."

Shu is at headquarters. His face is tensed in concentration, in front of an immense screen, a giant planisphere where the whole of Elwon is displayed. It is studded with tiny winking points, rapidly increasing in number.

"What's the situation?"

"Ah, Kohl! I didn't hear you arrive. Look, it's a disaster. All Elwon is affected. I don't know if we will have enough men to be able to deal with it."

"Can we talk? I think we have other options".

Shu hesitates. His eyes shift from Kohl to the screen to his advisors who are coming and going around him with serious and unreceptive expressions.

"Five minutes, Kohl, not more. I can't give you more."

"It will be enough."

"Fine, as you wish. Come."

Shu leads him into a small office adjacent to the main room, where he sinks heavily into a large armchair with a deep sigh.

"Kohl, the situation is in danger of fast becoming uncontrollable. Did you realise that? This has never happened on Elwon. Our Dynasty is at stake – I can't afford to make mistakes."

"You won't make any mistakes, Shu, trust me. Trust yourself."

"May heaven hear you!"

"Good start!"

Shu forces a quick smile at Kohl's joke which he's not sure is timely.

"I'm only half-joking. Listen, Shu! Now you have access to temporal energy, go down into yourself and *feel* what I'm going to say to you. All of this is OK, do you hear me? Despite appearances, it's OK. It's not a total madman telling you this, it's me – Kohl. I'm not given to flights of fancy, and the ordered survival of Elwon is as important of me as it is to you. What's going on is a foretaste of what awaits us with a Collapsus. Shu, it's just a warning! It's up to us to show that we have weighed things up and understood and that we are reacting as circumstances require – with the intuition of the instant and its consequences and not by a reflex conditioned by our past. Do you understand? Take the scope of the instant, weigh up all the information it gives you, open up to this wide and innate knowledge and let yourself be guided by the awareness it brings. Shu? Do you hear me? Let yourself be guided by time, by everything the moment contains. Make your decision from that place, that moment and nowhere else."

"I'm not sure I can do it."

"I'm going to help you, Close your eyes, Shu, and sense the goodwill I feel for you, for Eneter and for Elwon. Open up to this energy and be inspired by it."

Resistant for an instant – he really has got better things to do – Shu then lets himself go under Kohl's persuasive instructions. He lets his mind relax, free of any injunction or focus. He feels his thoughts become calm and then evaporate like dew in the sun. The unfamiliar and beneficent vibration gradually takes the place of his thoughts, or more precisely reclaims its place, as if his own thoughts were foreign to him. That lasts for a moment and then an image comes to him, so surprising that he has to hold back his laughter and opens his eyes.

"It's ridiculous!"

"What is?"

"What came to me – it's bloody ridiculous. I have just seen a magnificent beach, a dream beach like one in an illusion village. I don't know where that came from, but it's clearly has nothing to do with anything!"

"And?"

"The waves were furious, smashing in gusts on the coast, beating it mercilessly with all the regularity and constancy of an energy from a long way off; there was an impressive spouting of foam and a mist of spray."

270

"Perfect. And what's your conclusion?"

"Nothing in particular." He hesitates for a moment. "It was almost insurmountable, but still I got a feeling of balance. Neither the waves nor the beach are threatened. Each has its place. Like a superb interplay of energies within a powerful but stable dynamic."

"That's exactly it!"

"Exactly what?"

"What's going on right now in Elwon. It's a balancing act between rational immutability and the logic of order on one side and the furious creativity of the moment on the other. This apparent opposition is exactly the stable dynamic you talked about."

"Ah yes, maybe we can look at it that way, but what can I deduce from it to help me decide what to do? Don't forget what's going on next door, and especially what's going on outside."

"Do as the beach does: contain the wave but don't push it back. Be unmoveable: use the strength of the wave itself to push it back, but don't add yours to it – the wave's strength is quite enough."

"So I should give our squadrons the order to maintain their positions, not to move or push back, but to hold, not take over the illusion villages?"

"Precisely."

"And why would you want me to trust an image glimpsed in a moment of calm – perhaps an illusion – to make a decision this important?"

"Because it came to you precisely at the moment you had this decision to make; it came to you from precisely the moment of calm that you are talking about, and it was not forced upon you by anyone else! It belongs to you, proposed to you by that part of you that is permanently connected to the present potential. This intuitive visualisation is one of the simplest ways to access temporal energy and its instructions. It's what we call a connection. It's as simple as that. Check, here and now, without tension or intention, how you would feel if you took that decision and if you didn't take it."

A heartbeat later, Shu breathes in slowly.

"Yes, it's quite clear. You're right. I'm even quite impressed by the real consistency I feel around this decision. It must be the right one. OK, so we'll do as we've said, but I still want to cut off the electricity supply to all these crazy villages!"

He gets up and walks with renewed energy towards the vast control room.

"And what are we going to do about the creepers?"

"Leave us to take care of them. We have to go back to the Garden, with some of your most trusted men. Send a team of calm and reliable men there, as that's where this problem needs to be resolved. Above all, you should give the order that the creeper trunks must never be attacked with flashguns! Under no circumstances - it's absolutely essential – do you understand? It really must not be done. Maintain calm and order and that's all. At worse, evacuate the most threatened buildings."

"Evacuate! Do you realise what you're saying?"

"Yes, I do, but it would be a wise decision. It's up to you when to take it. I think your teams know how to manage the logistics."

"Hmm...I see. There's no time to lose."

At the same time, a similar conversation is taking place a few yards from there. In the building opposite, Jiù and Akané are assessing the situation with the Memory.

"What's your analysis, Memory?"

"The latest data indicates that the Eneter forces won't move. Nonetheless, the state of balance remains under threat. To bring back order, the convergence between the Garden and Elwon, and between you and Eneter, should be accelerated. Above all the inhabitants have to succeed in converging – they must make this synthesis between the instantaneous creativity of the Garden and L1 logic. Otherwise, the madness will continue, and it will be very difficult to stop."

"What do you suggest?"

"Memory recommends that you go to the Garden with Eneter, and do what is needed there. Then you two should both successfully undergo synthesis. From that point, Memory will also be able to assimilate and spread it on Elwon via the Zeitgeist in an almost immediate and generalised way."

"Why? Surely you don't think that we haven't completed this synthesis?"

"If it were the case, none of what is happening would have happened. There persists in you some mistrust of Eneter because Eneter remains powerfully mobilised against you. The antagonism is still alive, especially among some of your number who resist this convergence. Only one of the Dissidents, whose identity is only partially known to you, has truly experienced it – but that's not enough."

Jiù is perplexed. The prospect suggested by the Memory gives him a sense of unease and mixed feelings. It seems to him that there are other possibilities he should explore. More than anything he feels a degree of uncertainty that is making him hesitate. He opens up to Akané about it and her response is quick and final.

"The very fact you are resisting and doubting proves the Memory is right. We haven't completed convergence. I don't even know if we've started it, nor what form it should take. If we had, what the Memory recommends would seem obvious to us. I suggest, then, that we follow its advice and do this experiment. We'll do it together this time, rather than separately."

"You're probably right. But I feel something else is going on that we need to pay attention to and I can't focus enough to identify what it is. Let's meet up in the Garden."

When they emerge from their transition, they have difficulty recognising where they are. Instead of their eyes being drawn to the valleys and meadows they were used to, they see only a kind of half-arid steppe with scattered stems of long grass mixed with pebbles. Instead of the light breeze, a strong wind whips up clouds of dust that twirl in whirlwinds between the tufts like a sterile kind of pollination. Kohl is there too, sharing their consternation.

"It's really awful."

"Yes, but it's not irremediable. It's up to us to do something about it."

They go to Kohl's house, now resembling a mountain refuge lost in the scree, its little walls reflecting the heat of a blinding sun. Half a dozen men are waiting for them there. A good sign – they are not armed. It seems as if Shu has understood.

"Good afternoon!"

"Afternoon. We've been sent by Shu who told us to put ourselves at your disposal."

"Thanks for being here. Have you had something to eat and drink?"

"We've just got here, but we wouldn't say no. It's so dry!"

Kohl goes into his little house that he's astonished to find still cool and welcoming. He calls to them all:

"Come in! It'll be easier to chat inside."

They all follow him, breathing a sigh of contentment, relieved by the peaceful atmosphere of the house. They sit down and drink in silence, some waiting for orders, others completely open to the circumstances, letting the energy of time bring to them a glimpse of what is to come.

"Gentlemen, we are here in order to re-establish together the broken balance that is creating the disorder you've seen on Elwon. It's important that, like Shu, you trust us, and above all that you feel totally safe with us and about the events that are taking place. So, if one of you feels any concern, please let us know about it now."

One of the guards clears his throat, as if getting rid of what dust remains in it.

"We'd like to understand a bit what is going on."

Jiù calmly begins to speak.

"You're right, that's quite legitimate. You see, we erected our Dynasty on the order of pure reason, and logic has been the foundation of our civilisation. By doing this we've successfully constructed the technology that surrounds us and fulfils our needs. But equally we have completely eliminated the infinite creative power of the instant; we have channelled and limited it with all kinds of principles and rules to such a point that our society is now governed by machines, the most powerful of which,

Memory Central, thinks and acts for us. We no longer know how to create, except in ridiculous ways, and we've forgotten that was our reason for being.

"A few of us, in growing numbers, have found, whether by accident or not, this creative force that appears in strange instants – autonomous moments full of life that we have called connections. We have let this energy – which comes to us from time – imprint on us, fill us up and guide us. We have discovered the incredible richness of the instant, like a fan opening onto thousands of possibilities, each with its own vitality. We have touched and begun to use this energy, and it brought us here, to this Garden where the power of the present potential was always evident, in a continuous present."

Jiù stops for a moment, absorbed by nostalgia for what he had discovered and the inexpressible sense of well-being he had felt here. Kohl continues:

"But this Garden was cut off from Elwon. A powerful antagonism had grown between our two realities. This could not be, and therefore convergence began between these two worlds. However, force was involved and so it went wrong, for the simple reason that we were in complete opposition and could therefore share nothing – or very little; not the energy, nor the knowledge, nor the awareness that this force bears in it. And from there on, disorder came to Elwon which lived only by order, and aridity invaded the Garden which was nothing but abundance. Do you understand?"

"So we've come here so you can share with us what you know, is that it?"

A joyful expression lights up the three friends' faces.

"That's absolutely right: it's exactly what we're going to do. We have to recreate the balance between us that we've broken and that circumstances are obliging us to re-establish. We're going to share with you, as I've done with your boss, everything we know about temporal energy. Without hiding anything about it from you – because it doesn't belong to us, or more precisely, it belongs to you as much as to us. We are all only its custodians. What do you think?"

In a hesitant voice one of the guards ventures:

"Is there a risk? Does it hurt?"

These words are received with laughter and Akané replies:

"Forgive our laughing! There is absolutely no danger – this energy is part of you and isn't foreign to you. So nothing bad can happen to you. But I really understand your question – it comes from the conditioning we've all received – the cosy comfort of Elwon which has gradually eliminated everything – insects, flowers, emotions – in the name of our safety."

"I suggest one or two of you do the experiment with us; the others will be witnesses and will be able to see that nothing happens to them."

A hand is raised, then two, three, four.

"We would like to volunteer."

"Perfect. Here's what we are going to do. We are going to stay silent with our eyes closed. Totally relaxed; be calmly present to everything around you, simply curious as if you were using your senses for the first time. Don't worry about anything, not about you nor about the others. In this inner silence, a kind of energy will come, borne by the discovery of the moment. Let it rise: it's like the resurgence of a deep wellspring that becomes ever more powerful as your thoughts are calmed. Don't try to avoid thinking either – it's complicated, tiring and useless. Visualise instead your mind spreading; everything happening around you is falling inside it, whether you can see it or not; feel your thoughts melt like ice in the sun – above all don't hold them back. Let yourselves go."

"Is that it?"

"Yes, that's it. In order to feel temporal energy, to discover the joy it brings and let yourself be carried by it, it's enough to be totally present. It's as simple as that and that's how it begins. When you have accessed it once, you can return as much as you want. We'll explain how to use it."

These calm and simple explanations have ended up convincing the guards, even the most hesitant ones. They all close their eyes and surrender to the peace and quiet. Suddenly, more quickly than they expected, they each feel the inner vibration that Kohl has described. It rises and invades them, covering them like a quiver on their skin. Now they understand: they have instantly acquired this immediate and innate knowledge, as if they knew everything they needed to know, without it being formulated. With this understanding comes an unknown and powerful jubilation, caused by nothing in particular, which gives them a profound sense of their identity. They are filled up with themselves as if they were discovering their true natures for the first time. They all open their eyes. Some tears fall, without sorrow. They are moved by an intense exultation.

"Wow!"

Apart from this brief aside, which conveys their emotions precisely, there is a prolonged silence as the only alternative to what they have just felt.

"Now we can talk to each other without breaking the silence."

Jiù and Akané smile as Kohl's inner voice makes them all jump. Instinctively the Eneter agents reply in the same way.

"Can we communicate using our thoughts too?"

"Yes, and over immense distances. I propose that we now carry out together what we call a connection: still bathed in this energy, we are going to feel together the whole of what is in the present – all the potential realities, what leads up to this very instant and what it is in the future. This complete perception will give us a collective vision of our present and of what we can do with it. Is that OK? Is it clear enough?"

"Perfectly. Tell us what to do."

"We're going to go into active mode. Hold on to this energy that you've now discovered, and widen your attention as I showed you. Don't think about anything, but be attentive to what your senses tell you, the images that come. Observe them as suggestions but don't make any choices, don't have any preferences, let them go through you as if you were watching a rapeed go by. If you express a preference or a choice – that is, if you focus on one of those options – then you will transit, which means that you will project yourself in that reality, which you will then make happen like the one you chose. Do you understand? That's why we say that thought creates our reality. It would be more exact to talk about the thoughts we appropriate, that we make our own. That's one of the rules you need to know when using temporal energy."

"What are the other rules? Are there a lot?" asks a slightly awestruck voice.

"Only two. One is the law of causality: if you create a reality, you must accept to experience it and assimilate the consequences; the other one is that of free will – no-one can interfere with the reality you choose, no-one can stop you, although you can be accompanied if you accept to share it. This brings me to something I also said to your commander, Shu: this energy is more powerful when you share it. That's why it rose up so quickly within you."

He goes on, speaking with his inner voice to Jiù and Akané:

"Help me to surround them and if you feel one beginning to transit, go with him."

Silence falls and brings with it the almost-tangible peace that envelops and contains them. They have a vision of Elwon, its long roads now empty and crowds of people talking to and questioning each other. The anxiety has now disappeared, to be replaced by calm astonishment and an almost childlike pleasure before this new situation – it's as if the city could now be used for something other than moving between places. The entire city has become a moment! The wide attention of Jiù and Akané is suddenly attracted by one of the men whom they sense is focusing. They decide to go with him. All three of them materialise next to Shu in the huge control room. The guard, slightly dazed, pats his body and his arms, partly reassured.

"How did I do that?"

Jiù and Akané burst out laughing, attracting Shu's attention, who turns round and comes over, briefly greeting Jiù and Akané. Jiù turns to the guard who doesn't seem to know how to behave with his superior.

"It's nothing. We all mess up the first time – it's normal! I flunked my first transitions too. It doesn't matter – it only means that you are particularly receptive to this energy. I think that, when Kohl mentioned your commander, your sense of hierarchy got the upper hand and you focused on Shu, and that brought you here!"

Shu says, in an amused voice:

"It's impressively effective, isn't it? If I had told you I had done this myself, you would never have believed me. You would probably have referred the matter to your direct superiors. Therefore I deemed it preferable to let you have the experience. I think you'll agree I wasn't wrong!"

"So we can use the teleport without the control panel?"

"It's nothing to do with the teleport now. You can now transit; you can move about in space at will by using temporal energy. We are going to have to get organised, establish the rules; otherwise it's going to be a big mess."

"Don't rush into creating new rules. We'll see about that when the time comes. But speaking of rules, I should tell you something else. You can also transit in time. Moving in space is what we call level one transition; moving in time is level two. I'll explain it to you when it becomes necessary."

"How is the situation developing Shu?" asks Akané looking questioningly at the large control screen where a myriad of dots is blinking in a disjointed rhythm.

"Kohl was right, it seems to have stabilised. We have no doubt avoided the worst. We haven't had to intervene and our men have remained in control of events. Well – as much as possible, anyway. But we are having trouble curbing them. I think we are lacking a key factor that would help us return to nominal."

"I suggest we go and join the others. Together we will have a better chance of finding the solution."

"Let's go."

They are all in the little room in Kohl's house. The guards greet their leader's arrival with a slightly surprised nod. They are all quiet again – they don't want to move; rather, in the palpable peace surrounding them, they too are trying out this new instinct of letting things occur rather than causing them to happen. Suddenly they hear the shy and hesitant impact of scattered fat drops of rain falling on the roof like light footsteps. The splashing quickly intensifies and the shower soon becomes a torrential downpour they contemplate through the open door. A damp coolness comes with it in waves, rich with all the aroused scents of the earth.

They get up, absorbed by the deluge, and spontaneously go nearer to the door, each gripped by the same gratitude. They had forgotten how good it was when it rained – a renewal for the earth, for plants and animals, and for people. Some of them hold out their hand to savour it. One of them moves the others aside and goes out. His arms held out and his face towards the sky, he tastes the rain and surrenders to it. Why is he doing that? He doesn't know, but it's no doubt his way of becoming part of what is around him, whatever happens. One, two, three others, and finally all of them follow him. They laugh and spin around like children, slowly at first, and then faster, as if they were drunk on the water. Then their movements slow and they become still, welcoming each drop that falls as if in conversation with the sky. They go back in, shake themselves like dogs and dry themselves with whatever is at hand.

It's strange, but this instant of simple and fleeting happiness, totally inconceivable in the presence of a hierarchical superior, seems to have united them more than sharing temporal energy has. Their eyes don't just meet any more; they search each other out, both astonished and delighted at what they just did together. When the shower is finally over, they go out. Before them spreads an immense stretch of short new grass, a valley newly remade, its horizon blocked by the serrated outlines of countless city skyscrapers.

"Elwon. We're in Elwon. The Garden has disappeared!"

They look around them and find they are on the edge of one of the vast fields of captors on the city borders: the valley acts as a wide frontier between the city and the solar field where weeds are starting to grow between the gantries. Kohl, Akané and Jiù look at each other and then Kohl says, his calm voice still vibrant with the energy they have just shared: "Everything's fine – we've succeeded. By experiencing a connection together and sharing temporal energy completely – by uniting – we have restored the balance. So the Garden has become useless and it has incorporated Elwon. We can return to the city – we've finished what we had to do here. I suggest we transit to Juno. Gentlemen," he adds to the guards, stunned as they are by these unthinkable events that could be from another planet, "we are going to accompany you in your first transition."

Jiù and Akané have sat down a few yards away.

"Are you thinking what I'm thinking?"

"Yes. I too feel a need to be still for a while, to weigh these moments instead of jumping from one event to another. Kohl has no doubt his own reasons for setting such a fast pace, but I feel lost in it. As for myself, I – or rather we – want something else. Not to understand or control, but I want to taste what is going on. I know what is waiting for us in Elwon. Like you I sense in myself what these united energies bring, but there is something else. I'm certain of it and I don't want to miss it."

"I have exactly the same thoughts. Let's tell Kohl."

Once Kohl has been told of their intentions, they both move away from the little group. They find a cropped grass meadow behind the house where they stop in order to survey this new landscape calmly. The city must surely be unrecognisable!

In the middle distance, there is a light movement in the air as their new allies transit. Only a whirl of heat remains to mark the place from where they disappeared just an instant ago. Alone at last! Instinctively they savour this sensation they had expected: a subtle exultation as they feel time's meanderings curl up inside them and in the space between them. They want to enjoy to the utmost every piece of this instant. They look at and listen to this new landscape with intensified attention.

Then, with an almost imperceptible movement, their view gradually rolls up, like an image on the wall of a bottomless well into which they are letting themselves sink. Everything slows and then freezes; energy envelops them and radiates from everywhere. This moment of present potential is going to be unique – they know it and wouldn't miss it for the world. For the first time they are witnessing a connection in preparation. They feel the vibrations of time condensing stroke by stroke and fast binding together like a compound. The strokes become lumps, and before their astounded eyes, a new instant forms and becomes an exact moment, an immense vision with busy people passing through it, machines going by, life in movement.

Veils resembling holograms show them the joys, hopes and memories the moment contains, and the past or future events that are linked to it, like so many potential realities, as if life wanted to show them how it works: all the possibilities that a moment bears. And this life seems to be charged with a special energy, at the same time an invitation to contemplation and action. Insatiable, they gaze upon this slow motion genesis, their hearts enthralled. Suddenly their eyes meet, full of gratitude; their hands join, they lie down and the free movements of love come to them naturally.

And while their bodies are still joined, their connected minds both open at exactly the same moment. An inner space is revealed that they can see through the same eyes: they watch as the Zeitgeist uncoils its immense and colourful whorls, they feel them brush against, play around and finally touch them. It settles on them, as if wanting to share with them the energy of this unique moment. The slow to and fro of vivid waves in the sky accelerates until suddenly their sublime arabesques silently explode and are dispersed in a myriad of sparks which fall continuously on Elwon like a shower of stars.

The connection! They realise together, as if an obvious fact had occurred to them both, like a germ nourished by this cosmic rain, that the connection they witnessed being born has gone beyond them and, carried by the Zeitgeist, has magnified to contain the whole of Elwon. They guess that this vision born in them corresponds with a transformation of all Elwon's inhabitants, as each has been touched by one of its fires. The power of the instant has up till then been accessible to all who wish to draw on it, and now it's enough just to settle on it. They discover that, in the moment they have just lived, not turned towards one another and absorbed in their own reality, but both aware and filled with what surrounds them, a kind of stillness has been created, a moment where life has immobilised so that the world around it could have the time to taste it, to calmly explore everything the present offers and weigh what suits it best.

From this precise moment they have seen two shafts of light burst out, simultaneous and absolutely synchronous, one headed towards the past and the other towards the future; and they realise that like a pregnant woman, each instant bears in it all the pasts leading up to it and all the futures that come from it, created here and now in the present, instantaneously and not as the fruit of a chain of events. The more powerful the instant, the further the rays of light plunge into the infinity of time.

They rediscover this aptitude now given to everyone to create his or her own reality, simply to choose it by updating the entire instant that is being lived. The incredible power of the present potential then deploys, not only within them, but around them, and now for all Elwon's inhabitants.

Slowly the glow fades until finally disappearing. They are naked under the night sky with Juno before them, shining with a thousand lights, like everywhere else in Elwon.

"Wow! Whatever just happened, it's absolutely magnificent!"

"Phenomenal! Do you feel it? Elwon has become the Garden. Now we are all Dissidents!"

They laugh like children after a prank at the absurdity of this, but their laughter is suddenly cut short.

"All of us? Wait, something's wrong. There seems to be something missing, like a snag in the weft of time, a kind of linearity still forcing its way in – as if some of us had not been affected."

They are sitting facing the city and Jiù feels something like a string straining towards the sky, attached to a balloon that's on the point of being snatched away by the wind.

"Yes, I feel that too!"

"That's not good. The transformation absolutely has to be complete – otherwise there will still be opposition. I think that's why the transformation didn't happen last time – it was stopped by a solution of continuity that carried on developing. That has to be avoided at all costs."

Silence surrounds them once more, but it's not long before they exclaim together:

"Jon!"

"Doràn!"

———

11 - Connection

Jiù and Akané have transited towards their friend Leh, hoping to find Jon. They have found no-one. They are near a small, low, house in a sort of courtyard behind a guard's post just outside a little mountain village, but all the buildings are empty. There is no sign of life, no sign of Leh. They've connected to Kohl so as to make a concerted decision.

"So that's the situation. What do you think, Kohl?"

"Well, everything's going well over here. Transformation is in progress everywhere. We have reports from Newton, Juno, Petrow, Buneiro, and they've all been affected – I'll tell you about it. But like you, we are concerned: communications have been cut with AsiaPac and we have no news from Beihaï. Shu has lost contact with Doràn. The region is isolated from the main frame, but they have a secondary network they use. Nothing is filtering out and Memory Central doesn't have enough data. I sense the situation is not without danger. I'm going to ask Shu if he can send you some guards."

"I'm not sure that will be necessary. Wait till we tell you to."

In active mode, they scan the surroundings looking for a clue, for a direction. Before them a little path slopes downwards invitingly. They decide to follow it, feeling decisive but amazingly relaxed. Filled with the energy that makes the present shimmer, they have time for themselves. Suddenly Akané whispers:

"Follow me – I know where he is."

With a determined air, she increases her pace, sometimes slipping on a loose stone. Jiù follows her several steps behind, astonished as ever by her prodigious intuition. They walk for a long moment through a mineral landscape, arid and stony, crushed by the heat. Sweating and panting, they skirt around a damaged enclosure, and reach a tumbledown low wall running on from a few buildings, some of whose roofs have collapsed. Everything seems to have been uninhabited for a very long time. She stops, and says in her inner voice:

"It's here. Be careful."

They feel a distracted presence and guess there is a guard dozing.

"Perhaps there are others. I can feel where he is. I'm going to transit to behind him."

Jiù sees his companion disappear. He goes towards the dilapidated opening, as relaxed as possible but ready for any eventuality. A few yards in front of him in the shade of a porch, a guard with a confused bearing and scruffy appearance is sitting. He's alone. On seeing Jiù, he scrambles to his feet, surprised.

"Halt!" he yells.

He had evidently not heard Jiù arrive nor expected his presence. He looks around for his flashgun. Akané is behind him, as silent as a cat.

"Don't look for it," Akané says softly, holding the weapon in one hand while the other stretches out towards the guard, to stop him searching.

"Sit down!"

The guard obeys.

"Where is he?"

The guard points towards the vaulted entrance of a cellar with a weary, resigned and almost relieved gesture. Jiù takes the flashgun from Akané's hands and says in his inner voice.

"Go on in – I'll stay with him."

"Leh?"

Akané's call in the darkness finds no response. After taking some time to get used to the gloom, she moves carefully up to a little door that she can just make out in the half-light. She pushes up the latch and finds Leh tied up, sitting on a low, unsteady stool, wearing an inhibitor that she quickly takes off him before releasing him.

He breathes deeply as if he had held his breath all this time. He hasn't lost any of his impassibility, though, and Akané finds herself admiring his immutable patience.

"Have you been here long?"

"Thanks. I don't know – two to three days perhaps. I lost all notion of time."

"Come!"

She guides him towards the outside where, scrunching their eyes up against the blinding daylight glare, they join Jiù.

"Hello Leh! I'm pleased to see you again."

"Hello Jiù!"

The memory of their joint adventure in Beihaï comes back to them and a smile lights up Leh's drawn features. Their reunion is interrupted by an inner question from Akané:

"What shall we do with him?"

"We leave him where we found Leh and free him before we leave."

While Jiù takes the guard to the cellar, Leh walks around to stretch his stiff limbs, letting out some satisfied grunts.

"Look, I've found something to eat. OK, Leh, what happened?"

"I don't really know much. We forgot they could trace Mia. Doràn surprised us. They took Mia away at once and Jon must have followed. I don't know where they are. They put an inhibitor on me and then you found me."

"What state of mind was Jon in?"

"I wasn't able to talk to him, but he looked totally unreceptive. I think there's a huge conflict going on in him. I'm not at all sure how he got on."

Once they've had something to eat, they sit in the relative cool of the shade of an imposing tree in the little courtyard. This time, they don't want to get it wrong. An idea suddenly comes to Jiù.

"Memory, have you more data now? Can you give us a report?"

"Official communication is down, but the data from the Zeitgeist indicates that Doràn is moving towards Beihaï at the head of quite a large and well-organised battalion. They have relays in Beihaï. Their aim is to take control of Eneter headquarters and then overthrow Shu. They have identified a window of opportunity in the fact that Eneter forces are all mobilised around the current disorder in different parts of the city."

"What is the risk to Mia and Jon if we intervene?"

"Mia is under their control with an inhibitor. They are forcing Jon to be in active mode and are controlling his brain activity in order to prevent any initiative by you. 80% and 40% risk of fatal incident."

"And what is the risk to Elwon if they succeed?"

"Opposition will be maintained. The Collapsus will be delayed but its probability is 75%."

"How long before they reach Beihaï?"

"An hour at the most."

"Thank you."

There is absolutely no question of launching into another chase – they want nothing to do with that reality, and would be sure to lose their bearings. They've learnt from experience and now, hardened reality-makers, they choose a different one. Feeling relaxed, they gradually let themselves go as they lean against the rather rugged trunk of a moderately welcoming tree. In active mode they contemplate the arid plain stretching out below them. They seem to be napping, but in fact they are observing the air that vibrates with the fluctuation of the present potential being deployed.

Jiù exults, now familiar with the exercise: he gradually feels himself becoming an integral part of everything that surrounds him, things and people, space and time. This reality becomes the precise instant he chooses – everything that moves and lives is intensely part of him, just like he is part of each of these events. So everything becomes energy which rises up and takes hold of him again as he follows its progress from his centre towards his extremities.

Any feeling of urgency has gone; from now on it's all about contemplation; he is simultaneously the landscape and the circumstances that come up. He is, in the plenitude of the moment; and he immediately feels the coils of time organising irresistibly around him. He sees all its options as lightly shimmering rays. In fact, he holds on to none of them. You should never try to control this energy – he knows what would happen. On the contrary, you should let it deploy, be part of it. He knows what is at stake – what he and Akané just missed on the edge of the Garden: beyond the energy that is driving them, it's all about awareness. That's what needs to be shared with the whole of Elwon – that's what's at stake. It's not about persuading Doràn, let alone about stopping him. His mind needs to be touched, that's all.

Jiù knows he can connect to Doràn directly, meld with him, thus sharing this total awareness without forcing anything on him.

"Akané, Kohl, Leh, Jon – it's Jiù. I'm going to connect to Doràn, I'm going to meld with him. I'm going to share the awareness of the energy of time with him and I hope to cause a connection that we will then live together. Wherever he goes and whatever he does, I will be with him. Please be ready to help in case unforeseen circumstances interfere."

"Be careful, Jiù. We have never transited to that level of awareness. We don't know what the effects will be!"

Is it the heat or the novelty of the experience? Jiù's body does not disappear, but it becomes totally lifeless, and that of Akané, who was watching over him, begins to vibrate imperceptibly.

Several hundred kilometres from there, an interminable line of transports and rapeeds advances along a scorching track amid clouds of dust that are raised by its passage. Doràn stands in the first vehicle following the rapeeds that head up the procession, scanning the horizon. Behind him, Jon and Mia – who is wearing an inhibitor – are sitting.

"You see, Jon, as I said to your friend Jiù, I have absolute power over everything that happens on Elwon. I'm in command. Nothing can escape me, not even your DIY energy jobs. I control the teleport now and its entire infrastructure. I don't know what you did to Shu, but he's become useless, he will be relieved of his duties and judged for high treason. I will see to this personally. And now it's I who has authority over Eneter and his forces are all following *me*. You are going to see Beihaï fall and then one by one all Elwon's hypercities. From now on, the High-Council is me."

"Aren't you afraid of the Collapsus?"

"That's all tripe. Nothing will happen to us. Eneter has been managing energy for generations, so we know exactly when and where to use it. I can assure you that after centuries of control, the future of Eneter is perfectly under control – we have nothing to fear. The real danger comes from people like you who are rising up against the established order, who haven't understood that what the world needs is stability. And that's all."

"If you only knew how right you were!"

"Be quiet. Don't force me to repeat that I get tired very quickly of your little oppositions. You're like a stubborn mule drowning in convictions and false hopes."

Jon says nothing. Doràn hasn't noticed that, during this conversation, Jon has eased closer to Mia and their hands are now joined. They have gone into active mode and can now talk to each other, the vibrations of their inner voices passing via their hands, like a whisper.

"Where are we?"

"Don't worry – we are in a transport with Doràn. I reckon Shu has joined our cause. So Doràn has rebelled and is at the head of a detachment going towards Beihaï that he wants to conquer in order to hold AsiaPac."

"Have you managed to contact the others?"

"No, my brain activity is under surveillance. It's lucky they haven't been able to detect us at this weak range. Trust me, time is on our side!"

Beneath his confident and conquering exterior, Doràn is nonetheless anxious. It's impossible that Shu remain inactive. He's going to react, and what Doràn needs to do is guess how. He thinks about it, bringing into play all his knowledge of the way Eneter functions so as to anticipate the range of possible reactions available to Shu. Suddenly, while he is lost in his reflections, an almost imperceptible variation in his field of vision attracts his attention. It's as if the air had vibrated in an unusual way. Are they going through a warmer zone? Has there been an energy change on the transport? His attention aroused, he scrutinises his surroundings intensely. A calm inner voice suddenly speaks to him.

"Make the convoy stop. Have a break. The men are tired."

"What the hell is going on now?"

He recognises the voice as his, but not the thought it conveys, as if it does not belong to him. Wary, he turns towards Jon, who is dozing in the back with Mia.

"Jon, what are you up to?"

Jon looks at him in surprise, with a hint of mockery, like a student facing a teacher who's been caught out.

"Nothing, I can assure you."

Frowning, Doràn watches Jon and Mia for a moment, but nothing more happens. He glances at the brain activity monitor but doesn't see anything abnormal. He's about to resume his observation of the interminable chalky ribbon of the track in front of him, when a voice announces on the intercom:

"We request permission to stop the convoy and have a break. The men are tired."

Doràn is struck by the coincidence. At the very moment the thought surfaces, it finds its correspondence in reality. What is this mess?

"Permission granted. We'll stop for ten minutes, no more."

Doràn sits down. It's hard to admit, but he's exhausted too. The tension of the past few days has been particularly intense, so this break is actually very welcome. It will allow him time to think properly, to get some distance from events. He says to the pilot:

"Watch over the prisoners and wake me in ten minutes if I'm asleep."

"Affirmative."

His drowsiness turns quickly into a heavy and agitated sleep. Someone who rarely dreams, he starts having hallucinations that he can't explain. In the distance he sees the familiar outline of Beihaï's towers recede, dwindle and sink into the darkness, eluding him as twilight grows around him. He finds himself quite alone in a desolate landscape, on a gloomy and lifeless plain, with not a hill to break the monotony that stretches as far as the eye can see. He can't see himself but he is gripped by an unfamiliar solitude. The feeling of danger is oppressive and there is that voice again, this time repeating over and over again: "You can still stop it all."

He wakes up sweating despite the perfect temperature of the driver's cab. The dream doesn't tell him anything worthwhile, but he's never been one to attach any importance to dreams. It's time to move on, forget this nonsense cluttering up his mind. But again, the thought comes to him:

"Before moving on, you should consult your officers about preparations for your entry into Beihaï. The end of the day would be more suitable."

He doesn't know why, but this voice worries him. It's not threatening, but it is totally unexpected. And yet he can't deny that what it's suggesting seems to correspond to his own thoughts. Could it be a retort from Shu? Impossible. None of this is like him at all – neither the tone nor the intention; and above all, he would have heard about the technology being used. And what could be the explanation of the coincidence with the demands of his staff general? Well? The intercom calls him again:

"Commander? Perhaps it would be wise for us to consult one last time to prepare for our entry into Beihaï. We recommend waiting till the end of the day."

"Here we go again," Doràn says to himself, and then out loud: "Stay on standby – give me five minutes."

He needs to think: all this is totally unlike anything he's ever known.

"That's great! You're right – that's how to do it," the voice says to him, like a whisper inside his head. "Take your time to understand, to analyse. There's no hurry."

Doràn freezes in awe and he can't repress the inner question that he hasn't yet dared formulate:

"Who...who are you?"

"I am deep thought. I have a maximum of data on your environment and the effects of your potential decisions, and can analyse circumstances and guide you towards the best opportunities."

"Are you connected to Memory Central?"

"I could be but I'm not using it right now. It's not the Memory that is guiding me: I have access to all information on the present and on its consequences. This knowledge gives me an awareness and a analytical level that is far beyond your faculties – not because of limitations in your ability to think, rather in the elements at your disposal that you can take into account."

"What guarantees do I have that this is not a plot or a trick to my detriment?"

"You have the choice as to whether to listen or not. Your free will is unaffected. The only thing I allow myself is to keep talking to you."

"And if I refuse to listen to you?"

"I'll be quiet. From now on I will only talk if you ask me."

Doràn falls silent too, totally bewildered. He understands nothing of what is happening to him, nothing of this inner dialogue that is so out of character for him. Is it fatigue, heat? Is it because of events in the Garden? Fear suddenly attacks: perhaps I was contaminated! He looks at his two prisoners in a way that is both ill-intentioned and fearful, as if they were carrying some lethal virus.

"Commander, what have you decided?"

The voice emitting from the intercom with some impatience pulls him out of his reverie.

"Come and see me in the briefing room."

He goes towards the back of the transport where presently a dozen officers of different ranks wearing worried expressions come in successively.

"Commander, we feel menaced by an unidentifiable threat. We have consulted each other and we all feel the same. It seems there are some parameters that are not under control."

"Like what?"

"We don't know, but we think this sensation we share should be taken into consideration and that we should take another look at the deployment plan together."

Doràn has trouble hiding his stupefaction. What is this rigmarole? His officers talking about sensations? Sharing? Anything else? But what the hell is going on, for God's sake? He can't let the situation elude him, not now! He needs these men but he can't let this kind of state of mind have a free rein. He needs to bring them to their senses, immediately, so they can see through what they have undertaken – to take the key parts of Beihaï. Once success has been secured, then we'll see what to do with these half-wits.

"Sensation? What's all that about? Explain yourself, and I hope you are going to be precise – my patience has its limits."

"We have checked and consulted the onboard computers. The balance of power is not favourable to us despite the officers who are in place: we should optimise the surprise effect and limit targets to the absolute minimum."

Idiots! They've used the onboard computers. Memory Central must know now – not only about their movements but also about their intentions. And if the Memory incorporates this data, not only will Shu be able to locate them, but they could also warn Beihaï, which will be able to ready itself.

"But I expressly forbade you not to use the calculators!"

He is about to give free rein to his anger in the face of this unbelievable error – disobedience during a mission – when the inner voice interrupts his intentions again.

"Wait! Reassure them before punishing them – you need them. Try to understand their motives and intentions."

"You shut up!"

"Remember what happened just now – your need to think. You don't have enough elements to allow you to make a decision and act on it. Take into account the whole situation."

Doràn says nothing. Even if this voice is intolerable, he is obliged to come round to its arguments. First he has to get a grip on himself. His officers, silent witnesses to his inner dialogue, take the initiative, half reassured that they haven't yet incurred his fury.

"Commander, you need us. What we ask is that you take into account our intentions and motives as parameters in your decision."

"And they are?"

"We think it's preferable to avoid confrontation. It would be wise to resort to it only in an extreme situation. We think that a combat between Eneter forces would be detrimental to L1 order, which guarantees the redundancy of violence. Elwon has prospered by this rule. We, more than anyone, should not infringe it. None of us wants to oppose the status quo, and yet – taking into account the different parameters – it's obvious that we are heading towards confrontation. That has to be reconsidered."

"What do you suggest?"

"Simply to rally them. They mustn't let themselves be overcome by disorder. So, conviction should be enough – we don't need to put pressure on anyone."

"Go back to your transports. I'll communicate your orders. Leave me alone now."

Once his officers have left, Doràn is totally perplexed. For some unknown reason, he feels that this game has begun badly and that its dynamics are beginning to collapse. Everything was under his control just ten minutes ago. What parameter did he neglect? This conversation with his general staff was unpredictable, and yet it happened. And it wasn't just one or two of his subordinates – in that case he could easily replace them and keep control – but all his senior staff got together, as is if bitten by the same idea. It's incomprehensible and certainly very complicated. He needs time and knows he hasn't got any. Above all, he needs help, but where can he find it? In desperation, he turns to that inner voice that had offered its help just a moment ago.

"What would you do in my place?"

"What do you think of their intentions and motives?"

"I don't give a damn about their motives! All I want is for them to serve me, but they are doing just the opposite!"

"That's because you haven't explained to them that you are acting exclusively in your own interests, or possibly in theirs too in the event that you accept to share with them – or some of them – the profit you expect to get from your actions. Without these indispensable elements, they think they are acting for the good of Elwon, and are therefore stuck in a contradiction. You're the only one that can get them out of it."

That's true, undeniably. If he's going to get what he wants, he has to find partners. All at once he understands Shu's motives: he wanted him as a partner to help him achieve his aims. Shu couldn't take power alone. Doràn suddenly understands the implacable logic that explains Shu's recent behaviour: when he discovered their partnership wasn't working, he joined the stronger side. He is now certain that Shu has joined the Dissidents. It can't be any other way. Either to use it to his advantage or because he's realised that the Dissidence was going to be established in Elwon. That may depend on the balance of power.

These thoughts illuminate him but at the same time plunge him into an abyss of greater complexity. Shocked, he discovers the unfathomable extent of the increasing number of ideas and thoughts that arise as soon as he asks himself questions about what should be done. He understands how much the authority that Eneter gave him helped him in his tasks (it's quite simple – no-one ever opposed him), but at the same time limited his thinking, as if to protect him from it. He realises that he is what is known as a man of action. That is, someone to be used. Just this phrase has the power to make him furious. He has to recognise, though, that he is not programmed to assimilate a range of hypotheses, contexts and opinions. It's quite simple, he doesn't know how to.

"Can you help me?"

"Only if you really want it. As you've noticed, you are not well-equipped to take care of your own interests; there are so many parameters in the present, but also in their possible consequences. In the present case, you have three options."

"Which ones?"

"You could identify and enlist the support of a partner – someone from your general staff or a subordinate. This option gives you wide-ranging choices, but the results are uncertain, and you'll need some time to be able to bring it off. Or you can go it alone. With this option the choice is simple but the result is difficult to predict given the number of parameters that need to be taken into account: either to seize power with the expedients available – for example Memory Central – or to run away (never!). Or else you could join Shu and make the same choices he has recently, and I can tell you he's doing well from it. It's also the option that offers *you* the widest choice, and for that reason I would recommend it."

"And the option of continuing to Beihaï?"

"At the moment, this is no longer an option. Your general staff has faced up to you and they won't accept to go on without an open and convincing discussion with you. That's not to mention your soldiers whose loyalty is not guaranteed under such circumstances."

"This is hell!"

"That's your opinion, but it's a question of perspective! You see it that way only because you are insisting on taking a direction that no longer corresponds with anything, so no circumstance can be helpful to you any more. You have disconnected from time and the reality you want to create at all costs is no longer linked with anything except your will and your stubbornness. You're hanging on to an illusion, Doràn! It's not reality.

You are on an ice floe that is melting in the sun! Jump off the floe, change your perspective!"

"And then?"

"Well, you can choose to come back to the reality that's connected to the world and to others. You just have to let go and you'll be brought back immediately."

"Without being able to control anything? No thanks!"

"You have to get over this desire to control. Look at the impasse it has brought you to. Rather than controlling, try to participate. It's by creating reality with others that you control your future – it's really something. Your reality can only have meaning if it is shared with others; otherwise it's yours, certainly, but it's no use to you. Do you see the strength of a shared reality? But conversely, a reality that's lived by you alone has to be abandoned quickly. That's what I suggest at the moment: come back to a reality that you can share. Doràn! It's by sharing that you can create."

Doràn says nothing after this silent dialogue. The moment extends, strained like an expectation; then the voice goes on:

"You know what you remind me of? A child holding on to his almost-empty purse because it's his, even though behind him there's an open safe. He doesn't want to use it because others have access to it too. Do you see how ridiculous that is?"

"Go to hell with your crap about reality and sharing!"

Doràn feels shut in and trapped, and that increases his fury. He's doesn't even have the peace of inner silence with that voice that he knows he'll find there, acting as an irritating witness to his most secret thoughts.

He's made his decision. He's going to go it alone. He'll go and see Shu and tell him his way of thinking. He turns to the pilot.

"Give me your flashgun and open the door."

The guard hesitates.

"Go on – move it!"

He turns to Mia.

"You. Come with me. Get out – quick!"

He pushes Mia unceremoniously and they jump to the ground. Suffocating in the furnace of this rocky land choked by the midday sun, blinded by the unbearable intensity of a light that comes from all around, he makes for the first rapeed of the convoy, dragging Mia behind him. With an irritated gesture he says to the astonished pilot through the porthole:

"I'm taking your rapeed. Get on the transport."

He makes Mia get in and closes the cockpit behind them. Instantly he feels the coolness of the air conditioning in sharp contrast with the rock-melting heat. He heaves a sigh of relief and almost relaxes: something pleasant at last. He starts the rapeed at full speed, turning back towards the station they have just left. Calm gradually returns to him, helping confirm he's made the right decision, as he sees the convoy disappear far behind them. As if things were becoming simple again. Once at the station he stops the rapeed and, with determination, dives into the teleport installation, pulling Mia after him. The voice starts up again.

"Careful – don't do that, the station is on standby. You'll have to reactivate it or you won't have enough energy. I'd advise you to wait at least an hour."

"Shut it!"

He turns on the control screens, flicks a few switches and picks up a portable keyboard that he automatically fixes on to his arm.

"Doràn, don't do that. You don't have sufficient energy to transit. Wait till the level is nominal."

Doràn does not reply and continues moving around, imperturbable. He takes the inhibitor off Mia, who blinks and looks around her, trying to understand. He puts a portable keyboard under her arm too, which he hastily configures.

"Listen carefully. We are in a teleport terminal and we're going to transfer to where Shu is. Your keyboard is coupled with mine so I know you are coming with me. You had better do exactly what I say; otherwise your companion Jon, who's stayed in the convoy, will be in big trouble."

"Mia? It's Jiù. Don't worry: everything's alright – I'm with you. Forget Doràn's threats – Jon is not in any danger. I'm going to try to reason with him, but meanwhile you should relax and as soon as I say, transit immediately to Kohl. Don't worry about anything else. Do you understand?"

"Yes. What's going on?"

"Nothing serious. The transformation has started on Elwon, but Doràn is resisting it."

"I'm ready."

Mia relaxes and moves back a little, away from Doràn.

"Wait Doràn!"

Jiù continues in a strangely calm voice, but Doràn can't help sensing a kind of anxiety in it which, rather than alerting him, only delights him as it signifies the defeat of another adversary. Yet another! He knows this anxiety so well, having spotted it systematically in the countless interrogations he's led. It always heralded the fact that the suspect was about to give in and that he had won.

"Doràn, analyse your situation. There is not enough energy in the accumulators even for you to transit on your own, let alone both of you. You know it. You have to wait at least an hour for you to transfer, and two to take Mia with you."

Doràn is not listening, cut off from his own faculties, tetanised by his determination and a cold rage magnified by his frustration. He drums the coordinates of the Juno control room on his forearm – he knows he'll find Shu there. That's normal procedure when trouble breaks out in Elwon. Eneter's general staff gathers there to manage the situation. Actually, he should be there himself. So that's lucky, as it's exactly where he's going.

He initiates the procedure and behind him the teleport condensers gain power with their characteristic humming. A slight ozone smell is released into the room.

"Mia, now!"

Mia disappears without Doràn noticing. He is looking at his teleport terminal; he presses the trigger and it's his turn to disappear, but instantly, as if the overload were too great, the whirring dissolves, a dry crack follows and then an eternal silence closes in on the now still room. The overvoltage condensers are flat and have not been able to provide the intensity necessary for the transfer. Doràn has left but he will never arrive. No-one knows where he is, except Jiù, whose thoughts went with him up until the moment of his final desire.

There, in the abandoned village, Akané senses a change in the tension of his body. With Leh's help, she has been supporting Jiù in this unusual transition, transmitting the energy he needed, while at regular intervals Leh has gone to a nearby spring to get water for Akané to drink and to dab Jiù's face with, to alleviate the fire of the stony sultriness crushing them.

Akané feels that Jiù has come back, that his mind once more inhabits his body, which is resting but no longer unconscious. A slow sigh swells his chest at last and he weakly opens his eyes.

"Water, please."

He drinks and lets the water flow freely over his cheeks and neck, eyes full of gratitude for it, for Leh's joy and Akané's relief.

"I failed."

"Jon and Mia?"

"Jon is in the convoy. Let him know that Mia is safe. She must be near Kohl, but I didn't bring Doràn back. He wanted to transit with the teleport, but there wasn't enough energy accumulated and the transfer was interrupted just after he left."

He tells them in detail everything he witnessed, about his efforts that, in the end, were useless. They remain silent, frozen by the thought of Doràn's fate, the horror of which all three of them – and especially Akané – can fully comprehend.

308

"He's lost?"

"Yes, I'm afraid so. I wasn't able to stop it and I don't know where we would find him. I don't know if I'd have the capacity ... or even the possibility," he adds, remembering Doràn's cold determination. "We could perhaps try something, but not from here. Meanwhile, we have to tell Jon."

"You rest; I'll take care of it."

They get up at last and, in the failing sunlight, face the little valley below. They contemplate the track winding between the scattered trees, twisted by the wind and by their efforts to find a little water. This torrid land is certainly not hospitable, but people have lived here. In this place where only the essential survives, they feel a sort of drifting gratitude: life is possible even here. Above all they know that beyond the arid hills, they are together again. They sense that this time, the transformation they were hoping for is going to come to fruition.

Silence falls again, this time lasting until nightfall, on this village at the end of the world.

———

12 - Redemption

"So that's what happened. I'm sorry."

Jiù falls silent. They are reunited with their friends in Kohl's little house on the edge of the solar field. Shu is among them, as well as several Eneter officers, who, fascinated by their experience and knowing that their lives have irreversibly shifted, want to know more. Now it's Shu's turn to speak.

"You acted in the right way. I'm so sorry Doràn didn't listen to you, but I'm not entirely surprised. He made all this so personal, invested it with such an unusual emotional intensity. That's what lost him. But that's the way it is. We have to forget him and take care of what is in store for Elwon – there's going to be a lot to do here."

Kohl smiles at this quick conclusion that is so totally in line with L1 dogma. Any emotion is fatal in the end. Order must prevail at all costs and, in the end, people are secondary. Undeniably, the marriage between cold reason and the creative intensity of the present is going to beget some interesting results! Calmly, he interrupts:

"There is perhaps a way of finding him."

Everyone present turns towards him in surprised expectation.

"I think he's still synchronised with Mia, not only via the tracers, but also because he thought he was going to transit with her. He must be looking for her wherever he is. We should be able to reach him via her."

"What's the risk?"

"That depends on Mia."

He turns towards her.

"How are you feeling?"

"Not too bad, but it's as if I had not completely come back; I have memories and images that are embedded in my head, and it's like having bad jetlag. I'm not totally myself yet."

"I'm not surprised. What are you getting from Doràn?"

"Nothing in particular. Strong emotion when he's mentioned but I don't know what that comes from. Maybe because of what he put me through? Or because it's my fault he's where he is?"

"Don't think that; but besides that – there's nothing in particular bothering you physically?"

"No, nothing."

"Mia, I'm going to suggest an alternative that it's up to you alone to decide on. Whatever your choice, we will respect it. Either we can leave the trackers in place for Doràn to find us – but it won't definitely work, and it will still be uncomfortable for you; or we deactivate them, which frees you but definitively removes all hope of bringing him back to our time. What do you think?"

"It's a complex choice – I need some time. Can I wait before deciding?"

"Of course."

He gets up and goes out without another word. After a while, Jiù and then the others join him where he is standing in silent contemplation of the town that encloses the horizon.

"What do you feel, Jiù?"

Jiù knows that it's not just a random question. Like in the children's playground, Kohl is calling on his ability to consult the instant, his unusual capacity to perceive what is present in the moment and all its potentialities.

"I feel the energy of the Zeitgeist beating with enormously intense pulsations that now unceasingly bathe the whole of Elwon. It has become like a vast nervous system in a gigantic body, preparing us for action. I have just understood why we talk about real time when we talk about the instant – it's the only moment in which we really find the reality of time. All the rest is only evanescence. I feel that with all these comings and goings of the Zeitgeist between us, the Memory has become our common ability for sharing and redistribution. Convergence has clearly finished and transformation is at work."

Jiù lets himself go even further into the vision that is taking shape, all the while describing it for his comrades.

"It's as if the Memory was being diluted in each of us: it's pouring into us everything it's accumulated, concentrating from now only on the function of communication and transfer. I feel that it's indicating to us that what is important from now on is us, all connected to one another, each with his or her capacity to access the energy of time, with his or her ability to construct his or her own reality. I already see some of us making astonished experiments with these possibilities, and the more advanced among us are already mixing their realities, discovering how they combine ad infinitum. It's moving fast in an endless loop of positive feedback. I sense a countless number of futures becoming reality, as if the present potential were being infinitely multiplied."

Everyone is listening to him, filled with this new reality he's describing which is already so familiar to them. Kohl's eyes are closed: with each one of his senses he's savouring all the details, all his hopes of this new time that he has been preparing for so long.

"Thank you, Jiù, for describing that to us. That's exactly the challenge waiting for us: to make our realities fit in with those of others and make them serve each other rather than being in contradiction. Besides, that's what the Zeitgeist is going to be for – to build the connection between the times of each one of you."

He turns back to the little group that is gazing at the town as if they wanted to make out everything within it.

"Shu, Eneter is going to need training and adapting and this probably needs to happen quite quickly. I suggest you delegate the responsibility for energy to a special department, so as to both continue exploiting the solar fields and at the same time – and above all – coordinate access to temporal energy. The History department will need to be given the job of synchronising the countless simultaneous realities that are going to emerge everywhere in Elwon. Culture is going to facilitate the integration of all this creativity and that's not negligible. Do you agree that we should re-form the High-Council to pilot all this? I suggest it should be in charge of communication along with Memory Central, with the help of the Zeitgeist, like before. And I propose we become members."

Shu, dazed, is listening, and does not even seem to notice that Kohl has taken the initiative and that he himself, who has been used to giving orders for so long, is receiving them! He's having trouble following all these developments, disconcerted by how they follow on from each other and especially by their speed. Everything is sudden, immediate and above all so new! But at the same time he can't help noticing that Elwon order is totally intact. It's as if everything that had gradually been organised over time had been in preparation for this moment. Everything seems to be happening in a kind of continuity and what he dreaded – a great upheaval in Elwon – hasn't, in the end, come about. This not only surpasses his hopes, but also anything he could have imagined.

The little group is standing together. They are feeling rather than seeing the spectacle before their eyes. They all sense reality deploy before them and within them, at once familiar and outrageous, as if what they had lived up till then was only a small-scale model of the potential their Dynasty contained. The feeling of power emerging from everywhere is truly fabulous. They feel they are bathing in an immense energy that soaks into and penetrates them, leaving behind a sense of exultation they absolutely have to share. Clearly, incredible forces are at work transforming their civilisation, like the luxuriance of a life extending as far as the eye can see into the desert when conditions are finally right.

Then Jiù starts to describe aloud this vision they are already sharing in their united thoughts.

"Look – in all neighbourhoods, people are getting together to share their new abilities. In some places, whole sectors are already unrecognisable. Uniformity has been shattered.

"It's funny. It's as if all the inhabitants were waking up after a long sleep and were discovering loads of things to do that they had forgotten about.

"The really incredible thing is the Memory's prodigious analytical capacity: in the end it has come to the conclusion that its role from now on is to preserve the intense circulation of thoughts, ideas and realities that is the Zeitgeist. Memory Central is at the heart of sharing. We know enough now for our knowledge to be constantly increased by exchanging it."

Kohl stops them.

"It's not about knowledge any more, Jiù, but about awareness. That is the outcome of Elwon's transformation. We have gone from an era of knowledge to a time of awareness, and that's where we are now. It's the awareness we share and that goes beyond the capacities of our hyper-calculator that has served us so well. From now on it is at our disposal for that reason, and for no other. It was programmed to facilitate this passage. Now that it's actually happening, it has reached its limit and is returning to its primary function."

"I remember – it said to me one day: 'My function is to bring you back to your history so that you can surpass it.' That's exactly what you've just said, and what is happening, but I hadn't understood."

They look at each other with pleasure, not so much at the size of the task ahead of them but at the immensity of the possibilities they are discovering and which are just waiting to be made reality in Elwon. They are all smiling; some of them have tears in their eyes.

"I had not imagined that it would happen like this – a whole civilisation discovering the awareness within it, the irrepressible force of life..."

"Jon!"

Mia's anguished voice suddenly interrupts them, reminding them of a forgotten memory. She reels, and Jon catches her before she collapses at his feet.

"Doràn?"

"I don't know. I'm really cold and my heart feels crushed by anguish."

She's unsteady on her feet and trembling as if from a strong fever. They exchange meaningful looks: they can't leave things as they are, something has to be decided.

"What's your decision on the trackers?"

"I don't know. I think I'd be happy if you removed them..."

Akané has sat down next to her sister and is gently massaging her head which is resting on her knees. Once again she goes into active mode to embrace the present and be in total communion with her. She feels Mia's fear, oppressive to her on two counts: her concern about what is happening and Doràn's own fear that has wormed its way into her. For it's about him, holding on to the memory of Mia like a life-force. As for Akané, she knows very well what he might be feeling in this solitude beyond words in the infinity of time – a solitude that nothing resists except the determined will to survive. She knows, suddenly and unavoidably, which course of action to take.

"I know what we're going to do. I think it's going to work."

Her voice is firm and detached. She's not asking for confirmation or offering an explanation, only stating a fact.

"We're going to deploy a timescale again. Mia will be the pivot and we will spread throughout the times that Doràn lived, the ones he may want to hold on to. As for me, I'm going to go and look for him. I'll move along the ladder. As I look like Mia, this should help him."

"No, Akané, I should do it."

"I don't think so, Jiù. He may still feel antagonism towards you. And if he recognises your voice, that might push him away rather than attracting him. And besides," she adds, unable to suppress a shiver, "I already know this uncertain time he's lost in. I can't say it's exactly familiar to me, but it's not completely foreign."

"Leh, if you can position yourself in the past, right next to Doràn's last transition, that should help us."

Kohl smiles slightly at the knowing look between Jiù and Leh who are already preparing themselves for the efforts they imagine they are letting themselves in for, then he turns to Shu and the Eneter officers who are following the conversation without really understanding what's going on.

"We're going to spread out over time as kind of points of reference for Doràn. If he finds one of us, we must hope that he has enough energy and good judgement left to join him or her. Stay with Jiù and do exactly what he tells you – he'll explain more."

They all sit down where they are and gradually attain the inner state where their energies widen and intermingle. One by one they disappear like bubbles in the sun.

Straight away, Akané finds herself in total darkness and silence, projected in an unfathomable abyss, knowing neither where the surface is, nor how she got in, nor whether she will be able to get out. She is seized by a short instant of panic as if the immensity and the memory of her past terrors had aroused in her an unconquerable fear.

Akané floats in nothingness. She feels her sister close by, and focusing on Kohl, she's about to launch herself in his direction when she suddenly freezes in fright. Two staring eyes emerge from the void, coming towards her.

"Doràn?"

The eyes stop a short distance away and scrutinise her. Doràn's halftone body is floating there, blurred by a kind of static that she doesn't immediately understand.

"Can you hear me? I've come to bring you back to the present. Let me guide you."

"Who are you?" His voice is indecisive, filled with both anger and hope.

"I'm Akané, Mia's sister. Do you remember me? You came to meet me at the G13 station."

She is suddenly struck by the reversal of the situation. She's about to rescue from the infinity of time the very person who had once pushed her into it. This propensity life has of offering reciprocity for any circumstance does not cease to amaze her.

"Why should I trust you?"

"I'm here to help you get out, not to push you in deeper – you're doing that fine by yourself! Look at you! You're already only the shadow of yourself. If you don't decide, you're going to disappear."

"You're her sister?"

"Yes."

"Why do you want to save me?"

"Because Mia can't forget and feels guilty. She feels responsible for what's happening to you. The best option for you and for her is that you make it out of here."

She feels wavering uncertainty in him, a conflict of energies between his still keen anger and the pressing need to survive, like a high-intensity oscillation. She suddenly understands that this is the very cause of his evanescence; this ambivalence, this agony of indecision between contradictory urges is perturbing the awareness he has of himself. He is more lost to himself, to what he wants to be, than to the infinity of time, and she still feels the need to help him.

"Doràn, calm down, relax. Even here, there is no hurry; we have all the time in the world. You are not lost any more – I can offer you a way out, but first you have to choose for yourself. It's up to you to choose, calmly, the path you prefer between your frustration, this anger that's blinding you, and your desire for survival. I won't influence you, I won't advise you, but you have to make the move. I'm simply here to bring you back if you choose to live."

All the while, Akané is struck by what is happening to her. The memory of her old terror when she herself haunted this place has disappeared. She waits, impassive, in the heart of this bottomless darkness. She finds herself contemplating without fear this limitless void where things are only potential with no form of reality, as if she had nothing to fear, or even as if it were protecting her. She knows she's a foreigner here, but welcome at the same time – now time lives in her; it's she that carries it rather than being lost in it. She is its womb and it is making her strong. For Doràn she feels only a patient but distracted attention, and has no stake whatsoever in which decision he makes. She's simply waiting for him to make it, whatever it is. Time is in her.

Doràn's pacified voice startles her.

"OK... I believe you and I'm ready to follow you. How are we going to get out of here?"

"Concentrate on me; don't take your eyes off me and keep on trusting me. I'm going to focus on the present I've come from and you will automatically follow me."

The events of the Garden are just a memory: Kohl and Jiù are walking side by side down the streets of Juno. The string of rapeeds has considerably reduced, most people now preferring to get around on foot – they have time for themselves. As in Jiù's vision, they form scattered groups that stop and talk with an intense curiosity that brings them closer. Life has been re-created spontaneously in Juno as in all the other towns; in little groups and pockets, the present is reinvented on every street corner, each person experiencing his or her still unexplored potential. They all look astonished: of course, what is going on is endlessly surprising, but they are also amazed at themselves, at what they haven't done for such a long time, at what they can share and envisage together.

Jiù and Kohl are ambling along without paying attention to where their feet are taking them, when they reach the foot of the gigantic L1 Memory building.

"Come with me – I'm going to show you something."

Kohl takes Jiù to the higher floors and to the office that Jiù recognises instantly as his father's.

"Look at the message Doràn has left!"

On Kohl's holos, Doràn's face appears, tired and gaunt as if after a long illness, but full of gratitude. The short message has clearly been recorded somewhere in the Garden.

"I wanted to thank you all for coming to get me. Thanks especially to Akané for what she did for me even after what I did to her, but to you too, because I know you were supporting her." He pauses and then adds: "Thank you. And I'm sorry."

There is a brief glow at the end of the recording, before which they remain pensive, as the holos switches itself off.

"It's fabulous. Akané was extraordinary."

"Yes, she's a brave woman!" Then Kohl adds: "Welcome to my office, Jiù."

"Thanks."

An indefinite period lapses before Jiù realises what Kohl has just said.

"Your office?"

"Yes – the one you saw your father in for the last time."

Jiù suddenly feels cold all over and his thoughts freeze, incapable of order.

"I'm afraid I don't understand!"

"Jiù, are you sure my voice is really not familiar to you?"

"Kohl, what are you saying?"

"Jiù, your father didn't die in the cruiser accident. He disappeared. I wasn't going to let myself be eliminated, after all! So I decided to disappear. I transited to Sehn and with the active complicity of Elea and her incredible talent for regeneration, I continued to live under a different identity. To escape Eneter – it seemed more convenient to let them believe that I had really disappeared. Thus I changed personality completely and only my voice stayed the same. I always feared it would betray me. As for you, I didn't expect to see you mixed up in this affair and certainly not so closely! When we detected your experiments, Orion and I agreed that I should be the one to accompany you and train you. We decided to let life do its work and let ourselves be guided as to the right moment for me to unveil myself. Secretly I always hoped you would recognise me."

"You're my father? Kohl?"

Jiù is completely stunned. So this father that he believed lost twice over is here, alive, in front of him? Exhausted by all he has just lived, shaken up by totally contradictory emotions – a mixture of anger and joy, relief and alarm - he feels like he's losing his footing and no longer knows what to do or say. His thoughts frozen in a prolonged instant, he gently squeezes his father's hands as if to reassure himself he's real and tell him what he can't otherwise express. Hesitantly, he goes towards the window that gives onto a view of Juno. He looks at the city, absent-minded, letting his gaze wander from one tower to the next, from one horizon to the next. After a long silence, he starts to talk again, without turning his head, like an island of logic battered by an ocean of confusion.

"But – why did you not say anything to me all this time?"

"You have to understand – I wasn't sure how our adventure would turn out and if something had happened to me, like it did to Orion and Elea in the Garden, then I didn't want you to lose me once more. I also preferred you to experience it all independently of me and above all I hoped not to create a kind of vulnerability in you. If Shu had found out, we would all have been in great danger. And I should add – although it's something I discovered afterwards – that it was really pleasant to share all those moments with you without being constrained by a father-son relationship."

"Who knew?"

"Memory Central because it kept my biotics, but I requested it be kept secret, knowing that I would reveal it to you in the end – unless I had to disappear again."

"Who are you going to tell?"

"I don't know yet if it's necessary to unveil myself to anyone other than you."

Kohl moves closer to Jiù. In silence they look together at the hyperpole spread at their feet. There is nothing to say.

"Father, it's too much, everything I feel. I don't know what to think. I need to find myself again. Forgive me, but I need to be alone."

Jiù leaves the room without turning back. He is in exactly the same state of mind as at the beginning of this adventure, when Kohl had explained to him the path he was about to go down: the intense desire to drop everything and run away. He feels betrayed and manipulated. He's not sure of anything any more, neither of himself nor his senses. He's back at square one, as if everything he had experienced was merely a memory, an imagined and non-existent reality. He suddenly feels very alone; there is an immense emptiness in him, a space that needs filling, a whole life to replace.

Without thinking, he has aimlessly wandered back to the little house on the edge of the Garden. He sits in the little meadow that it is now adjacent to, and looks at the city lying beneath a totally clear sky. He lets himself be touched by the timid heat of the setting sun which gives landscapes such a deep density, such a warm colouration of plenitude and calm. This moment that sadly doesn't last, the beauty surrounding him, the final heat of the sun dipping behind the horizon – all of this helps slowly restore calm to his thoughts and peace to his being. In the silence enfolding him and within him, he has only one thought: Akané!

"I'm here, Jiù."

He turns around and finds her standing there behind him, her face at once serious and joyful, her black eyes shining intensely in the mottled light of the sunset, with those movements of her hands like a slow dance, so particular to her. As usual, she surprises him.

"I didn't want to bother you. If you hadn't called me, I would have left you in peace."

They are now both sitting facing the scarlet sun that ignites the sky dashed with purple clouds. Birds hurrying like latecomers shoot through the air before them. Like a song, the vibration and perfume of the earth rises up from the soil that has spent the day absorbing the sun and now restores it. They know that this is reality within them. The beauty of the earth like a jewel. This peace and this immensity, this immutable order deploying around them, have always been theirs. They contemplate their world and what unites them, even if Jiù still feels emotions rising up in waves, like sobs, when he thinks of his father. He feels Akané looking at him and turns towards her. Her face is peaceful, lit by the last hues of the day. Unusually beautiful.

"I'm pregnant, Jiù."

He looks at her, his eyes suddenly flooded with tears.

"Akané!"

He doesn't want words, nor thoughts, nor voice, either inner or outer. He doesn't want anything else, neither to speak or hear; he doesn't want time any more. Just looking is enough right now. He takes her hands and endlessly loses his eyes in hers.

Only then does he open up to life again, overcome with gratitude for all it contains, all that it gives in the infinity of the present, and to the rising joy that he does not hold back. Laughter comes, first in their eyes, then to their lips, understated then irrepressible and impetuous. Together, they let it out, like revenge, or an endless call to the sky.

———————